THE LOST BOOK 4

SWORDS AGAINST THE NIGHT

PETER NEALEN

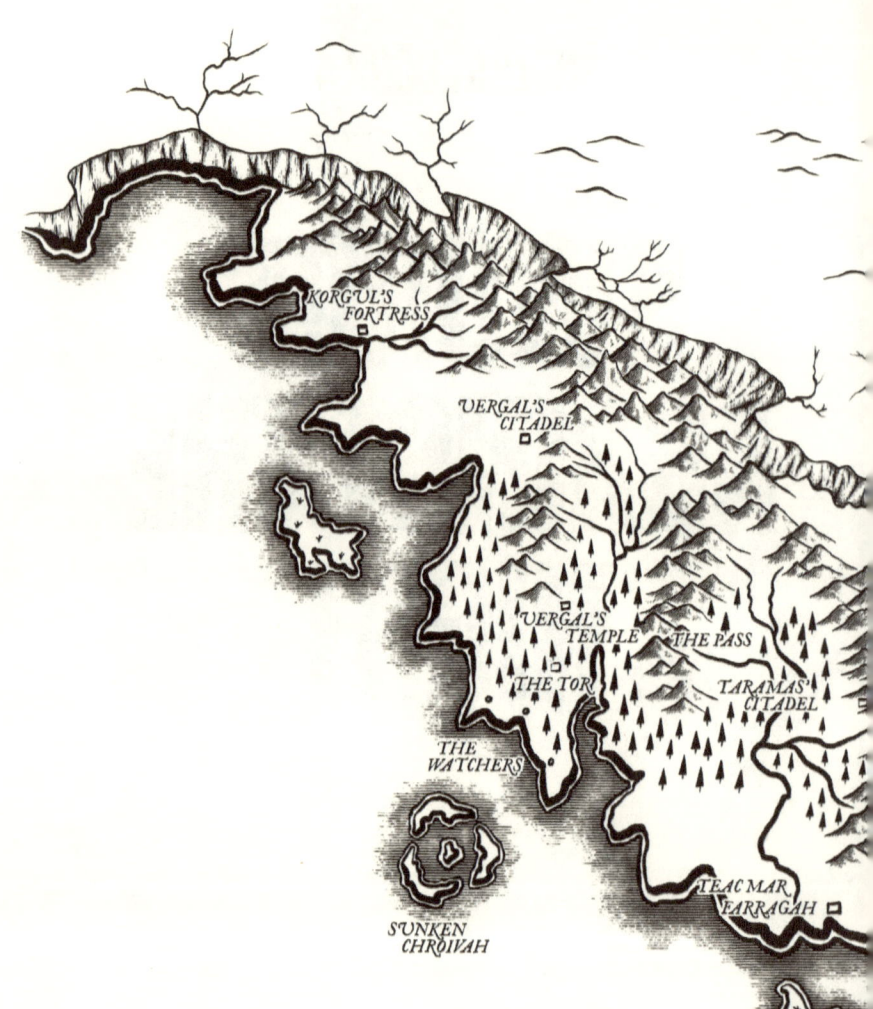

KORGUL'S
FORTRESS

VERGAL'S
CITADEL

VERGAL'S
TEMPLE   THE PASS

THE TOR   TARAMAS'
                 CITADEL

THE
WATCHERS

                              TEAC MAR
                              FARRAGAH

SUNKEN
CHROIVAH

THE LAND of
ICE & MONSTERS

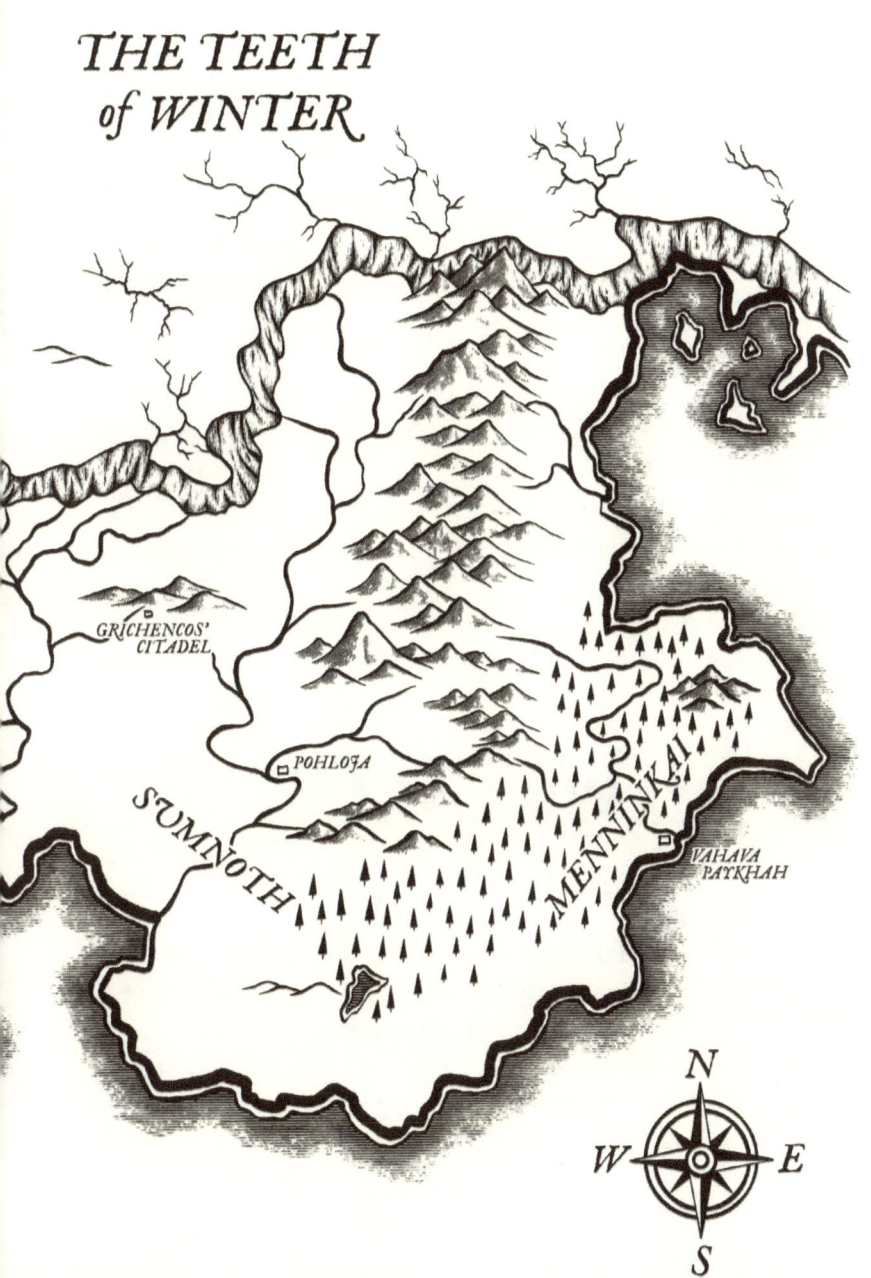

THE TEETH
of WINTER

GRICHENCOS'
CITADEL

POHLOJA

SUMNOTH

MENNINKAI

VAHAVA
PAYKHAH

N
W E
S

WARGATE

An imprint of Galaxy's Edge Press
PO BOX 534
Puyallup, Washington 98371
Copyright © 2021 by Galaxy's Edge, LLC
All rights reserved.

ISBN: 978-1-949731-80-4

www.forgottenruin.com
www.wargatebooks.com

CHAPTER 1

THE wind whipped through the rigging, making the lines sing and the sails snap. Nachdainn stood tall at the tiller of the *Radala Farragah*, keeping us on course as the white-hulled, high-prowed ship skimmed over the waves, rocking with the swell as we sailed west.

If we looked to the south, we could see the Isle of Riamog, the white snowcaps of the mountains that formed the island's spine standing out starkly against the deep blue sky, the green of the hills beneath shining like an emerald in the sun.

"Conor!" Nachdainn called over the creak of the rigging and the song of the wind. "Loosen that line next to your hand!"

I reached for the rope, seeing almost immediately what he was talking about. The wind was putting enough strain on the sail that I had to let up the pressure before something tore.

As I leaned over the rail to let out some of the line, I glanced over the side.

And froze.

There was a shape in the dark water below us. It was just deep enough that I could only see a part of it, the rest lost in the gloom of the deeper water. But I could see enough to make out a massive, blunt head with a down-turned, fishlike mouth and a single, glaring eye staring up at the ship. At me.

"Conor!" The line was singing with the tension of the wind, and I quickly let out some of the rope, loosening the complex knot that Nachdainn had taught all of us before we'd set sail. The tension eased, and the sail flapped a little more but was no longer on the verge of tearing.

Gunny Taylor had seen my hesitation, though, and he crossed the deck, weaving between the lines, sea chests, and various other bits of carefully crafted equipment that kept the *Radala Farragah* moving efficiently through the sea. He came up next to me without a word and peered over the side, but the thing had vanished. "What did you see?"

I quickly and briefly described what I'd observed, keeping my voice down. I didn't know that it was anything but a whale, but the Deep Ones had attempted to assail the Isle of Riamog before, and we'd had more than a few fights with them and their monstrous minions ourselves, most recently aboard this very ship, far to the north.

Gunny's eyes narrowed as he scanned the water, deepening the crow's feet around them. He had to be thinking the same thing I was, remembering the sea serpent that had attacked the *Radala Farraghah* just off the coast of the Menninkai's lands.

Still, there wasn't much we could do if the Deep Ones did have their eye on us. Not yet anyway. It wasn't as if we were carrying depth charges. "Keep an eye out. I'll tell Mathghaman and Nachdainn." He nodded toward the rigging. "We'll continue on until something tries to eat us."

I just nodded. That fittingly described our standard operating procedure, these days. There was no shortage of monsters and other threats in this strange world where we'd found ourselves stranded almost a year and a half before, and while I hesitate to say that we were getting used to it, there's a limit to fear. You develop a sort of equilibrium, where watchfulness is balanced with an acceptance that life is short, and better lived well than turned into a constant nightmare of worry and nerves. Some of us had found that out in combat zones back in The World. Some had discovered it here.

Some of us had needed to relearn it, since so many of the threats in this world are so weird.

Nachdainn was already steering us back toward the Isle. We weren't out there just for the wind and the sun, or even lessons in seamanship.

I glanced at the short, stocky men gathered near the stern. Rigged out in lamellar armor and chest rigs, most had hand axes at their sides and M110s close at hand. The Menninkai were ferocious fighters. We'd seen that graphically illustrated when we'd fought beside them at Vahava Paykhah, but they were still figuring out how to fight like Recon Marines. Ten of them had accompanied us when we'd departed Menninkai lands, and they were still integrating into the platoon.

With only twelve of the twenty-nine of us who had come through that mysterious fog bank left, the face of 1st Platoon, Force Recon Company, I MEF had changed quite a bit, and when Orava had approached with nine of his kinsmen, asking to join us, we'd accepted without much hesitation.

They adapted quickly, but unlike the Tuacha da Riamog, who have certain preternatural gifts that we can't match, and had picked up rifle marksmanship as easily as if they'd been born with a long gun in their hands, the Menninkai had to train just like we did. Which was why we were out there on the water, practicing maritime insert and extract. We'd already done two landings that day, and we had gone a little bit farther out this time, which had put us into the deeper water of the borderlands between the Isle of Riamog and what could only be considered the Deep Ones' domain.

A voice was raised, and I looked up to see Orava pointing off to starboard. I followed the line of his pointing finger, and felt gooseflesh go up on my arms.

It was late summer around the Isle of Riamog, and while the occasional thunderstorm was plenty common, fog on the water in the middle of the afternoon was not.

Before anyone could react, that wisp of cloud on the surface billowed up and out, coming apparently from a point barely a few hundred yards from the ship. Nachdainn called out from the tiller, his voice loud and strident, ordering the sails be reefed and the sweeps out to back water. The oars were pulling almost immediately, but it was too late. The fog spread and grew until, only a few moments after it had appeared, we were completely engulfed.

Thinking of the unnatural mists we'd come through to reach this place, I suddenly wondered. Were we about to be yanked back to The World?

Did I *want* to go back?

I didn't have time to think that through before the keel scraped on what felt like solid ground. If we hadn't been backing water, slowing precipitously already even before the mist had engulfed us, everyone aboard the ship would have been thrown to the deck by the abrupt halt.

We had just run aground, in the middle of deep water, miles out to sea.

After a moment, as I regained my equilibrium after the shock of that impact, I realized it felt like we were *rising*, being lifted above the water level. When I lurched to the rail and peered over the side, I saw only wet rock and silt beneath us. An island was rising out of the ocean, stranding the entire ship high and dry. It was still emerging, too, as the ground beneath us shuddered and shook like an earthquake.

The shuddering stopped. The mist seemed to thin, but only to reveal more flat, slimy rock, strewn with some seaweed and what looked like the flopping bodies of fish or eels. Strangely, the mist only appeared to be thinner off to starboard, where it had first appeared. The port side was still engulfed in gray.

The wind had died altogether, and the sails hung slack from the yardarm. Everything had gone quiet. Every man aboard the ship, Tuacha, Marine, or Menninkai, watched, weapons ready, listening and waiting.

A thin, hoarse voice called out from the murk. "Conor! Conor, help me!"

I swallowed, hard, as gooseflesh ran up my arms. I looked at Gunny, and saw that he'd recognized the voice, too.

It was impossible. That voice belonged to a dead man.

Sergeant Able Stanley had been killed that first night, only minutes after we'd come through the mists, his head ripped off after a sea troll had lunged out of the water and dragged him down into the depths. He'd been gone for months. We *knew* he was dead. We'd seen his corpse when it had bumped against the boat.

Yet, that was unmistakably his voice out there in the fog, somewhere on this strange island that had seemingly risen out of the sea in a matter of minutes.

"We've got point." I quickly loaded my M110, checked that my sword was still on my hip, and went over the side.

Whether or not it was Stanley—and I suspected that this was some trick of the Deep Ones from the get-go—I'd been called out. We take care of our own. That had included our missing Marines who had sided with Dragon Mask, all those months before in the north, and had extended to putting them down when Zimmerman had tried to finish what Dragon Mask had started, committing horrible atrocities to free the Outsider known as Vaelor. Furthermore, our time in this world had started to affect my own thinking in other ways.

I'd been called. I would answer.

And whatever slimy, unholy *thing* out there was challenging me, using the voice of my dead pointman, was going to regret it.

CHAPTER 2

THE ground under my boots wasn't just bare rock. Silt and slime squelched beneath my feet as I advanced, weapon up and searching the mist and cloud for threats. Rodeffer, Farrar, and Santos spread out in a wedge behind me, the Tuacha team with Mathghaman in the lead off to our left, Gunny and Bailey's Team Two to the right.

Within a hundred yards, the ship had disappeared into the fog behind us. The entire world had turned into a wet, gray dome hanging low over slimy rock and silt.

We seemed to be moving uphill, and that thin, quavering cry continued to come from in front of us: Stanley pleading for help.

I wanted to ask Mathghaman about that. We'd seen strange, unearthly things here. We'd *seen* the dead get up and walk. Of course, as Mathghaman explained it, they were never the same person as the actual dead men. They were simply evil spirits of some sort wearing the corpses like a skin suit.

I'd taken the lead too quickly, though. Sometimes just assaulting through is the best course of action in an ambush—and I had no doubt that this *was* an ambush—but there's something to be said about taking stock and considering contingencies and options before you go charging in.

Stanley's dead. You know he's dead. This is just some trick to draw you out.

But who—or *what*—wanted *me*, specifically? It had called *me*.

Well, I was going to find out, one way or another.

The ground got steeper and the footing more difficult. It wasn't that the terrain was particularly rough. In fact, it seemed oddly smooth, like a section of ocean floor had been lifted up to the surface. It was slicker than snot, though. A few dying fish flopped nearby, but nothing else moved in the mist but us.

Something dark loomed in the fog ahead. As I slowed my advance, my M110 coming up, the fog cleared a little bit more, to reveal a quintet of strangely asymmetric, cyclopean stones standing straight up out of the ground.

They were huge. I mean each one had to be almost a hundred feet tall. At first glance, they looked like ancient megaliths, slabs of stone pried out of a mountainside and erected by the hand of man, but as I got closer, I saw that every square inch of each had been carved, covered in twisting, intertwining designs, every one of them discordant, asymmetrical, and disturbing. Fanged mouths sprouting from the midst of masses of tentacles devoured fish, sharks, and men, all being torn, stretched, and twisted in agonized ways. Eyes that almost seemed alive sprouted from random places throughout the carvings.

Every one of the stones was covered in glistening slime.

The monoliths crowned what now appeared to be a domed hill rising up out of the sea. At first, from below, it looked like they stood around a flat courtyard, but as

I came closer, careful not to look too closely at those sculpted eyes in the slimy monuments, I saw that instead they were placed around a steep-walled pit, a cenote that descended straight down into the earth.

Something made me stop short. Some warning in the back of my mind made me reluctant, at best, to stand on the edge of that shaft and look down. I didn't know what I'd see, but it was a risk I didn't want to take. I put out a hand to halt the rest of the team. Mathghaman, flanked by Bearrac, barrel-chested and black-haired, on one side, and Fennean, slender, golden-haired, and quick, to his other, moved up on our flank, getting closer to the pit, though each of the Tuacha held those sleek, engraved, elegant rifles of theirs at the ready. Bailey and Gunny held a little farther back.

That was when I realized that Stanley's cries had ceased. The only sounds were the faint squelch of our footsteps in the mire.

No. There was another sound. A deep, subsonic rumble.

That wasn't it, either. The whole island shuddered, ever so slightly, in a not-quite rhythmic pattern, as if something massive was striking the ground.

It was. The shudders got more pronounced, though the monumental stones above us didn't even quiver. Something was definitely coming.

A massive, webbed-fingered hand reached up out of the cenote and gripped the edge of the pit. Then another. And another. And another.

I think we all took a step back as the massive thing came up out of the pit, its shoulders filling most of the space between the standing stones.

It loomed over us, its head an enormous dome covered in bony plates, relatively small eyes—even though each one was probably the size of my head—watching us from low in that dome, surrounded by spined ridges. A wide, lipless gash of a mouth split the enormous skull immediately below those slit-pupiled eyes, fringed by a beard of writhing, snapping eels.

Its body was roughly humanoid, except for its sheer number of arms, a mass of scaly appendages, tipped with more of those webbed-fingered hands than I could count.

Those baleful eyes were fixed on me, as were those of just about every eel in that strange beard.

"So." The voice was weirdly modulated, as low and rumbling as it was. Its tone rose and fell oddly, with a harmonic in it that sounded almost like a whale song, except different, more disturbing. There was a discordant note to it that was almost like fingernails on a blackboard. It was a sound of primeval chaos made manifest. "The thief has come out of his hiding place." One of those huge hands pointed at me. "That sword belongs to the rightful rulers of this world. Long have those who rebel against their masters hidden it. Now it is found again, brought to my very doorstep by the insects that would dance upon the surface of *my* realm."

It leaned forward, a dozen of those slimy hands gripping the cyclopean stones to either side. "I am not, however, without mercy. The masters might desire your destruction, but I find little interest in your small, pointless lives." It leered, its mouth gaping, revealing row upon row of needlelike, translucent teeth. "Leave the sword, and you may go free. My servants hunger, but I will restrain them if you give me what I want. Lay it down here at my feet, and you may return to your ship and your accursed isle unmolested."

Almost as soon as that strangely vibrating voice ceased, a mass of slithering sounds came out of the mist around us. I glanced over my shoulder, just for a moment, knowing that I was taking a hell of a risk by taking my eyes off that monstrosity in front of me, to see a nightmare coming out of the fog.

Sea trolls, their too-large eyes and too-wide mouths gaping, waddled toward us, leaning forward hungrily. They weren't alone, either. Slimy, hunchbacked things with splayed legs, blunt heads dominated by toothy mouths, and long, flat, spatulate tails dragged themselves alongside. The bloated corpses of drowned men, slender spines wrapped around their limbs from inside, stumbled along crablike behind the trolls. Standing taller than any of the rest, bluish-skinned giants, nearly seven feet tall and dressed in armor of shining, rainbow-colored scales, came behind, armed with spears of bone and coral. They looked almost human, except for the color of their skin and their huge, fixed, fishlike eyes.

So, we really had walked into a trap.

Fortunately, I doubted that these things knew quite what the boom sticks in our hands were capable of.

I turned back to the many-handed giant where it leaned over me, slime and seawater dripping from its fangs and those writhing eels that formed its beard. "You want this sword? All of this for a blade?" I needed to stall. Already, Gunny and the others were starting to adjust their positions as the advancing monsters closed in on us. My team backed me, facing the Deep One.

"Not just any blade. Did you but know what you carry, mortal." A massive hand stretched out. "Give me the sword. It belongs not in your feeble hands. It should have remained lost, if not in the masters' grasp."

I looked down at the sword that hung at my belt. Taken from the body of one of the Dovos nal Uergal in the north, I had wondered about it ever since. When I'd found it, its hilts had been wrapped in greasy skins, but its blade, balanced like a feather and forged of some smoky steel that never seemed to take a notch or a stain, and could cut through the most powerful eldritch monsters we'd faced like a hot knife through butter, had been something different. Mathghaman had said it was a blessed weapon. He had then told me to continue bearing it.

I'd wondered if I would ever get to know the real history of that sword.

I didn't think I was going to learn it now, though. Not from a Deep One. Anything that called the Outsiders "masters" wasn't to be trusted.

I glanced to either side. Gunny was ready. Bailey, next to him, gave me a look that suggested that he was a little jealous that I might get the chance to kill a Deep One while he was keeping the sea trolls and assorted other sea monsters off my back.

Mathghaman simply met my eyes and nodded. He was ready. I looked up at the eel-bearded giant with the hundred hands.

"Go to hell."

CHAPTER 3

I snapped my rifle to my shoulder and shot the Deep One in the eye. At least, that was what I was aiming for. Mathghaman and the other Tuacha all fired at the same moment, and the giant reared backward, stung though clearly not that badly hurt.

At the same moment, Santos pivoted, dropping to a knee and leveling his Mk 48 at the mob of trolls, drowned men, and other monsters behind us. With a stuttering roar, he opened fire, tearing into dozens of them with a long, ravening burst. Steam rose from the suppressor as he let off, only for Applegate, next to Bailey, to lay into them with Team Two's belt-fed.

Ordinarily, machinegunners trained to fire five- to eight-round bursts, to preserve the barrel. The *Coira Ansec*, however, King Caedmon's mystical cauldron that would grant you whatever you asked of it, *if* you asked right, produced barrels that we still hadn't been able to melt down. So, under the circumstances, neither Santos nor Applegate was too worried about short, controlled bursts.

Bullets chopped into rubbery flesh, tearing chunks out of the sea trolls in a way our 5.56 rounds hadn't that first night. The hunchbacked quadrupeds were a little tougher, but if it's flesh and blood, and not sorcerously reinforced, then 7.62 will usually kill it. One of them went up on its hind legs, writhing and hissing, as more rounds smashed through the alligator-like scales on its belly, and it went down.

I was still shooting at the Deep One, which was now shielding its eyes with about twenty hands, which was probably the only reason it hadn't tried to smash us yet. Most of the rest were still holding it up out of the pit. It suddenly lunged forward, though, four hands slamming down on the wet rock and silt, sending up geysers of mud and shaking the ground as they hit.

It was time to go. A Deep One wasn't an Outsider or a Warlock King, but it may as well be. We were not prepared to try to kill one.

"Back to the ship! Stay together!" Mathghaman's deep, resonant voice boomed through the mists. His rifle thundered again, and then we were moving, even as the Deep One began to haul itself up out of the pit, a dozen of those hands swinging and flailing for us. It didn't seem to be all that quick on land, but its reach was still long enough, even without the sorcery I knew had to be forthcoming sooner or later, that we had to make tracks *fast*.

Bailey's team's concentrated gunfire had torn a gap in the oncoming wave of fishy monstrosities, and soon we were driving into it in a wedge, weapons barking as we went, each bullet finding one of the Deep One's creatures. The sea trolls died pretty quickly, and while they usually took a bit of punishment, if you hit the hunchbacked quadrupeds in center mass or the head they went down pretty easily.

The drowned corpses, on the other hand, were a problem.

I shot one that lurched in front of me as I drove forward, charging over the bodies of several sea trolls. I hit it with three rounds, two in the chest, one in the head, and didn't even slow it down. It wasn't moving that fast or that well, but it kept coming as if nothing had happened.

Realizing that whatever was controlling the corpse wasn't easily hit, I let my rifle hang and swept out my sword.

Sometimes, there are things in this world that don't go down to just bullets. That was a lesson we'd had to learn the hard way. Sometimes that was because of sorcery. This time, it seemed to be because I was fighting a dead body being puppet-mastered by some sort of deep-sea parasite.

Or maybe it *was* sorcery. It didn't make that much difference, as I swept that bitter blade through rotting flesh and bone, hacking off first a grasping arm, then a leg. The thing tottered and fell, and I kept going, ignoring its remaining, grasping arm. Whatever was controlling it, it couldn't get it back up with only one arm and one leg.

Then we were in the thick of it.

We were close enough that while Rodeffer was still shooting at close-range, and even taking a couple contact shots, I couldn't sheathe the sword and get my rifle back up. Sweeping the M110 to my back with my off hand, I blocked the thrust of a bone-tipped spear and found myself face to face with one of the fish-eyed giants.

It was fast, bringing that spear back quickly before sending it darting for my eyes. I got the sword up in time to knock it aside, then grabbed the spear with my off hand. I'd been training with Mathghaman Mag Cathal, the King's Champion, and so I wasn't nearly the slouch with that blade that I had been, once upon a time.

With a hard yank, I actually brought myself closer to the blue-skinned thing, since as strong as I'd gotten, I still wasn't going to budge that creature. I just needed to be closer, though. I turned my lurch into a lunge, bending my forward knee a bit farther than I needed to so I could get the point underneath the two slimy hands holding onto the rough-textured spear shaft.

It was faster than I'd calculated, though, letting go with one hand and slapping my blade down while snatching its leg back. I twisted the sword and slashed its hand deeply as I withdrew the sword, bringing it back in a tight circle to strike again.

Then Farrar, having just dropped the monster closest to him, turned and double-tapped the creature in the head.

The strange blue humanoid dissolved into a puddle of slime, leaving the spear in my hand.

Farrar's bolt locked back on an empty mag, and then half a dozen sea trolls were lunging toward him from the flank. I reached out and shoved him behind me, knocking a troll's head off with one ferocious swing, the head tumbling to the muddy ground and a fountain of watery blood spouting from the severed stump.

Then Mathghaman and Bearrac came barreling through, blades rising and falling, spilling blood and slime wherever they struck.

Our wedge formation got tighter as we continued our drive through the press, wreaking as much destruction as we could. Gunfire barked, mostly off toward the flanks, because even in the strain of the moment, we were all entirely too conscious of the fact that the *Radala Farragah* lay ahead of us. *Know your target and consider its background.* Those of us at the point of the wedge hacked through the monsters with swords and axes.

An explosion *thump*ed out in the mist. I knew the sound of a 40mm grenade. It was followed by two more shortly thereafter.

The monsters were attacking the ship, and Gurke's team, along with Orava's Menninkai, were fighting back with some of their most effective weapons.

The Menninkai had been very interested once they'd learned about the thumpers. When we'd explained what mortars were, they'd gotten downright intense.

Suddenly, as I hacked down another sea troll, my sword cleaving through its neck and shoulder, cutting clear to the center of its chest before I drew the blade free, I saw open ground ahead. We were almost through, the mob of trolls, blue-skinned giants, and other things having parted before the ferocity of our assault. They'd encircled us, drawn by their gigantic master behind us, but their numbers had been thin enough that we'd just blasted our way through.

The Deep One thundered a discordant call behind us, shaking the ground and stabbing through my head with a lance of pain. The monsters didn't seem to either fall back or come at us with any less ferocity, though the blue-skinned spear-carriers weren't pressing in toward us the same way the more animalistic sea trolls and flat-tailed alligator things were. Those were getting hacked to bits by swords and axes or chopped down by bursts of machinegun or rifle fire.

We had our opening. "Run!" Gunny roared. We burst out through the hole in the press and started sprinting toward the ship.

As we did, the ground shook again, then again, harder. I almost stumbled the second time but caught myself and kept moving.

It took a second to realize what was happening, but after a few more paces I could *feel* the ground dropping beneath us. The Deep One was sinking the island it had raised, probably hoping to trap us in the water, out of our element, before we could reach the ship.

We just leaned into it and put on more speed. My breath burned in my throat and lungs, but I was probably in the best shape of my life, and while the Tuacha probably *could* have easily outrun us, they didn't try, keeping close as we kept going.

I glanced over my shoulder. The monsters were slowing as the gap between us and them opened up. We were faster on land than anything that lurked in the depths, even if it was humanoid. That was why the Deep One was trying to pull the ground itself out from under us.

Water was starting to run over the rocks and silt, and even as the *Radala Farragah* started to loom out of the mists, I realized that we were going to be wading up to our knees by the time we reached her.

Gunfire barked from the deck, and a couple more thumper rounds *thud*ded into the monsters trying to crawl or swim toward the hull, throwing up geysers of water, colored pink by blood and chunks of rubbery meat. Just behind me and to my right, Mathghaman's horn sounded, a deep, thunderous blast, warning our brothers in arms aboard the ship that we were coming and to watch their fires. We had radios again, but trying to talk on the radio while at a dead sprint is difficult, at best. The horn worked better.

The water was now about mid-calf, and we still had fifty yards to go. A massive, crocodilian thing reared out of the water right in front of me, its jaws agape, but I didn't even slow down. Leaning to one side, I slashed it through the side of the mouth, almost severing one entire side of its jaw, the blade only binding slightly as I tore through its skull. It splashed flat in the water and mud at my feet as I pounded past it, leaking dark blood into the greenish seawater.

Then I was at the side, knotted ropes falling from the rail to give us a way up. I didn't start climbing immediately, but stopped and turned, sheathing my sword and bringing my rifle back around, searching the murk for targets. The wind was picking up, though it wasn't so much dispersing the mist as it was lashing us with increasingly heavy rain, as the sky above seemed to get darker. Thunder rumbled, or maybe that was just the Deep One's roar.

The water was rising faster. It was up to my waist now, and I had to stand up. "Watch the flanks!" Gunny roared. "They've got deeper water there, and they can come at us faster!"

More gunfire roared out at our enemies, but I still didn't have any targets.

"Conor! Get aboard!" Bearrac was by my side, on his feet and with his rifle back in his hands, facing the way we'd come. "Before we have no ground to stand on!"

If it had been anyone else, I would have objected, staying until the last. Gunny might have prevailed on me to go first if he was the last man on the ground. But the Tuacha have strengths that we don't, and I knew that I was going to have a harder time getting aboard than any of them. So, I slung my rifle, turned, grabbed the rope, and started to climb.

The rain was getting fiercer, the wind plucking at me as I climbed. I could feel the ship rocking as I mounted the side of the hull, and the sails, reefed as they were, had begun to flap in the wind. A storm was rising fast, and I strongly suspected that the Deep One had summoned it.

Bearrac and Diarmodh suddenly leaped out of the water to either side of me, reaching the rail in a single bound each, grabbing it and vaulting over, just before Bearrac seized my rope and started to haul me the rest of the way up, hand over hand, his massive arms knotted as he pulled. I'm not a small man, though Bearrac makes me look like a boy in comparison.

Mathghaman was the last one aboard, vaulting over the rail just as I dragged myself onto the deck. Mathghaman had alighted gracefully, as if he'd just jumped over a fence, but I landed with more of a wet thump before I hauled myself up to face the enemy, my rifle coming back into my hands as I loosened the sling.

The land was gone, vanished beneath heaving, white-capped waves, studded with the heads of ravenous sea monsters that were now swimming toward us far faster than they could run. The wind whipped and whirled, hammering us with sheets of rain while black clouds, lit occasionally by forks of lightning, began to spin over us.

I couldn't make out Nachdainn's roar from where he leaned on the tiller, but the oars were already out, and, as the sea rolled and dipped beneath us, we began to claw our way out of the storm.

Toward the line of white spray ahead, where a ring of rocks had risen out of the sea to block our way.

CHAPTER 4

NACHDAINN'S crew had seized the oars as soon as the *Radala Farragah* had begun to float again, and they were pulling as hard as they could, even as the ship seemed to corkscrew in the battering winds. The waves crashed against her hull, threatening to tip her over twice, even as Nachdainn fought to keep the bow pointed into the waves, the crests smashing over the prow and washing the deck with brine a dozen times before we'd gone half a mile toward that deadly line of rocks.

That deep, thrumming, atonal bellow sounded again, vibrating through the ship's very timbers. The Deep One, no longer limited by its bulk above water, was in the depths beneath us and moving.

Most of us had been through storms aboard the *Radala Farragah* before, and we'd learned how to cope. We were all crouched low against the rail, where we weren't interfering with the oarsmen, most of us quickly tying ourselves in with sling ropes and carabiners, weapons pointed outboard, watching for targets. We couldn't do much to help the crew sail the ship, but we could sure shoot anything that tried to climb aboard.

Tying ourselves in was absolutely necessary under these conditions. We were all packing enough ammunition, not to mention the green-enameled mail shirts under our chest rigs, that we'd sink like rocks as soon as we hit the waves, no matter how strong we were at treading water.

It's hard to tread water and fight off a dozen sea trolls, too.

I glanced forward. The surf was pounding against the rocks, some of them just under the surface, others jutting out of the water like jagged, black teeth. I didn't see much of a gap, but given how straight a line Nachdainn was steering, he must have spotted some way through.

Then I saw that one of the rocks wasn't a rock. It was a bony-crested head, big as a house, with beady eyes near a massive gash of a mouth, and the eels that made up the Deep One's beard lashing at the water just beneath.

"Give up the sword and live, mortal! Or else I will smash your ship and swallow you whole, to suffer for a lifetime in darkness and pain!" The voice burbled through the waves, seemingly vibrating through the timbers of the ship herself.

"It really wants this blade," I muttered.

Mathghaman, untethered but holding onto the rigging with a grip that would only release when he was dead or chose to let go, heard me. "Indeed." His eyes were narrowed as he stared through the lashing rain at the ancient evil lurking in the water, his reddish-brown hair and beard plastered to his head and neck. "One wonders why it does not try to simply swat this ship and take it from the debris as we sink into the depths." He looked down at me then and held out his hand. "Come with me."

It took a second to undo my sling rope and get it stowed, in this case looped around my shoulders. I gripped his wrist and he hauled me up, before we both started to work our way forward, clinging to rigging or the rail where we needed to. The deck heaved under us, and I had to stop and just hold on several times, a lot more often than Mathghaman did. True to his nature, he showed no impatience, nor did he leave me behind, but lingered and waited until I regained my footing.

It's humbling to live, train, and fight next to a man like that.

We finally reached the prow. The oarsmen were pulling hard, though the waves made it difficult to keep a constant rhythm, and even the Tuacha sailors occasionally clashed oars as a sweep skipped out of the water. We were making progress toward that forbidding skull, but slowly.

Mathghaman gripped me by the arm and leaned in close, raising his voice to be heard over the cacophony of the storm and the creaks and groans of the ship itself. "I do not think that this creature can stand the touch of that sword, unless it is willingly given up, sacrificed to its evil, and so tainted. That is why the Dovos carried it, instead of a Fohoriman. Hold onto it, and do not surrender it. *That* is why it has not destroyed us yet, and that is what will give us our opening. Hold fast, Conor, and fear no darkness."

That's more easily said than done when you're riding a corkscrewing ship through a tempest, toward a Deep One the size of a whale and a line of rocks that could probably tear the guts out of even a Tuacha ship.

As we got closer, though, I started to see what Nachdainn was trying to do. The Deep One itself wasn't filling the entirety of the gap. It probably thought it was sitting in the only navigable part, but there were lower rocks to either side, mostly invisible except where the surf crashed and spouted spray into the gray curtains of rain. The gaps were visible as calmer spots, though whether they were deep enough to get the *Radala Farragah* through was anyone's guess.

Knowing the Tuacha, it was entirely possible that Nachdainn could see clearly just how deep the water was from his perch up on the tiller, despite the waves and the foam and the driving, windblown rain.

The Deep One rose up higher out of the water as we drove nearer, its massive head casting a shadow even in the darkness of the storm. A deep, greenish light seemed to flicker in those malevolent eyes.

It lashed out as we got closer, and I stood higher in the bow, my sword in my hand. One of those many hands suddenly snatched at the prow itself, and I slashed at it. It wasn't my strongest blow, since I was holding onto one of the forward lines for dear life, but I still nicked it.

The thing snatched that hand back as if it had been burned. If I'd needed any further indications that the Deep Ones were evil in a way that went beyond mere wickedness, that was it. The only other things that had reacted that way to that sword were creatures of the Outer Dark, the oily black monstrosities summoned by the disciples of Vaelor.

The Deep One rolled away from the ship, howling in agony, and I caught a glimpse of its hand, whitened and cracked around the gash I'd given it, just before it vanished into the water along with the dozens of others.

Then it hit the ship with its tail.

With a resounding *boom*, the *Radala Farragah* was knocked hard to port, as two of the sweeps snapped like matchsticks, the *bang*s as they were splintered and smashed even louder than the deeper *crack* somewhere down in the hull at that savage impact. If we'd been just a little bit closer, that hit would have smashed us against the rocks.

The Tuacha didn't cry out in pain, though I knew that some of them had to have been wounded by the snapping oars. It wasn't their way. If Recon Marines believed in suffering in silence, the Tuacha took it to a whole new level.

I barely hung on as the ship heeled over and skidded through the waves. Mathghaman reached over and grabbed the strap of my chest rig, just to make sure I didn't go over the side.

He wasn't just standing there watching and keeping me from falling overboard. His deep, resonant chant, calling on Tigharn to smite this monstrosity of the abyss, or at least protect us from it, rolled out over the waves and the wind.

We were getting closer and closer to the rocks, Nachdainn shouting out for the oarsmen to hold their course and speed, the drum still sounding the cadence from just forward of the tiller. Mathghaman and I held on as we plunged into another trough, and the crest of the next wave hammered me to my knees, but I still didn't lose my grip on the sword, which was also secured to my wrist by a thong, one of better quality than the crude rawhide that I'd first used in the north.

When we came up, punching *through* the crest of the wave more than riding over it, the rocks were barely fifty yards off, and we were closing fast. I took a deep breath as I spat seawater over the side. Nachdainn was steering us toward an awfully narrow gap, if it even was a gap.

The Deep One rolled underneath us and hit us again. Its tail struck far harder than the sea serpent in the north had, lifting the keel halfway out of the water, as the entire ship's structure groaned and creaked alarmingly, the impact as we dropped back to the surface so hard that it jarred my teeth together painfully.

When I cleared my eyes, I saw that we were right on the rocks. Nachdainn let out a bellow, leaning hard on the tiller to avoid the knife-edged promontory just beneath the surface, and the oarsmen pulled as hard as they could, sending the ship racing toward the narrow slot of calmer water between two of the jagged, toothlike rocks. That assonant bellow sounded behind us again, a sound of utter chaos and rage.

And command. The rocks and the Deep One weren't the only dangers we faced in that moment.

Sea trolls were already swarming up and over the rocks like insects. From the added height, as we flew into the gap, they leaped like demented frogs onto the rigging and the rail.

The Deep One let out another roar, and whatever it did beneath the surface, it sent a new wave, higher and faster than those that had already been battering us, surging out from behind us. It caught the stern, even as the sea trolls clambered aboard, and slewed the ship to one side.

We hit the jagged rock with an awful *crunch*, the impact throwing Marines and Menninkai to the deck. A few of the sea trolls were knocked loose, tumbling across the deck and quickly dispatched by Conall and Eoghain. I barely held on, and even Mathghaman was nearly jarred from his place in the bow, but then we were through the slot, out into the open ocean.

It wasn't a huge improvement, as the storm was getting worse and we still couldn't see more than a hundred yards. And we had easily a dozen sea trolls aboard.

One had leaped on Kainu, one of our Menninkai teammates, clamping its jaws down on his neck and shoulder. Even as he spurted blood and yelled, he was still stabbing the thing repeatedly in the side, going at it like a monkey with a screwdriver. Watery blood spilled out on the deck, mingling with his own, even as his blows weakened.

A moment later, Orava waded in and split the thing's flat skull with his axe.

Three more were scrabbling along the deck toward Mathghaman and me. We turned to face them, feet planted wide to try to offset the heaving of the ship on the massive swells, staying low to keep from getting bowled over by the vicious gusts of wind.

Mathghaman met the first when it leaped at him, his blow practically cutting it in two. With a twist of his upper body, he flung the suddenly limp corpse over the side, flicking the drops of blood from his sword as he snatched his blade back into a low guard.

I had a split second to see that out of the corner of my eye before the next one lunged at me, but it was a hair too slow. I was already set, and I thrust my sword into it as it leaped at me. The blade sank to the hilts in its pale, fishy belly. It snapped at my face with its too-wide mouth and razor teeth, but it was already dying, its struggles quickly weakening as I ripped the blade upward and eviscerated it like cleaning a fish. Its bowels gushed out onto the deck, and it flopped as I twisted the sword to lever it off.

Two more came at me, and Mathghaman was too occupied with the big one that had jumped on him, grabbing his wrist with its clawed hand, to help. I charged, almost lost my balance as the deck fell away beneath me, and my swing at the left one's head turned into a slash at its knee. Scaly, rubbery flesh parted along with cartilaginous bone, and the thing fell on its face, hissing and shrieking, while I ducked past it and, bringing the sword around in a tight arc, split the second one's skull just as it grabbed me. I felt its claws scrabbling against my mail, but only for a moment. It crumpled, twitching even more violently as I wrenched my blade out and ran the point straight through the first troll's spine.

When I looked around, there were only Marines, Tuacha, and Menninkai on our feet, breath heaving nearly as violently as the deck, many grabbing for handholds if they hadn't already been holding onto a mast, rail, or line with one hand while fighting with the other.

The oars continued to sweep, threshing through the water as we rode through the waves. The rain seemed to have lessened, just a little, but then we heard that awful moan behind us again.

The Deep One hadn't given up, and the storm raged on.

CHAPTER 5

THE storm hammered the ship with rain and wind, rocking us violently with massive swells, and enormous creatures surged through the waves behind us, though none of them surfaced far enough to see them clearly, especially through the sheets of rain. The clouds had gotten thicker and darker, flickering with lightning, the titanic thunderclaps drowning out even the howl of the wind.

As we got farther from where that eldritch island had been raised from the sea floor, the wind began to favor us some, probably against the Deep One's wishes. The Tuacha had continued their chant, joined by Nachdainn as he steered, the oars still heaving to speed us on our way, fighting the swell and the crashing whitecaps with every stroke. Now, as we rode the waves in keeping with the ship's name, Nachdainn stopped chanting long enough to command the sails to be set, if only by half.

We scrambled to help the Tuacha crew unfurl the sails just far enough that they'd give us a bit more speed, hopefully without tearing them to shreds with the force of the wind. Then we were really moving.

The rain began to thin, and the light ahead of us got pale, brightening with every yard we cut through the waves. Then, almost as if it had appeared out of nowhere, another ship was ahead of us, high-prowed and white, her sail furled and her oars out, stroking hard against the wind. Another Tuacha warrior stood in the prow, holding on with one hand and raising his other as he called out across the water, his voice faint against the thunder, wind, and rain.

Mathghaman answered him, and the other ship started to come about, turning to join us on our flank.

A few minutes later, we sailed through a fine mist of rain, flanked by a dozen more Tuacha ships, making good time toward the distant, still sunlit green and white gem upon the sea that was the Isle of Riamog.

It seemed almost as if the Deep One and its minions didn't want to clash with that many Tuacha, because while we could still catch glimpses of something huge occasionally breaking the surface behind us, whatever it was it didn't close the distance much. The storm, however, was spreading and growing, following us as we bore in toward the Isle, blackening all the sky to the north, stretching from horizon to horizon.

That Deep One might be wary about crossing swords with a Tuacha fleet, but it still didn't want to give up.

We raced toward the Isle and Aith an Rih ahead of the storm. It had begun to gain on us again, and by the time we reached the harbor, hours later, it was raging unchecked, hammering us with rain and hail while thunder and lightning blazed and cracked overhead.

King Caedmon himself stood on the quay when Nachdainn brought the *Radala Farragah* to dock, though the wind had died down a little as we'd entered the shelter of the bay. The rain and hail were still just as fierce, though the king hardly seemed fazed. A towering figure clad in silver mail and a gold cloak, his white hair was plastered to his head and shoulders, but he was unbent and refused to flinch before the stinging impacts of the rain and hail.

As impressive as most of the Tuacha are, King Caedmon is the only one I think I've met who makes Mathghaman seem ordinary by comparison.

Mathghaman let Gunny take the lead as we climbed up onto the quay. That took a moment. Before anything else, we had to get Kainu's body off the deck and taken to the Houses of the Dead with honor. He'd died in combat, and he was one of ours. He hadn't been able to speak a word of English, and even his *Tenga Tuacha* had been rough, but he'd still been one of ours. He'd been a scrapper and while he'd been a man of few words, I'd seen his flat face light up whenever he *got* something we were trying to teach. The man had fought on the first wall at Vahava Paykhah, enduring the onslaughts of the worst the Lasknut and the Dovos could throw at the city's defenses, but you wouldn't know it from the way he'd handled himself. He'd been just another guy. One who could take a beating and dish one out just as easily, without complaining once.

We barely knew him, but we'd miss him.

King Caedmon bowed his head and turned to follow us as we bore Kainu's body on a litter through the rain and hail toward the city, the white stones of the walls still as bright in the storm as if the sun was out. He didn't say a word. He wouldn't until we had set Kainu down.

There weren't many people on the streets as we trudged up the hill toward the great, domed temple of Tigharn, beneath which lay the Houses of the Dead. It was a long hike. The temple was the highest structure of

Aith an Rih, built on the shoulder of the towering mountain named *An Staighre Chun na Bhflaitheas*, the Stair to Heaven. It stood even higher than the great round tower of the palace.

It took nearly two hours to reach it. From the air, the temple would form a tripart knot, three great circles overlapping in the center, topped by golden domes. The gilded doors were decorated by bass reliefs depicting shining, winged messengers coming to the Tuacha when they had first awakened on the Isle of Riamog. Two more such messengers were carved into the glittering white stone to either side, their wings extended over the doors.

We passed through those massive doors, but instead of mounting the stairs that led up to the main part of the temple, we turned aside and started down, into the candlelit catacombs beneath.

The Houses of the Dead were cool and dry, lit by sconces along the walls, tended by the brothers who saw to the dead and prayed for their souls. I'd been down there once before, but since all of our fallen up to that point had needed to be buried or burned far from here, none of us had had much reason to visit. I'd seen enough to know that they were a maze, but, fortunately, one of the black-robed brothers came and motioned silently for us to lay Kainu's body on a plinth not far from the stairs that led down into the crypts.

His eyes had been closed and his hands folded atop his lamellar breastplate. His cloak had been wrapped around the awful wound in his neck. Orava laid his weapons by his side. The Tuacha brothers, their faces hidden by their cowls, didn't react that I could see. The Menninkai shared their faith with the Tuacha, but some of their smaller traditions definitely weren't shared by the Tuacha.

"He will be cared for." The lead brother's voice, deep and sonorous, drifted out from his hood. "You may rest, knowing that."

We nodded, though I think we all paused a little to look down at our little brother's corpse before we turned and trooped back up into the temple foyer.

King Caedmon had not accompanied us into the Houses of the Dead, but had stayed at the entrance to the sanctuary, waiting silently. He still didn't speak as we came out, but beckoned as he turned and headed back outside, into the rain.

Up there on the mountainside, we could see the full sweep of Aith an Rih and the great bay, though now it was mostly obscured by sweeping gray curtains of rain and hail. The wind had picked up and plucked at us brutally, cutting through our wet clothing, even though aside from the camouflage utility trousers we all still wore, most of it was now wool and linen.

The king, of course, didn't seem remotely affected by the weather.

"Come. We have much to discuss." He started down the long staircase that led to the plaza before the temple.

We followed, Gunny taking the lead next to Mathghaman. It was a long trek, into the teeth of the wind and rain, but we hunched our shoulders and made it happen.

I was getting old enough that I hoped to one day see the end of "It ain't rainin', we ain't trainin'," but it wasn't going to be that day.

Following the winding road down the mountain, we finally came to the palace, passing under the massive yet delicately arched portico and into the shelter of the foyer. A fire burned in the center of the great, wheel-shaped chamber, and we all sort of gravitated to it. Even the king held out his hands to the fire. It was summer, but the wind and rain were *cold*.

He nodded to two of his bodyguards, men in tall helms and white cloaks, and with a pair of deep bows, they turned and left. Finally, King Caedmon turned to us. "Tell me what happened."

Gunny gave a quick, dispassionate after-action report. The king listened silently, his eyes fixed on Gunny, without glancing at any of his own men for corroboration. Even if we hadn't earned that respect from the Tuacha through rescuing Mathghaman and his companions, then going into the Land of Shadows and Crows to find Sister Sebeal, not to mention taking a hand in keeping Vaelor from walking the earth again—we couldn't exactly take all the credit for that, since it had been Cairbre's sacrifice that seemed to have, somehow, sealed the Outsider back in his stony prison—he still would have bent all his attention to Gunny's report. Like Mathghaman, it was just the way he was.

Once Gunny was done, King Caedmon turned his eyes to me, then to the sword at my side. A faint frown furrowed his brow. "Hmm." He folded his arms and thought, studying that blade. I looked down at it a little self-consciously. Was I going to have to give it up? I suddenly found I didn't like the idea very much.

After all, Mathghaman had told me to continue to carry it when I'd offered it to him, down in the tunnels beneath Taramas's citadel. I'd been through a lot with that weapon.

"We have long believed that there is more to the sword you bear, Conor McCall, than meets the eye." The king raised his gaze to meet mine, and I found I was somewhat reassured. He was thoughtful, but that wasn't the expression of a man who was about to make a demand. "It seems that the truth of its nature and its origin have begun to emerge. Sadly, not only to us. It would appear that the enemy knows what you carry, as well. Perhaps better than we."

Before I could ask what he was talking about—a common thing with the Tuacha, we'd found; they didn't just hand out information willy-nilly—the two bodyguards returned with two other men in tow.

While neither matched the Tuacha for height—few mortal men do—both were tall, big-framed men, both with somewhat aquiline features. Each man wore a knee-length tunic, richly embroidered with what looked like coats of arms, over woven breeches and soft leather shoes. Short capes covered their broad shoulders, and I couldn't help but notice the massive forearms protruding from their mid-length sleeves. I'd been training long enough to recognize a swordsman's physique when I saw it.

Both wore their hair long. The man with dark brown hair wore his down to about the level of his jaw, the other, a reddish blond, had his somewhat longer hair bound back in a ponytail. Neither had a beard, but wore long, flowing handlebar mustaches. The darker haired one, with a red griffon on a blue field on his tunic, had a nasty scar running along the line of his jaw, while the blond man, whose tunic bore a raised golden gauntlet on a field of green, had obviously had his nose broken more than once. These men were clearly wealthy, but they were fighting men, not fops, and it showed in every line of their frame and bearing.

They'd also been through hell. Their tunics and capes were rumpled and still damp, and their hair was in disarray. Both looked exhausted and ragged.

They each bowed from the waist. "King Caedmon. We come at your summons." The dark-haired man spoke *Tenga Tuacha* with a slight burr, though his diction was noticeably better than any of ours, and we'd been living with the Tuacha for months.

He looked us over, taking in our odd clothing and accoutrements, a mix of US Marine and Tuacha weapons and gear. There was a combination of curiosity and wariness in his eyes, even as they descended to the hilt of the sword at my side.

The king answered their bows with an inclination of his head. "Lords Fortrenn and Galan. May I present my Champion, Mathghaman Mag Cathal, and his companions, led by Gunnery Sergeant Ronald Taylor."

The two men bowed again, and we all sort of vaguely and uncomfortably nodded in reply. A faint shadow might have crossed the dark-haired man's face, to which Mathghaman chuckled slightly.

"Forgive my companions, Lord Fortrenn. They are warriors from a distant land, and they are unaccustomed to bowing or kneeling before any mortal man. They mean no disrespect or discourtesy."

That was arguable, actually. Anyone who has ever had to salute the likes of Captain Sorenson knows what it feels like to bend the knee. Which was one more reason we weren't doing it now.

Fortrenn—I gathered that was the dark-haired man— inclined his head with a slight wave of his hand, as if to accept the apology and dismiss any offense that might have been taken. Then his eyes moved back to me and the blade at my side. He stepped forward, pointing to it. "If I may ask…" He hesitated, then looked me in the eye. I saw the same curiosity and wariness in his eyes that I'd seen before. No, not wariness. Not quite.

This man, this tall, proud fighting man who went by "Lord," was actually nervous. And slightly in awe.

"May we see that sword?"

I had my hand on the hilt already, almost defensive-ly, and I looked at Mathghaman, then the king. King Caedmon eyed me gravely. "You are its bearer, Conor. He is asking you."

There was something about the way he said that. As if carrying this blade was somehow far more important than being a team leader in this platoon of foreigners brought to his land by means unknown and supernatural. As if it set *me*, specifically, apart.

I looked down at the sword by my side. I'd known there was something different about it from the moment I'd first wielded it in battle. The question had always been what exactly that something was. Maybe I was about to find out. I suddenly realized that the king already knew, and that I had changed, somehow, in his eyes due to that knowledge.

I drew it out of its scabbard and held it out, blade par-allel with the floor, for Fortrenn's inspection. Lord Galan stepped up next to him then, his eyes wide as he beheld the weapon in my hand.

About three feet long, the blade was a smoky gray, shining brightly only along the thin edge that never seemed to require sharpening. Runes I'd never been able to decipher ran down the fuller. The hilt was of the same smoky gray steel, inlaid and set with gold. The downward-curving quillons were carved with gilded, roaring lions, and a rune that looked an awful lot like a Greek Chi Rho was set into the round pommel, gold inlaid in the steel. The grip was wrapped in black leather which seemed to be every bit as robust as the metal.

Fortrenn reached out a hand toward the hilt but halted only a few inches away, withdrawing it reverently. "So, it is true."

"What?" I frowned as I watched him. "What do you know about this sword?"

He looked me in the eye. "You do not know what it is you bear?"

I shook my head. "I found it in the hands of a dead Dovo nal Uergal in the north. I know it cuts through just about anything, never takes a stain, never gets notched or even dull. Oh, and it makes things from the Outer Dark burst into flame when you hit them with it. Other than that, your guess is as good as mine." I glanced at King Caedmon, but he was still holding his peace.

Fortrenn glanced at Galan, then the king, then turned his eyes back to the sword. "Lord Galan and I each had a dream, the same dream, some weeks ago. In it, this sword rose above the Isle of Riamog, over the western sea, and a voice told us that the Sword of Iudicael had been found." He looked up at me then. "We had to come.

Not only to see the sword from the Age of Heroes and Martyrs, but to beg the aid of its bearer."

I frowned and glanced at King Caedmon. "Well, now I know what its name is, but not much more than that."

The king took a deep breath. "The Age of Heroes and Martyrs was the darkest, and at the same time, one of the most glorious ages since the advent of The Summoner and the fall of the old world. During those short decades, many men and women stood against the growing darkness. Many fell, but the foundations of those kingdoms which still stand against the darkness today were laid then.

"At the darkest hour, two shining messengers of Tigharn descended from the sky above the battlefield at Thaurthuid. Calling themselves Iudicael and Categyrn, they handed their swords to the kings Feradach and Kyrator. With those swords in hand, the forefathers of the men of Silabor and Commagan won a great victory. They lived longer lives than most men, in the years that followed, and held the line against the Outsiders and their armies of monsters for many years."

"Wait. Commagan?" Bailey frowned. "Wasn't Commagan the empire that destroyed Colcand and Tethba? And then tore itself apart?"

Fortrenn and Galan had glanced sharply at my brother from another mother as he'd interrupted the king, but Caedmon was unruffled. "Indeed, Sean. The very same. Few are the kingdoms that have endured the temptations of power that the Outer Dark offers."

He continued. "As all too often happens, both Silabor and Commagan became complacent in the protection that the Swords offered. Commagan in particular began to rot from within. The Sword of Categyrn was stolen by a pretender to the throne, who then vanished. It has not been seen since. The Sword of Iudicael, which you now bear, was borne north by the king of Silabor many ages ago, after the fall of Commagan, to challenge the abomination which then squatted in the temples, drinking the people's blood in sacrifice. His ship was blown off course and he never returned." He nodded toward the sword in my hand. "He must have been shipwrecked in the north, and the sword fell into savage hands. Such is the fate of those who think too highly of their own strength and believe that protection from on high comes free of responsibility."

"Word has spread from the savage lands that the Sword of Iudicael has been seen again." Fortrenn took up his story once more. "Not to us, but spies captured in Cor Legear have been looking for any lore or news concerning either it or the Sword of Categyrn." He looked around at us. "The Emperor of Ar-Annator has learned of strange warriors who ventured into the lands of the northern corsair tribes and even into Lost Colcand itself, bearing what sounded much like the Sword of Iudicael. Now, he seeks to find the Sword of Categyrn.

"Our own spies have told us of dark stirrings within the Empire. Necromancies within ancient Commagan ruins. Revenants that stalk the waking world, searching for the sword. Our truce with the Empire holds, but King Uven fears it will not last long if the emperor finds the Sword and turns it against us. He has already awakened dark and terrible forces in his quest to find it."

He went down on one knee, then, and I was a little taken aback. "We have been sent through storms and monsters to find the bearer of the Sword of Iudicael and beg his help in this quest.

"We must find the Sword of Categyrn, before the darkness does."

CHAPTER 6

WHEN I looked at Gunny and Mathghaman, Mathghaman simply inclined his head, and Gunny just said, "It's up to you, Conor."

That wasn't the way it was supposed to work. Gunny was our de facto platoon leader, and if Mathghaman had demurred from taking that role, he was still the closest we had to such a figure. I was just a team leader. Yet, because I was carrying the Sword, this somehow fell on me to make the decision.

I wasn't prepared, but as I looked down at the blade in my hand, I couldn't bring myself to say no. "I'll go." I looked around at the rest of the platoon. "Whether any of the rest will, I'll leave up to them."

Gunny and Bailey both snorted derisively at that, almost simultaneously. As if I'd just said something supremely stupid. Santos laughed a little. That drew some frowns from Fortrenn and Galan, but I was getting the impression that the two of them were used to a far more formal and mannerly society than a bunch of Recon Marines. At any rate, they were laughing at the idea that I'd go myself while the rest of the platoon stayed back.

A few minutes later, we were getting down to the brass tacks of mission prep.

Of course, the storm outside was still raging, and we couldn't leave that day anyway, not without casting off against the incoming tide. So, with the basics of the planning over, we retired to the palace's guest quarters for the night.

I found Mathghaman standing just inside the portico that looked out over the bay. The candles and the fire within his quarters flickered and guttered as the wind continued to howl, lashing the front of the palace with rain and hail. The storm hadn't abated at all.

He turned as I got closer, though I hadn't made a sound. I'd always been good at moving silently, and while his senses were far more acute than mine, I suddenly had the impression that Mathghaman had been expecting me.

"Conor." He turned back to the window. He was just far enough inside that the rain and hail couldn't reach him.

I stepped up next to him. Lightning flickered across the sky, splitting the clouds a moment before a massive thunderclap shook the palace again. If anything, the storm seemed to be getting worse.

I wasn't sure how to ask this. Mathghaman was a brother, and at the same time, he was far more experienced and wiser than any of the rest of us. Questioning him like this felt wrong, but at the same time, I knew that he'd always been reticent about handing out information when not asked specifically. But something about this really bothered me.

"Did you know about this sword?" I hadn't put it aside since the meeting in the foyer of the palace. I'd never left it far from me since the north, but now it seemed even more vital to keep it within arm's length.

"Did I know?" He continued to watch the storm. "No." He turned to me again. "I knew that it was an extraordinary artifact, but understand, the Swords never came to our Isle before they were lost. There have been tales of them, but I have not been particularly familiar with them." He smiled slightly. "I am not all-knowing, Conor. Nor is the king. That you had stumbled upon a weapon of great power was unmistakable, but what weapon it was, we did not know. There may even be drawings of the Swords within our archives, but if they are there, I have not seen them."

I expected that if he had, he would have recognized it. The Tuacha are gifted, and I suspected that Mathghaman had a memory that could only be described as "photographic."

He gripped my shoulder. "This *is* your quest, Conor. *You* had the decision to make, and you chose to embark upon it. We will go with you, and we will stand with you. But there is more to what is happening that we can see from here. That you bear the Sword of Iudicael is not mere chance. Mere chance has little to do with the Two Swords. I cannot say to what end you picked it up, but you must understand that there *is* an end. Time will tell what purpose lay behind such a find. And even then, you might not know for certain. The truth may only become clear after you are dead."

From anyone else, that might not have been particularly comforting. Coming from Mathghaman, however, it didn't sound nearly as grim as it might have.

Maybe I was just getting used to thinking along slightly different lines after nearly a year with these people. I understood the point Mathghaman was making. Taking a deep breath, I nodded.

There were powers at work in this world that didn't always reveal themselves or their purposes, for good or evil. Sometimes, just like back in The World, the only thing you could do was do the right thing and accept what came.

Together, wordlessly, we watched the storm rage.

* * *

If we'd hoped that the storm would have abated by morning, we were sorely disappointed.

The wind howled, bending the trees nearly double, and the rain continued to sweep across the Isle, lightning repeatedly striking the mountains to either side of Aith an Rih. If not for the sheer volume of rain and hail, the forests would doubtless have been set ablaze.

From the roof of the palace, King Caedmon, Mathghaman, Gunny, Fortrenn, Galan, and I stood and watched the storm. Through the sheets of rain and hail, something dark could be seen on the water, far out in the bay. I couldn't make it out, not even with binoculars, but I almost didn't need to.

I knew what it was. I could almost see those eerily glowing green eyes just above the surface of the water, glaring toward the city and the palace. The Deep One hadn't given up.

"A persistent creature, is it not?" King Caedmon's voice was dry over the howl of the wind. "It seems that the Deep Ones require some reinforcement of the lesson we taught them some generations ago. Do you not agree, Mathghaman?"

Mathghaman inclined his head gravely. "Indeed, my king. Still, the wrath of such a creature is no small thing."

"No, it is not." King Caedmon looked over at the two men of Cor Legear. Galel, I'd learned, was the name of their tribe, if you could use the term "tribe" for a people with a civilization that seemed very High Medieval. "It has already shipwrecked our friends here, and they were not even its quarry."

"Weren't they?" I wondered. When all eyes turned to me, I tried to keep my own gaze locked on that distant dark spot on the water, even as the rain swept across it, hiding it from view from time to time. "That thing was after the Sword, and it's a creature of the Outer Dark." When Fortrenn's and Galan's eyebrows both went up, I explained. "The Sword's touch burned it. That's only happened with things that came directly from the Outer Dark. Vaelor's summoned minions." I nodded toward the dark spot on the bay. "When I cut it, the wound got scorched. That's the only explanation I can think of. Anyway, if it knew that I had the Sword of Iudicael and tried to ambush us to take it, then the word about the Swords must be getting around. Maybe it knew that Fortrenn and Galan were coming to seek help finding the Sword of Categyrn, and it wrecked their ship to stop them."

"It is possible." King Caedmon nodded thoughtfully. "You are right Conor, that the Deep Ones are Outsiders, though of a lesser order than the so-called 'elder gods.' They are rebels, just as the Fohoriman Warlock Kings and other such monsters are, who sought escape from their masters' ire in the depths. They have eyes and ears wherever the sea meets the land, and I doubt not that word of this quest reached them. Whether or not that one sought to kill our friends in the shipwreck, however, it failed, and it will be harder by far to sink one of our ships." He glowered out at the sea. "Still, it has been many years since any of the abominations of the deep dared to come so near to our shores, let alone assail the Isle directly. This must not be borne."

He turned and started toward the stairs. "Mathghaman. Summon your companions. We have preparations to make."

* * *

When Recon Marines hear "mission prep," we tend to think in concrete, material terms. We think about packing rucks, drawing ammo, planning primary, alternate, and tertiary routes to the objective, coordinating with insert and extract platforms, working up comms packages, that sort of thing. And we did that, for a good chunk of that day. By just before sundown, we had rucks packed, extra ammunition and explosives loaded aboard the *Radala Farragah*, comms checks with the new radios we'd gotten from the *Coira Ansec* done—they were *good*, to the point that I had begun to wonder if they actually used radio signals, or were some kind of Tuacha magic or miracle—and the Menninkai had not only their own personal weapons and gear packed but the three mortars that Gunny had finally agreed to let them ask the *Coira Ansec* for, as well.

The Tuacha, however, had additional preparations to make. And it had been Gunny's idea that he and I should join them, especially given my status as Bearer of the Sword of Iudicael.

We joined the vigil in progress. It had started right at sundown, in the temple on the shoulder of the mountain. The sanctuary was dark, lit only by candles. The golden glow barely reached the high, vaulted ceiling above, where the echoes of the chant reverberated. It rolled and soared, reminding me of the chant that our Tuacha brethren had sung against the thing of the Outer Dark that had come to our fire after the death of Fearghanagaidh, far in the north, only somehow this was greater by far.

King Caedmon himself knelt at the base of the dais at the far end of the sanctuary, leading the chant. Behind him, fully two hundred Tuacha warriors, in full armor and with their weapons and helms laid out neatly before them, followed. Mathghaman himself knelt at the king's right hand.

Gunny and I took this in, not sure what to do. One of the white-robed brothers who tended the temple appeared at Gunny's elbow and ushered us to a place near the back. He didn't say a word, which seemed fitting under the circumstances. Neither did we.

With a glance at each other and a vague shrug—neither one of us had gotten a handle on the ancient language that the Tuacha used in prayer or invocation—we settled down to wait.

I didn't know what was going on, really. I'd found that I was praying a lot more in this place than I ever had before, but I was still unsure about a lot of things here. Something about that chant, though, raised goosebumps on my arms, the kind you get when you realize you're in the presence of something transcendent, something powerful. It's the kind of gooseflesh you get when you hear a piece of music that doesn't just sound good, it pierces clear to your soul. It makes you want to do great things, to rise higher than yourself.

I couldn't join in the chant. I didn't know the words. But I didn't want to leave, either. So, I settled in next to Gunny as we laid our rifles, my sword—the Sword of Iudicael—and Gunny's axe on the floor in front of us, went as still as I could, closed my eyes, and listened to the chant.

* * *

I knew that all-night vigils were a pretty common practice among the Tuacha. Mathghaman had conducted one before he'd faced Bres, outside of Vahava Paykhah. It was a sort of mystical mission prep that made them a lot harder to touch with sorcery. The fact that two hundred or more of them were conducting this vigil meant that King Caedmon was serious as a heart attack.

That thing out there in the water should be afraid.

As the morning bells tolled, the first gray light of dawn, late and muted on account of the storm, leaking through the windows of the temple, the king brought the chant to a haunting conclusion. Slowly, the echoes died, until the temple was wrapped in silence.

Only then did the king take up his weapons and his helm and stand, turning to stride down the aisle toward the great doors. He glanced over at us and nodded as he passed, the rest of his warriors filing two by two behind him.

Mathghaman, Bearrac, Fennean, Diarmodh, Conall, and Eoghain waited for us. I found that my knees were not what they'd once been, though I made a supreme effort not to limp as we joined them, since none of the Tuacha looked even remotely tired or stiff after kneeling on the stone floor all night. Of course, I'd never known the Tuacha to sleep quite the same way we did, but still.

It was the principle of the thing.

We wrapped our cloaks around ourselves as we stepped out into the morning, immediately assaulted by the wind and the flying rain and hail, as a pair of lightning bolts hammered down onto the hillsides to either side of the temple, the thunderclaps immediate and brutal. If anything, the storm had intensified even more during the night.

We were in for a hell of a fight.

We followed the king down to the harbor, weaving through the streets of Aith an Rih as the storm raged and thundered overhead. He strode toward the harbor and his own ship, the *Shlae Scaehon*, his head high and his purpose undeterred.

Gunny nodded toward the house near the piers where the rest of the platoon had taken shelter during the night. Bailey, Gurke, and Orava were standing in the doorway, watching the procession of Tuacha warriors go by. We joined them a moment later.

"Everybody saddle up." Gunny looked around at all of us, Marines and Menninkai both. "It's go time."

CHAPTER 7

TWENTY ships plunged into the heaving surf in the bay, led by the massive *Shlae Scaehon*. With three sails to the *Radala Farragah*'s two, the king's ship was more than formidable. How formidable a Deep One would find it was another question.

The sea surged and rolled, and it took every bit of seamanship that Nachdainn and his crew possessed to keep us on course. That was saying something, given how skilled those guys were. The wind was too bad for the sails, so they were furled, the oarsmen pulling hard and Nachdainn leaning on the tiller to compensate for the wind and the waves.

We were all tied in again, braced against lines, spars, and rails, weapons held ready. I didn't know what we were going to fight, but given the battle we'd gone through just to get clear of that mysterious island, we had to be prepared for every watery nightmare the Deep One could summon.

Through the wind and the rain, I could just make out King Caedmon himself, standing in the *Shlae Scaehon*'s bow, his cloak whipping behind him in the wind, his spear in his hand. He was bareheaded, unlike most of his warriors, holding onto one of the forward lines with one hand, otherwise unmoved by either the wind or the heaving of the ship beneath him.

The Old Man was *pissed*.

I didn't know why that old slang term for a commanding officer had popped into my head right then. When looking at the king, standing there ready for a fight with a creature far, far larger and more powerful than him, though, way out in front of everyone else, it seemed to fit.

Caedmon was hardly the picture of a king that we'd grown up with. His white hair and beard notwithstanding, he was still physically powerful, and he didn't shrink from action or hide behind his responsibilities of government.

From what I'd seen, the Tuacha didn't require a whole lot of government, anyway.

Mathghaman, Bailey, Gunny, and I were in the bow. Applegate and Santos were just behind us, covering either flank with their Mk 48s. Chambers was in the stern with another, flanked by Huuhka. I don't know for sure what his name means, but Huuhka was one of Orava's biggest guys, who had basically muscled his way up to the Menninkai team's Mk 48 and said, "Mine."

If they'd had their way, all the Menninkai would be carrying Mk 48s. When we'd first started marksmanship training, they'd all shown a certain propensity for accuracy through volume. It had taken some serious war stories about trekking and fighting across the Land of Ice and Monsters with ever-dwindling combat loads to get them to settle down and concentrate on "aim small, miss small." Huuhka had still held onto the belt-fed, though.

The rest of the platoon was lined up on the flanks, armed with rifles and 40mm thumpers. We would probably be the deadliest ship in the flotilla, if you didn't take into consideration just *how* deadly a Tuacha warrior is, even buck naked and with only his bare hands. Failing to take that into consideration would not be a good idea.

Noita, who ran the Menninkai mortar team, was probably chewing nails as he watched the water over his M110. He didn't get to blow anything up this time. Gunny did *not* want him lobbing mortar rounds around from a rocking deck while there were friendly ships in close proximity.

We were getting close to drawing even with the two great headlands that jutted out to either side of the massive bay. So far, nothing had hit us except the storm. The dark shape that might have been the Deep One, or might even have been that mysterious island, uprooted and moved into the entrance to the bay, still lurked out there, but so far it hadn't moved.

King Caedmon had said that it had been a long time since the Deep Ones had dared to sully the Isle with their presence. It seemed that they were still reluctant to get too close, but a blockade wasn't off the table.

Then the king's ship crossed some invisible line, and the fight was joined.

Two massive creatures came slithering up through the waves, one of them breaching the water to reveal a head that was mostly mouth, lined with jagged fangs, and two clawed feet instead of flippers. It was probably as long as the sea serpent we'd fought in the north, if not longer, its powerful tail still winding through the sea behind it. It didn't try to wrap itself around the ship like that sea serpent had, though. It grabbed hold of one of the rails with one of those clawed feet, snapping several oars in the process, and hauled itself up, jaws agape, to attack the men on deck.

As scary as that thing was, though, it was no match for the dozen or so Tuacha warriors who leaped to meet it, blades and spears flashing in the lighting overhead.

Two spears rammed through the thing's lower jaw, one from the side, the other driven up from below by a red-haired Tuacha who slid onto a knee beneath it. He thrust upward so hard that he just about nailed the thing's jaws shut.

Three others attacked that clawed paw with axes and swords. Blood spurted as they hacked deep into it, and in only a few strokes, it had been severed, and the creature rolled over and vanished back beneath the waves, taking that one Tuacha's spear with it.

Then we couldn't watch anymore, as a raging mob of sea trolls attacked the *Radala Farragah*.

They surfaced close, as if whatever was directing them had learned from the last time, when we'd cut them to pieces with concentrated firepower. They were suddenly right there, about ten yards off the side, butterfly stroking through the water, leaping out like flying fish to grab onto the oars and climb aboard.

Closer or not, while they might have gotten close enough not to get turned into chunks by the thumpers, they still weren't too close to shoot.

I didn't have to lean out very far, still braced against the prow, to bring my M110 to bear, canted to bring the offset red dot alongside my scope to bear. I blew the first troll's brains into the next one's eyes, then shifted and double-tapped the one that had just thrown a scaly arm and webbed hand over the rail. My first round went through that gaping maw, the second liquefied a huge, staring eye, and then it limply fell off the side of the ship, vanishing into the water, though not before wiping out a couple more of its fellows.

Unfortunately, there were a *lot* of those things. So many that they made the mob that had attacked us on the island seem like a street gang in a mid-sized city compared to an army. That hundred-handed abomination must have been gathering them for the entire last two days.

The rail was suddenly swarming with the things, and I just dragged my muzzle across the mob, riding the trigger reset as I leaned into the gun, glad that I was tied to the prow as the ship rose and fell beneath me. I wasn't even bothering to get a good sight picture, but just squeezing the trigger as I kept the muzzle flat, my hand clamped firmly around the handguard, twisting my upper body to rake the entire group with fire as I dumped the mag.

At that range, I could hardly miss. If I had, Gunny would have been fully within his rights to thrash the snot bubbles out of me afterward, if we survived. Skulls shattered, throats were torn open, and rubbery, scaly, limp corpses tumbled off the rail, most into the water, though at least two landed on the deck.

Then my bolt locked back on an empty mag, just as one of the blue-skinned, long-haired, fish-eyed spearmen vaulted over the rail.

I already knew that going toe-to-toe with one of those things was going to be brutal, but I didn't have time to reload, and I didn't want to stay entirely on the defensive if this was going to go sword versus spear. So, I unclipped the carabiner that was keeping me secured to the prow, cinched down my sling, and drew the Sword of Iudicael with one hand, my shield with the other. The shield wasn't a full-sized round like I'd trained with initially. It was more like a buckler, about nine inches across, just big enough to cover my fist with a little bit of overlap to either side. It fit on the Sword's scabbard without getting in the way too much, especially if I was carrying a ruck.

Just in time, I swept the blade up to intercept the bone-tipped spear as it lanced toward my throat. In the frantic heat of the moment, I blocked with the edge instead of the flat, like Mathghaman had taught me.

I cut the spear in half with less effort than cutting through a stem of grass.

The fish-eyed man gaped, and I lunged at him, plunging my sword through his chest. He looked down at the blade that transfixed him, and then melted into translucent slime.

I didn't know what these things were, but more of them were coming on deck now, and my footing wasn't getting any better as the Tuacha flotilla came out of the meager shelter of the bay and into the *really* rough seas.

Taking a swing at a blue figure just as the ship heeled hard to port, caught by the wind and the sea and starting to corkscrew no matter how hard Nachdainn leaned on the tiller and roared for the starboard side to back water, I started to overbalance. My blow only sliced down the side of its face and its shoulder, and I almost fell. It still flinched back from the blow, getting tangled with two more of its fellows that had come over the rail behind it, but it wasn't out of the fight, and its spear hammered into my mail-clad side. It didn't penetrate, fortunately, but it hurt like hell, and it knocked me sprawling.

Instead of trying to hold my ground and recover, I threw myself into the movement, hitting the deck on my side while I lashed out with as powerful a backhand cut as I could muster from that position. It cleaved rubbery flesh and bone, lopping off the nearest spearman's foot, and he fell as I whipped the point up to catch him.

There was nothing human in those wide, fishy eyes as the thing gaped over me, then disintegrated. I rolled away just in time to avoid being drowned in the cascade of slime.

A hand had grabbed me by the chest rig and hauled me to my feet, as Mathghaman—who apparently hadn't bothered to tie in—stepped between the blue-skins and me. His own sword flashed in the eerie light, and more of the strange creatures dissolved into puddles of slime.

With my feet under me, I saw that it had been Gunny who'd picked me up. I nodded to him, and we both turned to face the oncoming tide of monsters, blades in hand.

Mathghaman had cut a swathe through the group that had been climbing the side, though, and we had a momentary breather.

In that moment, King Caedmon's voice rang out over the waves, louder than even the storm. I couldn't make out his words, as he used that ancient tongue of prayer and invocation, except this time, the tone was different. It was unmistakably a command, with the kind of force behind it that made you instinctively stiffen to attention.

It was a command, and at the same time, it was a challenge. Something about the power of those words reverberated through the air and made the hair on my arms stand on end. The very atmosphere seemed to crackle in that moment.

And the Deep One responded.

With a deep, moaning roar, it erupted out of the ocean like a mountain being born. Its hundred hands lashed at the water as spray fountained from its breach, its huge mouth gaping as it roared its hate, the eels that made up its beard writhing and hissing. The *Shlae Scaehon* rocked as the waves beat outward from the thing's rise, but King Caedmon, still standing in the bow, seemed unmoved.

Drawing back his arm, his spear glittering in the faint light of the sun, he chanted a single verse, loudly calling on Tigharn.

It's hard to describe what happened next. As he flung that spear, in one of the most powerful casts I'd ever seen, it was as if all the lightning in the clouds above stabbed down and gathered around it, until it was a brilliant, blue-white bolt arrowing straight at the Deep One's face.

It struck with a massive thunderclap and a flash that momentarily blinded me. I blinked at the green spot in my vision, turning desperately back to face the blue-skinned creatures, but they were gone, the last ones leaping overboard, one of them taking a burst of machinegun fire in the back and dissolving into slime as it hit the water.

When my vision finally cleared the wind had died down and the storm was already dispersing, the rain fading to a fine mist from the driving downpour it had been before.

There was no sign of the Deep One. The waves still rocked the ships, but the monsters had fled. A beam of sunlight lanced through the rapidly disintegrating clouds.

Nachdainn steered the *Radala Farragah* closer to the king's ship. Several of the Menninkai were heaving the torn and shattered bodies of sea trolls overboard. Mathghaman turned to look at us, and Gunny and I both took stock. My team was all in one piece. I got thumbs up from Farrar, Rodeffer, and Santos, and I passed it along. Gunny got similar signals from Bailey, Gurke, and Orava.

Mathghaman had climbed into the prow again, and as we came alongside the *Shlae Scaehon*, he raised his hand and called out to the king, who stood tall and straight in the bow of his own ship. "My king! We set sail for Cor Legear!"

"Go with my blessing, Mathghaman Mag Cathal." King Caedmon's voice boomed across the water. I felt his eyes on me. "And all who go with you. Conor McCall! Bear that Sword worthily and well, and do not forget from whence it came!"

I raised the sword in front of my face in salute, as Mathghaman had taught me. The king returned it gravely.

Then Nachdainn was steering us to the east, the sails unfurled and catching the wind as we set a course away from the Isle of Riamog.

It would be a long while before we saw those emerald shores again.

CHAPTER 8

THE sky was dotted with white clouds on the northern horizon, and the breeze was brisk and cool. I eyed the clouds as I stepped up into the bow next to Galan. I was getting better at reading the weather again. I'd spent a good chunk of time before the Marine Corps living in the mountains, and I'd gotten pretty good at reading the signs then. Some of that skill had slipped, but living in the open as much as we had since arriving in this world was bringing it back.

"Might be another squall coming." I leaned against the rail, watching the clouds. We'd been through a couple already on this voyage, though none nearly as bad as the storm the Deep One had raised against the Isle of Riamog.

Galan had straightened as I'd approached, but now he relaxed and leaned his elbows against the rail next to me. "I am no seaman." He chuckled slightly. "Nor am I a farmer. Perhaps that is a failing of mine. I have always left such concerns to the men who cultivate my lands."

I glanced over at him. That crooked nose and his big, scarred hands didn't bespeak a man who shrank from the difficult, but here he was admitting that he was somewhat more sheltered than even we were, by comparison to some in this place. I couldn't tell if that was a matter of pride to the Galel nobility or not, but Galan, at least, seemed somewhat abashed to admit it.

It had been a week since we'd departed the shores of the Isle of Riamog, and while Nachdainn had made it abundantly clear that he would tolerate no shirkers aboard his ship, the knights had done what little they could and otherwise generally kept to themselves. I was hardly a social butterfly—none of us were—but we had to break down the wall, as intangible—and, I suspected, unintentional—as it was.

"So, what do you do with your time?" It wasn't the most tactful of questions, and I halfway regretted it as soon as I asked. I'm not the greatest conversationalist, either.

He glanced at me. "Much the same as you. We train. We patrol our borders. We hunt. There is little time for other concerns."

I wondered at that. Hunting can take up a lot of time, I knew, but everybody has *some* leisure, and even as hard as we trained, we'd still had spare time during our stays on the Isle.

Galan looked over at me when I didn't reply immediately. "It is our role. This is strange to you?"

I shrugged. "We don't tend to get too caught up in roles." I realized that that needed a qualifier. "At least, among Recon Marines, we try not to. 'Jack of all trades' is one of our mottos. We work and fight in small teams. If one man goes down, everyone else has to be ready to take up the slack." I looked up at the distant clouds. "I guess some of us extend that to other endeavors, too." I turned and nodded toward Gunny, who was working with Pöllö on some knots while a couple other Menninkai watched.

"Gunny Taylor once told me that it's not enough for a man to be a great warrior. He has to be a *man*, first and foremost, or he is out of balance. That was why many of our ancient warriors composed poetry, or the samurai practiced tea ceremony." Galan wouldn't know what the samurai were, or even what tea was, but he nodded, nevertheless, with a glance at Gunny.

"He is a wise man." He turned back to the side and looked down into the water. "Perhaps I spoke without being clear enough."

He stared at the water with a frown for a couple of minutes. I just waited. If we were going to trek and fight with these men, we needed to get to know them, and right then, that meant letting Galan talk.

"I have gathered, from what you have said, that you and your fellow 'Marines' come from a rich society, one that has been largely at peace for a very long time." That might be arguable, given my own experience, but when you boiled it down, he wasn't far wrong. The vast majority of Americans *had* been at peace to such a point that they found violence almost unthinkable. "As such, you may pursue whatever profession you wish, as you wish.

"We, the Galel of Cor Legear, have no such luxury. Ours is a kingdom under siege, to an even greater extent than the Isle of Riamog. Despite the Deep Ones, the Tuacha have the sea to defend them. We do not. Half of our eastern border is open ground, without any obstacle between us and the Empire of Ar-Annator, once mighty, but now so thoroughly corrupt that the emperor himself offers sacrifices to the Outer Dark. Oh, a truce has been declared between us for many years, but that truce does not apply to the brigands and nomads of the grasslands to the north, whom the emperor's generals allow or even encourage to slip across our borders."

I snorted. "Hybrid warfare."

That drew a sharp glance. "What?"

I shook my head. "Just an academic term from where I come from. It means ways of waging war without formally declaring it, thus avoiding open warfare, and the mass destruction that came with it." I met his gaze. "We had weapons that could level an entire city in an eye-blink. No one wanted to invite such an attack, but they still wanted to wage war, anyway."

Galan nodded his understanding and turned back to the sea. "It is a coward's way of war. Yet it is one that has kept us under threat for generations, ever since the truce was signed."

He looked at me out of the corner of his eye, as if he was debating whether or not to speak his mind. "Where you come from, a man may choose his profession and his destiny. In the kingdom of Cor Legear, we are born to our roles. There can be no other way."

I nodded, suddenly realizing that this wasn't an aristocrat trying to put a common foot soldier in his place. This was a fighting man speaking to the Bearer of the Sword of Iudicael, defending the fact that his knowledge wasn't as extensive.

"Well, we've still got a lot to learn about this place, too, I guess." I looked over at him. "Not least about your people and your kingdom. If I may ask, don't let us make idiots out of ourselves when we get there?"

It took him a second to figure out what I'd just said. The idiom only slightly translated into *Tenga Tuacha*. When he got it, though, he smiled and nodded. "There will be those who doubt you, I should warn you." He nodded toward my rifle, which I had slung across my back. "Your weapons are not what we are used to, at least not in the hands of servants of Tigharn."

What immediately came to mind was a knightly code of honor and the old objections made to crossbows. "You don't use archers in combat?"

"We do. In fact, every one of us is trained in the bow, on foot and on horseback. Many of us prefer the sword and lance, but against the Avur, a man must know how to use the bow, or else be shot to a pincushion before he can close the distance." He shook his head. "No, it is the sound and fury of your…" He trailed off, frowning.

"Rifles?" I supplied.

He nodded. "Rifles. Yes. There will be those who view them with distrust, even after seeing them used in action against our foes. They may not be outright sorcery, but to some, it will seem far too close." He sighed and turned to look at me. "Understand, our people are proud. We have faced a great and terrible empire and its vassals for generations, nearly always on our own. You are companions of the Tuacha, and we have seen you fight, and both facts will lend you standing. But some of our people may not be so easily won over."

"Fortress mentality." I'd run into it before, mostly in Syria. Some of those Kurdish fighters had been fighting long enough that they looked down on men who were arguably far better warfighters than they were, just because they'd been at it longer.

"Yes." He nodded. "That is a good way to describe it."

I sighed a little. We'd gotten lucky, working with the Tuacha, and then meeting the Menninkai when they were in truly dire straights and desperate for help. The Tuacha were on a whole different plane, so with only a few exceptions—the revered, deceased Cairbre came immediately to mind—they didn't have much reason to resent us. They were faster, wiser, stronger, tougher, and longer-lived than any of us. The Menninkai had seen us stick our necks out for them, and as a people, they were of a practical enough mind that they didn't get too weirded out once they saw that our weapons and explosives were chemical and mechanical contrivances, not sorcery. Hell, just look at how eager Noita was to start dropping live fire mortar rounds on enemy foreheads.

The reality of life is, though, that not everybody's going to like you for being you. Even if you're a great ally, they still might not like you, for a lot of reasons. And if the Galel of Cor Legear were as proud as Galan said, we might have a long, uphill slog ahead just to prove ourselves.

Of course, carrying the Sword of Iudicael at my side would carry a lot of weight. Even as I thought it, though, I remembered that the Swords hadn't saved their respective kingdoms.

There was a lesson there. I just had to suss it out.

Before I could say anything else, a call came from the starboard side. We both turned to look. Moireach, one of Nachdainn's senior men, was standing atop the rail, holding onto the rigging with one hand, pointing off to the south.

I couldn't see what he was looking at. Neither could Galan, who shaded his eyes with his hand, squinting against the glare of the sunlight off the waves. Pulling my rifle off my back, I brought the scope to my eye, scanning the horizon in the general direction Moireach had been pointing.

There. They were small and distant, and after a moment, despite the movement of the ship, I could tell that they weren't sailing in our direction, but there were definitely ships out there. And they had red sails.

Moireach stepped down from the rail. "Not a good sign. The Clan of Suth rarely fares so far north."

I kept watching those blood-red sails in the distance. I didn't know a lot about the Clan of Suth, aside from a passing mention Mathghaman had made some time ago. He'd classed them with the Fohorimans in the north, which told me that they were not anyone we wanted to clash with in a lone ship.

Fortunately, if they spotted us at all, they had no interest in us, because they kept going west, and vanished over the horizon a few hours later. Still, it was yet another reminder that we sailed through hostile seas.

* * *

As the sun went down, I looked off to the stern. The waves rolled and heaved, but I saw no sails. Nor did I see any wake that suggested anything beneath the surface was following us.

That didn't mean that nothing was there. I knew it. The ocean was wide and deep, with a lot of water for the Deep Ones and their minions to hide in.

I hoped that King Caedmon had killed that thing. Even if he had, though, would another one come after us? I had no way of knowing what had put the hundred-handed thing on our trail, but I was pretty sure that whatever that creature I'd seen from the rail had been, it had seen me and told its master. Or maybe the Deep One had been looking through its eyes like a drone feed.

There were uncanny things in this world, above and below the surface of the water, and we couldn't afford to discount any of them.

As I looked out at that vast expanse of rolling waves, I was all too conscious of how far from land we were, and how small our ship was. Tuacha construction was endowed with a sort of power that made it very hard to break, but not impossible. And while we had the most powerful weapons and the greatest warriors—that I knew of—on the face of the planet aboard, we were still very far out and very alone.

And the water beneath us was very deep.

CHAPTER 9

COR Legear was a rocky country, the green-clad hills rising above stony cliffs that jutted straight up out of the sea. White gulls wheeled and cried overhead as we sailed in toward a sheltered bay beneath the castle of Lemmanonius.

Quite a few fishing boats bobbed on the waves as we moved in, none of their white sails even half the size of our own. As we got closer to the cliffs, Mathghaman ran our standard up the main mast, and it was answered with a banner bearing a red tower on a white field, flanked by a pair of blue fish, fluttering from the crown of one of the castle's turrets.

The castle itself was a massive block of stone, a round tower at each corner, gray and weathered, perched atop the highest promontory along the cliffs, with a sheer drop from the walls to the sea. There were no battlements, each tower being topped by a conical roof, but there were plenty of arrow slits studding the walls of the keep and the towers both. There weren't many places that an enemy could approach without being targeted with a rain of arrows.

A few larger openings might have been chutes for boiling oil, hot sand, or rocks. And those were only the defenses on the seaward sides, where you'd have to climb a spray-slick, sheer cliff to get up to the walls, anyway. As near as I could tell from the deck, the landward side was the *only* place the castle could be approached, and to get there meant climbing the steps carved into the rock from the piers on the bay at the face of the cliff. And those steps were overwatched by more arrow slits and murder holes.

Lemmanonius was a formidable defensive bastion. From the way Galan and Fortrenn were looking at the horizon around and behind us, instead of at the castle, I suspected that it had seen a lot of action, too. I remembered what Galan had said about brigands and Avur raiders and imagined that there were probably plenty of sea pirates in that mix, too. I'd seen the maps of Cor Legear. The country was a peninsula, and the Empire controlled not only all the land on the other side of its border, but a long way down the coast, too.

The thing about this place that we'd all had to sort of get used to was that while sorcery tended to make rebellion against the powers that be difficult, it was still a pre-industrial world —or post-industrial, I *still* hadn't figured out which—where unless some wizard had a real bone to pick with you, enough to send a summoned critter after you, enforcement could only happen at the speed of a good horse, max. That meant that there were still going to be plenty of outlaws in hard-to-reach places.

If the emperor could weaponize those outlaws against the Galel, then he killed two birds with one stone, keeping them out of his hair while simultaneously giving his enemies a perpetual headache. I didn't doubt that the conditions of the truce were such that if the Galel pursued the raiders across the border or onto imperial shores, then the truce would formally be over, which was a hell of a deterrent.

It was a cunning strategy, one that I'd seen plenty of times back in The World. Hell, my entire career had revolved around it, even if nobody could quite bring themselves to admit the fact.

If there were pirates nearby, however, they were laying low for the moment. I wondered, as I watched the bobbing fishing boats on the waves, how many of them were loyal, and how many were spies for the pirates? I was sure there were a few. There's no society, no matter how traditional and clannish, that's airtight. Gold will loosen tongues and loyalties, and blackmail's even better than gold, if you can make it happen.

Still, it was a quiet passage into the bay, and when we drifted in toward the stone quay, Nachdainn's crew throwing out the fenders, great knotted balls of rope to cushion the wooden side from the stone, there were a dozen men standing on the height above, waiting for us. The older man in the center was dressed in a long blue tunic and red cloak, leaning on a staff. Two younger men, in similar garb, stood next to him, while the rest were men at arms, leaning on spears, dressed in short mail shirts over white wool tunics, breeches, and closely wrapped boots. All but the old man and his two attendants—his sons or nephews, judging by the family resemblance in their faces as we climbed the steps from the pier and got closer—wore tall helms with carved cheek guards.

"Lord Achivir." Fortrenn stepped up ahead of us and clasped the old man's hands with his own. He and Galan were still in their well-worn and slightly ragged travel clothing, since their armor hadn't made it out of the shipwreck off the coast of the Isle of Riamog. They'd been clothed in new tunics and breeches on the Isle, but they'd changed back into their heraldic tunics again as we'd neared the coast. "It is good to see you again."

"And you, Lord Fortrenn." The old man's voice was creaky with age, and he coughed as he looked past the two Galel knights at us. "You have been long away."

"A mission for the king." Fortrenn turned and held out his hand to introduce us. "These are those allies from the Isle of Riamog that he sent us to find. Mathghaman Mag Cathal, the King's Champion himself, and his companions."

There was something about Fortrenn's reserve that prompted me to keep my head down and my mouth shut, but Achivir studied us all keenly, though he seemed to watch me most closely of all. He was staring, to be honest, and it wasn't comfortable. All the same, I couldn't exactly tell the castellan of an ally's fortifications to put his eyes elsewhere before I stabbed them out, but I had the sudden urge to say just that.

Now, where did that come from? I put my hand on the sword, half-unconsciously, as I met Achivir's gaze, unblinking. After a moment, he blinked, as if just then realizing that he'd zoned out, and his eyes drifted elsewhere.

I glanced at Mathghaman. He wasn't looking at me, but he was watching Achivir closely, what might have been a faint frown creasing his brow. He'd noticed something, too.

"Come. There is warm fire and good food and drink. I am sure that after such a long voyage, you all long for solid ground and proper dining." Turning toward the steps, Achivir started up as his men at arms stepped aside. His staff clicked on the stone as he mounted the stairs, one of the younger men hurrying to support him.

The other young man, who appeared to be the senior of the two by a few years, watched us for just a moment longer before he turned to join them. With his blond hair worn in a glorified bowl cut, the young man wore thin, wispy mustache that was still more substantial than the other's. The haircut almost covered up the fact that he only had one ear. All that was left of the other was a gnarled bit of scar tissue. Old boy had been in a fight or two, even though I guessed he was barely over twenty.

There was something odd about the way he looked up at his father or uncle, then back at us. Almost as if he was pleading. Then, without a word, he turned and followed Achivir up the steps.

I caught Bailey's eye. Mathghaman might have kept his misgivings subtle, but subtlety wasn't one of Sean Bailey's strong points. He was full-on scowling suspiciously when he met my gaze.

Gunny was suddenly there beside him, whispering in his ear, and I watched my friend struggle to bring his expression under control. I could almost hear Gunny telling him that he needed to think about social camouflage a little bit more.

"Something weird's going on here." Santos kept his voice low as he stood at my elbow.

"When *isn't* something weird going on whenever we leave the Island?" Rodeffer was slightly louder, as always, but not so loud that he could be heard very far up the stairs, where Achivir was still climbing, his men at arms falling in behind him and the two younger men, even if we hadn't been speaking English.

"It's the *Isle*."

"Shut up, Farrar." Santos looked at me. "What do you think's going on?"

"I have no idea, Vince." I looked up as we fell in behind Mathghaman and the Tuacha. "Might just be local politics. This Achivir seems to know Fortrenn, but who knows what kind of relationship they've had in the past. And did you notice that he didn't even look at Galan? These are touchy, proud, clannish people. There might be some old grudge or slight that we don't know about at work."

"Great. Back to fucking Afghanistan, with swords."

"Let's hope not." My yardstick for that sort of thing might be Syria, not Afghanistan, but still.

We followed Achivir and his entourage the rest of the way up the steps in silence, while the gulls screeched and cried overhead and the surf crashed against the cliffs below.

* * *

While we hadn't been able to see it that clearly from the sea, the peninsula actually narrowed sharply just in front of the gate. You might be able to get six men across on that land bridge, but you'd be exposed to everyone on every floor of the castle above. Not my idea of a good time.

The gate was a huge double door behind an oak and iron portcullis, set between two towers that jutted out from the front wall of the castle. The portcullis was currently raised, the iron points looming over our heads as we passed through the massive portal. The whole gate was probably twelve feet wide and twenty feet tall. The doors themselves were about a foot and a half thick. I could only imagine how much they weighed, and what it must have taken to lift them into position and get them fastened to hinges that could bear their weight, not to mention getting them just high enough off the ground that they could be opened and closed.

There was no open courtyard, since the castle was more of a tower than what we usually thought of as a "castle." The terrain itself provided most of the defense, leaving off the need for a curtain wall. Any outer wall, like those of Vahava Paykhah, would have only been about twenty feet long, anyway, unless they were set so far back that there would be a half-mile killing ground between the outer wall and the keep.

The castle itself, though, was huge, easily the size of Vahava Paykhah's great hall, if not bigger. Achivir led the way through the vaulted gatehouse, past a second set of portcullis and doors, and into the reception hall.

Nearly as tall as the gatehouse, the hall was relatively narrow, with four doors to either side, and two fireplaces, only one of which was currently lit. A dais in the center of the room bore two seats, side by side, though at a glance, I would have guessed that only one was being used. The cushion on the left-hand chair had started to gather dust.

We didn't linger in the receiving hall, which was empty anyway. There were two stairwells just behind the dais, and Achivir led us toward the one on the left, nearest the fireplace that actually had a fire in it.

The stairs wound upward in a tight spiral, with doors opening onto hallways at every floor. We went up four floors before Achivir led us out into the hall, and then into the dining room.

Both fireplaces were lit in there, and candles burned on the trestle tables that circled the room. Two servants were placing platters and cups on the tables as we entered, and they left quickly.

I watched them leave, my expression carefully controlled. Aside from his bodyguard and the two younger men, so far, we hadn't seen anyone else in this castle except for Achivir. And his staff seemed…small.

"Come, be seated." Achivir took his place at the head table, set across the room with two doors behind it. The two younger men sat down to either side of him, while the rest of us found seats on the benches at the side tables. There was just enough room for all of us.

I noticed that Achivir had started drinking from the fairly large goblet on the table as soon as he'd sat down.

The platters in front of us were mostly laden with bread and roasted seabirds. Each man also had a sizeable brass goblet in front of him, and when I grabbed mine and sniffed it, I smelled a pretty strong wine.

Gunny hadn't sat down yet. He suddenly leaned over my shoulder. "Make sure none of the boys get ripped tonight." He left it at that.

I fixed Rodeffer and Farrar each with a glower. Rodeffer's nod was easy, as if I hadn't needed to remind him, but Farrar's was a little more sheepish.

"So, Lord Achivir." Fortrenn held up his goblet. "What news? As you said, we have been away for some time."

"Very little." Achivir took another deep draught of his own goblet, draining it, and banged it on the table, prompting a very nervous-looking young woman in a plain shift and apron to hurry in with a jug to refill it. "It has been very quiet of late. Downright boring." He took another swig and looked across the table at me. His eyes suddenly bright, he leaned forward. "Tell me, is that *truly* the Sword of Iudicael?"

There was something disquieting about his sudden intensity. Apparently, I wasn't the only one who thought so, either. Galan was watching Achivir from the opposite table, a cleft between his eyebrows. He had his own misgivings about this situation.

"So I'm led to believe." I took another bite of the roast fowl. It was greasier than I tend to like, but that was water birds for you, and this wasn't exactly a restaurant where I could ask for something else. I felt the same discomfort radiating from several of the others in the platoon, though I couldn't exactly look around without potentially betraying my suspicions.

I didn't know what was going on here, but Gunny's order to go easy on the alcohol was feeling more prescient by the minute.

Achivir studied me for a long moment after my noncommittal reply, then took another swig of wine. He leaned back, then, and seemed to recall himself. "It is quite remarkable. We live in a time of legends returning." Another swig. "Legends."

The conversation kind of died away after that. Achivir was clearly preoccupied, and while he seemed to have realized that he was being a bit too focused, his eyes kept straying back to me. I didn't care for it, but there was little I could do when it was our host who was staring and being a weirdo, and neither Mathghaman nor Gunny seemed ready to do anything about it.

Finally, after what felt like an interminable amount of time, Achivir rose from his seat. "You have come a long way, and doubtless you are weary. I have had chambers prepared for you, on this very floor. I hope that my table provided you refreshment, and now I will leave you to your rest while I attend to matters of pressing importance." His voice kind of trailed off as he spoke, as if he was searching his memory for what business he had to see to.

I glanced at the older of the two young men, the one who had lingered at the pier. He was watching Achivir, his face composed but his eyes hooded. When he noticed me watching him, the look he gave me was strikingly alarmed. As if he was begging me to do something.

Then Achivir got to his feet and clapped his hands. Two of his bodyguard entered, along with an older woman in a plain dress, apron, and cap. "My servants will show you to your quarters."

Clearly, the meal and the awkward conversation were both over. We all stood and followed the woman and the guards out into the hallway.

Our chambers weren't big, but we shouldn't have expected "big" in a castle this size. There were also only seven, so that we had to fit one team in each. That was no big problem. Hell, even in those relatively small rooms, we had more space than we'd had aboard ship.

Our escort had barely disappeared through the door when Santos turned to me. "Okay, I'm no hearts and minds sort of people person, but that dude is acting weird as fuck."

"No, he is." I moved to the door and listened. "I don't know what's going on, but something's definitely off. And Galan thinks so, too."

"I think old boy's son, or whoever he is, knows." Rodeffer spoke up from where he sat on the floor next to his ruck. There was only one bed in the room. "Dude looks freaked the hell out."

Santos looked at him with a raised eyebrow, probably somewhat surprised that our pointman had picked up on that. "Yeah, he was watching everything a little too closely."

"You think he's in on it?" Farrar asked.

I shook my head. "From what I saw, he's scared. And not in the 'I hope I don't get caught' sort of way." I moved to the door, cracking it open and peering out into the hallway. "More like he's being held hostage, or something."

Even as I looked out, Gunny came out and spotted my open door. He walked down the hallway, and as he passed the door, without looking over, he said, "Team leaders, in my room, five minutes."

My watch was still working, but I'd left it behind. It was so far off the time of day that it was next to useless at that point. We were all getting to the point where we didn't really need watches anymore, anyway.

Gunny kept going, and I turned to Santos. "At least one man's up at all times. Weapons stay within arm's reach." I hardly needed to say it under most circumstances, but there had been some grumbling about going easy on the alcohol. We were supposed to be in friendly territory, and that mindset could be a trap in and of itself.

Santos and I had some experience with "friendly" territory on earlier deployments. After our little sojourn with the Dovos nal Uergal, everyone else should have the same mindset, but after our time with the Tuacha and the Menninkai, both of whom were now our actual brothers-in-arms, it bore some reinforcement.

I did leave my rifle behind, but I was confident enough in my skill with the Sword of Iudicael by then that I was comfortable with it alone in close quarters. Get us into a big fight in the open, and I'd definitely want the M110 again, but, for now, it was a bit easier to squeeze into a small castle room without a long gun on my back.

Galan and Fortrenn had both stepped out of their room when I walked out into the hallway and headed for Gunny's room. None of us said a word until we were all gathered in Gunny's room.

"Is it just me, or is it a little weird that a castellan out on the edge of nowhere knows about the Sword of Iudicael?" Gunny opened the proceedings as soon as he'd shut the door behind him. Mathghaman watched Galan and Fortrenn, his arms folded.

"It is strange." Galan's frown was now far deeper than it had been at the table. "Most have heard the legends, but that news of the Sword's reappearance should have come here?" He shook his head. "It seems unlikely."

Fortrenn was even more certain. "Few outside King Uven's court knew of our mission. That Achivir should have heard of the Sword's reappearance, let alone that its Bearer was coming here..." He shook his head. "Something is amiss. He is not himself. I have known Achivir since I was a lad." His eyes strayed to the door, and by extension, the rest of the castle. "This quavering old man is not the lord I knew."

"Do we need to break out and make a run for it?" Gunny was thinking about the mission first and foremost. The Galel's internal problems and espionage were of lesser priority.

Fortrenn's face clouded at the suggestion. He didn't like the idea of running. Truth be told, neither did I, but Achivir's eccentric behavior wasn't the mission.

"We need Lord Achivir's horses." Galan was much more phlegmatic about it than Fortrenn. Probably because he didn't have a history with Achivir. He sighed. "It is *possible* that someone spoke out of turn about our quest. It has been some months since we departed Cor Legear itself. Perhaps word *has* spread. Such news is not likely to stay secret for long. The return of even one of the Swords is sure to get tongues wagging. As for Lord Achivir, he *is* an old man. How many years since you have been here, Lord Fortrenn?"

Fortrenn thought for a moment. "Nearly ten."

"You see?" He looked around at all of us. "I do not say we should not be watchful. But Lord Achivir was placed here as castellan for long and honorable service to King Drosten, King Uven's father, long may he rest in peace. It is possible but unlikely that he is up to some intrigue. Yet we are all warriors, and all prepared and watchful. The very fact that we are having this discussion shows how dangerous it would be to attempt to attack us during the night.

"Let us set a watch, and be wary, but it seems reckless to me to assume ill intentions on the part of our host, and to strike out on foot during the last light of day. Let us wait and see."

Mathghaman nodded, then. "There *is* something going on here. I cannot say what, exactly, but our Marine comrades are correct. Something is not right. Perhaps we will have a chance to put it right before we depart. At the very least, we may have some more useful news to carry to King Uven than simply the fact that his castellan on the coast at Lemmanonius is acting strangely."

On that note, the meeting broke up, and we headed back to our rooms in the dying, reddish light of sunset as it filtered through the arrow slits along the hallway.

I had a feeling it was going to be a long night.

CHAPTER 10

FARRAR shook me awake. The room was pitch black, and I quickly grabbed for my helmet and NVGs. Something was wrong, but in the fog of slowly-dispersing sleep, I couldn't tell what.

I only heard the song after I got my chest rig on, my PVS-15s showing me a dim, grainy, green-tinted view of the room as the rest of the team got up and grabbed for gear and weapons.

It was weird. I can't describe it, not really. It was a bit like whale song, but more melodious, somehow. It was the kind of sound that made you want to go to sleep.

All the same, as I grabbed the Sword of Iudicael, something struck me about it.

The strange, haunting melody that made the eyelids heavy was laid overtop another, lower sound. It was hard to hear over the keening song, but it was there. Somehow, I could hear it more clearly with the Sword in my hand. It was almost as if, now that I knew what the Sword was, it was helping clear my head.

Maybe I just thought that the Sword gave me some kind of protection, and that cleared my thoughts and made the underlying tone clearer. I don't know.

Whatever the case, I could hear a lower, discordant, hateful song overlayed by the sweeter tones that were trying to lull us into a deeper sleep. The longer I heard it, the more it reminded me of the Deep One's voice.

The whole team was up, weapons in hand and ready, though even in the dim green image in my NVGs I could tell that everybody looked bleary. I couldn't hear anything outside except that song, and I wasn't inclined to just sit there and wait for whatever was outside to come inside. We had one door, one way in and out, and that's never a comfortable feeling in a combat situation.

I wasn't going to make one of my guys go through that door first. All the same, as I moved toward it, Rodeffer stepped in and beat me to the punch.

He reached for the bar, only to find it was already open. That was bad. The door should have been secured. It *had* been secured when I'd ended my last watch. And I didn't think that either Farrar or Rodeffer had opened it. Not consciously, anyway.

Pulling the door open, he kept his muzzle just above his hand, then he went into the hall, his rifle dropping level as he stormed out, covering one direction while I moved out behind him, facing the other way.

Just in time to look straight at the wide, staring, lidless eyes of a seven-foot giant wearing a coat of shimmering scales and carrying a bone-tipped spear as it came out of the stairwell, padding on squelching feet as it moved carefully toward the first door.

It saw me easily enough. Anything that is adapted for deep water shouldn't be bothered by darkness, but I had my own advantage with my PVS-15s. Canting my rifle, I put the red dot on its chest and double-tapped it, hammering two shots into its center mass so fast that the harsh, suppressed *crack* was almost a single sound.

It staggered, but it didn't turn to slime. I kept driving forward, smashing shot after shot into it until something finally broke, and a cascade of ichor slithered to the floor.

More came behind it, and I kept shooting, dropping two more before Santos was beside me, sending a short burst from the Mk 48 down the stairs, tearing three more to shreds and flooding the steps with their liquid remains.

The others behind weren't slowed by the cascade of slime, but they fell back. The song intensified, getting louder as it wafted up the stairs, and I felt a moment's vertigo. Or maybe it was just the incredible fatigue that felt like it was weighing down my limbs.

"We'll hold the steps. Farrar, start beating on doors, get everybody up."

"With me, Conor." Mathghaman and Diarmodh were suddenly beside us. If he'd been anyone else, I suspected that Mathghaman would have been somewhat frustrated that we'd beaten him to the punch. As it was, he was impassive, his rifle leveled down the stairs. Without looking, I already knew that Bearrac and the other Tuacha were probably covering the other stairwell.

Weapons at the ready, we started down the stairs.

I'd trained a long time on close quarters battle, or CQB, but it had always been based on the assumption that the bad guys had guns, too. It was a little different when "close quarters" meant bad breath distance with blades and clubs, but the tactics really hadn't changed.

Keeping my muzzle aimed down the steps, ready to engage anything just as soon as it stuck its head out, I started down.

Steps in a castle are often a defensive fortification in and of themselves. The steps leading up to the gate of

Unsterbanak's castle in the Land of Shadows and Crows had been asymmetric, no two steps the same height. It had made fighting up them a nightmare. These were even, though, and I was able to descend smoothly in the near darkness, even with my NVGs almost blacked out by the lack of illumination, without stumbling.

I saw movement, snapped the rifle up, and blew a hole through a blue-skinned monstrosity's forehead, right behind those massive, staring fish eyes. Its head disintegrated to slime as it snapped back from the impact, spattering the wall behind it.

I stumbled. The song was filling my ears, and despite the fact that I could clearly hear the low, assonant hatred underlying it, I could still feel my limbs weighed down like each one weighed a ton. My eyelids were heavy and gritty, and I just wanted to drop right there and go to sleep.

I fought it off. Fortunately, Recon Marines have a *lot* of experience with sleep deprivation. We can be falling down exhausted and keep going. Patrol Phase makes sure of that.

I still bounced off the wall as I kept descending. The fish-eyed giants—the Tuacha called them "*eac uisge*," I'd learned on the voyage east—were still falling back, unable to get close to us with those spears while we were still shooting them. Bullets traveling at over twenty-five hundred feet per second can be a lot more daunting than arrows or even blades, even for unnatural monsters that aren't really alive.

If I was really being thorough, I would have cleared the next floor down, but something drew me lower, toward the great hall. Something told me that the real fight was there. These things were there for us, not for Achivir or any of his household.

We still took care to cover each doorway with a rifle muzzle as we passed. We might be bypassing the bulk of the castle, but that was no reason to get sloppy. And there was enough uncanny weirdness in the air that we couldn't trust *any* opening as we passed it.

I paused just short of the entrance to the great hall. I could see the stone floor ahead, along with a small slice of the room itself, but not much more than that. What I could see, however, was not lit by firelight or candle-light. A weird, blue-green glow seemed to shine through the doorway and over the floor. It reminded me of the bioluminescence that I'd seen many times while doing night scout swimmer inserts.

Santos gave my shoulder a squeeze. I knew it was him because it was harder than anyone else in the pla-toon would have done it, and his Mk 48 rattled as he hefted it to point the muzzle at the ceiling, the belt shift-ing in the 100-round pouch.

Keeping my rifle up, the red dot just below the lev-el of my eye, I went into the great hall, pivoting hard to clear my corner as I stepped out of the fatal funnel, clearing the way for the rest of the team and hopefully avoiding an arrow or a thrown spear.

What I saw next stopped me, though, even though my finger was already on the trigger.

Lord Achivir stood in the very center of the great hall, still in the same long tunic and cloak he'd worn at table. He looked like he was in some kind of ecstasy, his face blissfully blank, his eyes vacant. I could see that even through NVGs, though I flipped them up pretty fast in the bright glow that illuminated the entire hall.

That glow was coming from the eyes of the woman on Achivir's arm.

To describe the woman as "curvy" would be putting it mildly, and I don't mean that in the euphemistic way that some people had started to use it to describe morbid obesity, back in The World. She was stunning. She had a body that would tempt a saint, and she wasn't being shy about it, either.

The off-putting part was the fact that she was green, her teeth were pointed like a shark's, she had kelp for hair, her eyes were apparently radioactive, and she was singing that disturbing song, the really bad parts of which I could make out a lot more clearly now.

She swayed as she held onto Achivir's arm, staring at us as her song got louder. I felt the fatigue wearing me down, and my rifle suddenly felt like it weighed fifty pounds. My helmet got heavier, and I started to nod as I stumbled back against the wall.

Then Mathghaman's rifle spoke.

The Tuacha rifles didn't look it, but they were, somehow, integrally suppressed. They were really wondrous artifacts, and a testament to what the *Coira Ansec* could do. I *knew* that they were still rifles, not magic wands or something, since I knew they were, in fact, magazine fed, and used the same bullets ours did. They were just uncanny, in much the same way the Tuacha often were, themselves.

Mathghaman fired once, the report a harsh *crack* that echoed from the high ceiling above us. He hit the woman right between those glowing eyes, putting them out in an eyeblink. She dropped like a puppet with its strings cut, dragging at Achivir's arm as she fell, hitting the floor with a wet slap.

The song went silent, and the remaining eac uisge fled out the open gate, rushing past the sleeping men at arms slumped in the gateway.

At least, I hoped they were asleep.

Eyes and weapons turned to Achivir. If we'd hoped that he'd snap out of it, we were disappointed. He twisted toward the dead creature at his side, his face contorted with grief, and sank to his knees with a wail.

"Lord Fortrenn. Lord Galan." Mathghaman stepped forward, looming over Achivir.

"We will gather the household." Galan was already moving toward the slumped figures of the guards, his sword in his fist. "We will have answers before this night is done."

* * *

The fireplaces roared, and every candle in every sconce in the hall was lit. I stood near the dais with Mathghaman, Gunny, Bailey, Gurke, Orava, Galan, and Fortrenn. The rest of the platoon was spread out around the hall, though if the locals noticed the fact that they were in an L-shape, with my team and Bailey's behind us and the rest lined up down only one wall of the hall, they were already too scared to react to it.

It's a lot easier to gun down monsters without shooting each other from those relative positions.

Achivir knelt almost where he'd collapsed, his hands on his lap, his head bowed. He wasn't so much remorseful as he was catatonic. He'd barely moved since Mathghaman had shot that merrow in the face, and he hadn't made a sound since his first keening cry of grief had died away.

The two younger men who'd accompanied him stood to either side of him, and the rest of the household, smaller than I'd expected, stood behind. There were only about fifty men at arms, and they'd all been disarmed until we got this sorted out. Aside from them, there were about ten servants. Cooks, maids, the steward, that sort of thing. It was far fewer people than I'd expected for a castle this size, but Fortrenn explained that most of the garrison lived in the farms or the fishing village down by the beach. This wasn't an industrial society. Most of these people still had to grow or catch their own food.

The younger of the two young men was still standing by Achivir, his eyes fixed on the floor. The older, the blond guy with the bowl cut and only one ear, had stepped forward. At some point, the two of them had been introduced as Allcallored and Broichan, Achivir's sons.

"Our mother died some years ago." I thought the older man was Broichan. "She was visiting her family in the south, and the wagons were waylaid by brigands on the way home. She fought them when they tried to take her and was cast down on the rocks and killed.

"My father mourned her for a year, as custom dictated, then he took Angharad as his new bride." While he kept his expression as neutral as he could, I could hear more than a little resentment in Broichan's voice. "She was never strong. She died in childbirth last winter, and my father was devastated."

He glanced toward the doors, beyond which we'd tossed the merrow's corpse. It had already started to smell, less than an hour after its death. "Only months later, that creature came among us, disguised as a fair maiden from the north. It blinded my father and offered him sympathy and comfort. In time, he became the man you see here." He motioned toward the kneeling, stricken old man behind him, who was now rocking slightly.

I kept a close eye on the castellan. I'd seen grief transform itself into insane rage in a heartbeat before.

"And you did nothing." Fortrenn wasn't having it. "An abomination of the Deep Ones had taken command of one of his majesty's coastal fortresses, a lynchpin of the kingdom's defenses against sea raiders and Deep Ones alike, and you simply sat here and watched?" The knight was clearly getting a little pissed. The fact that he'd apparently known Achivir years before seemed to intensify his anger. "Could you not even attempt to get a message to King Uven?"

The young man hung his head then, much of his anger suddenly lost in shame. "We were prisoners here. You must understand! It would have killed him, had any of us tried to flee! And the eac uisge were always watching."

"The eac uisge must needs seek the water from time to time. They could not stay on land all the while." From the glitter in Fortrenn's eye, I started to suspect that he was gearing up to hang everybody in the room. I glanced at Gunny. I wasn't sure we could allow that.

Bearrac's massive hand closed on the knight's shoulder. "Easy, lad. A merrow's song is not easily shrugged off, and do not underestimate the power of the Deep Ones once they had the castellan in their grasp." He looked at

Achivir. "The old man is certainly to be blamed for falling for such a ruse in the beginning, especially if his wife was so recently in her grave, but the lad was caught as well as any of the rest of them."

Fortrenn's expression didn't soften, but Galan stepped up close to him and whispered in his ear. After a moment, his shoulders slumped ever so slightly, and some of the taut rage seemed to drain out of him. Finally, he nodded with a sigh, and turned to me.

"It seems that the forces of the Outer Dark are mobilizing to oppose our quest even more than we had suspected." He stroked his mustache thoughtfully, then grimaced, looking down at Achivir. "Lord Achivir stands disgraced, and he must answer to King Uven. Yet, we cannot leave Lemmanonius leaderless." He turned his baleful stare on Achivir's sons. "Caught they may be, yet those who did not fight cannot be left in command of such a vital coastal outpost until their honor has been cleared."

Galan looked over the crowd behind Achivir's bent form. "Who is the senior warrior here?"

The men at arms looked around at each other. Finally, a red-headed man with a wispy beard stepped forward. "That would be Pidarnoin, my lord. He is not here. His farm lies to the north, nearly a league."

"Find a horse and go fetch him." Galan's voice was firm. His eyes swept the rest of the people in the hall, few of whom would look at him.

Fortrenn nodded, and turned to me again, as if I was the commanding officer, instead of just the guy who had picked up the Sword. "I fear that I will not be able to continue to accompany you on the quest. Lord Galan will ride with you, but I must stay here and assume the watch over Lemmanonius until King Uven appoints a new castellan."

He turned to Galan, who bowed slightly. There was some formal passing of the torch going on there, as if Fortrenn had been the lead, and Galan now had to take the responsibility for the quest upon his own shoulders. I didn't know how the chain of command worked in Cor Legear, but that it was there was obvious.

"Now, since it will be some time before that man returns with Pidarnoin, I suggest we set a watch on these, just in case, and take what rest we may before the morning."

CHAPTER 11

IT wasn't exactly the most restful remainder of the night, but we made the best of it. We'd already had a watch set, so that wasn't that much of an adjustment. Going back to sleep after finding out that the Deep Ones' minions had already been in that castle, and had been there for a long time, was a little more of a hurdle.

Those of us who had slept in the Land of Ice and Monsters, not to mention Lost Colcand, Ruined Tethba, and the Land of Shadows and Crows, could manage to sleep just about anywhere, though.

The few remaining hours before dawn were quiet and uneventful. The only sounds in the castle were the roar of the surf below and the whisper of the wind through the arrow slits and between the peaks of the towers. No eerie songs, no strange, damp footfalls squelching in the remains of the eac uisge. The slime had already nearly completely dissolved by the time we'd gone back upstairs, as if it couldn't stay in the world above the waves for that long.

By the time day dawned, the man at arms Galan had dispatched had returned with a massive specimen of a man, who looked like he could barely straddle a horse without breaking its back. Pidarnoin was six foot five if he was an inch, with a barrel chest and not much of a neck. He was the kind of man that you really didn't want to get his hands on you in a fight, especially since each one of those mitts was the size of a dinner plate and calloused to all hell.

He was waiting in the great hall when we came down, standing tall before the rest of the castle's people. Most of them were still napping in the corners, though it didn't look like Achivir had moved since the night before.

"Pidarnoin." Fortrenn might have been formal and firm the night before, but he clearly knew this man. "It has been many years."

"It has, my lord." Pidarnoin had a voice that matched his appearance, as gravelly as if he'd been drinking whiskey and smoking cigars his whole life. "Would that your return was under better circumstances."

The Galel weren't speaking *Tenga Tuacha*, not quite, but their language was similar enough that I could even understand Pidarnoin's words through his thick, gravelly brogue.

"Did you know what was happening here?" Fortrenn still hadn't gotten over the fact that, apparently, none of the castle's people had lifted a finger to stop the merrow's takeover.

The big man didn't hang his head or shift his feet, but he did look uncomfortable. He clasped those massive hands in front of his tunic. "My lord, I knew that not all was well, but that the denizens of the deep had suborned the Lord Achivir... No, my lord, I did not know." Those big sausage fingers clenched suddenly. "I would have wrung the unlife out of that foul creature myself, had I known. It was cunning, my lord."

Fortrenn sighed. There was anger in the sound, though less intense than the killing rage he'd shown the night before. "So it would seem." He straightened. "In King Uven's name, I have taken command of this castle until such time as he sends a man to replace me. Will you swear loyalty to me as my First Spear until such time as the king orders me to step down?"

Pidarnoin stepped forward and went down on one knee, holding up his hands, clasped together. Fortrenn took them in his own. "I do so swear, Lord Fortrenn. Until death or my king release me."

Fortrenn released Pidarnoin's hands. "Rise, my friend." He looked around at the militiamen Pidarnoin had brought with him. For the most part, while none of them were as massive as the new First Spear, they were all cut from the same cloth. These guys worked hard and fought harder, and they probably occasionally did the latter for fun. There were plenty of cauliflower ears and busted noses in that group of old salts.

"For those who have not yet heard, though I doubt they are many, your lord Achivir has betrayed his king and his land for the lies of a merrow." There was a bit of a stir at that, though it was small enough to suggest that Fortrenn's assessment of the speed of whispered tales in the local environs was pretty spot on. These people made the Lance Corporal Underground look slow. "Lord Galan will take him to face judgement before King Uven. In the meantime, I shall serve as Lord of Lemmanonius, with Pidarnoin here as my First Spear. We have been invaded by the creatures of the Deep Ones, and I must now rely upon each of you to be even more watchful than before. All who served in this castle on a permanent basis must now be viewed with suspicion, and they are being held in the catacombs beneath. It is not to my liking, but I need tell none of you how serious such dalliances with the things of the depths are."

There was another murmur at that. I saw a few warding signs made, and there were quite a few hard looks among the men Pidarnoin had gathered. I suspected that Fortrenn was being far more merciful to those who had been practically prisoners to their lord's delusions and the merrow's lies—not to mention the threat of its eac uisge bodyguard—than most of these hard-eyed fishermen and farmers would be. They'd probably lived their whole lives under the threat the Deep Ones' creatures posed, unless I missed my guess, and they would *not* be amused that the man responsible for their protection had sold out to those same creatures.

Fortrenn dismissed the militia, and they bowed, not quite in unison, several reaching up to tug at their forelocks, before dispersing, several of the older men gathering around Pidarnoin for more detailed instructions. The big man's voice was a foghorn as he started to direct his men to take up the defenses of the castle, telling some of them to bring some of their sons, daughters, nieces, and nephews to fill in for the other functions of the place.

Fortrenn, meanwhile, beckoned to Galan and the rest of us, and retired to the stairs that led up to the dining room.

We gathered around the big table, Fortrenn now standing in front of the high seat where Achivir had held his place. He leaned on the worn and scarred wood of the tabletop and looked around at us, his eyes settling on Galan.

"Well, my old friend, I fear that you must now take the quest upon yourself without me. Of the twenty of us who set forth, you are the last one upon the path." He hung his head a little. "I would not have it so, but duty holds me here."

Galan simply inclined his head, almost a faint bow. He had little to say, and Fortrenn didn't seem bothered by it. He looked around at the rest of us. "Horses will be saddled within the hour, and you may resume your journey. I regret asking that you take Lord Achivir with you, but he must face judgement, and better that he reaches the king's justice sooner rather than later."

"We'll see to it." Gunny's voice was firm. While it seemed like we had a weird sort of confused chain of command going on, between the knight, the Tuacha King's Champion, and the Marine Gunnery Sergeant, when it came to the platoon's course of action, even Mathghaman would yield to Gunny's decision, if the two of them were ever at loggerheads, which I had yet to see happen. For all the disparity of background and character between us and the Tuacha, there was a greater mutual respect and smoother communication in this mixed unit than I think I'd ever seen before.

Fortrenn turned to a sideboard and drew out a jug and cups. "Come then, my friends, if I may call you that after so short a time. Let us share one last drink before you set out upon the mission I may no longer pursue."

* * *

The Galel horses weren't quite as stocky as the Menninkai mountain ponies, but they were still solid, shaggy animals, and well-broken to the saddle and reins. We'd all gotten a lot better at riding since we'd arrived in this place, and while it took a few miles for the horses to get used to us and vice versa, we still didn't have any trouble with them, aside from the occasional mount wandering off the road when the forage looked particularly good. There was Chambers' horse, which had been clever and blown up its stomach while being saddled so that the cinch hadn't been tightened down all the way. Chambers' saddle had started to slip to one side after half a mile. Chambers had cussed the animal soundly when we'd stopped so he could tighten the saddle, drawing a disapproving look from Galan, who still hadn't quite adjusted to the roughness of our manners.

Maybe he was right to frown. We were the outsiders here, after all.

As we rode, Galan joined me. I wasn't the commander, but he seemed to have gravitated to my side as the man who carried the Sword of Iudicael. I didn't object to his company. He seemed like a good dude, though my upbringing might have initially made me bristle a bit at any presumed aristocracy.

We rode in silence for a little while, winding along the hard-packed dirt road through the fields and patches of wind-twisted forest, heading up into the rocky hills swathed with green. It was a couple hours before he twisted in his saddle and looked back at the mule where Lord Achivir, his hands bound to the saddle with rawhide cords, rode with his head downcast. Then, as he turned back forward, he shook his head.

"This is not good, Conor."

"I don't doubt it." I could tell he had something on his mind, more than just the fact that one of the Galel's vital coastal fortresses had been infiltrated.

"That a man such as Achivir should be seduced by the very monsters he swore to protect his castle from…" He shook his head again. "It bodes no good for our people. Where else have the forces of our enemies wormed their way into our confidence?"

I wasn't sure what to say to that. I'd gotten to know Galan a bit on the voyage, but I still didn't know enough about his people or the situation around Cor Legear to have much in the way of insight. But I'd seen a few things in my time. "Look, I don't know anything about Achivir's history. I'm guessing, though, that he didn't get appointed castellan to a vital coastal defense fortress without proving himself worthy."

Galan nodded. "I never knew him the way Lord Fortrenn did, but his deeds were well known, even in my country to the north. He held the line at Cor Turling, and when the pirates from the Fiachla Cloic raided his lands when he was a young man and took him prisoner, he escaped, seized a ship with a handful of his cousins, and hunted them down so thoroughly that they dared not budge from their harbors for nearly two years."

I kept scanning the hills beneath a blue sky studded with fluffy white clouds while I gathered my thoughts. "There was a time, when I was younger, that I would have thought that might be enough. A man's put his life on the line, sacrificed and fought to preserve his people and his family, then he's good. Solid. I've seen a lot since then, though. Watched an officer—granted, not one I ever trusted—go bad. Watched an NCO go worse." I used the term "Second Spear" instead of "NCO," since the *Tenga Tuacha* doesn't really have a term that better translates to "non-commissioned officer." "A year ago, I never would have thought a Tuacha could turn to the enemy, but I've seen that, too."

Galan looked a little startled at that, his eyes flicking to our Tuacha companions and then back to me. "Truly?"

I nodded. "As sure as I'm here talking to you." I paused for a moment. "I don't want to go into details. I think that Mathghaman should be the one to tell you that story, if he's of a mind to." That was unlikely; he'd been tight-lipped as all hell about it with *us* for months. "But yes, I've seen it." I shifted in my saddle a little. I was getting to be a better rider, but that didn't mean I'd *mastered* the skill. Far from it. "My point is that nobody's incorruptible. We've all got to be on our guard."

It was something that had bothered me since we'd confirmed that Captain Sorenson, Staff Sergeant Zimmerman, Staff Sergeant Gonsalves, and Sergeant Owens had—apparently willingly—joined Dragon Mask's quest to free Vaelor, an ancient eldritch abomination, from his prison under the ice sheet known as the Teeth of Winter. While none of them had been what I might have called close friends, they'd all been Marines, with the training and the expectations that went with it. That they'd so easily sided with those savages, and even resorted to human sacrifice in an effort to set Vaelor loose, had gotten a lot of us thinking.

Especially about what *we* might have done if we'd been cut off and reliant on the Dovos nal Uergal for survival for that long.

That thought drew my eyes to the hilt of the sword by my side.

While I had really come to appreciate the advantage the Sword of Iudicael gave me in close combat, I couldn't help but remember the story of its loss, and the fact that I'd found it in the grasp of one of the Dovos nal Uergal, a blood-drinking savage who had picked it up from some battlefield after it had passed through who knew what hands. It had not been in the good guys' grasp for long before it had passed out of knowledge.

That fall into darkness bore thinking about, especially when it came to planning the way forward. I didn't want to go that way.

It was a sobering thought as we rode higher into the hills.

* * *

We slept under the stars and the trees for the first couple of nights. While we'd made a good fifteen miles away from the ocean by the time we stopped the first night, we still set a watch. Some of that was purely due to habit. We weren't on the Isle of Riamog anymore, even though the Galel of Cor Legear were supposed to be the good guys.

The specter of those eac uisge hung over us all, though, and no one was willing to let our guard down, even as we put more distance between us and the Deep Ones.

Around the fire that night, I asked Mathghaman, "Have any of the Deep Ones ever come ashore? I mean the Deep Ones themselves, not their minions."

Mathghaman never looked directly into the fire. I was sure that he could without affecting his night vision, given the Tuacha's eerily adaptable eyes, but I'd never seen him do it. He watched the perimeter and the shadows beyond the firelight, instead. "They can. They are not of this world, though they are lesser than the things we speak of when we refer to the Outsiders. They chose the depths because of their temperament, not their nature."

"That's not good." Gurke was already looking back the way we'd come, then looked at me. "If they *really* want that Sword…"

It wasn't a comfortable thought.

"Then we will fight it just as we fought it before." Mathghaman didn't seem overly worried. Though his gaze rested on me for a bit longer, his eyes straying to the Sword of Iudicael, where it now leaned against a tree next to my rifle.

"All right, stand to comes early. If you're not on security, hit the sack." Gunny knew that we could very well go on for hours with increasingly dire speculations about increasingly spooky threats. We'd done it before, and we were currently better rested than we had been in months, the previous night notwithstanding.

Still, as I lay down with my weapons next to my head, the stars twinkling through the branches above me, the thought wouldn't leave. What terrible forces were currently in motion, all seeking the Sword that I had just picked up, seemingly by chance, in the north?

* * *

After three days' riding, we reached another castle.

We'd seen a couple more in the distance as we'd made our way inland. The entire country seemed to be

studded with them, which kind of made sense for a kingdom under permanent siege from irregular forces as well
as the vast imperial armies off to the east. Many of them
were similar to Lemmanonius, little more than towers or
keeps set on high ground with command of the surrounding terrain.

Arborth was a little different. A round keep was set
atop the peak of the hill, surrounded by thatch-roofed
buildings and three rings of earthworks, all topped by
stone walls. Herds of cattle roved over the green hills in
the distance, outside the mosaic of stone-fenced fields
that covered the flatter ground beneath the castle.

A small knot of riders, clad in mail beneath brightly colored tunics, wearing slightly conical helmets with
equally brightly colored horsehair plumes flying from
their peaks, came out of the gate and cantered down
the road toward us. Since Galan had lost his standard
in the shipwreck and was currently wearing borrowed
armor—though he'd saved his sword—we were flying
Mathghaman's silver banner with a golden rune in the
center, a recognizable Tuacha emblem that shouldn't
freak anyone out when they saw our strange, motley
assortment of riders coming. Between our unfamiliar
weapons and equipment, not to mention the differences
between the Tuacha's gear and ours, we had to present a
pretty odd sight. Better to put their minds at ease before
there were any misunderstandings.

Provided the enemy hadn't gotten to this place, too.
It didn't *seem* likely, but there was a river running through
the rocky land only a few dozen yards from Arborth's
outer walls. I didn't know if the Deep Ones could reach
inland through the rivers, but it seemed possible.

I also didn't know if the Deep Ones were the only enemies we needed to worry about. Fortrenn and Galan *had* said that the Empire of Ar-Annator was looking for the Sword of Categyrn.

The riders came all the way out to meet us, about two hundred yards from the walls. The man in the lead, a tall, spare-built man with a long, graying beard who wasn't wearing mail, but a fine coat of small, circular metal scales instead, raised his hand in greeting, then cantered forward to greet Galan with a clasped hand to forearm.

"Lord Galan. It has been too long."

"Lord Girom." Galan returned the handclasp and then turned to wave to us. "Allow me to present Conor McCall, the Bearer of the Sword of Iudicael, and his companions."

I blinked a little at that. Bailey and Gurke both shot me a look. Gurke's expression was the physical embodiment of "what the hell," while Bailey just smirked. Gunny chuckled faintly. Orava muttered something under his breath in the Menninkai's tongue, but otherwise was as impassive as ever.

"Moving up in the world, Conor," Santos said quietly.

If the Tuacha were insulted at being described as *my* companions, none of them showed it.

The truth was, this wasn't *my* quest. It was Galan's. But I could hardly say that without contradicting Galan in front of the older man, and something told me that wouldn't be a great idea.

Girom looked me over with a faint frown, taking in my odd equipment, including the rifle slung across my chest, hanging just above my saddle horn. Then his eyes moved to Achivir, and they widened. "Lord Achivir?"

"Just Achivir, now." Galan's voice was cold. "He rides with us to face the king's judgement." He motioned toward the castle. "If we may impose upon your hospitality for the night, Lord Girom, I can tell you more."

Girom studied Achivir for a moment before he turned his horse. "Of course, you are always welcome under my roof, Lord Galan, as are your companions." He glanced over the younger man. "It seems that you have met with some misfortune of late. Perhaps I can outfit you with more fitting accoutrements before you go before the king. Come with me."

* * *

The firelight flickered on Girom's weathered, lined face as he looked around at us, something close to shock etched across his features. Galan had just finished describing the events at Lemmanonius.

"Achivir gone over?" He shook his head and took another swig from the bronze cup in his hand. "It hardly seems possible. It is true that he seemed little like the man I remembered, the last few times I spoke with him. But to have allowed himself to be enmeshed in the nets of a merrow…" He sighed and looked down into the cup before taking another drink. "It seems that no one can truly be trusted any longer."

"We can trust the king, I think." Galan had put his own cup aside, and now leaned on the wooden table with both elbows. "He sent us on this quest, after all."

"A quest that has so far proved nearly disastrous." Girom waved his hand at the younger knight. "Only one man of how many still pursues it?"

"Twenty." Galan's voice was grim. "And yet, we *did* find the Sword of Iudicael, and its Bearer has agreed to come with us, along with a fighting force the likes of which I think our enemies have not yet imagined."

I wasn't so sure of that. Sure, we had rifles, machine-guns, explosives, and now mortar support, but in a world where I'd seen monsters blasted to a fine, black mist by sorcery, I didn't think that was quite as awe-inspiring as Galan might have hoped.

One thing I'd noticed since we'd arrived was that the modern fantasy that firearms would be so shocking and outside of pre-industrial people's experience that they'd think they were instruments of the gods didn't actually work out that often. I shouldn't have believed that it would, really, when I thought about it. The American Indians had sure adjusted to them awfully quick, and with only a handful of exceptions, there really weren't any records of them worshiping the white man as a god. People recognize tools for what they are, even if they don't necessarily understand how they work.

The Menninkai and their near obsession with mortars were a prime example.

Still, I wasn't going to gainsay Galan in front of Girom, and he wasn't *entirely* wrong. We did things differently, and so far, our strange fusion of ancient and modern warfare had stood us in good stead.

Girom glanced around at us and at the weapons stacked against the walls behind us. We weren't going to let them far out of our reach, not after what had happened in Lemmanonius.

"Still, be cautious." He lowered his voice as he leaned forward. "There is an emissary of the Empire at court. There is sorcery on the air. Lord Carvorst lies near death, and none can say why. Rumors have reached us from the east, rumors that the emperor has forged pacts with dark powers thought long buried. You must step carefully."

"We had heard such rumors at court, even before we departed," Galan said, but Girom shook his head.

"Not like this." The castellan's voice dropped still more. "They say the emperor has awakened the Thirty."

"Truly?" Galan's face went slack with shock. "Is he such a fool?"

"Perhaps. They say he has become more and more obsessed with ancient magics and artifacts in recent years." Girom raised his cup. "I salute any man who would continue on this quest, knowing that such monsters might lie in wait for him."

"I gave my word." It was a simple reply, but it spoke volumes, and Girom nodded grimly, and maybe a little sorrowfully.

"Fear not, Lord Girom." Mathghaman's deep voice resonated through the firelit room. "Even the Thirty may fall again."

"Who—or what—are the Thirty?" Bailey asked.

Girom glanced at Mathghaman, but the King's Champion shook his head. "That is a subject best discussed in the light of day, Sean."

He didn't need to say much more than that. We'd gotten used to such things, in this world where dark and sinister forces are always lurking, waiting for an opening. It went against the grain a little, when we wanted all the intel we could get, but you adapt, or you die.

Or worse.

We left it at that and called it a night.

CHAPTER 12

IF Arborth had been larger and more impressive than Lemmanonius, even it was a hovel compared to Cor Legear.

Massive, slightly sloping walls encircled the fortress, standing high on a promontory overlooking miles of rolling hills and forests. Big, square towers with red-tiled roofs studded the walls, and similar but larger towers stood at the corners of a much larger stone keep inside. A small city lay sprawled beneath those walls, and we'd been riding through farmland for most of the way since Arborth. There was a smaller curtain wall around the city, but it didn't appear quite as hardened as Vahavah Paykhah. The people probably retreated to the castle if the city came under attack.

With Galan in the lead, we rode up the main thoroughfare toward the city gates, eyes fixed ahead and trying to ignore the stares we got from all and sundry along the road. There was a fair bit of traffic, both coming and going. Young and old, men and women, most on foot, though there were still quite a few either on horseback or riding wagons.

We weren't expecting the kind of reception we'd gotten at Arborth, at least I wasn't. Gunny was his usual self, his eyes hooded, a faint sardonic look on his face, watching everything, keeping most of his thoughts to himself.

"Remember what I told you about leadership challenges, Conor?" he'd said to me once, when I'd mentioned how little he talked sometimes. "I *can't* just say whatever comes to mind. I couldn't when Sorenson was alive, and I can't now. Your dad didn't tell you everything he was thinking, did he? Don't answer that. The point is, as long as I'm running this show, and as long as you're all a bunch of wild men who would take just about *anything* I say as an excuse to run amok if I don't pay very, *very* close attention to my words, I've got to maintain that bearing. We're brothers, but there's still got to be a chain of command."

Mathghaman, though he wasn't technically a part of that chain, carried himself in much the same way. He didn't pour his soul out to any of us. He'd told us about Bres because he'd had to. We had needed to know.

When I thought about it, I didn't usually confide in Farrar or Rodeffer, either. I talked some things out with Santos, when need be, but we all look to someone older and wiser than ourselves to figure things out. So, Gunny held his peace most of the time.

Bailey was riding next to me, as Galan moved forward to take the lead as we got closer to the capitol. "You know, except for the Isle, this is the nicest part of this world I think I've seen since we got here." He was looking around at the green fields and the trees waving in the faint breeze in between them, as well as the stout, timber-frame, thatched-roof houses. "I could get comfortable here."

"You'd be going stir crazy within a week." I understood what he was getting at, but I also knew Sean Bailey. "If you settled down here, you'd be riding out within a month to go pick a fight with somebody."

"Hey, that shouldn't be too hard, from what Galan's said." He smirked and looked admiringly at the handful of people pacing the oxcart that was rattling along the road toward the castle as we passed them. "These people are constantly fighting off bandits and nomads. Plenty of combat to go around. And the women are awfully good looking, from what I've seen."

I had to agree with him there, though the Galel women were perhaps more earthy than the ethereal beauty of the Tuacha. There was a certain distance between us and the rest of the Tuacha, even given the brotherhood we'd forged with Mathghaman and his companions. They were different, and there was no getting around that. Even if we survived the wars and lived to be bent, white-haired old men, they'd all probably still outlive us by centuries.

There was a welcoming committee coming out to meet us as we neared the main gate, even if it was only two horsemen backed up by what looked like close to a company of men on foot, geared up and ready for battle, their arms and armor similar to Achivir's guards, though of different colors, mostly red and gold. Unlike Girom, they came partway outside the city walls and halted on the road, waiting.

We rode up in good order, a double column with our pack animals in the rear. It wasn't the most tactical formation, but we hadn't come under attack since we'd left Lemmanonius, though we'd been on alert the entire time. Galan didn't seem to think that we had to worry so much here, despite Girom's warnings about the Empire's emissary. Any mischief in this place, surrounded by the might of the Galel king, would probably be on the sly and in the dark, anyway.

Galan held a hand up in salute as we rode nearer. Girom had been as good as his word, and Galan was now decked out in much finer armor than he'd gotten from Lemmanonius's armories. A shirt of tiny round scales glittered in the sun when they peeked out from beneath the blue cloak and red linen tunic that he wore over them. His helm was tall, of burnished iron braced with bronze, and bore a blue-dyed horsehair crest that bobbed in the wind. There hadn't been time to get a standard made, so his spear was unadorned, but Bearrac still bore Mathghaman's standard, and a Tuacha banner carried some serious weight.

"Lord Galan!" The lead horseman looked about twelve. I was sure he was older than that, but he was a lot younger than Galan, that was for sure. "You have returned." His gaze traveled over our group, and he faltered a little. "Lord Fortrenn?"

"Lord Fortrenn lives." The fact that Galan didn't address this kid as "Lord" anything told me something. He didn't point, but he looked over his shoulder toward where Achivir still rode his mule, as mute and dead-eyed as he had been since we'd left Lemmanonius. "I would speak to the king about him."

In other words, "Mind your place, youngster."

The kid, to his credit, picked up on the message and didn't take offense. At least, not that he let show. Facing this bunch of hard cases, that was probably smart. We were all carrying a few scars that we hadn't been when we'd first arrived in the Land of Ice and Monsters, what felt like a lifetime ago, and from what I'd seen, nobody tangles with the Tuacha da Riamog on a whim.

"Follow me. The king is currently in council, but I will take you to the fortress." I traded glances with Bailey, and the look on his face said about what I was thinking. There was no way this kid knew what the king was doing. He was trying to save face.

We rode through the city. It was about what you might expect from such a place. It wasn't quite the mire of filth like the movies usually portray medieval towns, but it wasn't a rose garden, either. Most of the houses were only one story, sturdy timber frames with thatched or shingled roofs. The roads were dirt, though they were hard packed enough that there wasn't much dust. There was plenty of manure on the track as well, as we hardly had the only horses on the street, and there were more than a few mules and oxen, too.

Strangely, most of the animals around here looked a lot more like those we were used to from back in The World than what we'd seen in the north. The barrel-chested, blunt-muzzled mutant horses that the Dovos and some of the Fohorimans rode were nowhere to be seen, and the oxen looked more like oxen and not like some kind of prehistoric aurochs. Even the sheep looked normal, in comparison to the black, five-horned animals the corsairs kept.

Even as we slowed down, because there was a large oxcart in the way just ahead of us, I saw a couple of kids with wheelbarrows dart out into the street and start shoveling the manure into the buckets. It was one way to keep the streets relatively clean, and probably got used as fertilizer. Waste not, want not.

Reaching the base of the promontory, the kid led the way up the winding, switchbacked trail toward the castle gates, leaving the infantry at the small stockade near the bottom with a simple hand signal. There wasn't room for them on the path up to the fortress, at least not without spreading the column out to a quarter mile or more, and Galan's presence meant they weren't needed anyway.

Unless they were supposed to be an honor guard, in which case I guess the kid was getting his back for being put in his place earlier, out at the city gates.

The hill was even bigger than it had looked at a distance, and so was the citadel atop it. It was old, too, just judging by how weathered the stones were. Cor Legear had stood for a *long* time.

The path twisted its way up to the gate that stood above the town, flanked by two of the massive, square towers. The gate was open at the moment, which was a change for us. Ten men in red tunics over scale coats, their iron helmets burnished and gleaming in the dappled sunlight, spears held at order arms, flanked the gateway as we rode through.

We found ourselves in a wide courtyard, slightly narrower than the killing field that had extended between the first and second walls of Vahava Paykhah, but just as empty. I guessed that the fortress's position atop the steep and rocky hill made the killing ground less necessary. The defenders would be able to wreak absolute havoc on anyone trying to climb that path against determined opposition. The bodies would be stacked like cordwood at the bottom of the hill.

The kid led the way toward the inner gate, a quarter of the way around the hill. I watched the battlements of the main citadel above us, but there were no guards in evidence. They must only post up in time of emergency. I guessed there wasn't a whole lot of call for an alert while the region was at relative peace, to the point that the main gate was open. The guards were probably staged inside the towers unless there was a general stand to.

Steps hewn out of the solid rock of the hillside led up to the inner gate, and we dismounted there, leaving our horses to the small army of young men with mud on their boots waiting to take their reins. Galan spoke sternly but quietly to one of them, pointing to the pack animals with our rucks on them. He was probably telling them that if they screwed with our stuff, they might well blow themselves up.

None of our explosives were primed, but it never hurts to treat them with respect, anyway.

We formed up into a loose column before we mounted the steps. Since Galan had armed himself with Girom's loaned arms and armor, we were all geared up, too, though we'd put our helmets aside for the moment. We still made for a pretty subdued, drab assembly compared to Galan and our small honor guard. We were still Recon Marines, and so our mail shirts were enameled green, our chest rigs over them were still green, and we were still wearing our MARPAT woodland camouflage trousers and tan boots. Over it all, we each wore the Tuacha cloaks we'd been given, which appeared green, gray, or brown, depending on how you looked at them.

The Tuacha were dressed in much the same sort of way, as were the Menninkai.

Add in the rifles and our four belt-feds, and it was an odd-looking group that walked up the steps. We didn't leave our weapons behind, since Galan didn't either. I guessed, from what I'd seen of these people, that being always armed was a fact of life, much like it was with the Menninkai.

The kid led us through a guardhouse and a short corridor that led to the great reception hall. It might have been the twin to either Achivir's or Girom's great hall, except it was considerably bigger and brighter. If I'd expected the interior of the citadel to be gloomy, given the small and high-placed windows we could see from the outside, I was in for a surprise. The walls were all whitewashed and hung with colorful tapestries, and in places where the windows couldn't cast a lot of light, bright lamps were burning throughout the day and into the night. This might be a fortress, but it was also home to the king, and so it was kept as bright and cheerful as possible.

The twin thrones that stood upon the dais at the center were painted blue, red, and gold, with braziers blazing next to them. Red and blue tapestries hung behind the thrones and against either wall, and a red carpet had been laid out leading up to the dais, flanked by several classic bear rugs, the animals' jaws gaping wide.

A small knot of men were gathered around the dais, though the thrones were currently unoccupied. None wore armor, though all were armed, with daggers or swords at their sides. Like all the rest of the Galel I'd seen so far, they wore bright colors, with lots of yellows, blues, greens, and a few reds, the man at the center dressed from head to toe in red and blue.

He looked up as we approached, Galan's arms and armor clinking slightly as he walked, while our gear made hardly a sound. He was a young man, younger than I'd initially thought, with hawkish features framed by jaw-length auburn hair and a short, trimmed beard. His eyes lit up as he saw us, and he shoved his way through the group impatiently. "Lord Galan!"

Galan and the honor guard all went down on one knee as the young man in red and blue approached. "My lord king." So, this was King Uven.

If I would hazard a guess, I would have placed him in his early twenties, younger even than Galan. He didn't have anything like the weight of presence that King Caedmon bore, but he was a fraction of King Caedmon's age. He did carry himself with an assurance and charisma that couldn't be denied, though.

He seized Galan by the shoulders and drew him to his feet. "Why did no one tell me you had returned?" He looked around at all of us with that same quick, fiery impatience he'd shown as he'd parted his council to come and meet us. "Where is Lord Fortrenn? And the others I sent with you?"

Galan's face was grave as he gave his king the news. "We were shipwrecked in a terrible storm off the coast of the Isle of Riamog, my king. Lord Fortrenn and I were the only ones to survive. As for Lord Fortrenn, he was kept back by pressing concerns that arose on our way back to your court." A meaningful glance at the crowd of councilors communicated the fact that he didn't want to say more with too many ears around.

King Uven was sharp. He didn't need much more than that. I saw his eyes flick to Achivir, who stood bound behind the Menninkai, and while he betrayed very little emotion, the flash in those piercing, light blue eyes showed that the wheels were turning, and he was putting a lot together on very little explicit information.

With a grave nod, he looked over the lot of us, his brow furrowing a little at the sight of our strange weapons and equipment. "Did you find the man you sought?"

Galan turned to me, then, holding out a hand in invitation. "I did. Conor McCall, Bearer of the Sword of Iudicael, may I present my King, Uven, son of Drosten."

I stepped forward, somewhat unsure of how to proceed. We'd discussed all kinds of tactical contingencies on the way, but somehow protocol hadn't been a part of it. That was a bit of an oversight, but I guess that after some of our experiences in places like Syria, where a lot of the cultural briefs we'd gotten before heading overseas had turned out to be incomplete or to have put too much stress on the wrong things, we'd decided to kind of play things by ear. Sometimes that worked, but right then, I kind of wished we'd figured out how, exactly we were going to approach a meeting with local royalty.

King Caedmon had never demanded or expected any great deference on our part. He got it in function, if not in form, just because he was the sort of man who commanded respect by his very being. King Uven was different, though, and I wasn't entirely sure if I should bow my head slightly or salute him. Or just give the greeting of the day and call it good. After all, he wasn't *my* king.

He beat me to the punch, though, looking down at my belt and holding out a hand, almost reverently, toward the blade at my hip. "May I see the Sword?"

I couldn't help but take a look around the room, as all eyes were then on me. The kid who'd led our escort was staring at me with an intensity that could be awe or might be hostility. Most of the councilors, mostly men older than King Uven by a decade or more, were watching me with hooded eyes, their expressions blank and unreadable.

Slowly, so as to avoid giving anyone nearby the wrong impression, I drew the Sword out of its scabbard, holding it out with the blade laid over my forearm. It glistened in the light of the fires and the sunlight that filtered down from the arched windows high above.

King Uven stared at it raptly, reaching out a hand slowly. He touched the blade with his fingertips, just above the guard, then drew his hand back and put it to his chest. He met my eyes then. "Thank you." He took a step back, gazing at the sword in my hands. "I never thought that I would see such an artifact, when I first learned at my grandfather's knee, as a boy, about the coming of Tigharn's messengers and their bestowal of these weapons on the men of Silabor and Commagan." He turned, then, looking back at one of the councilors, a large man going to fat, his beard carrying more gray than brown. "Would you not agree, now, Lord Talargan, that while the darkness is indeed stirring, all across the face of the world, Tigharn has not entirely abandoned us? If these great tokens have once again come to the light of day?"

The big man didn't like being called out like that, but he couldn't very well challenge his king. Especially since it looked like King Uven was ready and willing to throw hands if it came to it. There was a rough edge to the young king, and, up close, the scars and callouses on his hands were more evident. He was a fighter, King Uven.

"Darkness, my king?"

I might not be the greatest of wordsmiths, but something about the voice that echoed from the back of the room just made the word "unctuous" seem fitting.

The man who stepped out into the hall was clearly Galel, though the only way to really tell was in comparison with the men who followed him. His complexion was redder, his hair brown, and his features were fleshier than those of the men who filed in behind him. He wore similar clothing, though, eschewing the bright yellows, oranges, blues, greens, and reds of the rest of the Galel for a longer tunic of midnight blue, trimmed with gold, with a black cape over it. Except for the length of the cape, his garb was identical to the pale man who walked behind him. That one was tall, spare, and hatchet-faced, with long black hair that fell straight from a widow's peak to his shoulders.

"Must you continue to use such language, Your Majesty? I have told you before that our guests find it… provoking."

I saw the flash of anger in the king's eyes as he turned back toward the dais and the little entourage that had just come out into the great hall. His jaw worked under his beard as he clenched his teeth.

"Lord Brule." Apparently, the bluff, rough-around-the-edges king had a certain degree of diplomacy in him.

I would have bitten the man's head off. "I do not recall summoning you."

Okay, he could be *somewhat* diplomatic.

Brule apparently realized that he was on thin ice, because he bowed, deeper than I'd seen any other Galel do. It only made him seem oilier and more obsequious. "Forgive me, Your Majesty. Our guests saw the new arrivals coming through the gate and requested an introduction." He looked at us, then, and I didn't like the look in his eye. "They could not help but be intrigued at the sight of such visitors."

Brule wasn't the only one studying us carefully. That tall, skeletally thin man behind him, who looked far too old for his hair to be as black as it was, was watching us even more intently, and had been since they'd entered the hall.

We'd received haughty stares before. Hell, as a Marine, I was used to them. Even more as an enlisted Marine. There was more to this than just arrogance, though. I remembered what Girom had said about sorcery being in the air.

This man was dangerous, and he knew who we were now, even if King Uven hadn't said a word about our identity.

Don't ask me how I knew that. I could read it in his eyes.

Apparently, so could King Uven. "These men have nothing to do with the emissary from the Empire of Ar-Annator. You may return to the diplomatic chambers. When I am ready to receive them, I will send for you." His voice was cold, but there was a deep, dark vein of anger running through it.

Fortunately, Brule picked up on it, bowed, and ushered the embassy out. That tall one with the widow's peak kept watching us until he had to turn fully toward the door.

The king watched them go with an unblinking, baleful stare until they had all disappeared into the hallways beyond. Only then, with a grim exchange of glances with several of his councilors, did he turn back to us.

I'd noticed that one of the men he'd locked eyes with before turning our way had been Talargan, the same one he had chided for holding too grim an outlook.

"Forgive me, my friends." He was clearly still pissed. "I have been unable to rid myself of these sneaking spies lurking about my castle as 'emissaries' for the last week." He turned to Galan. "No doubt you will require some time to rest and prepare before we set out."

That *we* caught my attention, and from the way Gunny's eyebrow went up, it caught his, too. Galan didn't even blink, though.

"Of course, my king." He inclined his head toward the rear of our formation. "Of course, there is the other matter…"

"Of course." King Uven huffed a deep breath, a combination of impatience and frustration. "Lord Vepogenus, take Lord Achivir in hand, until such time as we can hear his case." He looked toward the rear of the cluster of councilors. "Lord Gurthinmoch, as you are castle steward at the moment…"

A wide, jolly-looking older man, his flyaway hair and beard both snow white, boomed out, "Of course, my king, of course. Lord Galan, Lord Mathghaman, Lord Conor, if you will follow me?"

He'd apparently figured that the "Mac" at the front of my last name was close enough to the "Mag" of the Tuacha's patronymics that "Call" must have been my father. He wasn't, but I could see why he might think so.

Galan immediately started to follow the jolly oldster, and we just sort of fell in behind him. A few glances might have been shot at Achivir and the king's council, with even more at the door through which Brule and the imperial emissary had disappeared.

We might technically be in friendly territory, but the enemy was already there, too.

* * *

Gunny waited until the door shut behind Gurthinmoch before he turned to Galan. "Okay, just why did the king say, 'before *we* depart?'" He folded his arms. "He's not coming with us, is he?"

"It is the Galel way," Mathghaman said from where he stood near the fireplace. "The king must lead, not simply rule, and if he stays in his castle, feasting and drinking, rather than going abroad to do great deeds, he will not long be the king. Uven has shown no tendency to laziness or timidity in the short time he has ruled. It would have surprised me a great deal if he did not seek to come on such a quest as this. It is what Galel kings were born for."

"Unless the emissary refuses to leave." Galan was leaning on the windowsill, looking out at the courtyard below. "It is concerning that they are here now, of all times. We have long known that the Peruni have spies throughout our lands, and not all of them of flesh and blood." He looked up at the sky. "Do they know of the quest?"

"If they're looking for the Sword of Categyrn too, then probably." Bailey was fiddling with a knife, which might have seemed odd or slightly threatening to anyone who didn't know him. "If I was looking for a high value target that I didn't have a precise location for, I'd be snooping around to see if the opposition had any information that I didn't."

"So, the king of Cor Legear has invited himself on the mission as a straphanger, and we're just going to go along with it?" Gurke didn't like the idea, and since he was sort of our platoon nay-sayer, he had to put it out there. Gurke wasn't a bad dude, but he had a contrary streak that had really come out since we'd arrived in this world.

"Are you going to tell the king who gave Lord Galan the quest in the first place that he can't come along?" Bearrac retorted.

"We don't fight the same way these Galel do." Gunny wasn't arguing, but he needed to put it out there, anyway. "You guys have gotten used to it. I doubt a king like Uven will be all that *willing* to."

"Do not underestimate him." Galan turned away from the window. "He is young, and he is brash, but he has a quick mind and no small amount of courage."

"If his mind is made up, it will do little to argue with him." Mathghaman spoke with his usual authority. "It would be best, rather than to worry about the king, that we be on our guard tonight. I fear the emissary of Ar-Annator holds us no good will."

"You think we should set a watch tonight?" Gunny was studying Mathghaman closely. The King's Champion was curiously disturbed.

"It would be prudent."

He was thinking deeply when we left to go to our respective chambers, in an eerie echo of the night we'd spent in Lemmanonius.

Cor Legear might be friendly territory, but it was just as spooky there right at the moment as it had been in the Land of Ice and Monsters.

CHAPTER 13

NOTHING happened that night, or for most of the next week. Galan was busy during the days, gathering supplies and pack animals for the journey. The rest of us didn't have that much to do except try to find out as much about where we were going as possible.

We didn't see much of the king. He was busy, mostly with the trial of Achivir, which we didn't attend, and handling the emissaries. On the rare occasions we did see him, he was mostly grumbling about the latter.

It seemed that his accusations of spying were probably pretty spot on. So far, the emissary had wasted an immense amount of his time with socializing, without ever coming right out with their reason for being there. Furthermore, it didn't appear that they had a schedule for when they were going back east.

That was a problem, because King Uven was still determined to come on the quest, but he couldn't leave as long as the emissary was still hanging around, so we were stuck in an endless planning and prep loop, long after any further rehash of what vague information we had about the last known whereabouts of the Sword of Categyrn got repetitious.

Rather like the quest for Vaelor's throne, that intel consisted mostly of vague and archaic legends written down in crumbling manuscripts that were copies of other manuscripts long turned to dust. It turned out that there were at least three versions of the story of the Sword's loss, with different thieves involved each time. However, the vision of its return was remarkably consistent. It would appear in the last chapel in the Commagan Empire, unlooked for, when it was needed. This vision, seen by a prophet named Draal, was the same across every legend, even down to his name, though it was apparently spelled slightly differently in each.

The question was where the last chapel really was. The ruins of the long-dead Commagan Empire were vast, and there hadn't been too many records kept when it tore itself apart. Naturally, there were at least a couple of possibilities. We planned to investigate the two that seemed most likely.

Some said that the last chapel of the Faithful had stood in Gremman, on the Cardeleven Sea, which bordered the northern marches of the Empire of Ar-Annator. Others claimed it must have been in Myrgarak, a couple hundred leagues south of the Sea, on the Borala Plateau. Apparently, most of the disagreement stemmed from comparisons about which city was the most heavily defended, and Myrgarak had been much more heavily fortified. However, as the old scholar who had been helping us, Arcois, pointed out, the Commagan Empire had wholly gone over to the worship of Thoggudan by the time of its splintering and fall—a disintegration and fall largely driven by Thoggudan itself—so figuring out where the "last chapel" had stood was mostly a matter of guesswork. It would have been underground long before the inhabitants of the last stronghold—wherever that had been—had gone insane and torn each other to pieces.

Unfortunately, we'd exhausted the information available in the small library within Cor Legear within three days. Still, the king wasn't ready to leave. We'd hardly seen him all week, and Galan, Gunny, and Mathghaman had tentatively worked out a plan to make for Myrgarak first. It was closer, for one thing. If the Sword of Categyrn lay there, we'd save ourselves a couple hundred miles of riding or walking.

Finally, though, Uven ran out of patience.

He stormed into our apartments, fuming. "Enough!" He stabbed a finger at Galan. "Are you ready to depart in the morning, Lord Galan?"

Galan was slightly taken aback at the king's outburst. Uven was dressed to ride, most of his court finery put aside in favor of rougher trousers and a shorter, quilted tunic. "Of course, my king." He didn't say that we'd been waiting on the king for the last four days. That would have been impolite, and Galan was remarkably polite compared to a platoon of Recon Marines.

As for us, we stayed quiet. King Uven was obviously pissed.

"Good." He took a deep breath and seemed to calm down a bit. "I have had enough of these simpering easterners. They still cannot come to the point after two weeks!" He threw himself into a chair, which creaked under his weight. The King wasn't as big as some of us, especially Bearrac, but he wasn't a small man, nevertheless. With a sigh, he continued. "I know why they're here. But I have exhausted my obligations to cater to them. There will be a banquet tonight that I cannot escape, but then they must leave." He looked around at us. He hadn't been that present during the planning, but he'd gotten to know the basic lay of the land in the platoon, as confusing as it might be to an outsider. "I would have you join us, though with the Peruni still attending, I would understand if you declined."

Honestly, for a young king, Uven was a pretty decent dude.

"We shall come." Mathghaman didn't ask the rest of us, but he probably had a better read on the situation than we did. It said something about how much we'd come to trust him that nobody objected, not even Gurke. "I should like to see more of these Peruni." The Peruni, we'd learned, were the tribe that had founded the city of Ar-Annator and formed the backbone of its empire. There were quite a few other tribes involved, but the Peruni were the rulers, and therefore they formed most of the Empire's army and aristocracy.

The king nodded his appreciation, but he didn't seem inclined to leave at first. He let out a long sigh again, and I suddenly saw a young man who would far rather be out fighting or hunting but was trapped by statecraft.

No wonder he wants to come with us.

He looked over at me, then. I was drawing an awful lot of attention, being the Sword Bearer. It didn't appeal to me.

"How did the Sword of Iudicael come to you? I still have not heard the tale."

"My king…" Galan began, but Uven raised a hand to forestall him.

"I wish to hear it from Lord Conor himself."

Fortunately, nobody snickered at the king's use of the honorific "Lord," though I knew I'd get a full ration of shit from Bailey over it once the king was gone. I saw Gunny's eyes glint across the room with that faint deepening of the crow's feet around his eyes that told me he was laughing at my discomfort.

I would have done the same thing to him, if our roles were switched.

"It was entirely by accident," I admitted, looking down at the sword leaning against the wall next to me. "We'd just come through the mists and found ourselves in the Land of Ice and Monsters. Had to break contact with some sea trolls, then holed up in an old, abandoned fortress carved into the rock. The locals showed up and took some exception to our being there. They attacked the fort."

I waved to our other weapons, though they were far more powerful than the M4s and M27s we'd been carrying when we'd first landed. When King Caedmon had granted us access to the *Coira Ansec*, we'd all agreed that we wanted bigger bullets, given some of the things stalking around the wilds of this world. "We killed an awful lot of them before they changed tactics. I found the Sword on one of the bodies. He'd wrapped the hilts so he didn't have to look at the gold and the rune on the pommel."

Uven thought that over, studying the Sword, a faint furrow between his brows. After a long moment, he looked up at me, his eyebrows slightly raised. "Nothing in this world happens by accident. It may seem so, but while I may be younger than you, I have still seen enough to know that, especially when it concerns an artifact such as the Sword of Iudicael, there is no such thing as mere chance."

"You really believe that?" While he seemed slightly hesitant to ask the question, the fact that the king had engaged so familiarly lent Gurke some confidence.

King Uven didn't take offense at my fellow team leader's doubts. "Of course." He looked around the room. "While I am no loremaster, with a head full of figures and astronomical calculations, what are the odds that you should have been drawn through the mists from some far distant time and place, only to just *happen* to set your hand on the Sword of Iudicael, lost for all these long years?"

I had to admit, he had a point. From the look on Gurke's face, he didn't really have an argument there, either.

"It is not something I would wish to try to calculate," Mathghaman said.

Several of us were clearly chewing on it, while others were quiet and blank-faced. Despite all we'd seen and experienced in this world, we didn't come from a society comfortable with the mystical side of things. Marines especially tend toward a "God helps those who help themselves" sort of mindset. Some of that came from sheer necessity, coupled with the experience of those of us who had fought beside and against those of a more "Insh'allah" mentality. If you leave vital details to chance or providence in combat, it can get people killed.

One of the more religious NCOs I'd known, back in The World, had referred to that kind of negligence as "presumption."

"So, what? This was destiny or something?" Gurke still wasn't quite ready to accept it, especially as he looked at me. After all, why should I be the Chosen One, or whatever?"

"I do not know." Uven seemed vaguely amused by Gurke's obstinacy. "Yet it seems more logical to me that whatever power brought you from the place and time you came from intended for one of you to find the Sword." He stood up with a resigned sigh, knowing he had to get back to his duties as king. "Personally, I find that encouraging." He turned to leave. "I will see you all this evening, then. We depart in the morning."

Galan had come to his feet as his king had stood, and we all followed suit as he left. It seemed like the right thing to do.

As the door shut behind the king, Gunny drawled, "Don't let it go to your head, Conor. Remember what happened to the first Sword Bearers."

I didn't answer, as Bailey and Santos chuckled. I just looked down at the ancient, blessed weapon at my side and thought about it.

Unfortunately, the Sword itself didn't have any answers.

* * *

The great dining room was crowded and noisy. Between us, King Uven's court, and the emissaries, whom I got the distinct impression King Uven wished he could have banned, the place was packed. The Peruni—accompanied by their Galel toady, Brule—lurked at the end of one of the long side tables like a murder of crows, their dark clothing in decided contrast to all the bright colors the Galel liked.

We were probably somewhere in between the two extremes, dressed in blues and greens. Gunny had brought up asking the *Coira Ansec* for uniforms, but we'd all begged off. Service Alphas and Dress Blue Bravos might look good, but they'd be considerably out of place here, and they were uncomfortable as all hell. They'd also be tough to pack in the rucks. So, we were all in blue tunics and green trousers, of a somewhat similar cut to our cammies, but of finer cloth. None of us had brought combat gear into the hall, though in keeping with Galel custom, we all had blades on us. I probably would have invited King Uven's ire if I'd left the Sword of Iudicael behind, even if I'd been willing to let it out of my sight, which I wasn't.

Fires blazed in half a dozen fireplaces around the walls and more candles burned on the tables, lighting the room brightly. It was actually getting oppressively hot in there, between the fires and the body heat of the revelers, but I supposed it was a bit better than the cold of the north or the ocean wind.

King Uven sat at the head table next to his wife. The queen was blond and slightly heavy, her face flushed. She was no great beauty, but she had a warmth to her demeanor that more than made up for it. She was currently in animated conversation with the wife of Lord Guidid, her eyes sparkling in the candlelight.

Granted, I didn't have a lot of time or energy to watch the king, who was mostly holding his peace and watching his guests over the lip of his cup, because I was being plied with questions by a gorgeous redhead by the name of Derelei. Her green eyes always seemed to have that dewy gleam to them that's hard to look away from, and I was having a hard time stringing my sentences together in response to her eager inquiries about where I came from, what it was like to travel through the mists—it seemed that the Galel had legends about men becoming lost in the mists and coming out in a different time and place—and anything else she could think of.

Lord Cailtarni's booming laugh broke through the dull roar of conversation and the strains of music played by the minstrels gathered in the corner. Derelei blushed a little at her father's mirth. I hadn't heard what he'd said, but she had, and she was looking at me sort of sideways with a demure smile on her face, while Cailtarni, another big, barrel-chested example of a Galel knight, his bushy beard a badger-streaked blend of black and gray, his salt-and-pepper hair drawn back in a ponytail, grinned tooth-ily at me.

I got it, then, and smiled back at her. When I glanced around the table, I saw that while the Tuacha were as aloof as ever, and held in some awe by the Galel, and the Menninkai were mostly their usual clannish selves, every Marine had at least one pretty young Galel maiden plying him with talk.

My eyes strayed then to the Peruni from the Empire of Ar-Annator at the far side of the room, and the glow of Derelei's closeness and interest faded a bit. They were watching us, and there was no friendliness there. Not that I particularly expected any from the representatives of an empire that was, according to the Galel's intel, awaken-ing all sorts of eldritch horrors, and had even possibly set the Deep Ones on us. I didn't think that the sudden interest in the Swords of Iudicael and Categyrn was co-incidental.

That put me back on my guard. Derelei was delight-ful company, but I had to remember that we couldn't necessarily trust these people the same way we might trust the Tuacha, or even the Menninkai. After all, we'd already seen one of the Galel's lynchpin fortresses infil-trated. How deep did the rot go?

So, it was with some disappointment, but a consider-ably cooler head, that I turned back to Derelei's conver-sation, knowing that I had to step carefully and not get carried away by her beauty or her engaging personality. She noticed the shift, too, but a flick of her eyes and a slight narrowing as she momentarily glared at the Peruni told me that she knew just *why* I'd suddenly cooled. She didn't like the Peruni, either, and if I was reading her right, not just because they'd diverted some of my at-tention.

The rest of the banquet was perhaps a little less en-joyable, though Derelei didn't seem too upset when the king rose to his feet to announce that he was withdraw-ing, and we said our goodbyes. The Peruni left stiffly without a word.

Derelei offered me her hand as we both stood, and I took it awkwardly, not sure if I should shake it or kiss it. One thing I'd learned from the last few months, the women here operated by different rules than those back in The World, particularly in San Diego County.

As weird as it seemed, I bent to kiss her hand. Apparently, that was the right move, because she beamed like I'd just offered her a million dollars. When I looked up, her father was watching me closely. There was an approving look on his face, though, as he held out his arm and Derelei took it, letting him escort her from the hall, though not without a backward glance at me.

"Look at Conor. Straight-up ladies' man. When did this happen?" Bailey threw an arm around my neck, and I elbowed him in the side to get him off. That wasn't exactly the time or the place.

"Lord Cailtarni is probably thinking about the prestige it would bring his house if he married his daughter to the Bearer of the Sword of Iudicael." Mathghaman smiled as he joined us.

"You hear that?" Bailey grinned as he stepped out of my reach. "Conor's gonna marry a princess!"

"That's assuming we get back alive," I growled. That did put a bit of a damper on things. After all, we were stepping off on a long, hazardous infiltration into hostile territory the next morning. And I was pretty sure that those glowering, dark-clad Peruni knew it, too.

It was a more subdued group that headed back upstairs to our apartments.

* * *

While it was getting late, and I needed to get some sleep before we hit the trail the following day, I needed some air. The dining room had been sweltering, getting more so as the evening had gone on, and the night air out on the battlements of the citadel was bracing in comparison. Some of the smells of the town below came up to me, but the breeze was coming in off the ocean to the west, so it wasn't bad.

Clouds scudded across the sky, moving fast as they passed across the moon. The stars glittered brightly between them.

I studied that moon. It looked like the one I'd grown up with, and yet different. Frankly, the more I looked at it, the more I thought that it was close enough to be the same moon, only changed by a lot of time. I'd wondered from the day we'd first arrived through the mists whether we'd moved through space, time, or both, but now I was beginning to think that maybe we were on the same Earth we'd always known, only changed almost entirely out of recognition.

Mathghaman had told us the story of the coming of The Summoner. Whatever he'd been, the Summoning had broken the world on a level that made the fears of nuclear war my parents had grown up under seem like a kid's bad dream.

I'd probably never know. It probably didn't matter that much, if I was being honest with myself. We'd all pretty much given up on finding a way back. Dragon Mask had promised that with the power of Vaelor, he would have been able to send us back to our own time and place, but nobody who had survived the last months was going to try to go that route. At least, I hoped not. We'd risked life, limb, and sanity to stop Vaelor in the north, and we'd seen just what kind of evil he represented. Not to mention the fact that we were all pretty sure Dragon Mask had been lying the whole time, anyway.

None of the Tuacha had any ideas, either. They didn't know how we'd come here, and they had no idea how to send us back.

I heard a rustle behind me and turned to look, my hand moving to the Sword's hilt. The Peruni's glares had put me on guard.

Derelei stood silhouetted in the candlelit doorway, her hand on the door jamb. A moment later, she glided toward me, her skirts rustling on the stone as she joined me by the battlements, standing next to me and gazing out over the moonlit landscape below us.

"Does your father know you're out here?" Not the smoothest line ever, but I also knew that the last thing we needed was to get into a feud with one of King Uven's knights because we were too forward with the local women. Gunny had been adamant about that when he'd pulled us all in before the banquet. We'd been too busy or too exhausted for the most part to go chasing after female companionship in the Menninkai lands, though a few guys probably would have ended up with shotgun wives or whatever the Menninkai equivalent was if we'd stayed for too much longer.

"No." She laughed as she said it. "I trust you, though. Lord Galan would not have befriended a man without honor."

"You've known Galan a long time?" I guessed that was a safe subject. She was standing awfully close, and she really was a beautiful woman.

"Since we were children." She glanced at me with a smile. "He has always been like a brother to me, and he is betrothed to my cousin. You need not fear having him as a rival."

That was not where I'd been going with that. I swallowed and tried to think of a subject that wouldn't have Lord Cailtarni calling for my head in the morning.

While I was groping for words, leaning on the stone battlements, though, I heard something. A faint sigh? No, it was something else. Something a lot creepier than a sigh.

There it was again. A moan. A wail of despair combined with a distant scream of hatred.

I snapped my head around, my hand straying to the Sword again. I was still only carrying that blessed, mystical blade, instead of my rifle.

Derelei had heard it too, and she turned as I did, her eyes searching the shadows under the keep's towers, huddling next to me. I stepped in front of her, scanning the battlements around us for threats.

All I could see at first was darkness and the dappled moonlight on the towers above us. Nothing moved.

At least, nothing physical.

A faint luminescence began to coalesce in the shadows down the battlements to my left. It started as only a glow that might have been nothing but reflected moonlight, but it slowly grew, almost like a flame catching on a candle's wick. There was none of the warmth and cheer of a fire or a candle flame here, though. It flickered and wavered, a dim, greenish-bluish light that illuminated nothing.

The temperature up there on the battlements had just plummeted. I could see my breath, and my tunic was far too thin to keep the chill at bay. "Derelei, get inside." I drew the sword, unsure that it would do anything against whatever that was, but it didn't feel right *not* to have a weapon in my hand.

Derelei, however, shrank closer to me. "There is another one by the door."

I glanced that way, stifling a curse. Sure enough, another column of lightless phosphorescence was solidifying next to the door leading inside. We were trapped.

I could hear commotion inside already. Shouts and screams were punctuated by the sharp claps of suppressed gunfire. Something was going down within the keep, but I had a more immediate problem.

The phantoms drifted closer, the moans and distant screams of hate sounding louder and more strident. We were cornered, and there was nowhere to run. The wall behind us was sheer, despite its slight slope, and to go over the battlements would be suicide. At the very least, we'd break bones, and be stuck lying helplessly waiting while these things closed in on us.

I remembered similar things in the woods of the corsair lands, and Bearrac's warning not to look at them or even think about them too much, that attention drew them to prey on a man's mind. Yet it was a little too late for that, and there was something different about these things. They were singularly focused on us from the moment they appeared, floating toward us like transparent photographic negatives of cloaked men, their faces hidden by deep, tattered cowls, reaching out with clawed hands.

I stepped toward the first, holding the Sword of Iudicael up in front of me like I had confronted the great black shadow outside of Vahava Paykhah.

Unlike that thing, however, the drifting specter was undeterred, and just kept coming.

I was left with what a Recon Marine knows best. When in doubt, attack. I lunged, thrusting the sword through the specter's middle, right where the heart would be on a living man. I didn't know that it would do any-thing, but it was better than just cowering and waiting to get eaten. Or whatever some screaming phantom from the Outer Dark did when it got its claws on you.

The blade passed through without resistance and did absolutely nothing.

I withdrew quickly, stepping back into a guard, but not quite fast enough to avoid the swipe of that thing's clawed hand.

It passed right through my arm, or my arm passed right through it. I didn't feel a thing.

I figured it out suddenly. "They're illusions. They're not really here." I grabbed Derelei's hand and turned for the door, but the phantoms had done what they'd been summoned to do.

While I'd been trying to fight off smoke and mirrors, the real attackers had come up on the battlements.

Three of them stood in the doorway, advancing with a leisurely sort of menace. They had us cornered and they knew it.

Rather, they'd know it if they were human.

They had been, once. They were still dressed in the armor and quilted tunics they'd worn when they'd been living guardsmen. Those tunics were now soaked in blood from slit throats that sagged open like grisly smiles, and their eyes shone red from within.

Fortunately, none of them had weapons, but I didn't know what supernatural nasties were puppet-mastering the corpses. If there was a vampire involved, this could get really bad, really fast.

"Get behind me." I didn't know for sure that these were the only ones, but right now the length of the battlement behind me was clear, while these three shambling corpses were an immediate threat.

Always push the immediate threat.

Of course, they didn't have the courtesy of coming at me one at a time, so I had to move fast. I stuck one through the throat as it lunged toward me, quickly drew the sword back, and then stabbed the next one in the teeth.

I'd been kind of hoping that the blessed steel of the Sword might make them drop dead or fall apart at a touch. Of course, that was a long shot. I'd still had to cut Unsterbanak's head off to put him down, and he'd been dead for centuries. They reacted, flinching back from the burn that whatever was using the bodies felt at the touch of the blade, but they didn't go down.

As I drew the sword back from that second stab, I switched tactics, even as I kept backing up and kept myself between them and Derelei. She was scared; I could tell that much by the iron grip she had on my free arm. She wasn't panicking, though, which was good, though I could still hear her hyperventilating behind me.

Bringing the sword over my head and down in a short, tight arc, I struck the middle corpse right at the neck, sweeping its head off its shoulders with only the barest resistance. The fact that the dead man's throat had been cut nearly to the spine probably helped there. The dead skull, still in its helmet, toppled to the battlements.

The thing *still* didn't go down, even as I lit into the next one to my left and slightly closer. A dark cloud seemed to come out of the severed stump of the neck, forming the vague impression of a head, featureless except for two glowing bits of congealed blood where eyes should have been.

This was not going well.

I'd just lopped off a grasping hand that had grown blackened talons from the split flesh of its fingertips as the one I'd beheaded started to lurch forward again, outpaced this time by the two that still had their heads.

I could hear more gunfire down below, and more shouts. The battle in the castle was getting intense. I couldn't spare any attention from the immediate fight right in front of me, though. We were being steadily forced across the battlements, falling back from the shambling corpses step by step even as I hacked away at them, not slowing them down more than a little.

I knew what I was going to have to do, now. It still might not work, but it was better than nothing.

"Derelei, I need you to stand back and let me work." She let go of me reluctantly and shrank back against the battlements, and then I had room to swing.

I still couldn't maneuver as well as I wanted to, since I had to keep them away from Derelei. They were still closing in.

The only hope I had was speed, aggression, and brute force. And even that might not work.

Just as I got ready to go to town like a chimp with a meat cleaver, I felt a hand on my shoulder.

At first, I thought it was Derelei, and was about to tell her again to get to safety, but then I saw a glow out of the corner of my eye. It wasn't the sickly corpse light of the phantoms, which had disappeared now that their purpose was fulfilled. It was a golden-white glow that I only saw for a split second, but I knew it had been there.

I wasn't alone.

I can't say for certain that the presence of my mysterious guardian lent more speed or power to my blows. Maybe it did. Maybe it was just a confidence borne of knowing that he was there.

My first stroke severed a leg at the knee, the backstroke taking off another clawed hand as the corpse toppled to the battlements.

The next few moments turned into a blur of flashing steel and flying body parts. If I'd had any lesser weapon, it would have been a lot harder, but the Sword of Iudicael was sharp as a razor and probably wouldn't break if I ran a tank over it.

I went after the grasping hands first, since they were the closest and the nearest threat. About four out of the five remaining, I ended up taking a good deal of arm with them. Another head rolled, replaced once again by that blurry cloud of darkness with the same dim glowing red eyes.

By the time I was starting on legs, Bearrac and Fennean had come through the door, blades drawn.

The rest of the butchery didn't take long.

CHAPTER 14

KING Uven was in a roaring rage. His tunic was spattered with drops of blood and the naked sword in his hand had clearly seen some hard use.

"I want those barbarians on their knees in front of me *now!*" He paced the dais like a caged tiger, his bloodied fingers flexing around his sword hilt. "I'll have their *heads!* All of them, including that traitorous bastard Brule!"

"Was anyone else killed?" I realized I probably looked as savage as the king did, and the Sword of Iudicael was still naked in my hand, though as always it had not taken a single stain from the grim work I'd put it to. The things that had inhabited the corpses had drifted away like smoke as soon as we'd broken the bodies down enough, but there'd still been plenty of blood and bits of meat flying around.

"Aside from my guards?" King Uven's bark echoed from the rafters. "Men I've fought and bled with?" He stabbed his sword toward the rear of the hall, where the remains of one of the walking dead were being carefully bagged up. "I attended Denbecan's *wedding!*"

The king's fury was even more understandable. While the Tuacha were an exception, I still expected most political leaders to be politicians, and therefore likely to use

146

the people who answered to them as expendable pawns. That was certainly the way I'd seen things work back in The World, and the Dovos sure had treated everyone around them as a tool or a threat. Even King Karhu, from his throne on Vahava Paykhah, hadn't seemed to know every one of his men. But King Uven was different. He was the kind of leader who goes out of his way to learn his men's names. He'd probably spent as much time as possible on campaign, just to be a part of that brotherhood.

He *knew* the men who'd been murdered to furnish those eldritch things with vehicles for their hate. This was *personal* for him, and not just because he'd been a target.

A blood-spattered, mustached young man in trousers and no shirt rushed into the hall and bent down on one knee. "The Peruni are gone, my king. Their apartments are empty."

"*Find them!*" the king roared. His bellow almost seemed to have physical force. The kid without a shirt flinched, and two of the knights at the rear of the hall turned and left immediately, naked swords in their hands.

"Conor. Sean. With me." Gunny had his chest rig on and his rifle slung, with his axe in one hand and our chest rigs in the other, both of our own M110s hanging from their slings over his shoulder. We geared up quickly as we headed out after those two knights.

Gunny made straight for the gatehouse, rather than checking the rest of the keep. I thought I saw what he was getting at. If the imperials had disappeared from their apartments, then they were probably trying to get away. Either they knew that their attack had failed, or they were trying to get away before the survivors could react, figuring that their mission had been accomplished.

I had as little doubt as King Uven that the Peruni had been the ones to murder those guards and summon whatever had turned them into shambling corpses. You don't run for it after something like that if you don't have a guilty conscience.

The gatehouse guards were standing post, just as they had been the last time I'd seen them. They didn't react to our weapons or gear as we approached, guns up and ready to fight, though. In fact, they didn't seem to even notice us at all. We slowed as we got closer without either of them so much as turning his head to see who was approaching.

They were staring fixedly at the gateway, their eyes glassy, one of them swaying a little bit. Gunny snapped his fingers in front of one man's face, as Bailey and I watched the outer gatehouse. "Completely out of it." He brushed past me to continue out through the gatehouse. "Let's go."

The gate was open, though only so far that maybe a single horse could get through at a time. Granted, I didn't know whether the gates had been barred before, since the castle didn't seem to be on a war footing, but the guards' fugue state said about all that needed to be said.

We paused just short of the opening, just long enough to make sure everyone was up and ready for whatever we might find on the other side. I gave Gunny the nod and we went out fast. I hooked around the open gate, turning hard right to clear behind it, while Gunny took the left.

The steps and the steep hill leading down into the courtyard between the keep and the outer wall were empty and dark. I didn't have my NVGs on me, but I triggered my weapon light and played the white circle of illumination over the ground and the ancient stone wall. It went against the grain a little, but the boys with bows up on the towers didn't have NVGs, so it would help them out.

Nothing. The grounds were deserted and still. Not even a rat ran across the grassy gap between keep and wall.

"Let's keep going." Gunny wasn't quite ready to give up the hunt yet. "Keep an eye on the ground. I know I've got some trackers in this platoon, still."

Probably more than we'd had when we'd first come here.

Trying to find usable spoor in the trampled dirt and grass of the hillside, with a flashlight, was a losing proposition, though. Dozens of riders and even more men and women on foot had trampled that path, and that wasn't even getting into the oxcarts that regularly brought supplies up to the castle. Picking the Peruni's spoor out of that mess would be difficult in daylight, never mind with a weapon light in the dark.

We had to try, though. Santos, Farrar, and Rodeffer had joined us, while Baldinus, Applegate, and Synar had run up to the battlements to provide overwatch. While Santos set up on the gate itself with the Mk 48, the rest of us spread out and headed downhill, looking for any sign of our quarry.

We got all the way to the outer gate without any sign of anything out of the ordinary. It was as if nothing had happened.

The outer gate was ajar, too. I didn't think that was normal. The guards were still there, still alive, but just as out of it as the men up at the keep.

The king had come down after us, flanked by Galan, Cailtarni, and what looked like almost a company of armed and very pissed Galel knights. Torches flickered in the night, casting a wavering golden glow over the stones of the outer wall.

Gunny turned to the nearest guard, who was still staring blankly off into the night, through the gate and over the town below. He slapped the guy lightly on the cheek. No response. So, Gunny being Gunny, he applied a little more force.

I've sparred with Gunny Taylor before. Believe me, you don't want that man to hit you in the face when he's serious.

The slap turned the man's head halfway around with a *crack*, and he stumbled against the wall. A moment later, he staggered back to his feet, shaking his head, one hand to his cheek and a bewildered look on his face.

He looked around, his eyes focusing, and then saw King Uven, his face thunderous and a naked, bloodied sword in his hand, standing over him.

The poor kid looked like he expected to die right then and there. His eyes widened and he stiffened to attention, then sank to one knee before his king, though he clearly still had no idea what had just happened, or why Uven was standing there, his face a mask of rage, armed and spattered with blood.

"My k-king." I'd guess he was about to report his post, except then he looked around and saw six of the strangers with unfamiliar weapons standing around him, the gate open, and his fellow guards standing there staring out the open gate like men in a trance. "I…" He simply trailed off, at a complete loss.

"They were all like this." Gunny stepped forward before Uven could take out his wrath on the guard. "I think we know how the Peruni got out."

"Indeed." Mathghaman had slipped through the darkness like a shadow, and was suddenly just *there*, at the king's elbow. "A shadow races across the moors to the east. The emperor's lackeys are gone." He turned to Uven. "They are moving faster than horse or foot might carry them. To pursue them now would likely not succeed."

King Uven stared out into the dark, his jaw tight, his fingers working around his sword's hilt. Finally, he turned to the quaking guard, who was still down on one knee, staring at the ground. The kid knew he was in it deep. Even without knowing details, it didn't take a genius to see that something terrible had happened.

The king reached down and took the younger man by the arm, lifting him to his feet. His jaw was still clenched, and his eyes flashed with rage, but he didn't look at the guard at first. Not until the younger man was on his feet. "Wake the rest of them up." His voice was cold, though when he finally looked the guard in the eye, he relaxed slightly, and there was a faint warmth in his voice. "What is your name, my lad?"

"Domelch, my king." The kid's voice was still shaking, and he stood stiffly, hardly daring to look King Uven in the face.

"Domelch. You are of the town's levy?" The king's voice was almost gentle.

I glanced at Gunny. I didn't know *what* the king was going to do, but this sudden quiet after the storm of rage was concerning. Sure, the Galel's culture was a far cry from the savagery of the Dovos or the Lasknut in the north, and the Tuacha seemed to trust them well enough, but they were still ordinary men with ordinary human weaknesses. The king's behavior was giving me the willies. Were we about to watch him run the kid through with that bloodied sword, just to make an example of him, or even just to take out his rage?

"Y-yes, my king. I am son of Itharnan, the butcher."

"Tell me, Domelch, do you remember anyone coming to the gate in the last hour? To enter or leave?" King Uven still had his hand on the young man's arm, though his voice was still low and even.

The kid gulped. "No, my king. I mean, yes, my king. When you arrived, just now." The kid was scared spitless, and I couldn't exactly blame him. Gunny gave me a faint "down" gesture with his hand. We'd wait and see what happened.

That bothered me. I was supposed to be the Bearer of the Sword of Iudicael, a weapon supposedly handed down from heaven, or something. I shouldn't just stand here and let the king murder one of his guards in a fit of rage. *If* that was what was about to happen.

All the same, survival is survival, and we were a handful of men, currently scattered in small teams across the castle, and there were a lot of equally pissed off skullcrushers with weapons they clearly knew how to use with a great deal of skill right in arm's reach.

We'd put up with a lot in the north, dragging along with the Dovos nal Uergal through those monster-haunted woods, just because survival had demanded it.

I didn't care to be back in that position again.

King Uven sighed, then. He looked around at the other guards, who stood around the inside of the gatehouse, still at attention though most of them were looking at the dirt, ashamed to have been caught off guard.

"My king..." Cailtarni stepped forward, but King Uven let go of the kid's arm to lift a hand to forestall him. Cailtarni stopped, his words dying on his lips.

Looking down at his tunic, King Uven seemed to think for a moment. "Does anyone here have a rag?" It was an odd question, but one of the guards, apparently eager to make up for falling asleep on watch, if they could do that, quickly stepped up with a dirty rag that looked like they probably used it for keeping their armor clean.

I remembered reading once that the penalty for falling asleep on security in the Roman legions had been death.

King Uven took the rag, though, carefully wiped his sword clean, then sheathed it and handed the rag back with another deep breath. Looking around at the assembled guards, he cleared his throat.

"Under any other circumstances, you would all be flogged, at the very least, for falling asleep on watch." One of the young men, who still had his eyes fixed on the dirt, flinched at the king's words. "However, while you may not know what has happened, I do." He pointed to the open gate. "You were bewitched, lads. Every one of you. Count yourselves fortunate. Not only do I not hold you responsible for the Peruni dogs' escape, but you at least are alive, which is more than I can say for several of your comrades inside." Once again, a flicker of fury passed across his face.

"Is the truce over, then, my king?" I didn't recognize the knight who spoke, a tall, thin man with a long, morose-looking face, made more so by the drooping mustache over his mouth.

"It is." King Uven turned to the group of angry warriors. "The war arrow goes out tonight. They would not have done this had they not already been prepared to move against us once more." He turned to Galan. "I fear I will not be able to accompany you now, Lord Galan. With the war arrow going to the holds, my place is here." He was clearly trying very hard to keep himself composed, but I could still hear the disappointment in his voice. The king had been looking forward to doing some adventuring, but now his duties held him there.

"I shall go in your stead, my king, with your permission." Cailtarni stepped forward again. He looked at me. "It would be my honor to accompany the Sword Bearer, the man who saved my daughter's life."

Bailey elbowed me then, and I kept my expression carefully neutral. I could see him watching me out of the corner of my eye, though, and I could see the smug smirk on his face.

"Let it be so." King Uven turned to us, then. Mathghaman had moved to stand next to Gunny. "I fear, my friends, that haste is now of the utmost importance. That pig, Votozun, will be carrying word to Ar-Annator that the Sword of Iudicael is indeed on the board. You must depart first thing in the morning. There is no further time to wait."

"We have been ready to go for several days now, my king," Galan admitted. "We shall ride for Cor Hefedd as soon as it is light."

The king nodded. "I hope to see you off myself, though I mourn that I must send you without me." He turned to the guards. "Resume your watch, and if your minds begin to wander, strengthen each other! The night is far from over."

All of them sank to one knee, each man touching the forehead of his helm. The king turned and led the way back up the hill.

It's been said, back in The World, that no battle plan survives contact with the enemy. My experience tended to amend that old truism to say that no plan survives the first step outside the wire.

This one had already gone to hell in a handbasket before we'd even known the mission had been laid on.

Murphy will have his chuckles, though. We just had to keep pressing on.

CHAPTER 15

A patchy morning fog had moved in by the time we set out, riding north and east from Cor Legear, the sun barely a wan, pale disc on the horizon. There was a chill in the air, and everything was dead still. Even the animals didn't make much noise. The clop of our horses' hooves was strangely deadened.

Santos had urged his mount up next to mine, and he was looking around the fog. "This gives me the creeps, brother."

"After last night? I don't blame you." To tell the truth, I was every bit as on edge as he was, scanning the mists and the dark shapes of hills and woods as we paced along the road toward Cor Hefedd, the last castle before the border of Galel territory and the northern marches of the Empire of Ar-Annator. So far, everything was still, not even a breath of wind stirring the fog or the tree branches, but when you've barely slept after fighting phantoms and walking corpses, you get hyper alert.

Or you pass out in the saddle. My eyes were gritty with fatigue, but I was still confident enough that I'd be able to stay awake and alert on movement. I'm not wired to fall asleep easily anymore, and it takes a lot for me to relax.

Especially when I'm riding behind the Galel lord whose daughter I'd been alone with on the battlements the night before, just prior to everything going weird and deadly.

I still wasn't sure just why Cailtarni was with us, or whether I should be concerned. On the one hand, he'd stepped up when the king's responsibilities had kept him from accompanying us on the quest for the Sword of Categyrn. On the other hand, I wasn't sure where I stood with him. He'd made a point of staying near me, and while he'd seemed to take some pleasure and pride in the fact that Derelei and I had, apparently, hit it off, I was still leery. After all, she'd slipped away to join me on the battlements, and while I had managed to keep her safe when the walking dead had attacked, I probably wouldn't have been all that happy about my daughter sneaking off to spend time alone with a Recon Marine, especially not if I came from a clan-based, traditional culture like these people seemed to have.

On the other hand, it was conceivably possible that he really was hoping to marry her off to the Bearer of the Sword of Iudicael, and he was coming along to se-cure his investment. He sure hadn't seemed all that upset when she'd slipped out through the gate to put her hand-kerchief in my belt, with a whispered plea to bring her father back alive…and to come back to her.

I wasn't sure which possibility was more unnerving.

So, I had plenty of reasons to stay awake and alert.

Santos wasn't thinking about that, though he'd got-ten a bit of a chuckle when he'd found out that Cailtarni was coming with us. I'd gotten a few sly looks after that, which I'd done my best to ignore when they came from

Santos, Bailey, or Chambers. I *might* have snarled a bit at Rodeffer when he'd tried to make a crack, and he'd subsided quickly.

I *was* still his team leader. Despite the fact that we'd become more Recon than Marine by then, in the absence of Big Marine Corps and its strict protocols that we usually found hindering, at best, there was still *some* hierarchy. There had to be in a combat unit.

There was only so much guff I was willing to take from a dude five years younger than me and with a lot less time in Recon, anyway. That was, ultimately, what had always mattered, more than rank. How much time did you have in Recon?

The road wound around the hills and the woods, hardly taking a straight line for longer than a few dozen yards. It was a track packed down by the tread of feet, hooves, and wagon wheels, rather than a purpose-built road, like the Romans might have once constructed, that cut straight across the landscape. That meant the footing was a little less sure, and the terrain dictated the course of the road. That was good and bad. On the one hand, it provided us with a little more cover and concealment in places, and while we rode with Galel knights who dressed like peacocks compared to our browns and greens, that could always be useful. On the other hand, it was hard to avoid certain places that made for good ambush spots.

Fortunately, the fog burned off as the morning went on and we climbed higher into the rocky hills. The wind picked up, too, blowing east from the sea, which was still out of sight to the west, though we could still catch the occasional whiff of salt on the air. The road wound through and over the hills, which were getting steeper and rockier as we moved north, toward the spine of low, stony coastal hills that divided the northern half of the Galel kingdom from the Empire's western marches. The wind whipped along those grassy hilltops, and while there were still patches of woods, they were mostly down in the low ground, where there was water.

Those patches of wooded low ground were danger areas. And the second time we stopped to rest and water the horses, we got to see just how dangerous they were.

As we rode down off the road and into the willow-choked hollow where a stream burbled over mossy rocks from a spring up the hill, shapes moved in the shadows under the trees. Hands went to weapons, but Galan didn't slow or stop, so we followed his lead. Technically, he was the mission commander at the moment.

A moment later, though, Gunny whistled from his position halfway back in the column. I turned around and saw him signal that we should stop and dismount. I nodded and swung a leg over my saddle.

We weren't cavalry. To make matters worse, none of these horses had been trained to handle gunfire. As soon as we started shooting, things were going to get awfully chaotic, and that was just talking about the animals' reactions.

So, while the knights—about eight of them had come along with us, including four of Cailtarni's household, all younger men full of piss and vinegar—continued to advance, accompanied by the Tuacha, the Recon Marines and Menninkai swung down off our horses and got ready to fight our way.

We spread out to either side of the track, moving into the trees, while the guys who'd drawn the short straw—Synar, Franks, and Ohto—held the horses.

There was a lot more movement, now, as the band in the woods closed in. They were moving carefully, but even from what little I could see, there were a *lot* of them.

"Greetings, my lords!" While the Galel's tongue was different from the *Tenga Tuacha*, again, it was close enough that I could understand it if not speak it. The point was, I could understand it well enough to tell that this man who had just stepped out onto the stream bank, cloaked in green over a thick, brown gambeson, wasn't some accented yokel, or even a foreigner. His voice and his accent were as cultured as Galan's or Cailtarni's. He was rougher in appearance, but that might only have been due to his time in the woods. His reddish hair was long and a bit scraggly, at least the bits that stuck out from under his hood, and his beard hung nearly to the middle of his chest. He held a spear in his hands, and the hilt of a sword—a quite fine-looking sword—jutted from the sash around his waist. "I would say that it was unfortunate that you ventured into these woods at this time, but…" He shrugged. "Fortune had little to do with it." He gestured with the spear. "You are completely sur-rounded and outnumbered three to one. There is little to no room to maneuver. Get down off your horses, lay your arms on the ground, along with any valuables you might be carrying, and go back the way you came."

"So." Galan leaned on his saddle horn. He bore no lance at the moment. None of the knights did. Where we were going, it had been decided that lances would prove too unwieldy and difficult to get into action quickly.

Lances were for open battle, and best carried in threes, when there were squires along to carry them. We didn't have squires, and the knights hadn't brought them, either. This band needed to move fast and light. They had each brought several shorter spears, but they were all sheathed and tied onto the packhorses. His sword, however, would be quite deadly from horseback. "The son of Cinioch has found employment as a bandit and a crony for the Empire, rather than trying to restore his family's honor. How fitting." There was no fear in the knight's voice, only contempt.

The bearded man's face stiffened, and he stabbed a finger at Galan. "And how should I have done that, except by taking vengeance on those who drove my father to suicide?"

Cailtarni leaned forward in his saddle, still without reaching for a weapon, though there were easily thirty men in view, all with bows, spears, billhooks, clubs, and axes in hand. "No one drove your father to take his own life. He fell on his sword rather than face the man he'd cuckolded. He was a coward as well as a thief and an adulterer." He spat on the ground. "I see his son is following in his footsteps."

The bandit's face was pale, and the knuckles around the spear haft had gone white. "I had hoped not to shed blood today. Why should I waste any of my men's lives? The Emperor will get his wish, one way or another. But now I will see you all dead." He lifted a hand, his mouth opening to yell.

Bailey shot him between the eyes.

The shot *crack*ed across the little vale, the echoes deadened by the trees. The bandit's head snapped back, and he crashed onto his back, his spear clattering on the rocks in the stream. There was a sudden pause as every bandit in the trees froze.

"You boys might have us surrounded, but that just makes things simpler." Gunny still managed to drawl the words, even using the *Tenga Tuacha*.

Cailtarni was less perturbed by the gunfire than I might have expected, but then, he had been in the keep when our guys had discovered the hard way that those walking cadavers didn't go down when you shot them. Some of the younger lads hadn't been there, and a couple had flinched a little at the noise. Galan was utterly calm. After all, he'd already seen us shoot stuff a lot.

"Who's next?" Bailey was usually a quiet dude, even in his angrier moments, but he was still a Marine SNCO, which meant he could make himself heard without difficulty when the occasion called for it.

Now, while most people weren't immediately panicked by firearms here—and as I've said before, never really were in The World, either—there are other dynamics at work in a situation like this, too. These guys were thugs, bandits, outlaws. They were in it for what they could get. From their leader's words, it was doubtful that any of them were true believers in much of anything. They were greedy bastards at best, angry, bitter psychopaths who just wanted to take their own misery out on the world at worst.

That meant that there were few things that men like them would be willing to die for. And when we'd just smoked their leader without breaking a sweat, they were going to be thinking. Wondering if the reward that the

Peruni had offered would really be worth it if they didn't live to collect.

I guessed, as several started to fade back into the trees, that the son of Cinioch had promised that we'd just set our weapons down and meekly slink away with our tails between our legs, outnumbered like that. They wouldn't have to risk much.

Boy, did he read his own people wrong, never mind the rest of us. Even though none of the knights had yet drawn a sword, I'd seen just enough of the Galel's ways that even *I* knew that they'd never back down to a brigand in the woods. This would have been a bloodbath, even if we hadn't been along.

"There are still more of us than there are of you." The voice that came out of the trees was rough, but the man didn't show himself. "And the reward for stopping you is considerable."

"I'm sure it is. How many of you will live to spend it, though?" Galan was completely relaxed, though his hand was close to his sword hilt. This could get nasty in the next few moments.

More of the figures in the trees slipped away. As I watched, several more seemed to look from side to side, and then they decided that discretion was the better part of valor.

Within moments, as the others saw that their backup was dissolving, they turned and ran.

Galan sat up straighter in his saddle. His voice rang off the hills. "Did I not have pressing business, I would hunt the lot of you down and hang you for the wolfsheads and traitors you are! Be warned! Your days are numbered!"

There was no reply. Still, as we looked around, Bearrac ventured an opinion. "Perhaps a different watering hole. This one has a bad smell to it."

* * *

We finally paused for the night some hours and many miles later. With security set, we settled into a small hollow in the hills, which provided some shelter from the wind for us, the horses, and the fire.

"We're still being followed." I kept my voice low as I joined Gunny and Mathghaman up on the promontory where we were setting an OP in. The three of us wanted a better view of our surroundings as the sun went down, though Huuhka and Kärsä were already set in with optics and rifles, watching the long slope down to the valley that stood between us and the hills. We had about twenty miles to go to get to Cor Hefedd, at the base of the pass that was the doorway to the northern reach of the Galel kingdom. The sea was just visible off to our left, glittering in the last rays of the sun.

"I know. I saw 'em, too." Gunny was scanning the valley below us. "Interesting that they were riders, since everybody in that watering hole was on foot."

"I doubt they are the same band." Mathghaman was as unperturbed as ever, even knowing we were still being hunted in what was supposed to be friendly territory. "Those men, those 'wolfsheads,' as Galan called them, will have scattered to the winds. They would certainly not try to follow us further, not after Sean's little demonstration."

"Who's still after us, then? There can't be *that* many bandits running around this country, not with the people being armed and perpetually on a war footing the way they are." I hoped that my other suspicion, that there might be a feud involved, was wrong. After all, from the conversation about the late Cinioch's fate, it was apparent that such things weren't out of the ordinary among the Galel.

"There should not be, but we are in the borderlands now." Mathghaman lifted his eyes to the dark in the east, past the mountains. "The Peruni's servants will not all be Galel outlaws, this close to their territory. The Empire has long been known to hire the nomads of the northern steppes, east of the Wall of Scath, as auxiliaries. They are horsemen and keepers of sheep, and if they could get across or around the mountains, they would be eager to harry the farmlands here. Their lands are not fertile, and their lives are hard." His eyes narrowed. "They would have shamans with them, as well."

"Great." Gunny looked around the hilltop. "At least we'd have warning if any flesh and blood enemies tried to come at us here."

"They will wait still, I think." Mathghaman ran a hand over his beard. "A shaman runs a great risk, calling upon the forces of the Outer Dark, even those that they think are 'insulated' from the Outsiders themselves. They will probe us first, I think. Even then, they might not attack before we reach the castle." He put a hand on each of our shoulders. "We will do what we have always done. Stay alert, be prepared to fight, and trust in Tigharn."

He was right. There comes a point where you don't have enough information to plan in any greater detail, so you have to fall back on situational awareness, alertness, and training. There was a book I read, back in The World, written by a Delta guy. One of his little axioms, that had always stuck with me, was that you should "prepare more than plan." Plans die quick. Preparation gets you through those moments of chaos where the plan just went up in smoke.

We were back in our element. We just had to stay alert and be ready for whatever came at us.

And hopefully spot it coming early enough to head it off.

CHAPTER 16

IT was a quiet, uneventful night. We were up and moving at daybreak, heading down into that green valley below, following the road as it wound its way through the trees and the rocks on the leeward side of the hills.

I looked up as the sun crested the ridge ahead of us, and saw, just for a moment, a figure on a short, barrel-chested horse, briefly silhouetted against the sky on the next finger over, to our south. He disappeared quickly, going down the opposite slope, but I got the quick impression of a stocky man, almost matching his horse, carrying a recurve bow and a spear, his peaked cap pointed forward.

The rest of the day, as we rode down into the valley and across the woods and farmland, were quiet. We still spotted our shadowers from time to time, but they kept their distance. I didn't know if they were just scouts, or if their warband was just too small for them to be confident enough to attack.

Either way, we were unmolested as we made our way across the valley. It was near dusk when we finally rode up to the gates of Cor Hefedd.

The castle looked more like Lemmanonius than either Arborth or Cor Legear. A lone keep, perched atop a shoulder of the mountain, just on the west side of the pass, it was a single, thick, round tower, with a small, square addition to one side and a ramp curving around its flank to the gate halfway to the battlements. It looked just big enough for a small force to hole up inside and bottle up the pass. The farms nearby were relatively spread out, and only a handful of houses and what might have been shops were gathered in the hollow beneath the castle, notably with the keep itself between them and the pass.

A few lamps burned in windows that had not yet been shuttered as we came to the stable at the base of the path leading up to the castle. A lantern hung on a post just outside the stable doors, and an older man in an iron cap, a faded blue gambeson, and an equally faded red cloak leaned on a spear next to the post. Despite the faded and tattered look of his clothing and armor, his cap gleamed without a spot of rust, and the spear glittered in the golden light from the lantern. His hair and his short, neatly trimmed beard were gray, but his eyes were clear and sharp as he looked up at us.

He touched the rim of his helmet as Galan and Cailtarni reined in before him. "Welcome to Cor Hefedd, my lords." He looked past the Galel knights then, and when he saw the Tuacha and our rather more unconventional appearance and weapons, his eyes widened slightly. He composed himself, though. The Galel might not be as stoic as the Menninkai, but they were still a people who took some pride in not being easily rattled. He turned and whistled sharply, and a moment later a younger man with a hangdog look to him came out of the stables, looking even more morose as he eyed the column of men on horseback that was strung out down the rocky road below.

The old man turned back to look up at Galan. "I would suggest you leave your horses here, my lords. There is no space for the beasts in the keep above."

We dismounted then and handed our mounts and pack animals off to the haggard-looking groom, who didn't speak but managed by looks alone to communicate how put upon he was, having to care for this many horses at such a late hour. The sun was barely setting at our backs, so it wasn't *that* late, but he'd probably been dead set on an uninterrupted evening in a quiet corner with a jug before we'd showed up. Now he had a couple hours of extra work to do.

I'd been about to pull my ruck off my pack horse, but Gunny, after a look up at the keep, told us to leave the rucks, just taking the day packs off the tops. We didn't intend to stay in Cor Hefedd for more than a night.

Gurke was already telling Franks to stay with the horses, but Fennean stopped him. Gurke had been speaking English, but with the mind speech, the Tuacha understood anyway, even if the locals didn't. "These people will guard mounts and packs alike, Ross. It is a matter of honor and hospitality. To leave a watch would be an insult." He glanced at the old man, who was just far enough away that he didn't seem to hear. "They will not let anything happen to the horses, nor will they touch our gear."

Cailtarni was just close enough to hear. He snorted. "Were these still Fidach's lands, that would perhaps be less certain. Fortunately, his widow is more upstanding than he ever was." Shouldering his own saddlebags, though he still pointedly left his packhorse's load alone, he started for the path leading up to the keep.

I traded glances with Gunny, who shrugged. This place had been Galan's choice of destination, and he hadn't said anything about the locals being untrustworthy. Maybe Cailtarni just had a grudge. It seemed like the Galel were pretty touchy about some things, and I could see them holding onto vendettas, even if they weren't quite as vicious about them as, say, some Arab tribes I'd met, never mind Pashtuns.

With Galan and Cailtarni in the lead, we finally started our ascent to the keep. It was hardly the steepest climb we'd ever made, and without rucks it was pretty easy, but it would be a nightmare to try to fight up that narrow, rocky path while being pelted by arrows and sling stones flung from the battlements above. The entire route up the hill was covered by the keep's defenses, which also had a pretty good shot at the trail that wended its way down from the pass above, which was almost as narrow.

A bell tolled down below, and eyes turned that way while hands moved to weapons. The alert signal on the Isle of Riamog was a bell, and we were immediately looking for enemies. After a moment, though, Diarmodh looked back and chuckled. "Only two strokes, my friends. They are telling the keep that we are coming."

It was a somewhat rueful bunch of Recon Marines who relaxed with a few muttered imprecations. Some things we were still getting used to, even after this much time, and different methods of signaling in a world without radios or phones can get pretty inventive.

The hike took a few minutes, but by the time we reached the gate there were ten men waiting for us, in armor and carrying torches. Each carried a sword at his side, but they all touched a hand to their helmets as

Galan and Cailtarni approached them. From the looks of their gear, at least two were knights, particularly the wiry, weathered old man with the gold-chased helm.

The ten men formed a double line of five each, lining the gateway, lit by their torches. At the end of that short column stood a woman, wrapped in a voluminous cloak, with a boy standing next to her, carrying a lantern on a pole. She was handsome, if somewhat heavyset, her dark hair streaked with gray.

Galan exchanged greetings with the two men in richer gear, then strode between the others to bow in front of the woman. "My lady Loncheta."

"My lord Galan." She sounded tired. "What brings you and the likes of Lord Cailtarni to my doorstep?" The look she gave Cailtarni wasn't exactly friendly, though she still bowed, and Cailtarni returned it graciously. There was definitely some history there, and not all of it pleasant.

"We are on a mission from the king, my lady." Galan straightened. "We ask your hospitality for one night only. We shall be gone in the morning."

"Gone where, my lord?" She asked the question even as she turned and ushered us inside. The interior of the keep was dark and cold, at least compared to Cor Legear and Arborth. If the walls had been whitewashed once, it had mostly worn off, and the plaster had fallen away in many places, leaving the bare stone visible. A few tapestries hung on the walls, and the rushes on the floor seemed fresh, but there was an air of shabby neglect to the place. The handful of candles and rushlights on the tables against the walls of the reception hall, small as it was, only barely lit the space, leaving much of the ceiling in gloom. "We are at the limit of our king's domain. Beyond the pass are only the tribes that pay tribute to the Empire of Ar-Annator, and the mountains to the north are worse."

"Yet we must venture into that territory beyond, my lady." Galan didn't seem all that eager to go into details, and I decided I should probably keep my cloak over the Sword of Iudicael. I didn't know if Galan didn't trust Loncheta specifically, or if he was just concerned that word of our mission might get a little too far if it was spread around the borderlands like this.

Recon Marines are used to working with classified material. We could keep our mouths shut. We'd done a pretty good job of listening more than we talked so far on this trip, at least when we'd been around outsiders.

Of course, the Menninkai were putting us all to shame on that count. I think mostly because they were still the FNGs, and they knew it.

Loncheta turned to face us as the men at arms pulled the gate shut, closing off the night outside. The bar was slid to with a *boom* a moment later. They took security a lot more seriously out here on the borderlands, it seemed.

"This is not a good time to venture beyond our borders, my lord." She was in earnest, though she seemed to have picked up on the fact that Galan wasn't going to tell her exactly what we were doing. "The Empire has not yet ventured to cross the pass, but the tribes in the mountains and beyond have been more active." Her voice and expression turned bleak, as her eyes moved to the barred gate door. "As have their shamans."

That got everyone's attention. "Have they sent sum-monings?" Cailtarni asked, his antipathy for the wom-an's late husband forgotten for the moment.

"Nearly every night." She sounded even wearier than before. "This is a haunted place, my lords. I fear that you may have picked a poor refuge for the night, yet you will only face worse if you cross the border here."

"We have little choice at this point, my lady," Galan confessed. He turned to Mathghaman, who nodded gravely. Loncheta didn't seem to have noticed just who our Tuacha comrades were, though her eyes had rested curiously on our gear and weapons. They might have rested longer on Gunny, but that could have just been my imagination.

If I could confirm it, though, I'd certainly give him the same ribbing he'd been giving me about Derelei.

"Our mission is set, and our time is short. We must hazard the risks." Galan looked around the hall. The boy with the lantern had disappeared for a moment, only to reappear with several more youngsters and women. "Is this all the garrison of the castle?"

"I fear it is, my lord." Loncheta sank down in the high seat where she probably adjudicated the problems in the valley. "The last year has not been kind. The pres-sure from the tribes has only made matters worse."

Mathghaman had glanced at Bearrac and then Gunny. Both nodded. We were going to be on watch that night, anyway. We may as well help out with the defense of the castle while we were there, especially if we'd drawn more trouble to Loncheta's doorstep. If those tribesmen had been our mysterious followers, then we could be looking at an interesting night.

Galan had seen the exchange. He stepped closer to the seat, and Loncheta looked up at him. "Sadly, we can spare none of our party at this time, but we will stand the watch with your men tonight."

Loncheta nodded sadly. "I will have food and drink brought. It is little, I fear, but it is what we have."

I kind of felt bad at that, and from the look on Santos's face, he did, too. Unfortunately, we had a long way to go, much of it across open grassland where hunting was going to be difficult, and we couldn't spare much of the rations we'd packed.

While Loncheta's people brought trestle tables in and started to prepare a meal, we got down to the business of setting the watch schedule for the night.

* * *

It was past midnight when I climbed up to the top of the keep with Rodeffer, Farrar, and Santos. We'd gotten a short nap before our turn on watch had come up. Just long enough to feel groggy.

Orava and the Menninkai team were up there when we reached the battlements. I had to guess that they didn't get a lot of snow here, because the roof of the keep was flat, allowing for defenders to move around it as the threats demanded.

The Menninkai were all standing at the battlements, their weapons in hand as they watched the black bulk of the hills around us. The *Coira Ansec*'s version of our PVS-15s were slightly lighter and slightly better, which had prompted a few of us to start muttering that we should have given ours to the Menninkai and taken the new ones, but Gunny had put a stop to that. Ours would break down eventually, and *then* we could replace them.

None of them moved as we spread out along the roof. If it had been anyone else, I would have immediately suspected that something weird was going on, but it was the Menninkai. They were stoic, tight-lipped guys to begin with, and they had become even more so as they tried to earn a place for themselves in the platoon. They were tough bastards, nobody doubted that after we'd fought beside them in the north, but there were differences in the way we fought, and they'd wanted to join *us*, so, in true Marine fashion, we were making them earn it. Gunny had already put them through a brutal Pre-BRC to BRC pipeline, at least as much as we could in the time we'd had on the Isle, but there was still some integration that needed to happen.

While Santos moved up to cover the pass as best he could with that Mk 48—I'd commandeered the team's 40mm thumper, since Santos already had enough weight to carry with the machinegun, gorilla though he might be—I found Orava and joined him.

Orava was built like a fireplug, and no matter how many miles the man ran or rucked, he always would be. The faint epicanthic fold that the Menninkai all shared was almost imperceptible simply because the man always seemed to be peering at the world through an unimpressed squint. He was a good dude, he just looked like a powerlifter trying to do an impression of Clint Eastwood all the time.

"Anything moving?" The moon was down, so the wooded and rocky hills were awfully black against a starlit sky. The clouds had moved on, and it was getting chilly.

"Maybe." He pointed to the hills to the south. "I saw a glint up there. Like a reflection off metal."

I followed his pointing finger. I couldn't see the shine, but after a moment, I was pretty sure I spotted a shadow moving behind a tree. "Sloppy."

Orava shook his head and tapped his NVGs, all without taking his eyes off his sector. "I would never have seen it without these. They have been careful." He finally looked at me, now that he'd pointed out the potential threat. "I think that our nomad friends have worked their way around the long way, along the ridge."

"They can't think that they've got a hope in hell of taking this place." I watched the shadow, which had gone completely still, though I thought I could just make out what might have been the haft of a spear jutting from behind its shoulder. "Anything spooky?"

"No." He looked up at the starlit sky. "If they have a shaman with them, he is being careful." There was no small bit of venom in his voice. The Menninkai had been at war with their cousins and neighbors the Lasknut for generations, and the Lasknut had been led and ruled by sorcerers, if of the slightly less potent variety that worshiped the Fohorimans rather than the Outsiders directly. He had good reason to hate spell-slingers of any variety.

"We need to figure out a way to hunt those guys down first." I had plenty of bad memories of sorcery, myself, even from before Vahava Paykhah.

Orava sighed and turned away from the battlements. "I agree. Let me know when you think of something." He took a couple of steps toward the door and the stairs, then stopped. I could tell he wanted to ask something. He just wasn't sure it was the time or the place.

"What is it, Orava?"

He stepped back up to the battlements next to me. "Why do you think all of this has happened?"

"What do you mean?" I asked.

"I mean why do you think you came through the mists? Did Tigharn mean all of this just to make you the Sword Bearer?" His accent when speaking *Tenga Tuacha* was worse than mine, but he was understandable, and I could hear the hesitancy as well as the thoughtfulness in his words. He was trying to figure things out. "You have shaken the world already. Your quest drew the Fohorimans and their servants away from Vahava Paykhah, when it seemed like the city would fall any day. Yet how many have died along the way?" He looked at me, then, turning his head so he could see through his PVS-15s. "I am no lore-master, as Mathghaman said of himself. I do not know of any prophecies that might have spoken of your coming. Why now?"

"Hell, I don't know, Orava. If I did, I might have more of a plan." I rubbed my chin as I put a boot up on the battlement and leaned a gloved hand on my rifle's buttstock. "I'm sure a bad pick for some mystical, prophesied 'Chosen One,' if there even is any such thing." I glanced down at my hip, where the Sword hung, though at that distance it was a blur in my NVGs. "I don't know why I picked this up. Maybe it really was an accident, no matter what King Uven thought. Those things do happen, you know."

Orava shook his head. "No, I do not think so. I agree with the Galel king. That you should have come here through the mists already tells me that some greater power has some plan for you. I only wonder…"

"What that plan is? You and me both, brother." It wasn't something I could avoid thinking about, but it also wasn't something I was all that comfortable mulling over, either. What did this all mean? We were just another bunch of Recon Marines, not any different from any other platoon, except we'd had maybe an even more insufferable platoon commander when we'd deployed. None of us were exactly paragons of virtue, even if we were hard as woodpecker lips and very good at our job, which was getting into hard-to-reach places, spying out the terrain and the enemy, and if the situation called for it, killing the hell out of them. We didn't come from a background or even an organization that stressed honor that much. Sure, lip service was paid, but down in the Fleet, where the metal meets the meat, things are a lot murkier. Hell, even then, the leadership was probably a lot more morally flexible than the most degenerate infantry Marine. I'd seen officers and senior enlisted get away with stuff that would have landed a sergeant in the brig for a long, long time.

So, why us? Why me?

I didn't have an answer.

Orava, though, seemed to accept that. He shrugged and clapped me on the shoulder. "Maybe Tigharn will show us, someday." He turned toward the stairs with a yawn. "I need sleep."

I let him go, still watching that shadow out there on the mountainside. It still hadn't moved, but was just crouched there, behind a tree. If it was a man, he was set in for a while.

Maybe that was all they were out to do. Wait and watch, until we were over the pass—or in it—and then spring an ambush on likelier ground. Like I'd said to Orava, a small team was unlikely to try to raid a keep. There were ways—we'd done it to Unsterbanak, though technically that had been a trap that the vampire had laid for us, so naturally we'd made it inside—but without some significant numbers and preparation it was usually a bad idea.

My hand strayed to the Sword by my side, and I traced the carved lions on the quillons, still thinking about what Orava had said, and King Uven before him. I still didn't think that I was any kind of Chosen One. I didn't know why I'd found the Sword instead of anyone else. The weapon's history wasn't all that encouraging, either, no matter what our allies thought. The original Sword Bearers had gotten big heads and charged off to ruin. Maybe I was just one more set of hands for the Sword to pass through as a lesson to others.

I took a deep breath, looking up at the stars for a moment. Maybe all I could do was to try to be a better man and be worthy of the reputation that being a Sword Bearer seemed to carry with it. I'd kind of already started, since it had become evident just how important the mystical dimension was here. I'm not saying I was doing that great of a job, but I was trying.

Maybe that was all I could do.

I lowered my gaze and went back to watching that shadowy figure where he was crouched on the hillside across the road.

CHAPTER 17

OUR watch passed uneventfully. The shadow didn't move again before Mathghaman came up to relieve us and we headed back downstairs to get some sleep.

Orava might not have noticed anything spooky on watch, and neither had we, but the dreams once I finally got back to sleep were not pleasant.

I found myself alone on the plains, utterly lost. It was dark, and clouds hid the stars. My compass spun crazily, refusing to point north, south, or anywhere else. Not a single landmark met my eyes.

The wolves that ran through the storm-lashed grasses, though, were obvious enough, their eyes glowing like coals. I pivoted and snapped my rifle to my shoulder, but in typical dream logic, it failed to fire. I tapped, racked, and pulled the trigger again. Nothing. I had to run.

Strangely, when I turned to run, the wolves darted around to head me off. Soon I found that I could run in three directions—though I couldn't tell whether any of them were north, south, east, or west—but there was one place the wolves didn't want me to go.

There was something else in the background, too. I could never see it, but it was there. The wolves weren't just wolves. They were more like hunting dogs. There was someone or something out there on the plain commanding them, sending them after me.

I woke up before I could figure out what was going on, but the disquiet of the dream lingered. As I lay there in my Ranger roll, staring at the ceiling in the wan gray light of pre-dawn, filtering in through a high window or arrow slit, I could have sworn that I'd seen a face just before I'd awoken. A face with flat, hard eyes that nevertheless were both hostile and curious. As if the mind behind them was carrying out orders but still wondered exactly why.

As I sat up and gathered my gear and my weapons, even though it was still early enough that most everyone else in the reception hall was still snoring, I suspected that the nomads had indeed brought a shaman with them, and I'd just gotten a look at him.

I made my way back up to the battlements, looking out over the hills and the pass in the faint light filtering over the mountains from the east. When I brought my rifle up and peered through the scope at where I'd seen the shadow the night before, there was nothing. Old boy must have moved on with the onset of daylight.

Smart.

"Anything moving out there?" I asked Gurke. He still looked bleary, and very much like he really didn't want to be up there.

"We heard some movement about an hour ago." Gurke sounded about as sullen as he looked. "Didn't see nothing, though."

I nodded as I scanned the woods and the hills. We hadn't been able to see too much the night before, but the hills were low compared to some of the mountains we'd crossed. They were still quite steep in places, studded with massive boulders where they didn't turn to sheer, stony cliffs. The trees were a mix, with elms and oaks in the lower ground giving way to spruces and firs higher up. In some ways it wasn't that much different from the forests of the corsair lands, but the woods were thinner and lighter here, and the air was more temperate.

Some fog was moving in, but the wind was mostly southerly, instead of coming straight in off the water. It didn't look or feel like we were going to be socked in anytime soon.

I was glad of that. The hilltops got steep and jagged toward the pass, massive slabs of stone crowned with trees and low bushes on either side of the track. That wasn't going to be fun to negotiate, even in clear weather.

If there were lookouts up there, they were staying well hidden. This was going to be an interesting morning.

Not that we were used to much of anything else.

"We're heading out in an hour." Several of the castle's garrison were climbing up onto the battlements behind me, bowing their heads slightly and touching the rims of their helmets in thanks for the help we'd given during the night. I returned the nods, though I wasn't sure we'd helped much more than to give them a night off. The attack we'd been expecting hadn't happened. "Gunny wants everybody at the gate downstairs in thirty."

Gurke waved his acknowledgement. He was not a happy camper that morning.

It happens. Especially with Gurke.

I met Mathghaman on the way down. He stopped on the steps and eyed me in a way that told me he had something on his mind. "What is it?"

"Did you have any dreams last night?" Since that was hardly a normal question from Mathghaman—he was not a chatty man—I immediately figured he'd sensed something, something beyond the normal disquiet from nightmares.

"Yeah." I described the shadow wolves on the featureless grassland. His eyes narrowed and he nodded as I spoke.

"They do have a shaman out there, then. I thought I felt something last night." He turned his eyes to the narrow slot of a window high up in the stairwell. "Those wolves were the lesser spirits he summoned and sent to probe the castle."

"So, they know the Sword's here?" I didn't much like that idea.

"Perhaps. The spirits undoubtedly know." He lifted a sardonic eyebrow. "Whether the shaman himself knows or not is doubtful."

"The summoned things are keeping secrets?" From what I knew about the world of sorcery, it didn't especially surprise me. "What a shock."

"Of course. Such is always the risk in trafficking with such creatures." He turned and joined me on the way down the stairs as Gurke and his team started to descend from the battlements. "The imperials will not have told their auxiliaries everything, and they likely do not know everything, themselves. The emperor is a young man, but he is cunning, and from what we know, he is deeply steeped in the ways of the Outer Dark. If he knows that the Sword is moving, he will not have necessarily told his vassals, since he fears the power of such an artifact being turned against him."

I frowned a little at that, and Mathghaman noticed. He stepped in front of me and turned to face me, his expression stern. "Do not begin to imagine that carrying that Sword is more than it is. It is a relic, yes. It holds its edge like no other weapon, and it cannot break easily. There are things of the Outer Dark that cannot stand its touch—provided that the man who wields it uses it honorably." He pointed a finger at my chest, one of the more emphatic gestures I'd ever seen him make. "It does not make the man who carries it more than he is in himself. Remember that."

I nodded. "I'm guessing those kings who last carried these Swords didn't."

He nodded, somewhat like a proud father whose son just got it. "Indeed." He turned back the way we'd been going. "At any rate, while the emperor may or may not know that the Sword is on the field again, he will know that we must be seeking its twin. Even if he was not already aware of Galan's quest, the presence of Tuacha and Recon Marines in the Galel lands will have been a warning in and of itself."

I would have originally just thought that the Tuacha alone would have been of note to any spies, but the things of the Outer Dark seemed to have an interest in us. Unsterbanak had deliberately tried to lure us into his lair, just to find out who we were and what we were doing in this world. We still didn't have any answers, but that wouldn't stop the whispers.

If I'd been a bit more egotistical, that might have given me a big head, just like Gunny had warned me against. After all, *we* had been brought across time and space by mysterious powers and I had been personally granted the privilege of carrying a mystical weapon.

Except that we were still mortal men. That had been blatantly obvious from the beginning. Twenty-nine of us had come through the mists. Twelve were left. We had manifested no extraordinary powers. We were still the same fallible dudes we'd always been, just with better weapons and training.

I had heard my instructors in BRC say that the job is only ten percent physical. The other ninety percent is simply the mental stubbornness not to give up when you're wet, hungry, tired, and in pain. I'd found it was true a lot of the time, but it also came with its own pitfalls. That was where another quality that was not always emphasized enough comes in.

Humility.

A Recon Marine has to know what he's capable of, and his limitations. Humility is truth. Ego can get a Marine and his team killed.

In this place, it was becoming obvious that humility might be the only thing that kept us on the right side.

It was a sobering thought. It would stay with me as we finished getting our gear ready to go.

* * *

The sun was up over the ridgeline when we rode out. At least, when the main body rode out. My team and I weren't with them.

While we'd left our rucks on our pack animals, my team had slipped out on foot about half an hour before. We weren't going to outpace the horses, especially not the way we were going, but that was why we'd left early. We moved quickly into the woods while Eoghain and Diarmodh held overwatch with their elegant rifles and eagle eyes from the battlements, our cloaks over our gear and our faces covered in camouflage paint, getting into the thickest vegetation and rocks we could find before we started up toward the ridgeline.

While the Galel knights were definitely the kind of warriors who preferred a stand-up fight, they weren't dumb, especially when fighting the sorts of nomadic savages we were probably going to face here. They hadn't objected at all to our moving ahead quietly and carefully to get eyes on the pass and cover the transit.

I remembered what Galan had said on the voyage about how all the Galel learned to use the bow as well as the lance and sword. They were proud, honor-bound people, but they had no illusions that honor was a suicide pact.

It was a rough movement. The hills got steep as soon as we moved above the castle, and the woods were pretty thick. If we'd been carrying our rucks, I was pretty sure we'd have had a lot rougher time of it.

Of course, the terrain and the woods weren't the only problems we faced on that climb.

I'd always made a habit on patrol of looking up and around in a full scan about every three or four strides. Patrolling is more than just getting from Point A to Point B. You're moving through hostile territory whether the enemy knows it or not, and you've got to be alert.

I looked up past a gnarled oak and right into a pair of glaring red eyes.

Now, it might seem entirely logical, but red eyes are usually not a good sign. Especially when I'd just looked at that same spot less than a minute before and they hadn't been there.

It took a second to resolve the rest of the creature. It looked like it had been carved crudely out of a tree stump. In fact, I realized that I'd initially mistaken it for a tree stump.

I snapped my rifle to my shoulder. So far, nobody else had seen the thing, and I hesitated. It hadn't moved. It was just sitting there, staring at me balefully.

A gunshot, suppressed or not, would be heard across the whole valley. If the Avurs—Galan had confirmed that they were most likely the nomads we'd seen before, judging by the description of their arms and armor—were out there, they'd know that the column wasn't alone. They'd know that *somebody* was out on the flanks.

Yet getting my face eaten off by a forest goblin was not my idea of a good tradeoff for stealth.

The red-eyed thing saw that I'd spotted it and started to unfold itself. Long, knotty arms stretched out as it started to crawl toward us. At the same time, half a dozen more came out of the leaves and the rocks around us. They weren't moving fast, and from the toothy leers they wore as their oversized mouths creaked open, they didn't really know what our rifles were. They thought they had us flanked.

If they thought at all.

I shot the first one through that gaping mouth from ten yards away. The bullet smacked through its woody flesh with an audible *crack*, blowing what looked like moss, splinters, and a thick, milky sap across the rock behind it. The malevolent light in those red eyes seemed to flicker and go out, and the creature stiffened to immobility.

Santos opened fire with a short burst, then, even as Rodeffer freaked and hammered half his mag into the tree-stump goblin that had just come to life right in front of him. Santos was an artist with that Mk 48, even though as the ATL, he probably shouldn't have been carrying it. His eight-round burst chopped into three of the things as he walked his bullets up the hill, and somehow, without taking his finger off the trigger, he got most of those rounds into vital spots. One tree branch arm was shattered, another woody jaw was blown off, and a head that looked more like a tree burl than a head exploded, turned into a canoe by a pair of 7.62 rounds.

Suddenly, the remaining goblin turned around, a lot faster than it had moved before, and scampered backward, leaping straight over a massive boulder and disappearing.

"One, this is Five." Gunny hadn't given up the "Five" callsign, even though he could probably easily lay claim to the unit commander's "Six." "Status?"

I reached under my cloak and keyed my radio. It felt a little weird, using the radios again, but with dispersed operations like this, we kind of needed them. We'd held off for a long time, just because we weren't sure how much the spooky things out there might be able to listen in, but these weren't the PRC-152s we'd inserted with. These were *Coira Ansec* 152s. So, they were a little spooky all by themselves. "This is One. Just took contact from some small trolls or goblins. They look like tree stumps until they move, so be on the lookout. No friendly casualties."

"Roger." There wasn't much more to say. We still had some distance to go to reach the top of the ridge.

I moved up to join Rodeffer, who was down on a knee behind a boulder, carefully examining every tree and stump over his weapon's sights. That goblin had been a nasty surprise, though you might think we'd started getting used to weird things popping up where least expected by then.

Some things you just don't get used to. Bullets flying past your head close enough that you can hear the *snap* are one of those things. Weird monsters are another.

"Let's shift north." I kept my voice low, not much more than a murmur. "If we've got any more company up here, I don't want them to figure out exactly where we are or which way we're going."

He nodded. It was too late to keep them from knowing we were up on the ridge, anyway, and if the shamans were on point, it always had been. We had to try to maintain some unpredictability and surprise, though, and tactics are tactics.

Plus, assuming the enemy always knows everything is as much a recipe for mission failure as underestimating them, and is almost always wrong, anyway.

Rodeffer levered himself to his feet, looking down at the shattered corpse of the forest goblin with a faint shudder. I didn't think it was because these things were any more grotesque than anything else we'd faced so far—Vaelor's monsters from the Outer Dark had been *far* worse—but more because he hadn't seen it until it had already been at knife-fighting distance. Gene Rodeffer was a good pointman, and he took some justifiable pride in it. Getting jumped like that had to have him rattled.

We started to climb the hill again, moving even more carefully from tree to tree, rock to rock. The terrain got steeper, while the woods got thinner. Several times we had to backtrack downhill to get around an escarpment or big boulder.

I was starting to get a little stressed over how much time this was taking. While I might not be wearing my watch anymore, I was more attuned to the movement of the sun overhead, even in the forest, and I knew that the rest of the platoon had to be getting close to the pass already, while we struggled to get up to the top of the ridge. If we rushed it too much, though, we'd probably run into another ambush, only it would be worse the second time.

Rodeffer got to a massive, knife-edged rock that jutted from the mountainside, just below the crest, and took a knee. After a moment, he lifted his rifle to his shoulder, just over the rock, and then looked down at me.

There was only one reason he'd take his eyes off where his muzzle was pointing, and that was to make sure I'd seen it. Which meant he'd seen something and immediately identified it as enemy.

I was about ten yards downhill, and there wasn't a lot of cover where he was, but I couldn't see his target. Struggling a little against the steepness of the terrain and the occasional loose rock, I clambered up to join him, careful to stay low as I got to the edge of the promontory.

He had turned back toward his quarry, and now he pointed. "Just below that pile of rocks, left of the dead tree that looks like it got hit by lightning." His voice was so low that I had to lean in to hear him.

They were good. Even though none of them were wearing camouflage, it still took some searching to find the three Avur scouts where they squatted beneath the shadow of the stony pile that formed the crest of the hill just above the pass. None of them showed any shine. Any metal they wore was covered—if they were wearing any at all—and the colors of their tunics were obscured by the fur mantles they wore overtop and their careful positioning within the branches of the evergreens.

I keyed my radio. "Five, this is One. We have eyes on three OPFOR scouts with overwatch on the pass. We are directly north, on the west side of the ridge. Watch your fires in that direction. Moving in."

"Good copy, One." Gunny sounded like he'd expected just this. "Get one alive if you can. We'll leave it to you, unless you need a base of fire."

That was new. I'd done some kill or capture missions in Syria, but aside from our last mission in the north, which was supposed to have been a rescue, we hadn't really done it here. And I had no idea if these guys would even consider surrendering, even if we got the drop on them.

Santos and Farrar had climbed up to join us while I was on the radio with Gunny, getting down on security to the north and downhill. "Wait, we want to do what?" Farrar turned to look over the rock, but Santos cuffed him on the shoulder, and he hastily turned back to cover his sector. "Hitting some derka in his hut in the middle of the night's one thing. How are we supposed to grab one of these guys in the rocks while he's awake and ready to fight?"

"If we can corner him, maybe we'll take a prisoner." I was trying to watch the three tribesmen without looking directly at them. Sometimes humans tend to have a bit of a sixth sense when they're being stared at. It's not something you'll find in any Marine Corps manual, but it's a good skill to practice, watching a target without looking directly at it. "If not, we kill 'em and keep moving."

There weren't a lot of tactical options up there on that ridgeline. The steepness of the terrain and the thickness of the trees and bushes sharply limited our maneuvering room. I couldn't have set up an L-shape on these guys if I'd tried, and I was pretty sure they'd picked their position for just that reason.

"Echelon left. We'll sweep across. Stay low, stay quiet." I gave Rodeffer's shoulder a squeeze and he rose smoothly, clearly trying really hard to get over his earlier brush with the forest goblins. He was moving more carefully, each step rolling on the rocks and grass as soundlessly as possible, bent nearly double as he moved toward the Avur scouts.

I followed, while I had to duck in directly behind him before I could slip over the promontory and slightly downhill to offset. Farrar and Santos would have a little farther to go, but we were moving quietly and slowly, so there should be time to catch up.

Except that we'd barely gotten ten yards before a strange, warbling whistle went up from the trees at the base of the rockpile.

An arrow whistled out of that clump of trees and hit Rodeffer in the helmet. At the same moment, the three

Avurs we'd been stalking turned abruptly. Two snapped up their short recurve bows, though they didn't shoot immediately. The third went thrashing through the trees toward the crest on the other side of that mound of stones.

Rodeffer cursed as the shattered arrow went spinning off to his left and returned fire, though I didn't think he had a solid target. He just hammered five rounds at the trees. At least his helmet had held.

I shot one of the two Avurs in the OP through the chest. It wasn't a long shot, and right at the moment he couldn't see me, since I still had a low, scrubby evergreen between me and him. He kind of fell back on his haunches, looking down at the spreading red spot on his chest, in that split second before my trigger reset and my sights settled again, and my second shot took him just above the first. He fell out of sight.

Santos and Farrar were still behind us, but I pushed up, bellowing at Rodeffer to follow me, even as the second scout let fly an arrow. It smacked into my shoulder with bruising force, knocking me partway around, but my mail stopped it. Barely. It stuck in the armor and the gambeson underneath it, getting in the way as I snapped my rifle toward him, though Rodeffer beat me to the shot by a split second. His bullet took the man in the guts and the Avur doubled over with a shrill scream, falling on his face a moment later.

I pushed Rodeffer uphill. That should open a lane up for Santos and Farrar, and I wanted to make sure we weren't about to get flanked from the trees where that first arrow had come from.

I could hear the one who'd run as he crashed through the brush, letting loose with a strange, warbling yell.

As we got closer to the clump of windswept trees at the base of the small, rocky hill, I saw a body on the ground. It wasn't moving. One of Rodeffer's rounds, at least, had struck true.

We still closed in carefully, weapons up, scanning the rocks and trees around us. These Avurs were sneakier than we'd expected, and if they had a shaman, they could have all sorts of nasty surprises ready for us. The man was clearly dead, though, a ragged, livid hole punched through the side of his neck. Judging by the sheer amount of blood on his tunic and the surrounding ground, he'd been shot through the carotid. He'd been dead for a minute.

With Santos and Farrar on-line with us, we swept around the rocky mound to the Avurs' OP. The man Rodeffer had gut shot was still twitching, but a moment's look told us he wasn't long for the world. Rodeffer still kicked his bow and his spear away from his hands.

The man I'd shot was crumpled against the roots of a tree nearby, his eyes open and fixed on the sky. There was a small mirror next to his hand, with an oddly disturbing design carved into the bronze frame around it. As I looked down at it, I saw an eye in the glass, just for a moment.

It had been black, hard, and definitely not mine. And the mirror had been pointed at the sky.

Santos had moved up around the trees, and now he paced carefully toward the crest of the ridge, which was only a couple yards away from the OP. The pass lay below, and I could see Galan and Cailtarni, their armor shining and their crests lit up brilliant red and blue in the sun through the branches below.

Santos paused right at the crest, looking over his ma-chinegun for a moment before he bent, picked up a rock, hefted it, and then fastballed it down the opposite slope.

I might have heard a faint thump and a cry. Then Santos, without taking his eyes off his sector, turned his head to call out. "I think we've got our prisoner."

CHAPTER 18

THE Avur tribesman was silent and surly as we manhandled him down the slope. He was dressed simply once his weapons were taken away. The bow, knife, spear, and single-edged, slightly curved sword were finer than anything the Dovos had carried. That sort of stood to reason, given who the Avurs were working for. The Dovos were blood-drinking savages who were little more than expendable pawns to the Fohorimans, who noticed they even existed only when they needed some bodies to throw at each other. The Avurs were auxiliary cavalry and border raiders. Naturally they'd be better equipped.

His tunic was wool, dyed light green, and what I'd taken for a fur mantle over his shoulders turned out to be sheepskin. His breeches were also wool, and his moccasin-like boots were made of soft leather. The only metal on him was in the adornments on his belt, his knife, his saber, his spearhead, and the points of his arrows, which had some nasty barbs on them. I'd broken off the arrow that had hit me, but it had punched deep enough that one of those barbs was caught in one of the rings of my mail, and I'd need to take the shirt off and use a multitool to get it out.

We'd gotten to him while he was still down, a nasty lump on the back of his head, leaking blood into his long, dirty blond hair. When we hauled him to his feet, taking his weapons while Farrar and Rodeffer held security, I saw that he had a bone whistle around his neck. That probably accounted for the cry we'd heard.

An answering call went up from some kind of horn, just as we hauled him up off the ground. He'd been heard. Our enemies out there were alerted.

The question was, how many and where were they?

None of us knew how to talk to this guy. We knew *Tenga Tuacha*, but while that meant we could communicate with the Galel and the Menninkai, I doubted some Avur grunt was going to be particularly multilingual.

Santos tried anyway. "How many of you are there, and where are they?" While he'd let his hair and beard grow out, finally, Vincent Santos still looked vaguely like a shaved gorilla. He was slightly shorter than me, but considerably heavier, and when he was standing there with a machinegun slung across his chest and his hand on a blade, even a hardass had to be somewhat intimidated.

If this guy was intimidated, though, he didn't show it. His blank stare managed an awfully convincing impression of a man who didn't understand a word of what was being said. His eyes were flat and brown, and while they weren't as full of hate as a Dovo's might be, there was no give in this man. He was hard, weathered, and had probably killed more people than any of us had.

I scanned the slopes below us carefully. We had several miles to go through some rough country, but we were over the crest of the coastal mountains, and the rolling grasslands of the northwestern marches of the Empire of Ar-Annator spread out beneath us, receding into the distance. I could just make out the dark bulk of the shoulders of the Wall of Scath to the north.

If the bad guys were down there, they were about as well hidden as their scouts had been. Of course, the tree-clad slopes and twisting ravines and valleys of the foot-hills looked like they'd provide hiding places for entire battalions, and that was just from where I was standing. I was sure it was a lot worse than it looked.

"We don't have time to screw around with this guy." The bad guys were down there, somewhere, and if that weird mirror had been what I thought it was, the scouts had been reporting everything as the column had entered the pass. They knew we were coming, and they were probably already moving into ambush positions. "Let's get him down to the others. Maybe the Galel will know how to speak his language."

With his Mk 48 pointed at the sky, held in one beefy hand, Santos yanked the Avur scout to his feet. "Let's go, *cabron*."

With Rodeffer in the lead, Farrar taking up the rear, and Santos and I in the middle with our prisoner, we started down toward the pass.

It took most of an hour to get down to the rough pe-rimeter where Gunny and Mathghaman had halted the platoon just short of the crest. So far, so good. No con-tact. If the Avurs were out there, they were either waiting to see what had happened to their scouts, or else they were still far enough away that it was going to take them some time to close in.

Or else, they were already set in and waiting for us, farther down the mountain.

Galan and Cailtarni were standing near the edge of the perimeter when we deconflicted over the radio and came in from the wooded hillside above. "You caught one." Cailtarni sounded like he was more than a little surprised. "That is a feat." He glared at the Avur tribesman. "These savages rarely allow themselves to be taken alive."

"I hit him in the head with a rock." Santos brought the man up roughly with a jerk on his arm, then put a hand on his shoulder and with the kind of inexorable pressure that only Santos can bring to bear, slowly forced him to his knees. "Might have scrambled his brains a little; he hasn't made a sound since we got him up."

Cailtarni snorted. "The silence of a trapped animal." He glared at the shorter Avur tribesman. "Even an animal can be brought to heel, though."

Galan put a hand out to calm his older companion. He turned to the Avur scout and spoke. The language was harsher and more guttural than the *Tenga Tuacha* or the dialect that the Galel spoke, and I couldn't make heads or tails of it. It sounded a little bit Turkic, but I'd heard Turkish in Syria, and that definitely wasn't it.

The Avur scout stared sullenly at him, his mouth shut, without a flicker of expression or a word spoken.

Bearrac had seen what was happening, and I saw him whispering to Mathghaman. The King's Champion nodded, and Bearrac started toward us.

Galan's frown deepened as he continued to question the prisoner. He was clearly changing his line of questioning, but the longer the obstinate silence continued, the more irritated he got. I didn't think Galan, of all people, would get violent with an unarmed prisoner—in fact, I'd have been very surprised by then—but he was clearly getting riled.

Bearrac put a hand on his shoulder. "Allow me, my lord."

Galan somewhat reluctantly drew back, and Bearrac stepped up to the kneeling captive. For the first time, I might have seen a flicker of uncertainty in the man's eyes.

Bearrac didn't try to speak the Avur's tongue. He crouched down until he was even with the Avur's eyes and spoke in the *Tenga Tuacha*.

"I know you can understand me, tribesman."

The scout's eyes widened, and I saw real fear there.

"You know of what tribe I am?"

The man nodded jerkily. I traded a glance with Santos, who looked a little bemused. This was interesting. It seemed that the Avurs knew of the Tuacha and feared them. This might be useful.

Bearrac didn't even say anything more. He just held the scout's eyes and waited.

After a moment, it seemed that the strain was simply too much for our prisoner. He started talking.

He talked fast, words spilling out of him as if he had to get them out before they choked him. Even if I'd had any comprehension of the language, I probably never could have followed it. Bearrac, however, was a Tuacha. The mind speech means they can understand as easily as they can make themselves understood.

Soon, he cleared a patch of ground at his feet and began to draw in the dirt, asking pointed questions as he did so, looking up to fix the Avur scout with his gaze each time. Some were apparently answered in the affirmative, others in the negative, some with more details. I couldn't make out all of what Bearrac was drawing, but it was clear that he was walking the young man through a thorough tactical picture of the enemy's presence, positions, and likely plans.

Finally, with a nod that might have been in appreciation, were it not directed toward a deadly enemy who had just, for some reason, spilled his guts, Bearrac dusted his hands and got up. "So. The emperor, it appears, knows that some of the Galel have set out to find the Sword of Categyrn." He nodded toward the shell-shocked scout. "This one does not know about that part, but it stands to reason, and explains why three warbands were offered great sums of gold and precious stones if they kept any of the Galel from venturing past the mountains."

"Three warbands?" Gunny rubbed his chin thoughtfully. "How many is that?"

"Anywhere from three to five hundred men." Mathghaman's voice was grim. "Far more than this small band could hope to face in open combat."

"Open combat, yes." The wheels were turning in Gunny's head. "How far away are they?"

"They are not far into the hills, though there are more scouts and small bands of archers scattered along the path that leads down toward the main road to Ar-Annator. The Avur are horsemen, and dislike mountain fighting. They will wait until we get onto ground more fitting to their way of war. Then they will surround us and shoot us full of arrows while their shamans blind us." He chuckled, to the captured scout's obvious terror. "Or so goes their plan."

"Okay, then. We've got some breathing room." Gunny thought about it some more. "Conor, your team's back in the column. You've done some climbing already today. Sean, take your team up on traveling overwatch. Ross, you and Conor will switch out as need be. Orava, your boys are going to get a chance to prove how much they've learned and drilled with those mortars, so make sure you can get to 'em fast." He looked around. "We'll continue as we have, in traveling column with overwatch, until we get eyes on the main body and can adjust the plan from there.

"Be ready, gentlemen. I expect we'll get hit a couple more times before we make the plains."

CHAPTER 19

THE sun was going down behind the ridge to our rear when I saw movement in the trees.

I didn't stop my horse, though I did slow down and key my radio. "This is One. Movement right."

"I see it." Gunny left it that. There wasn't much more we could do until or unless whoever or whatever it was gave us an opening.

It was hard to say what I was looking at. It wasn't one of the Avur scouts. The overwatch team had spotted them twice, but after what had happened to the first team, they weren't eager to cross swords with us again. They'd faded as soon as they'd seen us. Even the overwatch team, Bailey's the first time and Gurke's the second, hadn't been able to catch them. It was possible that one of the Avur shamans had gotten word to them about what had happened, but it was just as likely that they'd heard the gunshots and the whistle, and they knew that nobody had come down the mountain afterward. We'd left our captured tribesman tied to a tree behind us. He'd get loose eventually, but we'd be long gone by then.

No, this wasn't one of the Avur scouts. In fact, I didn't think it was human at all.

It was next to impossible to get a clear look at it, even though it didn't seem to be really trying to hide. It reminded me of a creature that had stalked Rodeffer and me in the north, the day after we'd arrived through the mists and landed on the hostile shores of the Land of Ice and Monsters. It was *blurry*, as if it wasn't quite there, or was somehow out of focus. When it didn't move, I almost couldn't see it at all.

I'd driven the thing in the north off by pointing my weapon at it. I wasn't sure if I could have actually hurt it, but it had worked, somehow. Maybe I'd bluffed just enough.

But when I lifted my rifle this time, I couldn't see it at all.

"Damn thing's playing hide and seek."

"I see it." Mathghaman had ridden up next to me, and I didn't doubt he'd heard my muttered imprecation. His steely gray eyes were fixed on where I'd last seen that weird, blurry figure, but I still couldn't see anything there. Unless… When I concentrated, I thought I could see the faint gleam of yellow eyes staring out of the murk and the foliage.

"What is it?" I kept my voice low, even though I was sure that thing could probably hear me, anyway.

"Something one of their shamans summoned." He was still watching it, which made it that much more eerie that I couldn't see it at all. "More fool they." He twisted in his saddle, made eye contact with Diarmodh, and jerked his head toward the trees. The younger Tuacha warrior nodded, swung off his horse's back, and vanished into the woods.

A moment later, a horrific shriek went up somewhere in the trees. It was enough to make my ears hurt and raise gooseflesh on my arms.

That takes some doing, after some of the things I've seen.

Shortly after the echoes of that scream died down, Diarmodh came strolling down out of the woods and re-mounted, as cool as if nothing had happened.

We kept making our way down toward the plains, eyes out and even more alert than before.

* * *

On horseback, and having started fairly early in the morning, we could have made it down to the plains by dark. The foothills were rough, but they fell down toward the flatlands fairly quickly.

We halted before sunset, finding a rocky hill where we could set in security with a good view of the surrounding valleys and hills. We had good lines of sight and fields of fire across the valleys to north and south, out to about five hundred yards. A long shot at night, but easy enough during the day. Especially for a Mk 48, where you get your accuracy through volume.

Of course, one of the Tuacha could still probably shoot the wings off a fly in the dark at that distance.

Gunny pulled the team leaders in, joined by Mathghaman, Galan, and Cailtarni. "Okay, we haven't gotten eyes on the bad guys just yet. So, that's going to be the first task."

I was prepared to take the mission. As tired as I was, and as tired as I knew my team was, we'd been riding for the last several hours, and hadn't taken another turn on overwatch duties, so that made it our turn.

Mathghaman interrupted, though, before I could roger up. "Diarmodh and Fennean will find them."

That gave Gunny a moment's pause. We were coming up against that odd dichotomy within the platoon again. We were all brothers in arms, but I think that Gunny still hadn't completely wrapped his head around treating the Tuacha as another team. They were *other*, in a way that even the Menninkai and the Galel were not. Mathghaman's kingly demeanor aside, it just felt odd, giving orders to men who were somehow more than human, and were more than likely several lifetimes older than we were. There was still a lot we simply didn't know or understand about the Tuacha, and they weren't all that eager to ply us with answers, either.

Strangely enough, that had never come across as evasive or untrustworthy. They just didn't talk about such things, and it always seemed a little out of line to ask.

"Okay." Gunny seemed to collect himself. He wasn't easily rattled. He never had been. And I don't think that Mathghaman's announcement rattled him, especially. He was just tired and had to rethink the plan. "So, Diarmodh and Fennean will conduct forward recon tonight, and locate the enemy." He glanced at me. "You boys dodged a bullet, Conor."

"We would go." Orava sounded a little surlier than usual. After all, he and his boys, all nine of them, had been down on the path with the horses and the pack animals the whole day, holding security for the column. They hadn't had a chance to go out and do Recon shit.

There's an old saying in the community. "Everybody wants to be Recon, until it's time to do Recon shit." That wasn't the case with these tough, barrel-chested fighting farmers, but all the same, their training wasn't entirely complete, and there were still things that Gunny and I were a little concerned about. They were good, don't get me wrong, but they weren't entirely integrated into the platoon's SOPs yet.

"I know you would, Orava, but this is still your first real rodeo." Gunny could be a harsh taskmaster when the situation called for it, but he also knew how to take a more fatherly tack. "There will be plenty of opportunities. Besides, you've got a pretty vital role coming up once we get them nailed down."

Once again, we didn't have maps, aside from some relatively crude ones drawn on vellum from Cor Legear. So, planning had to happen with a combination of direct observation of the battlefield and glorified sand tables. And the light was failing fast for either one of them.

Gunny, however, had been looking closely at the terrain as we'd entered our lay up site and he had a pretty good idea of the distances involved and what needed to happen. "If we can pull it off, you'll set up those mortars here, Orava. If we need to move them down lower, we'll do that; that will depend on Diarmodh's and Fennean's reporting." He looked around at us again. "Gurke, you'll handle call for fire. We'll figure out exact locations once we get the initial recon reports back, but I want you and your team in an OP to the north by sunrise. Conor, Sean, you get the base of fire." He pointed out into the dusk. "You see that finger about half a mile south of here?"

I followed his gesture and nodded. A long finger of the ridge stretched out into the low ground, dominating much of the land around it. It was wooded, but in patches, the stands of trees little more than darker blotches against the slightly lighter grass and stones as the sunset died in the west behind the mountains. "Got it."

"That's probably going to be your best bet, *if* the enemy main body is accommodating and it's in range. I don't think I need to tell you what to prioritize."

"Shamans and chieftains." Bailey was chewing on a stalk of grass and drawled around it. "In that order."

"Why do they get to do the shooting while we just call mortars in?" Of course Gurke had to find something to complain about. I *almost* missed Zimmerman.

"Because they have more men and better long-range marksmen than you do." Gunny's fatherly understanding didn't extend to one of his veteran team leaders whining. "You've got the call for fire mission." He stared at Gurke with that unblinking, basilisk glare that could make just about any of us look for somewhere else to be. "Don't screw it up."

Gurke decided discretion was the better part of valor and shut up.

Orava had been watching him with that heavy-lidded stare that only our Menninkai team leader could summon up. It wasn't contempt, not quite. It was more like a long-suffering sort of disgust. He and his boys had put in long hours to join up, but they weren't quite up to standard yet, even though we were going into combat on a deep recon mission. He'd accepted their role, but here was an established team leader bitching because he didn't like his.

To make matters worse, Gurke was going to be giving Orava's team their fire mission and corrections.

Gurke, to his credit, caught the look. He didn't quite hang his head, but he at least had the good grace to look chagrined. "Roger that, Gunny. It'll get done."

Gunny nodded and dismissed the disagreement as if it had never happened. "That leaves the scheme of maneuver. Galan, Cailtarni, that's where you and the Tuacha will come in…"

* * *

Bearrac and Conall had been busy while we'd been planning, pacing around the perimeter and chanting softly in that ancient language. Hopefully, they would keep the shamans' summonings away from the perimeter during the night.

Not that we'd be there for all those hours of darkness. Diarmodh and Fennean had slipped away almost as soon as Mathghaman had tasked them with the advance reconnaissance. They had the commander's intent, and that was what they were going to go with. It wasn't uncommon among the Tuacha, and if we'd still been going by Big Marine Corps rules, that could have been a problem. We could trust their common sense, though. They were better men in the field than we were, and that was saying something.

We set a watch and started to prepare for our own movement. That didn't take all that long, actually. We were already carrying all we had available to us and what planning we could do without Diarmodh's and Fennean's report was minimal. So, we went over the basic situation and mission, and called it good. We needed *some* rest plan, so while one of us was up, the rest went down as well as we could.

It was going to be a long night and a longer day.

CHAPTER 20

WE moved quietly and carefully along the military crest of that finger Gunny had pointed out at sunset. The three camps that Diarmodh and Fennean had spotted not long before midnight were on the other side of that ridgeline, so unless they had scouts out, we were well concealed from the enemy.

Of course, the shamans had been busy that night, so we didn't dare get complacent.

I'd heard the strange sounds in the night while I'd been on security. Eerie cries had echoed across the hills, hoots and gibbering taunts from things we could never quite see. Whatever the shamans had brought across the veil, it was simultaneously noisy and invisible.

Maybe the Tuacha could see them. I hadn't even seen the gleam of eyes in the dark so far. That made it worse, somehow.

So, we picked our way along the slope with care, Rodeffer finding the nastiest route he could through trees and bushes, staying out of the open as much as possible, even though the sun wasn't going to be up for another two hours. I didn't know that it would hide us from the things the shamans had brought against us. Sometimes all you can do is follow your training, though, and hope and pray that it works. There's no SOP for hiding from preternatural creatures that aren't limited by the same physical constraints that you are.

Rodeffer paused and looked up. The moon was down, and it was *dark* out there, even on NVGs. The trees were little more than black shapes in the dark, and footing was a little uncertain, as was navigation. We hadn't gotten eyes on this side of the ridge from our redoubt on the hill the evening before, so we were having to guess our way along the terrain based on what we could remember of the shape of the ridgeline, which was currently little more than a darker line against the stars.

I moved up to join him, taking a knee beneath a light-ning-blasted cedar. "I don't think we've moved quite far enough yet." I pointed toward another outcrop, barely visible against the sky even in my PVS-15s. "That right there should put us where we want to be."

Rodeffer nodded, though he couldn't avoid a slight sigh. If he'd been more of a boot, I might have gotten on him about it, but he was as much a veteran as any of us by then. He was just tired. None of us had gotten more than around three hours of sleep, and the mountainside had been tough going, between the rocks, the trees, and the dark. There's a reason why the pointman carries the lightest load on the team. He's got to do most of the work on a movement.

Just as he got up to get going again, though, some-thing moved in the dark, just ahead. A faint rustle of branches and the crunch of the grass under something heavy.

Rodeffer froze. I brought my rifle up, looking for the source of the noise. Bailey's team was behind us. I knew that. We'd had visual contact only a few minutes before. So, whatever was up there was a threat.

It might only be a wild animal. That's still a threat. Even if it's not a predator, animals can compromise your position as clearly as a gunshot.

I searched the hillside, my blood going cold as I heard it take another step. Whatever it was, it sounded heavy, and it wasn't trying to be stealthy. I'd heard elk sound like that, but I didn't think this was an elk.

It wasn't.

It took a second to resolve what I was looking at in the dark. Night vision goggles still need ambient light to work, and there wasn't a whole lot available. But that thing was blacker than the night itself, once I laid eyes on it.

Before I joined the Marine Corps, I'd spent a year living in the mountains. I'd come face to face with a wolfpack not far outside Yellowstone. It had been a bad experience, but I'd managed to scare them off and break contact. The pack leader had been a massive black wolf, easily two hundred pounds or more.

This thing dwarfed that monster. It turned toward us as it climbed up on top of a boulder, its long, pointed ears silhouetted against the sky. Its eyes glinted in my PVS-15s.

It was four feet tall at the shoulder if it was an inch. It had to weigh three hundred pounds. Its growl seemed to shake the ground with a subsonic rumble, like the hillside was about to come down under our feet.

"Conor, is that a summoning or something else?" Rodeffer was already aimed in, his red dot hovering right in front of his NVGs.

"I don't know, but it ain't friendly, and I don't *think* it's natural, either." We'd run into various forms of wildlife on our long patrols through haunted and monster-infested wilderness since we'd passed through the mists, and I was developing a sense for these things. Even though NVGs wash out a lot of details, I could somehow just *tell* that this thing was far more intelligent than those wolves I'd faced in the Rockies, back in The World. There was a mind behind those baleful eyes, not just instinct.

Still, this thing was also clearly physical, unlike the shadow monsters that had been prowling around the edges of the Lasknut and Dovo armies that had besieged Vahava Paykhah. Which meant we should be able to kill it.

Could we do it without thoroughly compromising ourselves, though?

It came down off the rock, stepping down and stalking forward slowly but inexorably, those awful eyes fixed on the two of us. We weren't going to get much of a choice.

I wished we'd had Mathghaman or Bearrac with us right then. Wishes don't get you out of bad situations, though.

Rodeffer shot it first. I confess I flinched as the *crack* of the shot echoed down the slope. There was no disguising that. Even if some Avur shaman wasn't watching us through that thing's eyes, every ear for miles was going to prick up at that sound.

The thing stopped in its tracks, but it didn't die. It reared back on its hind legs, pointed its muzzle at the sky, and *howled*. There was a horrifying, eldritch quality to that sound that didn't come from any flesh and blood wolf I'd ever heard. And I'd heard a few.

I shot it again, then, putting a hammer pair into that massive, black-haired chest. Rodeffer was still shooting, dumping five more rounds into it as fast as he could pull the trigger.

It shuddered and howled once more, the sound turning hoarse and losing most of its strength before it trailed away and the thing seemed to shrink as it twisted and tumbled down the mountainside, finally fetching up against a tree about fifty yards downslope.

"Stay here." I didn't want Rodeffer to have to regain lost altitude. I'd do that, as bad as it was going to suck. Alone, though Rodeffer and Farrar were in position to cover me, I clambered down the hillside toward the twitching carcass of the monster.

As I got closer, I saw that it wasn't nearly as big as it had looked. In fact, as I stood over the dead wolf, it looked like just an ordinary wolf, torn and bloodied by the passage of no less than six 7.62 rounds.

I frowned as I crouched down, still a careful distance away just in case it wasn't all the way dead. Something about it was still off, even though it was definitely not three hundred pounds and six feet long. It looked... shriveled, somehow, its fur coarse and twisted, as if it had been scorched.

When I straightened, I couldn't quite suppress a shudder. I was sure of it, now. Something had been wearing a real wolf like a skin suit, and when we'd killed the wolf we'd banished it, and it had torn the hell out of the carcass on its way out.

I headed back up. We still needed to get into position and we had to do it quickly, now that the enemy knew we weren't bottled up on that hill anymore.

* * *

"They sure know something's up." Bailey and I had decided to collocate our teams, since the terrain was pretty rough and there was really only one spot where we could support each other. Bailey, Synar, Rodeffer, and I were set in among the rocks, watching the Avur camps on the valley floor below, while the others watched the flanks and our rear. We were the best long-range marksmen in the platoon, so we got the duty.

"Or else this is just their morning stand-to." I couldn't deny that there was an awful lot of activity down there. The three camps were all laid out in something close to circles, though they were a little ragged and disorderly inside those circles. Horsemen were hastily donning armor and readying weapons or packing their bedrolls onto their horses below us, while the three chieftains' pavilions were hastily struck. The men on guard, sitting their horses in rings around the camps, were all facing outboard, and it looked like some of them really didn't trust the other warbands, from the way they were watching each other. "If these are steppe raiders, they probably don't trust anyone or any place."

"You may be right." Bailey was watching through his scope, while I was on binoculars. It wasn't time to take a shot yet, though we had some pretty good lines of sight, even if they were going to be long shots. The wind that was coming up out of the south and swirling around the valley was going to make precision a bit iffy, too. This was no three-hundred-yard potshot. We were going to be stretching the capacity of our 175grain 7.62 rounds as it was.

I briefly wished I'd brought the .50, but that thing was heavy and unwieldy, and I'd decided against it just for mobility's sake. It was still strapped to my packhorse, back with the main body.

"Five hundred fifty-two yards to Eagle Feathers." I was ranging our targets. We hadn't spotted a shaman yet, so the chieftains had priority, and I was giving them nicknames for easier target identification. The nearest, a relatively tall, spare man with three eagle feathers sprouting from the onion-shaped peak of his helm, was just over five hundred fifty yards away. He would be the easiest target.

I shifted my rangefinder to the next, a stout, short, fireplug of a man with a tall lamellar helmet trimmed with wide leather cheek guards that looked like wings or giant ears on the side of his head. He had no crest like Eagle Feathers, but long black braids cascaded out from beneath the scale aventail behind the helmet. "Eight hundred seventy-seven yards to Braids."

"Armadillo is gonna be a hell of a shot." I had to search to find the third chieftain, but when I spotted him I saw why Bailey had given him that nickname. The man was armored from head to toe in scales, with a long coat of overlapping plates over lamellar greaves, lamellar shoulder guards and vambraces, and a ludicrously tall neck guard that made him look almost like a turtle. His spiked helmet was solid, but otherwise of a similar profile to Braids' lamellar helmet. His horse was as heavily armored as he was, and his retainers were still strapping the panoply onto the long-suffering animal.

If we hadn't been in a sniper hide, I might have let out a whistle as I ranged the third chieftain. "Twelve hundred ninety-seven yards. Ouch. I'm not sure a 7.62 is gonna hit hard enough at that range."

"Maybe he'll move closer." Bailey sounded slightly hopeful.

"Or we'll have to leave him to Gurke."

"That son of a bitch'll miss." There wasn't a whole lot of humor in Bailey's voice. Gurke had been a bit of an ambivalent younger brother among the team leaders to begin with, never quite committing when we disagreed until he saw which way the wind was blowing. As opposed to Zimmerman, who had apparently seen it as his sworn duty to take a tack contrary to whatever Bailey and I had agreed on. Now, with Zimmerman dead and presumably burning in Hell after trying to out-Dragon Mask Dragon Mask, Gurke seemed to have decided that Zimmerman hadn't been a bad guy to emulate, after all.

It was annoying, but I didn't have quite the same visceral reaction to it that Bailey did. "He's calling mortars. He doesn't have to be sniper precise."

Bailey just grunted, then keyed his radio. "Five, this is Two. We are in position and have eyes on three priority targets. Northernmost is out of range. Ready when you are."

"Copy." Gunny wasn't going to waste time or breath on unnecessary radio chatter. He'd always been that way, which I could appreciate.

Captain Sorenson had occasionally gotten downright voluble on the net, and it had been simultaneously tooth-grindingly aggravating and cringeworthy.

"Three, this is Five. You are weapons free in one-five mikes."

"Good copy." Gurke, for all his personal failings, wasn't asleep at the switch.

Fifteen minutes later, almost to the second, Gurke's voice came over the radio again. The pavilions were down and nearly packed, and the Avur warriors were forming up in the low ground, milling around as their horses smelled the coming fight and got excited. "Four, this is Three. Fire mission, polar."

"Send your fire mission, Three." Orava's voice was clipped over the radio, but if he resented being in a support role at all, there was no sign of it in his tone. He was all business.

The Menninkai were probably just stoked that they got to drop some mortar rounds on some real bad guys. They'd been itching to try them out for a while.

"Direction: nine three magnetic, distance three four hundred, down fifty."

Orava read the instructions back, after which Gurke finished off the rather obvious target description and method of engagement.

"Shot, over." The words had barely come over the radio when I heard the first *pop* as one of the mortars fired.

There was enough activity in the Avur camps below that only a few of the horsemen on security on the perimeter noticed the sound. They shifted in their saddles, their horses picking up the stress and starting to shift nervously, even as the first round whistled down out of the sky.

I was already on my rifle, the handguard nestled in a notch in the rocks, cushioned by part of my cloak. Bailey and I had needed to resort to rock, paper, scissors to decide who got which target, and I'd lost. Eagle Feathers was mine, while Bailey took the longer shot, on Braids.

I didn't see the impact, but I heard it a moment after, as the round came down with a faint whistle and struck somewhere north of Armadillo's partially disassembled pavilion with a heavy *thud* that reverberated across the valley. The chaos in the camp was immediate. Horns and whistles began to echo across the clearing, braying and skirling over the shouts of men and the screams of scared horses.

My trigger broke a moment later, my crosshairs just above and to the right of Eagle Feathers' shoulder.

While my position had been good, the recoil was still just enough to throw my sight picture off for a moment. When I reset, I saw grass where I'd been aimed before, just before Rodeffer announced, "Hit. Dead center, boss."

I didn't come off my scope, as much as I wanted to see if Bailey had gotten Braids with his first shot or needed a follow-up. There was work to be done. "Ten mils above, red tunic, lamellar helmet, shaking his spear and trying to rally."

Rodeffer took a second. "Got him. On you."

I made my elevation adjustment, hesitated for a second as I tried to read the wind, then sent it. The rifle's *crack* was drowned out by another *thud* as the second mortar round landed off to the north, sending more of Armadillo's Avurs into a frenzy. Even as I saw that I'd missed, while my target ducked for cover, I heard Gurke over the radio again.

"Fire for effect."

Rodeffer called out a right adjustment, and I shifted and shot the red-tunicked man through the side. He crumpled as the first sheaf of three 60mm mortar rounds came down out of the sky with a whispering banshee wail.

I did come off my scope then, just to assess the battlefield. We had a few moving parts to worry about.

That latest adjustment round had been right smack-dab on target. Armadillo and one of his retainers lay crumpled on the blackened grass under a still-dispersing cloud of smoke and dust, even as the next volley came crashing down with a triple *thud*, kicking gouts of dirt, smoke, and debris into the air, fragmentation slashing through any Avur horsemen and animals that were too close. They went down like wheat before a scythe, even as their fellows scattered.

Then the horn call came down from the pass, and the charge began.

Even with the chaos and disarray we were sowing by fire, we didn't have enough riders to face the Avur in a toe-to-toe fight. The Galel knights were good, but there were still only about eight of them, and six Tuacha. Fourteen riders would never manage to break five hundred men.

Unless they were Tuacha.

It wasn't Cailtarni or Galan in the lead as that tight wedge of armored horsemen came thundering out of the slot in the hills and onto the open plain. Mathghaman rode at the head, his sword in his hand, bellowing an ancient Tuacha war cry as Bearrac and Eoghain rode at his side. His voice rose even over the thunder of the second salvo of mortar rounds, roaring out a challenge in the

Tenga Tuacha, louder than any ordinary man could make himself heard.

It worked.

Gunny had thought of it first, sometime after the initial planning session, before Diarmodh and Fennean had returned from their reconnaissance. We'd seen the terror that the Tuacha had engendered in the captured Avur scout. So, we'd decided that we'd use it.

As soon as the Avur realized there were Tuacha descending on them, they panicked. Horses screamed and men yelled, shrill whistles and frantic horn blasts sounding across the open grassland, even as the mortars smashed even more of them into the dirt, bloody and lifeless.

Bailey and I had gotten back to work, finding targets where we could and knocking more of them out of their saddles or off their feet with aimed rifle fire. It got tricky, fast, given the swirling wind and the frantic movement as they ran for their lives. We had to keep the pressure up, though. We wanted them to run as far as their legs or horses could take them before they slowed down and started to think about what had just happened and tried to regroup.

We hoped to be far, far away by then.

I knocked a man clad almost entirely in boiled leather scales sprawling on his face as he tried to catch his panicked horse, then shifted and took a snap shot at another archer in a blue tunic and burnt orange cap. I caught him high in the shoulder and spun him halfway around before he threw himself into a ditch and I lost track of him.

Then I spotted a shaman.

He was the only one who didn't appear too afraid. Cloaked in black, not unlike some of the Dovos' shamans, he was dancing weirdly in the middle of the camp, twitching like an epileptic—or a man possessed. It hurt my eye to watch him. Whatever he was doing, something weird was going on.

I shot him dead center through the chest. He didn't drop.

I knew that I'd hit him. I was fairly sure, since I'd adjusted enough weight behind the rifle that I didn't lose the sight picture, that the bullet had gone right through him.

I dumped the rest of the magazine into him, just enough of a pause between shots that I could make sure I was getting back on target. Four more 175-grain bullets tore through him, the fourth one taking him in the head.

We never had trained for headshots in sniper school. At that kind of range, you go for a surer shot, and that's center mass. You don't try to get fancy. I'd hit him in the face solely out of sheer luck.

If there is such a thing.

His head snapped back and suddenly his frenetic movement stilled. He dropped as if every joint had suddenly gone slack.

The headache I'd barely realized was there started to go away.

"End fire mission and regroup." Mathghaman's voice rolled over the radio. "They are fleeing."

I came off the scope and saw that he was right. The Avurs were streaming across the low ground, leaving dozens of dead men and horses behind. This was no orderly retreat, either, but an utterly panicked rout.

I levered myself up from my position, pulling my rifle with me. "Let's go. We've got a long movement to linkup."

I just hoped that we could be far, far away from there before any of them even thought about coming back.

CHAPTER 21

THE next several days were remarkably uneventful. After linking up and getting back on our horses, we rode down onto the plains and headed roughly east, northeast. The wind whispered across the grass and stirred the leaves in the occasional grove of trees that stood sheltered around what little water there was in the low ground, but the only other sounds for days were the clop of the horses' hooves, the creak of our saddle and tack, and the low murmurs we never quite got out of the habit of using when we spoke.

Despite the quiet, there was something about that wide, rolling landscape that kept any of us from wanting to make much noise. Part of that was simply native Recon Marine wariness. We were in enemy territory, and we knew it. Granted, with the long lines of sight out there, noise discipline wasn't as vital, but there was something strange about those plains.

I couldn't see what it was that was bothering me, and I was looking. There were no weird obelisks, no shifting eyes in the grass. Even the birds overhead all seemed to be birds, rather than some leathery abomination summoned from the Outer Dark or someplace nearly as bad.

Yet I couldn't shake the heebie jeebies. There was something foreboding about the very atmosphere of that place, even as we got deeper and deeper in, the coastal mountains shrinking and finally disappearing below the horizon behind us. I felt exposed, as if there was some-one or some *thing* watching us, all the time.

I could tell I wasn't the only one, but for some reason none of us seemed to want to address it. We just hunched our shoulders, kept watch, and kept riding.

* * *

We were about a week out from the mountains, a thin over-cast blotting out the sky and turning the sun into a wan, pale disc as it neared the horizon behind us. It was getting late, and the oppressive sense of wrongness was only get-ting worse as we found a hollow to set in for the night. The wind got ferocious once the sun went down, and the horses needed shelter, not to mention water.

I kept my team up on overwatch, still on horseback for the moment, while the rest got down in the low ground by the spring and set in.

None of us had spoken. It didn't seem necessary, or wise. I'd just looked at Santos, then at Rodeffer and Farrar, and they'd all nodded. They all felt it, too, and none of us were all that eager to get down in low ground right then.

A distant croak sounded overhead. I searched the sky but saw no birds. There was something even more un-nerving about that. It seemed as off as everything else about this empty wilderness.

"Conor." Farrar was watching the south, and as I turned toward him, he pointed.

At first, all I could see was the rolling plain, and what might have been darker clouds to the south. Then I saw it. A cloud of dust, far off to the southeast.

Riders. Had to be. We hadn't seen any herds of wild cattle or aurochs here, even though it was the sort of landscape that would have been home to vast numbers of bison back in The World, once upon a time.

It seemed we hadn't shaken our pursuers altogether, after all.

No, that wasn't quite right. The Avurs had been to the west of here, and even though they'd fled ahead of us, most of them had gone either south or north. That cloud was being kicked up by a larger force, coming from the direction of one of the Peruni cities.

That didn't mean they weren't after us. Sorcery has a long arm, sometimes.

For a long moment, I just sat my horse, watching. The animals were all restless, though not yet nervous. They were alert, ears up and watching their surroundings. They didn't like this place, either, though it wasn't bad enough to panic them yet.

It was hard to tell just how far away that dust cloud was. Distances got deceiving out there. They could be almost a hundred miles off, or they could be only an hour's ride away.

I was about to call Gunny over the radio when Mathghaman rode up out of the hollow. He hardly needed me to point out the dust cloud. He spotted it immediately. "I do not think we should stay here."

"You don't have to convince me." The longer we stayed put, the antsier I got. I nodded toward the dust cloud. "That alone tells me we need to move."

"That's not all." Mathghaman inclined his head toward the hollow without taking his eyes off the distant dust cloud. "There are ruins down there. We should move. Gunny is trying to convince Cailtarni now."

"Ruins?" I hadn't seen anything that looked remotely like a single sign of habitation the entire last week we'd been riding across the grasslands. "There were people here once?"

He nodded gravely. "These plains were once the breadbasket of the Commagan Empire. Tens of thousands lived in the towns and cities that rose along the trade routes with Cor Legear, Tethba, and Colcand."

"The fall of Commagan." He'd told us some of the story, largely in response to the tale Almak had spun on the borders of Lost Colcand. It had been chilling enough there, thinking about the ancient abomination that had been the Outsider Thoggudan slouching its way across the landscape, leaving devastation and madness in its wake. Somehow, it wasn't any better here, knowing that this place had probably been scoured of life as that thing had passed. We'd seen what the vampire's footsteps had done to the land as it had walked abroad. An actual Outsider must have been far, far worse.

"Indeed. That is not all, however. If it were only ruins, I would not mind. There are symbols still carved upon the stones, though. Ancient, eldritch sigils." His expression was even grimmer than his voice at that point. "This was a place of unholy rituals. Even if Thoggudan destroyed it in his passage, there is a taint here that will draw things we do not wish to face in the dark. Assuming that they are not already buried beneath our feet."

I glanced over my shoulder. "Do I need to go down and stick my oar in? Galan seems to respect my opinion from time to time."

He shook his head. "I do not think so. Galan has seen what I have. He agrees. Cailtarni simply needs some convincing."

"Why not show him the sigils?" It seemed like a straightforward matter of sharing intel. But Mathghaman shook his head.

"These runes are not mere scribblings. They are an invocation." His eyes moved around the grasslands around us, though they were not wandering. He was searching for something. "They are spells of binding and worse. To look on such things for too long is not good for any man." He was still scanning, and I joined him even though I didn't know what I was looking for. "This is a bad place to stop."

Even without the threat of something weird lurking around that place, the more I looked at that cloud of dust in the distance, the less I wanted to be in the low ground for any great length of time. It might be good for the purposes of concealment, but as far as defensive terrain goes, it was no bueno.

I kept looking around, and my eyes narrowed. How had I missed that before? I pointed toward a rise to the north. "What about there? It looks like it might be a couple hours' ride, but it's elevated and looks a lot more defensible if those riders catch up with us."

Mathghaman followed my pointing finger with his eyes, and something changed. He hadn't quite noticed that rise before, either, which was spooky. Almost as if someone or something hadn't wanted us to see it.

Or else it hadn't been there a few minutes before, which was an even creepier possibility.

That sense of oppressive wrongness that had been haunting me the entire ride through these grasslands came back with a vengeance. Something wasn't right here, and I suddenly wanted very much to be far away from that spot.

Mathghaman kicked his horse's flanks, urging the animal up onto the highest point near the hollow, his face set and grim, as he peered toward what now looked increasingly like a low mesa rising above the folds in the plains just a couple of miles to the north. There was a sort of haze around it, which I really didn't like, and from the look on his face, Mathghaman didn't, either.

"Gunny!" His voice was thunderously loud in the eerie quiet of the plain. "Get everyone mounted and ready to ride. We cannot stay here."

Galan looked up from where he stood near the spring, watering his horse. "It is nearly nightfall."

"This is a trap. We must ride. *Now!*"

It was rare enough that Mathghaman raised his voice at all that the urgency in his words went through the whole platoon, even including the Galel knights, like a lightning bolt. I felt my hackles go up. Without any further question or protest, everyone quickly scrambled to swing back into the saddle, or quickly started throwing their gear onto their horses if they'd already begun to unload.

A moment later, a faint quiver seemed to go through the ground. The branches of the trees down around the spring seemed to rattle, the leaves shaking violently as if in a wind that I couldn't feel up on the higher ground.

My horse nickered and pranced nervously, tossing his head. He didn't want to have anything to do with this place anymore.

I reached down to pat his neck. "I hear you, boy. I don't want to be here, either."

One of the Galel knights, Elpin, cursed as his horse freaked out, rearing and neighing, her ears back and her eyes rolling in terror. Galan urged his own mount over to help, grabbing the mare's reins and helping to get the animal under control.

Another quiver seemed to go through the ground. I might have heard something else, almost a hiss or a long, low, poisonous exhalation. I suddenly thought of Mathghaman's words that the sigils were "spells of binding." What had they bound?

Whatever it was, it seemed to be waking up.

The others felt it, too. Gunny wasn't screwing around, and that earthquake had lit a fire under everyone else, too. In moments, the rest of the platoon was urging their barely-controlled animals up out of the hollow and onto the grassland.

Since we were already up on the higher ground and still mounted, my team took the lead, Mathghaman falling in with us. We moved fast, breaking into a canter, more to keep the horses from losing their heads and just stampeding than for any other reason, moving down the faint slope that lay due east of the hollow. Right then, I didn't want to have anything to do with that mysterious mesa that had seemingly popped up out of the ground, and Mathghaman seemed to agree.

As we thundered away, I could have sworn that the earth shuddered even more violently, and a sepulchral roar went up from the hollow behind us. We'd escaped just in time.

Except we hadn't escaped at all.

CHAPTER 22

WE rode hard into the growing darkness on the eastern horizon, the dust of what looked increasingly like a good-sized army to the south and a mesa that shouldn't have been there to the north. Behind us, the monstrosity that the ancient Commagan had bound at that spring roared and raged, though so far, whatever it was couldn't quite get free, because when I looked behind us, I saw nothing but the grasslands and the sunset at our backs.

When I turned forward again, the Avurs erupted from the plains in front of us.

Easily a hundred riders surged up out of the low ground about four hundred yards away, yelling and whooping, the red light of the sunset glinting on their tall lamellar helmets. The ravine where they had lain concealed was invisible below a rise in the grasslands just ahead, so they seemed to have sprung up out of the grass itself.

Gunny urged his horse into a gallop, catching up with Mathghaman and me. "We need to turn north! Get to the high ground!"

Mathghaman shook his head. "That is not a good idea."

Gunny stabbed a knife hand at the oncoming Avurs. "It's either that, or we get into a fight in the open, and we don't have the ammo or the time to get the mortars set up. I know it's a risk. I didn't see that place before either. But it's rock or hard place, and we can at least hold the rock for a little bit longer."

If he'd been any other man, Mathghaman might have cursed then. He hauled on the reins, and we came around sharply, heading up the shallow slope toward that ominous massif to the north.

Bearrac caught up. "This is madness, Mathghaman! You know what place this is!"

Mathghaman didn't alter his course a whit, though. "Gunny is right. An open fight here would be suicide. We will have a fighting chance in the ruins."

"If any of us can find our way out again." Despite his obvious misgivings, Bearrac fell back to his place in the wedge we'd formed as we rode toward the rock.

As we got closer, I started to see that it wasn't just a mesa. It was a ruin, an ancient, crumbling city atop a small mountain that rose alone out of the grasslands. None of the structures I could see were intact, hardly a wall standing more than halfway to the sky, their interiors open to the elements. There was at least some cover, though, if we could get into those ruins.

Whether or not we really *wanted* to I was seriously beginning to doubt, more than I had when I'd first noticed that the mesa had seemingly just appeared out of thin air. The Tuacha were tough, fearless warriors, able and willing to face down all sorts of otherworldly horrors. The fact that none of *them* wanted to go in there *really* gave me the screaming willies about the place. While they had been cautious, none of them had hesitated to go into Teac Mor Farragah, where things had been unleashed during the city's fall that were so evil even the Fohorimans had feared them.

Still, Gunny had a point. Even if we stuck to the outskirts, we had a better chance against the numbers we were facing if we had some walls to hunker down behind. Orava's guys could get the mortars up, and we could wreak all the havoc we wanted to among the enemy ranks from higher ground and behind some cover.

I still didn't want to go there. And as we reached the base of the mesa and started to look for a way up, I could tell that my horse didn't want to go up there, either.

Rodeffer found an ancient road leading up the side of the mesa. The outer walls—what was left of them—were set back from this shoulder of the massif, while they were set right against the sheer sides of the mesa elsewhere. The road switchbacked up a short distance before disappearing into a cleft in the mountainside, a dark, steep-sided slot in the reddish rock.

That was a fatal funnel and a half. But we had an abundance of bad options at the moment, and no good ones.

Rodeffer hesitated just a moment before entering that slot. He looked back at me, and I nodded. We were committed. He smacked spurs to his mount and surged up into the ravine, hitting the road at a gallop by the time he passed through the portal of rock leading into the shadows above.

Speed, surprise, and violence of action. Sometimes those three are the only things that are going to keep you alive.

I was right behind him, leading my spare mount and packhorse as I went. The road was steep enough to make it hard going for the horses, and we slowed considerably as we mounted the slope. I looked up as we rode, my rifle in my hands, knowing that I would have to get remarkably lucky to hit anything on the rim of that canyon while riding, but I really didn't want to get shot full of arrows or crushed by flung rocks. Even if all I could do was suppress an attacker up there, it would be better than just taking it.

The rim of the canyon, black against the fading light in the sky, remained empty and deserted, though, even as our hoofbeats echoed and re-echoed off the rock walls to either side. Then, after what felt like a small eternity, we broke out into the open, facing the shattered gates of the ancient city as the last of the sunset died, leaving a fading, bloody red smear in the western sky.

We slowed down and spread out as we faced that broken portal, its angular crown broken off and tumbled into rubble at the base of square pillars. Each one of those pillars had to be ten feet across. The towers to either side had also fallen in. Their remnants looked like dark, jagged teeth against the gray of the sky.

"We can hold this slot for a while." Gunny had come up to join me and was looking around appraisingly. "Unfortunately, that puts us in a defensive position with no way out. They can just as easily bottle us up here." He eyed the gates. "We're going to have to find a way through."

Bearrac's voice was harsh and ominous in the gloom. "No living man has passed through those gates and returned in many generations." He heaved a sigh, audible in the strange quiet that had settled on the top of the massif now that our hoofbeats had been stilled. "This is Barmanak."

I could almost hear Galan gulp. "Truly? I thought we had steered far enough south to avoid it."

"So we did," Mathghaman said. "Or, rather, we tried to. Yet this place is no longer entirely of the waking world. If the old evils that tore it asunder are stirring once more... Well." He looked around at the ruins and the lands around us. "It is hard to avoid that which seeks you out."

"This is why I would rather have braved the Avur." Bearrac's expression, even in the twilight, was grim. "Yet here we are, and we must either trust in Tigharn and venture where few have dared to tread for many a long year, or else throw ourselves into the midst of that vast host below us."

That prompted a look over the side of the mesa. That was when I saw that the southern force had indeed been far closer than we'd thought.

Just at a guess, I'd have to say that we were facing close to two entire regiments. About two thirds of that force was on foot, with the other third made up of armored men on armored horses, heavy cataphracts with long spears. They made Armadillo look light.

The larger force, centered around standards in the form of great half-circle fans atop tall poles, had linked up with the Avur auxiliaries and now faced the base of the mountain, though they kept a respectful distance. It was possible that the Avurs had warned them about our weapons, but all the same, from what Mathghaman and Bearrac had just said, it seemed equally likely that none of them wanted to get too close to Barmanak, particularly in the dark.

"We're not going in there at night." Gunny was firm. In fact, he hardly seemed rattled at all by the revelation that we'd been drawn and driven into a place of otherworldly horror, where men who dared to venture in never came out.

When I thought about it, I guessed it wasn't exactly a first for us.

"Set security and be ready to kill anything that comes up that ravine or out of those gates."

* * *

The night was black as sin, despite the fires burning below. I lay on my belly on the edge of the mesa, watching the enemy camp through my scope, trying really hard not to keep looking over my shoulder at the black stone walls behind me.

Barmanak stood on top of a red stone mesa, so why the hell were the walls black? I wasn't sure I wanted to know.

In the light of the fires, I could make out several different groups among the imperial battalions. Galan and Cailtarni had confirmed that these were, indeed, regiments of the army of the Empire of Ar-Annator. They were a long way from home, but if word had reached the Emperor that the Sword of Iudicael was on the board and involved in the quest for its twin, then he might easily have dispatched a greater force to stop it.

Either that, or we'd just crossed paths with the very force that had been sent out to look for the Sword of Categyrn itself.

There was enough variety in the equipment of the foot soldiers that I guessed they came from several different nations or tribes. Most wore coats of overlapping scales, some wore simple tunics, some wore mail, a few wore what looked like bronze breastplates not unlike some of the corsair armor from the north. Helmets ran the gamut from simple round caps to tall, crested, elaborate helmets with flaring cheekguards to full facemasks.

They all seemed to be armed roughly the same, though, with spears, short swords, and recurve bows. The exceptions were the cataphracts, who had long lances and shorter axes, though they all carried bows and arrows as well.

Mathghaman and Bearrac joined me, getting down in the prone to either side. "What do you see?"

"A whole lot of bad guys." I pointed toward the cluster of pavilions at the rear of the imperial camp. Most of the soldiers, even the cataphracts, had small tents or shelters made of their cloaks and spears. Only a handful had dedicated shelters. The weird part was that all the big, richly decorated pavilions surrounded a bare patch of ground. I hadn't yet seen anyone cross that courtyard. In fact, I'd seen several men pointedly go wide around it. "Most of the commanders look like warlords, but I think I've identified two sorcerers. One was wearing a black robe like that Avur shaman I shot a week or so back, but another one looks like some kind of ancient astrologer." Remembering that even with the mind speech, some verbal shortcuts don't entirely translate, I groped for a description. "Dark purple robe, tall headdress, staff. Everybody seems afraid of him, too.

"What is that?" Bearrac was peering at the half-circle of massive tents. "That figure in the open there, which none dare approach?"

I shifted my aim toward that bare patch of ground in the middle of the pavilions. I hadn't noticed anything there at first, but then, I didn't have a Tuacha's eyesight.

I blinked, trying to focus through the scope. It seemed difficult there, and the fact that very little of the firelight reached that open yard between the tents made it worse. Slowly, I started to make out what looked like a figure standing in the center of that open space.

There was something weird about it, and I found that, even though I couldn't make it out as much more than a blacker shadow against the dark ground, I really, really wanted to look somewhere else. I felt a chill go up my spine, and I didn't even know why.

Then the thing lifted up what I thought was a lantern, at first. It emitted a sickly, greenish glow, not unlike those phantoms that Derelei and I had faced on the battlements at Cor Legear. This actually cast some illumination, though, and after a moment I saw three men hurry into that circle of corpse light. Two were warriors and the third was the wizard/astrologer looking dude I'd just told Mathghaman and Bearrac about.

Even at that distance, I could tell they were nervous. No, not nervous. They were scared out of their minds.

That was when I saw that the mysterious figure wasn't holding up a lantern. It was holding up a severed head that glowed with that unnatural phosphorescence that made me think of rot and decay.

A severed head that belonged on its shoulders.

In that glow, I was finally able to make out the fact that the figure was that of a tall man, but without a head. Instead, it was holding its own head in its hand, while the other toyed with a long whip.

"One of the Thirty is here." Once again, if he had been anyone else, Mathghaman might have cursed.

"I guess that really means we're between the hammer and the anvil, then." I still hadn't gotten the full story about the Thirty, but if they were all headless horsemen, or whatever that thing was down there, then they were probably potent horrors we really didn't want to cross.

"Indeed." Both Tuacha drew back from the edge. "We will spend the night in vigil. Be alert." Mathghaman bent close. "If you hear a voice and cannot see who speaks, do not answer it."

On that comforting note, he and Bearrac moved away, leaving me to look down at the imperials and their eldritch commander below.

It was going to be a long night.

CHAPTER 23

THE sun had barely started to lighten the eastern horizon when the first assault came.

We hadn't gotten a whole lot of rest. The horses *really* didn't like it up there, and it was going to be a fight to get them into the city at all. So, we'd needed to have at least two men on horse watch as well as regular security.

The short periods of time when we hadn't been on one or the other duty hadn't been restful, either.

Mathghaman hadn't just been blowing smoke when he'd warned us about voices in the dark. They'd been quiet at first, but about an hour after full dark, they started to whisper. Low susurrations hissed through the rocks and the rubble of the gate. It would have been bad enough if they'd just been murmurs that could have been put down to the wind. I've been a lot of places where I've thought I'd heard voices until I'd stopped and really listened for a while, after which I'd realized that it had just been the breeze in the rocks, the trees, or the grass.

These whispers were understandable, though. That was the worst part.

They called our names, they asked what we thought we were doing there, they wondered if we were ready to face the hereafter, they told us we were all dead men and damned, and then they laughed. That was when it got really bad. The words had been whispered or murmured, but the laughter, high, shrill, and insane, had been at full volume, like someone had been whispering in our ears and then belted out a psychotic belly laugh at the same distance. Everyone could hear them, too. I woke up easily a half a dozen times to that maniacal, demonic laughter, not having heard what had been said prior.

I could sure guess, though.

The dreams…

There was no getting away from the dreams, either. I can't describe them except to say they were little more than disjointed audiovisual noise. I got vague impressions of blood, guts, and awful mutilation, all overlaid with screams, cries, and gibbering laughter. They were insanity distilled.

We were getting into position to rain death and destruction down into that slot in the mesa when Cailtarni's voice cracked across the morning stillness. "Where is Elpin?"

Everyone looked around, but there was no sign of the young Galel knight. "He is gone." Bearrac's words were like the pronouncement of doom. "We should pray we do not find what is left."

Then the enemy was moving, and we had other things to worry about.

Nearly a hundred cataphracts formed into a column and kicked their horses into a canter, their spears held in both hands as they rode up to the base of the mesa. We let them come for the moment. The firing angles were pretty extreme, and nobody wanted to lean out over the somewhat crumbly edge of the massif to shoot straight down. The odds that the ground would give way and spill you two hundred feet down to be dashed to pieces on the rocks seemed pretty fair. Especially in that place.

It felt like something in the mesa might *make* the lip collapse, just to see you fall.

So, we kept ourselves back and gathered at the mouth of the canyon, machineguns, rifles, and 40mm thumpers ready to engage the first elements that entered that slot.

If it had looked like a murder hole writ large to us as we'd started up, we were going to make it infinitely worse for anyone who came after us.

Orava and his boys were set back from the edge, invisible to the enemy forces below, mortars set up and ready, Ohto, Miero, and Lintu waiting with rounds already in their hands. Orava himself was just close enough to the edge that he'd be able to spot the fall of the rounds and call adjustments.

Gurke had drawn the short straw again, and Team Three was stuck on rear security. He'd complained bitterly, and he hadn't been the only one. Franks had *not* been happy.

Franks seemed to be more disturbed by the idea of facing the ruins of Barmanak than the prospect of missing out on the action, though.

He wasn't wrong, either.

We could just hear the thunder of hooves and the rattle and clink of equipment as the cataphracts rode up into the cleft, though we couldn't see them yet. Everything else was dead quiet. The wind had dropped to nothing. Even the voices had stopped, perhaps because the sun was rising.

Then Chambers yelled and let rip with a long burst from his Mk 48.

"Watch your fucking sectors!" Gunny barked. My team *was* watching our sector, though, so I turned to see what had just happened.

Chambers was pointing his belt-fed at a crack in the wall near the gate, practically hyperventilating. Bullet scars stood out white on the black stone. That crack was barely three inches wide, if that.

"Alex. *Alex!*" Gurke was next to him, just about snapping his fingers in front of his ATL's face. "What did you see?"

Chambers gulped and visibly forced himself to calm down. "There was a shadow." He looked up at Gurke, then saw me watching him, too. His expression turned almost desperate. "It was real! It was shaped like a man, but it was coming out of that crack, and it was *reaching* for me!"

Conall was at Gurke's elbow, then. "Do not let them touch you. Bullets will not hurt them, but they should still drive them off."

"Wait. So, he really *did* see something?" Gurke was being obtuse. We'd seen stuff every bit as freaky over the last year. He still pointed to the crack. "Nobody could get through that!"

I was starting to think that Gurke was just pissed that he'd been startled.

Conall leaned in close, his eyes still lifted toward the walls of Barmanak. He was the quietest of the Tuacha, now that Cairbre was gone, but it was a different sort of quiet. Less contemptuous and more contemplative. He looked older than the others, even though I was pretty sure he was actually younger than Mathghaman, his hair and beard shading to silver. "The shadow people are not men of flesh and blood, like you and I. Keep a sharp lookout, and do not let them catch you off guard." He turned grim. "I think we know what happened to Lord Elpin last night."

We were not in a good spot, that was for sure.

Then the first cataphracts came around the bend and into the cleft in the rock, and it was on.

Applegate and Santos opened fire with the Mk 48s first. Even suppressed, the rattling roar of 7.62 machine-gun fire in that narrow space was thunderous. The effects on target were even more devastating.

Bullets chopped through armor and flesh, tearing into horse and man alike. In moments, the slot was a chaotic nightmare of rearing, screaming horses and bleeding, broken, dying men.

Then Gunny launched a 40mm egg with a *thunk,* and the nightmare down there got even worse. At least the carnage was blotted out for a moment by the boiling black cloud of the ogive's detonation.

Behind us, the mortarmen hung and dropped, the rounds rocketing skyward with *thump*s made dim by the rattle and roar of rifle and machinegun fire. I couldn't see the fall of the rounds, but the uproar as they detonated among the enemy could be heard even up on the mesa top.

We could hold the imperials off from that position for as long as we had ammunition. There was only one way up onto that shelf of the mesa, and that was up that slot. Hell, even if we ran out of bullets, we could still throw rocks and do a lot of damage. We could stack them like cordwood until they got tired of the slaughter.

But that wasn't why we were there. This wasn't Masada, and we weren't the Zealots. And sooner or later, we were going to run out of ammunition.

We had to choose between braving the ruins or sitting up there until either we ran out of ammo, or we ran out of food and water.

"Gurke, you've got point." Gunny had stepped back from the slot as the surviving cataphracts backed off. The men in the rear must have seen enough of the carnage in the slot that they didn't push, but instead backed their horses down the road to the bottom of the mesa. It sounded like chaos down there, though, especially with the Menninkai still raining a disturbingly large portion of our mortar rounds down on the gathered imperial soldiers at the bottom of the mesa.

Then a voice shouted from below, and I felt a spike of pain behind my left eye. For a moment, everything went blurry. When I cleared my head, I saw that everyone else looked as punch drunk as I felt.

"It is the ruins or the Dullahan." Mathghaman swung into the saddle, leaning forward to murmur to his horse, which seemed to immediately calm down. The horses were in a bad way, between the ruined, haunted city on one side and the gunfire on the other. It took some doing to get mounted, and it would have even without the dizziness that had followed that shout.

"Quickly!" Eoghain was at the cleft still, covering our retreat. He fired, and as I fought to bring my horses under control and get them closer to the walls and the gate, I looked down through the dust and smoke that drifted and lingered in the slot, to see that headless abomination ride into the cleft.

I could see it more clearly now. It was shockingly tall; it probably would have stood seven feet if it had had its head attached to the stump of its neck. It didn't appear to wear armor, but only tattered black robes.

That whip wasn't just a whip. It was several human spines bound together with what looked like black wires.

Eoghain shot it three times, so fast that the reports blended together into a single, rolling thunderclap. It didn't even flinch. Nor did its mount, a hellish, skeletal thing with smoking red eyes. That thing looked far scarier than even the mutants that the Fohorimans had ridden, with the possible exceptions of the massive beasts that the Warlock Kings rode.

Eoghain reloaded, chanting as he did so. It didn't slow the thing down. It still had a long way to go yet to reach the top, but it was moving fast. It didn't look like it was galloping, but it was climbing as fast as if it were.

"Ride!" Eoghain shouted. He hammered the entire magazine at the advancing headless horseman, still not even slowing it down. "I will hold it as long as I can!"

I hesitated. I'll confess, it wasn't because I really *wanted* to stand there with him. That thing trotting up the cleft made me want to crawl into a deep, dark hole and pull it in after me. Every fiber of my being wanted to run. But as little as I'd really talked to Eoghain—he wasn't as quiet as Conall, but all of the Tuacha were a little aloof, a little standoffish—he was a brother. I knew I had to do what he said, but it went against the grain anyway.

"Go, Conor! I will be right behind you!" He was reloading, but before he slipped the magazine in, he whispered over it, his eyes turned toward the sky, just for a moment.

I forced myself to turn and head for the gate, pulling my horses with me, as Eoghain leveled his rifle again and opened fire once more.

His shots thundered down the cleft in the mountainside as we rode through the narrow gap in the rubble that lay across the gateway, into the ruins of Barmanak.

Horror came after us. Horror lay before us.

CHAPTER 24

WE were forced to slow as we worked our way through the wreckage at the gateway. The remnants of the towers and gates had been worn down by time and weather to mounds of detritus. Black dust rose from every hoof or boot as we scrambled over the wreckage. Nothing grew on top of that mesa, not once we passed inside the crumbling walls. It was a place of death.

A terrific *boom* shook the ground behind us, and a cloud of dust and smoke went up on the other side of the gate. I didn't know what Eoghain had done; I hadn't thought he'd been packing explosives with him, but sometimes the Tuacha were full of surprises, even when you thought you knew them.

A moment later, he came galloping through the gate behind us, his horse leaping over the rubble in the way. "It is slowed, but not stopped. It will take more than bullets and a satchel charge to stop one of the Thirty."

Mathghaman nodded his understanding from where he sat his horse near the center of our column. The ruins allowed for little dispersion, especially with horses.

I suddenly thought of the nightmare faced by armored forces in urban combat and suppressed a shudder. We weren't in quite the same position as Russian tanks in Grozny, but this was still a bad spot to get canalized, especially if those shadow people Chambers had seen could get through any size opening to come at us.

"We must make haste. Watch the flanks carefully, but speed must be our security. If it be Tigharn's will, we should be through by sunset." While he spoke with his usual, measured assurance, I thought I detected a hint of worry in Mathghaman's demeanor, even from several spaces back in the formation. If Barmanak was as sketchy a place as he'd said, it might just take a miracle from Tigharn for us to ever leave it.

None of the ruins stood very high. Again, it looked almost as if the place had been shelled into oblivion. The outer walls were far higher than any structure within, with the exception of a massive tumulus of rubble and jagged, broken towers that stood high against the eastern wall. It looked like it might have been a citadel once, or maybe a temple. The decay was too advanced to tell for sure.

It was eerily quiet, once the echoes of that blast had settled. Our horses' hoofbeats seemed awfully loud, even though they fell dead, without an echo. It was weird and unsettling. The dust rose and hung in the air as we rode through, getting into our eyes and throats. Everyone wore a thin layer of grit after only a few dozen yards. The silence never seemed to change. Even the inevitable coughs from the dust seemed muffled.

Worse was the fact that I started to see movement out of the corner of my eye after we'd gone less than a quarter mile in.

It was only ever just a flicker, right at the edge of my peripheral vision, and when I turned to look, there was never anything there. The thought of those shadow people nagged at me, and I searched every hole, every crack, every corner as I passed it. Nothing. Just that persistent flicker of movement.

Step by step, we followed the remnants of the streets, unable to do much else. The remains of the houses and bigger buildings were too stacked with rubble to ride through them, even though Franks tried, more than once. None of us were comfortable following those empty avenues. We expected each and every opening and pile of rubble to contain an ambush.

If this were any other ruined, long-abandoned city, that might not make much sense. Who could possibly be waiting for us here? But this was a world where ancient, malignant presences lurked, and while I had no idea what kind of history Barmanak had, it was already clear enough that it wasn't as abandoned as it looked.

As we rode past what might have once been a mansion or a small castle within the city, the ruined walls rising higher than any others nearby, I glanced inside to see a skeleton lying unburied just inside the broken doorway. It was completely intact from what I could see, and something about the way it lay there made me think that the man or woman lying there had died in considerable agony.

I reined in just a little, slowing as I studied the bones. There was something off there. I looked around carefully, but, aside from those weird, persistent, and disturbing flickers of motion at the periphery of my vision, I couldn't see anything but ruins, rubble, and our own column of horsemen. Something was warning me that we were in trouble, though.

The term "sixth sense" can be a bit misleading. While I can't deny that there is a decided mystical dimension to this world, sometimes that sixth sense here is the same as it is back in the time and place we had come from. The mind can unconsciously put together clues that the other five senses pick up without our noticing, and we get hunches that we can't necessarily point to a reason for right away. I was getting one of those hunches right then.

As the bones began to move, I realized what it was that had warned me, aside from their odd placement. There were thin, dark filaments holding the skeleton together, long after any natural ligaments and tendons should have crumbled to dust.

One of the Galel knights let out a yell. Bones were shifting and skeletons were rising out of the rubble all around us. They didn't make a sound, not even the rattle that you sort of expect from a walking skeleton after all those movies and video games. They were utterly silent as they rose out of the rubble and the ruins, jaws gaping in silent leers, their hollow eye sockets seeming to glare despite their emptiness.

There were hundreds of them.

Hardly thinking about it, I twisted in my saddle, snatched up my rifle, and shot the grasping skeleton right in front of me through the skull. Bone shattered, but the thing kept coming. Clearly, whatever was controlling it didn't need its cranium intact to do so.

I could waste ammo, or I could try something else. Letting the rifle hang, fighting to maintain control of my near-panicked horse, which was about at the end of his rope, I swept out the sword and brought it crashing down on the thing's shoulder as it grasped at my leg.

The smoky, blessed steel clove through bone and dark tendrils alike, but the effects were decidedly different. The bone just cracked. The tendrils shriveled and turned to dust as the blade of the Sword of Iudicael sheared through them. A chain reaction seemed to shudder through the skeleton, and it collapsed to dry, disconnected bones at my horse's feet.

I kicked the terrified animal forward. Fortunately, none of the horses had stampeded yet, though I think that was mainly because there was simply nowhere for them to go. They reared and stamped a little, ears back and eyes rolling in terror, but they huddled together as the bones of those long dead reached out for us.

Gunfire cracked up and down the line, but with little effect. "Blades!" Gunny already had his axe out and brought it crashing down on a tall skeleton that was missing its lower jaw. He proceeded to take the thing apart as efficiently as a man boning out a deer, though it took considerably more effort than my single stroke with the Sword.

I drove my horse up along the west side of the line, where more of the skeletons were coming out of the ruins and there was more room as the horses shied away from the dead. Two more swings caught two more of the undead things, one lopping off a skull, the other shearing through a ribcage. Both skeletons collapsed to piles of bones.

"Shift right!" Gunny cracked another skeleton apart, but there were just too many of them, and we were too spread out along that lane. "Find a defensive position!"

Gurke took charge as Franks fought his mount, grabbing Franks' horse's reins as he kicked his own into a gallop, heading for the next turn. More skeletons were coming out of the tumbled buildings, trying to cut us off.

Cailtarni took the head off one with a single swipe of his sword as he thundered past. We were pushing for distance now, so there wasn't time to do much more than that, even though that single blow wouldn't put one of those reanimated skeletons back in the dirt. Only the Sword of Iudicael seemed able to do that, and there was only one of me and one of the Sword.

More and more of those horrors were flooding the streets, grabbing for us as they grinned silently and grimly. There were shadow people slipping between them, too, and one of them writhed up to grab at Vihattu. He swung his blade through it, seemingly without effect, and while it didn't manage to grab him and haul him off his horse, it did touch him. He started screaming hoarsely, clutching his side where its hand had seemingly passed through him, doubling over in agony, and then he fell.

I was just close enough, due to the fact that I was riding up and down the column, slashing at the skeletons where I could reach them, that I got to him first. His horse was wild with terror, but there was nowhere for it to go. I couldn't get close enough at first, as his mount was flailing with its hooves, screaming, out of its head.

I reached down for him, though he was doubled up and keening in agony, his eyes going glassy. In fact, I could have sworn that they were going white, too, like cataracts were growing across them even as I tried to grab him and get him up.

Then his horse crashed down from its terrified rear, its front hooves barely missing me and caving in his skull.

I'm not entirely proud of what I did then. It was reflex, more than anything else. Vihattu was dead, and I'd barely avoided being hammered into the dirt by those flailing hooves. I slashed the horse's throat open before it could do any more damage. It screamed and staggered as blood spurted out and turned the dust to black mud. In only moments it had fallen against a ruined wall, kicking feebly.

We'd regret that. I had a feeling we'd need every animal by the end. But that horse had already killed one of us, and it was only going to get worse as time went on. Its terror had become a threat.

It still didn't feel good to slaughter a helpless animal in what amounted to an angry outburst at the loss of a man who was probably dying anyway.

Wheeling my horse around again, I held my ground as Orava and Noita leaped off their horses to retrieve Vihattu's weapons and ammunition. Noita was cursing bitterly, tears streaming down his cheeks, as he pulled magazines out of the dead man's chest rig.

Orava slapped Noita on the shoulder and turned to his own horse. The two of them mounted quickly, Orava shouting to me, "We're clear!"

Then we were thundering for the corner again, blades whirling, cutting down skeletons and trying to avoid the shadow people.

As I rounded the corner, I spotted a lumbering figure behind the mob of skeletons. I couldn't see much of it, but whatever it was, it was at least a head taller than any of the other skeletons that were now clambering out of every hole and shattered doorway in the city.

Step by step, we tried to avoid the bulk of the undead mob and make for the north gate—or what we hoped was the north gate. Those mobs seemed to be disproportionately thick to the north, west, and south, though, and we found ourselves steadily forced, by both the fleshless enemy and the rubble that was strewn across the streets—none of which were exactly straight or laid out in any kind of logical grid—toward the east.

The east, and the ruins of the citadel.

That thing was bigger than it had appeared from a distance. The dimensions of Barmanak were odd. Streets that seemed short turned out to be longer than they looked, and vice versa. That citadel had been a lot farther away than it had appeared to begin with. Now it loomed over us like another mountain.

Built of the same black stone as the rest of the city, it looked like it had once been a ziggurat, with pointed towers at the four corners of the second tier. It was in ruin, with three of the four towers completely collapsed, one corner of the third tier sloughed away in a glorified landslide.

The steps leading up to the gateway, halfway up the second tier, were choked with rubble. They had once been flanked by statues of what might have been animals or monsters. Those monuments had all been smashed, though one's head lay at the base of the ziggurat. It had been worn down by time and weather, but it still looked a lot like a stylized horny toad. With big teeth. Really big teeth.

Whatever had happened to Barmanak, I kinda figured that it had already been on a downhill slide beforehand. There was something about that smashed stone head that gave me the willies almost as much as the rest of that strange, twisted place.

The skeletons and the shadow people were closing in, mindlessly groping for our lives. Maybe worse. I got another look at that big sucker as we found a low, half-ru-ined wall halfway across the courtyard at the base of the citadel, where we might be able to set up defenses. It was another skeleton, but bigger than the rest and completely encased in armor. Great, verdigrised bronze plates cov-ered it in overlapping layers from throat to knees. It al-most looked like a walking ziggurat itself. Only its bony claws for hands and the leering, moldering skull peering out above the high neck guard and the domed helmet showed it for what it was.

My rifle was on my back then, and I had sword and shield in hand as I stood near the center, waiting for the enemy. There were an awful lot of skeletons, though. And even with the Sword of Iudicael, I still couldn't be everywhere at once.

They had slowed, though, as we took up defensive positions, keeping the horses as far from the undead as possible. Even as I moved up to a gap in the wall, know-ing that I had an advantage with the Sword in my hand that the rest didn't, the mob had stopped, still about ten yards away.

Everything went quiet then. Nobody was shooting—there was no point—and even the horses had stopped their frightened neighing. The undead didn't make a sound. The shadow people lurked, but they hadn't made another attempt to grab any of us.

Mathghaman and Gunny stepped up next to me, sword and axe in hand. I gulped as I looked at that army of bones, knowing just what it was going to take to carve our way through all of them. We didn't have the numbers, and we'd be exhausted and overwhelmed before we could knock down even half. That was assuming that they didn't get through on a flank or bring enough of us down by main force before we got to that point.

Maybe this was why no one ever returned from Barmanak. The weirdness of the place aside, there were enough undead abominations here to tear any adventurer limb from limb and add their bones to the horde.

Time seemed to slow down as we waited, breathing hard, weapons clenched in white-knuckled fists. We were too few to break out, but we couldn't just lie down and die, either.

That we'd come all this way only to be cornered in a dead city by its dead inhabitants was crushing and infuriating all at the same time. The quest couldn't end this way.

When that big bruiser shoved its way to the front and we braced ourselves for the charge, suddenly all those dark, empty eye sockets turned up to look behind us.

It might be a trap. But something told me that these things weren't that clever. I glanced over my shoulder.

A figure had appeared in the gateway at the top of the steps leading up the ziggurat.

It was massive, barrel-chested and brawny. Or maybe it was just bloated. It was clearly dead. The face was another skull, though a long beard still clung to its jaw. Dressed in heavy, pleated robes, it wore a tall, square-topped helmet atop that bony dome and held a curved sword in one blackened fist.

The figure held up that wickedly hooked blade and spoke. Its voice was deep and loud, while seemingly distant, as if it was coming from a deep well. The words were unintelligible, but they were about as comforting as the headless Dullahan's shout from earlier. My head immediately started to hurt.

That was probably why the skeletons weren't advancing. They were just bottling us up for this thing.

It leaped off the top of the steps then, and seemed to almost float down toward the ground. I had already turned to face it when Santos opened fire on it with the Mk 48.

While it's a heavy beast, the Mk 48's recoil is still no joke. There's a reason why machineguns are usually fired from a bipod or tripod. Santos was a beast, though, and he was equal to the challenge. He leaned into the weapon and hammered a long burst right into that thing's chest in midair.

If it hadn't already been dead, it would have been right then.

As it was, the storm of jacketed lead slammed it backward, and it hit the steps about ten feet higher than it probably intended to, falling clumsily and catching itself with one blackened, rotting hand. When it stood, drawing itself up to its full height, I saw that there were dim lights within its eye sockets, shading from a sickly green to a weird sort of purple.

Somehow, despite its fleshless face, I got the impression that it was *pissed*, and not just because we were interlopers. It was planning on tearing us to pieces anyway, but Santos had just burned down its dignity, so now it was doubly angry.

It raised that hooked sword, but before it could speak again, Bailey hit it with a thumper.

The *thunk* of the 40mm launcher was followed a split second later by the heavy *thud* of the detonation. The explosion threw the thing back against the steps again, and this time, when it heaved itself up, its robes were torn and smoking and it looked like some of its blackened, bloated flesh had been flensed off.

It was already dead, though. I didn't know what was animating that thing, but it wasn't going to get cast out easily.

I died as men die ages ago, pathetic mortals. That voice was as loud and as distant as ever, and I understood even those foreign words that seemed to emanate from the rocky ground beneath our feet. *Only cold travels in my veins. Soon your blood will run through them, for a little while. There is no escape from Barmanak for you, trespassers, just as there is no escape for me!*

It heaved itself up and darted toward us, only to be knocked back again by two more 40mm grenades.

They were flensing the rotting flesh off it, but still not stopping it. They forced it farther back up the steps, though.

I knew what I had to do. Scary as it was, bullets and explosives weren't hurting that thing badly enough. The Sword in my hand was probably the only thing we had that might.

Gritting my teeth, sword in one hand and buckler in the other, I waded in.

CHAPTER 25

BULLETS *crack*ed over my head as several of us poured more fire into the revenant. The gunfire staggered it, the sheer physical impacts at least keeping it from driving forward much farther. It did seem strange that not a single round had yet broken a bone. It stayed on its feet, cursing us as it staggered under the hammering we were giving it.

I realized I wasn't alone as I advanced on the thing. Cailtarni, Mathghaman, and Gunny had come with me, moving up to flank me on either side. Gunny had his rifle slung across his back and his own thumper, a standalone M203, slung at his side. His axe, which he had decided was more his speed than a sword, was clenched in both hands, while Cailtarni held an oval shield up, his sword point laid over the rim. Mathghaman was Mathghaman, striding forward with sword in hand, barely seeming to be on guard at all.

We started up the steps, and the revenant looked down at us. Those glowing points of unholy fire in its eye sockets seemed to light on the Sword of Iudicael in my hand. With a sepulchral howl, it leaped backward, clear to the top of the steps, and disappeared into the cavernous entrance to the ziggurat.

I kept going after it. Killing that thing—permanently—might be our only way out. If it was the source of the undeath out there, then maybe, if I put it down, the rest of the skeletons might collapse and then we could get clear.

That was what I was thinking, anyway, up until the point that Mathghaman reached out to stop me. "Be wary." He frowned as he looked up the steps. "This is a trap."

"This entire country is a trap." I didn't like the idea of following that thing in there, either. But if it was afraid of the Sword, then I might have a chance. "Just keep any of the other undead off me." I looked down at the sword and sent up a brief, wordless prayer. I still wasn't sure whether the God I'd grown up knowing was still present in this place, but I didn't have much else to go on.

I continued up the steps. The blackness of the opening loomed over me, getting darker and bigger as I got closer. The entire ziggurat was far larger than it had first appeared, and my legs were starting to burn as I got closer to that massive portal.

Finally, we reached it. There was no sign of the revenant, and there was nothing but unutterable darkness beyond that twenty-foot-high gateway. Gunny slung his axe and brought his rifle around, triggering the weapon light to disperse some of the cloying blackness just inside the entrance.

Weapons ready, we moved inside.

Even after I dropped my NVGs, I couldn't see much of anything. There was no source of light inside, and the black stone seemed to drink up what little illumination made it past the opening. The revenant had vanished into the darkness.

Going in there meant walking into an ambush. There was no doubt in my mind. But what else were we going to do, if we were going to put this thing down? If we turned our back on it and tried to break out, it would presumably come after us, even if we *could* just cut our way through the army of the dead by main force.

Gunny was thinking more clearly than I was, though. "Mathghaman. Do you think we can drop this gateway?"

The King's Champion looked at the massive blocks of black stone around us. "It is possible, but it will not be easy." It would probably take a good chunk of our remaining explosives.

Just then the decision was taken out of our hands, as the revenant suddenly loomed in front of me. I got my buckler up just in time to divert the vicious slash of that hooked sword, that might very well have taken my head off.

I didn't try to stop the blow cold. That probably would have shattered my forearm. That thing was *strong*. It felt like getting hit by a bull, and given how big it was up close, that wasn't far off. Whoever this thing had been in life, it was far larger and stronger than most men in death. I barely managed to redirect the stroke with my buckler.

It was fast, too. I'd barely ducked under that thunderous strike when it arrested its swing, reversed the blade, and brought it sweeping down in a vertical chop that would have split me in two if I hadn't sidestepped. As it was, I felt the wind as the blade clove through the air right next to me.

I got a cut in just before it arrested that stroke just above the floor and tried to take my leg off at the knee. It felt like hitting an oak, and while the wound blackened and smoked, it wasn't deep, and the revenant didn't seem as hurt as the creatures of the Outer Dark had been at Vahava Paykhah.

Still, that cut probably saved my life, because the revenant recoiled just enough to take a lot of the force out of its next blow, giving me a chance to leap backward and out of reach of that sweeping slash.

I realized then that I'd somehow been drawn deeper inside without noticing it. This thing was playing sorcerous tricks even as we fought, and I heard a gasp behind me. It sounded strangled and pained, and there was a heavy throbbing in the air, a thick, cloying stagnancy that made me want to cough. The pressure was increasing, and it was getting harder to catch my breath as this thing stalked me.

It *was* stalking me. It wasn't enough to just kill me. It was playing with me like a cat with a mouse. It backed off just a little after I cut it, and we circled. I didn't want to let it get between me and the entrance, but as it swung viciously again, parting the air with a nasty *hiss*, I had no choice but to step to the side and back to avoid it. Avoidance was the only way I was going to survive this, I realized.

The revenant was forcing me back, deeper into the darkened interior of the ziggurat. I could see the light of the entrance off to my left, and out of the corner of my eye, I could see the webs of darkness and the shadow people that the others were struggling with.

I ducked under another swipe, backing up to keep my distance. It hadn't escaped me that this thing had singled *me* out, drawn *me* in.

Young fool. That voice didn't seem to come from the leering, bearded skull facing me, but from somewhere beneath my feet. *That blade will not save you by itself. Its master cares not for your life. I will take it from you, bury it deep where no man will ever find it again, and then I will strip your flesh and leave you hanging in the dark until the sun itself is dead.*

The revenant darted forward, swinging for my head, and I ducked and backstepped. I had to get around this thing again and back to the exit. Right at the moment, though, it was all I could do just to keep my distance.

With a lunge, it brought that blade down again like a falling tree, only this time, when I dodged, it was ready for it. I just barely got the Sword and my buckler in the way of that stroke, batting it aside. It had put so much force behind the stroke that the hooked blade struck sparks off the stone floor.

Just for a moment, I had an opening. I darted in, hammering my buckler into its arm to keep it off me, and aimed a ferocious cut at its head.

It leaped back, though not *quite* fast enough to avoid a slash along its cheekbone. The blade left a black line along the yellowed bone, and cracks began to spread out from the cut.

With a roar that vibrated through the stones underfoot, it came at me again, and I almost lost my head as I stumbled on some rubble on the floor behind me that I hadn't been able to see. I didn't dare take my eyes off that monstrous, fast-moving corpse for a moment. I caught myself before I fell, but then I had to jump left fast, my rifle hammering against my back as I circled, still not quite fast enough to get around it. I deflected the hooked sword with blade and buckler again and again, as it kept forcing me, step by step, deeper into the dark.

I was beyond the narrow cone of illumination from the doorway then. All I could see was the revenant's silhouette, darker against the gray light cast on the basalt floor behind it, and those baleful, fiery eyes. Everything else was stygian blackness.

With a growing sense of desperation, I knew that I was going to lose. I was cut off, no matter which way I moved. I attacked again, trying to get inside the reach of that hooked blade, to get close enough that I might do some real damage before it could hit me.

Smacking my buckler into the inside of its arm, I stabbed at it. The point of the blade only went in about an inch or so before it hit me with its off hand and leaped backward a good ten feet, landing with an impact that shook the floor, even as I reeled under the force of that blow. My head swam and my jaw ached. I'd been hit before, but that backhand slap had been as bad as taking a full-force punch from Santos.

I suddenly had an opening, though, and I went for it. The revenant had jumped backward, leaving a gap of at least ten yards between it and the outside wall. I sprinted for the light, throwing myself toward it, praying wordlessly that I could make it without taking that sword through the skull.

It still hit me as I went past, but I'd judged my distance just well enough that only the tip touched my mail, and that hooked point went into one of the rings. I stumbled as it pulled me sideways, but when I dipped my shoulder I got the ring off the point and then lunged for the door again.

Gunny and Mathghaman hadn't been idly waiting at the door for me. Mathghaman cut through the last tendrils of a thick, black web that had snapped across the doorway as soon as I'd been pulled in by the revenant's ambush, and then both of them came through fast, charging toward me. Gunny hammered half a dozen rounds into the revenant past my shoulder, just to keep it off balance, while Mathghaman, sword in one hand, ran to me, grabbing me by the arm and hauling me roughly to my feet, practically flinging me toward the doorway.

As we rushed past Gunny, he let his rifle hang, snatched up his 203, and lobbed a 40mm grenade at the revenant.

He was too close, and the ogive bounced off the dead sorcerer to detonate somewhere behind it, but it was still close enough that frag sleeted through the thing's already tattered robes and scarred, rotting flesh, and the shock-wave knocked it sideways. I felt something hit my helmet as the explosion reverberated through that confined, stone-walled space.

Then Mathghaman and I were hauling through the door and down the stairs, Gunny turning and burning right on our heels. As we plunged out into the wan sunlight, I saw why.

Bearrac was holding a satchel charge with the fuse smoking. A very short fuse. As we passed him, he threw it inside, hard.

Then we were plummeting down the stairs as fast as we could go without face-planting on the stone.

The explosion shook the ziggurat, and a black cloud billowed out of the gateway, flinging bits of black stone over our heads. With a massive *crack*, the lintel above the door broke and caved in, and more shattered stone cascaded down from the eroded edifice, shaking the stones under our feet as we raced to stay ahead of the slide.

Apparently, dropping the entrance *wasn't* going to take all of our explosives. The structure of the ziggurat had been more unstable than we'd thought.

We reached the bottom as the rockfall ended, dust rising in a choking cloud behind us. The skeletons were still there on the perimeter, though it didn't look like they'd moved since we'd climbed up into the ziggurat in pursuit of their master. They stood, stock still like the dead things they were, their ranks an unliving wall between us and escape.

That duel had taken longer than I'd thought. The sun was already past its zenith.

Even as we panted for breath and tried to gather ourselves for the breakout, something shifted in the pile of stone behind us. I turned to see a slab of rock turn over and go bounding down the smashed steps. An unearthly howl reverberated through the ground beneath us.

That thing was still kicking.

"This is not the place to make a stand." Mathghaman turned grimly toward the line of undead abominations. "Prepare yourselves. We must ride out, or else we die here."

We saddled up.

CHAPTER 26

THE rest of the platoon hadn't been idle during the time I'd been inside, either. While bullets wouldn't hurt those skeletons much, hacking them to pieces at least seemed to put them down for a while.

Explosives would do the same job, only faster. We hadn't had the time or the space to use them before, but now we were ready.

Ranges were still too short for the mortars, and re-packing them would take too much time, anyway. But the satchels were another matter.

Three of them arced, smoking, over the wall. The skeletons didn't react, even as several dozen of them were blotted out in the ugly black plumes of smoke, dust, and shattered black stone, the *boom*s hammering at us even behind cover. Then we were on the move, charging out through the gap in the wall behind a volley of 40mm grenades.

Necessarily, the grenades weren't all that accurate, since we were shooting from horseback. That's the great thing about grenades, though. They only have to be sorta accurate.

Explosions blossomed across the lines of undead warriors, shattering bones and flinging them at lethal speeds around the ruins. I dropped one right at that big, armored bruiser's feet, and blew its lower legs to splinters. It collapsed like a falling tree.

The skeletons were slow to respond, even as more rocks tumbled down the steps of the ziggurat with another subterranean roar. If those things were little more than automatons, puppets of the revenant, then maybe it was so focused on freeing itself that it couldn't control its minions that well.

I hoped so.

We thundered out through the gap, letting the thumpers hang and drawing swords and axes. Blades rose and fell, aided by the weight and momentum of frightened but tightly controlled horses, smashing more skeletons and sending skulls and bones flying.

Then we were through and riding hard for the north gate.

More skeletons were coming out of the ruins around us, but they were slow and sluggish, easily evaded or knocked aside. The shadow people were more elusive, but they also seemed more cautious. I didn't know why, but I'd take it.

We still nearly got turned around a couple of times, but after almost an hour of frantic riding and occasional desperate fighting, still stalked by the undead, we came out onto an open boulevard with the gate just ahead.

I looked up at the sky, just to check. We *were* still going north. With all the strangeness around Barmanak, I wanted to be sure. It would really suck to go through all that only to find ourselves back at the south gate, with the Dullahan in front of us and the undead behind us.

Unfortunately, the north gate was in even worse shape than the south. We were going to have to ride over that mound of shattered stone that choked the gateway, and that was going to slow us down considerably, while the skeletons continued to close in behind us, slower than before but no less horrifying and inexorable.

"Team One!" I'd just about screwed us, rushing into the trap after that revenant. Now I figured I needed to make up for it. "Hold up here. We've got to cover the rest." I reined in, pulling my thumper back up to my saddle and hastily reloading from the bandolier hanging off the saddle horn.

A line of skeletons stalked up the boulevard, still a decent way off, but in a growing mob. Flipping up the leaf sights, I put the M79's buttstock in my shoulder, put the sights in the middle of the group, and corked off a round.

The *thunk* echoed off the outer wall above us, followed a moment later by the *thud* of the explosion. You can actually see the 40mm ogive as it flies through the air, especially out of the shorter M79. It hit in the middle of the street, smashing one skeleton to fragments and shattering several more standing closer to it.

The rest kept coming, utterly insensible to the destruction we were wreaking. I dumped another round into the nearest ranks, disintegrating several more in a dirty black cloud. My horse shifted and pranced back and forth nervously. He didn't like being that close to the undead, and he also didn't like the fact that I'd turned him around just when we were almost out of the woods.

None of our mounts were in the best of shape at that point. Farrar's kept trying to rear and was a hair's breadth away from panicking outright. We couldn't hold for much longer.

Another 40mm arced over my head with a *thunk*, obliterating another three skeletons. "Let's fucking *go!*" Bailey sat his horse on top of the mound of debris, reloading his M203. My team was the only one with an M79, because Santos was a traditionalist and had asked the *Coira Ansec* specifically for the Vietnam-era weapon. Bailey was alone, the rest of the platoon already on the other side of the mound.

I pulled my horse back around for one more shot. "You heard the man. Get a move on." Rodeffer and Farrar went first, Santos hanging back until I lobbed my last egg at the skeletons and turned my horse to follow.

We went over the pile of rocks and out onto the open ground outside. A steep slope fell away beneath us, leading into a wide badland of canyons and windswept rocks.

It took a few moments to find the remains of the northern road, and even then we had to slow down as we picked our way down toward the badlands, following the rest of the platoon.

Behind us, shadows flickered in the gateway.

* * *

The badlands were rough going. Most of the canyon floors were bare dirt and rock, seemingly scoured flat and smooth by floodwaters, so they weren't hard to travel over, but navigation was a bear, given the twisting maze of arroyos and gullies. We could kind of see the massif of Barmanak behind us for a while, but even that was soon hidden as we got deeper into the labyrinth of the badlands.

We rode hard for a while, until about an hour before sunset. Sunset down there in the canyons, anyway. Then we simply had to halt to take stock and gather ourselves. We circled up in a hollow beneath a rocky outcrop which would make a pretty good OP, with a clear view up and down the canyon. It was a decently defensible position and might serve as our night lay-up site, unless we got attacked first.

With Applegate and Chambers up on the OP with their Mk 48s, the horses tended to and calmed down—that was a good sign; they were considerably less agitated than they had been up on the mesa, which suggested the skeletons or other creepy-crawlies were still some distance away—the team leaders, Gunny, Mathghaman, Galan, and Cailtarni gathered to consider where we stood.

"We've used up most of our explosives, to include the HE grenades." Gunny's assessment was grim. "Somehow we also lost two packhorses in that nightmare, so that's a couple days' worth of food and water gone." He looked at Galan. "I sure hope we don't run into anything like that in Myrgarak. Or Gremman, if we have to go there."

Galan shrugged uncomfortably. "No man of the Galel—or any of our allies—have set foot in either place in generations. There is no telling."

"This was a dangerous sidetrack." Gunny looked around the group. "I'm not saying we could necessarily have avoided it, but it could very well end up costing us."

"It already has." Orava was grimmer than usual. No surprise; I thought Vihattu had been his cousin as well as his teammate.

"Yeah." We could all commiserate. We hadn't been able to retrieve his body in the chaos of that fight, but he was hardly the first platoon mate who'd fallen, never to be seen again, without burial or marker.

Gunny looked at Galan and Mathghaman. "What do we know about these badlands?"

"Little." Mathghaman didn't beat around the bush. He looked up at the stony walls above us. There was no way we could ride the high ground there; the ridges were razor sharp, sculped by wind...and maybe something else. The sense of the uncanny that had lurked around that spring where we had stopped just before being ma-neuvered into Barmanak was just as strong in the bad-lands. "Barmanak has long been a whispered tale, one more stronghold that fell into ruin during the conflagra-tion that destroyed the Commagan Empire. Its corrup-tion could not save it from the rampage of the abomi-nation that ruled the Commagan. Since then, it has been a ghost story, a ruin that few men have reached, while many have vanished in the trackless plains around it."

"Well, that's encouraging," Gunny said dryly. "We need to bear east. So far, the canyons have been forcing us north." He looked down at the rough map he'd been drawing in the dirt. "I take it we're not turning back?"

"Be kinda hard to, with that fuckin' army right be-hind us." Bailey was, as usual, blunt and to the point, never mind the somewhat more refined Galan in our midst. "Unless anybody really thinks they fucked off once we went inside the city." He spat into the darkness of a low overhang. "If it was me, I'd have put pincers out to either flank. Probably try to get some of those Avur nomads into the badlands to scout things out. We were up there for most of twenty-four hours. Plenty of time for men on horseback to get ahead of us on open ground."

Galan didn't actually seem disturbed by Bailey's vulgarity, as much as it translated. "The Avurs will be even more disquieted by these lands than we are. Even their shamans will be wary, fearing what they might summon in this place. The Outer Dark is very close here. I do not need to tell you that." His voice grew haunted. "One of the Thirty, though..."

"Yes." Mathghaman's voice was less haunted and more grim. "The Dullahan might well not fear the Outer Dark."

"What is a Dullahan?" Gunny asked. "I mean, I saw that it's a headless horseman, but aside from that? We saw some freaky stuff with the Fohorimans in the north, but none of them were toting their severed heads around. Hell, even the vampire died when Conor beheaded it."

"They have not been seen in many generations," Mathghaman said. "Some say they were The Summoner's original disciples, cursed in a way even the Warlock Kings were not, when The Summoner tore the veil aside and brought the Outsiders into the world. They are even more terrible than the Warlock Kings. That they have reappeared, and now seek the Swords..." He shook his head, his eyes far away for a moment, before they focused and moved from one to another of us, finally settling on me. "Dark forces are moving that have lain quiescent for many centuries. We must step carefully."

He kept his eyes fixed on me, and for a moment, he was not addressing the rest. "Those forces will not only seek to destroy our bodies. We must always be on guard.

Their traps can be as subtle as they are deadly, and they can read our hearts as well as our actions."

I nodded quietly. I thought I saw where he was going.

I'd relied on the Sword to give me all the edge I needed in that ziggurat, but at the end of the day, as potent as it was, as much as the creatures of the Outer Dark could not abide its touch, it was still only a sword. It was a weapon in my hand, and if I screwed up, it wouldn't save me. Not by itself.

Mathghaman held my eyes for a moment before he nodded fractionally and looked back at the others. That was the lesson I think he was hoping that I'd figure out.

I remembered the way Sister Sebeal had talked about the Staff of Nechtan. It was a relic, without power in and of itself, but only the lingering influence of the spirit of the man who had carried it. The Swords, I realized, were much the same.

I remembered the dead man I'd taken the Sword from, then. He sure hadn't been immortal because of it. He had rejected what it had stood for, and used it simply as a blade that did not break or dull, and had even covered it so that he didn't have to look at the symbols that spoke of its origin.

He'd died with a bullet or several in him, despite having the Sword in his hand. It was something to think about.

Especially as we delved deeper into these haunted realms, and the wish for *something* that might give us an edge got stronger.

As we continued to plan as much as we could for our next steps on the way to Myrgarak, I pondered that we probably needed to put more faith in the intangibles than in secret weapons.

After all, the Creed doesn't talk about high-tech toys or super weapons. It talks about Honor, Perseverance, Spirit, and Heart. The intangibles that keep a man going when all else is pain and fatigue.

We finished our planning session as the darkness descended over the badlands and strange, wild cries echoed through the canyons. There was a long way to go in the morning.

CHAPTER 27

IT took four interminable days to get out of the badlands. It was a four-day long nightmare.

Not that we got hit that entire time. Aside from several wrong turns and riding up dead-end box canyons, it was an uneventful half a week. No, it was the sheer, eerie *wrongness* of the place that got under our skins and had us sleeping only fitfully and looking over our shoulders all the time.

We weren't alone in that maze of twisting canyons and sharp-edged, weirdly shaped rocks. The wind whispered strangely, never far from a voice, murmuring just beyond the range of hearing. Our sense of direction seemed to constantly shift uncertainly, and the flickers of movement at the edge of our vision never went away.

The oppressive sense of being watched never went away.

On the second day, I could have sworn I saw the figure of a man standing atop a finger of white rock standing high above the canyon where we rode. When I looked up, though, a crow flapped away with a hoarse, mocking croak.

Water was getting low by the time we finally found a way out, up a steep slope of scree where the canyon wall had collapsed. We'd passed a few thin streams coming out of the rocks, but no one had ventured to suggest refilling our canteens and water bladders from them. Nobody wanted to drink any water that ran in that place. And at least a couple of us had drunk from Syrian or Afghan canals before.

My team was back on point by the time we rode up out of the gully and onto the plains again. We rode warily, rifles in hand, scanning the windswept grasslands carefully. Our physical enemies hadn't ventured into the badlands after us, but that didn't mean that Bailey was wrong.

At first, all we could see was more rolling hills covered in bunchgrass. A faint, dark line on the horizon might have been the Borala Plateau, where Myrgarak lay. It was in the right direction, at least, judging by the position of the sun.

I rode toward a slight rise just ahead, then dismounted and handed my reins to Farrar before I beckoned Rodeffer to join me. I'd be able to see farther up there from horseback, but I'd also skyline myself. Every little bit of knowledge of camouflage and concealed movement was vital out there, forced by the terrain and the reality of what we were up against.

We were becoming more and more like the Apaches I'd studied back in the day, especially out on those empty plains and without the pressure of Big Marine Corps looking over our shoulders. Too often, back in The World, our ops had been constrained by timelines set during planning and enforced by officers back in the TOC who were more worried about the plan than about the actual situation on the ground. That wasn't an issue here. Time was against us, yes, but that was more a matter of logistics and enemy action. We could afford to be patient, on a tactical level, anyway.

Keeping the terrain between us and the horizon, Rodeffer and I got low and started to work our way up toward the crest of the rise. We kept our heads on a swivel, watching every fold in the ground, careful to scan the skyline to either side before we moved higher with each step. It was slow going, but it was necessary.

The rest of the platoon was below us, gathered in the little hollow at the top of the slide, hands on the horses' muzzles to keep them quiet. They'd been restless most of the entire way through the badlands, for reasons it was easy enough to figure out. We'd been weirded out and disturbed. It had to be far worse for the animals. At least they weren't on the edge of panic anymore.

I froze only a few yards from the crest of the rise, the sandy soil crunching slightly under my gloved hands and my boots. I'd seen a glint of sunlight on metal, somewhere off to the southeast.

Turning my head carefully, I scanned for it. I didn't have to look far.

Those half-circle standards swayed in the wind under the brassy sky, above rank upon rank of footmen and cataphracts. The imperials had indeed come around the flank. They were waiting, though they were still at least three or four miles away.

Where were the Avurs, though?

I kept going, crawling up to the top of the crest on my belly, keeping my head below the tops of the bunchgrass. Peering through the stalks, I scanned the rippling plain ahead.

I couldn't see anything but the ground, the grass, the occasional stand of trees, and the wind stirring up little dust devils through the grass. I'd seen enough of that terrain, though, to know that there could be a battalion hiding out in the low ground. Those plains were not nearly as flat as they looked.

Against every instinct that wanted to get back to the rest of the platoon and make tracks away from that army sitting on the plains to the south, I stayed in place, motionless, watching and waiting. Scouting takes patience, and if you think you've seen everything in a glance, you're probably missing a lot.

There. A bird dipped toward the trees in a hollow about half a mile away, then suddenly veered off. There was someone or something down there. It was probably the Avurs, but it could be just about anything. Including the really freaky stuff.

I didn't *think* the Dullahan would have pushed forward by itself, but it was always a possibility. That was a sobering thought. As Mathghaman had said before, we needed to step carefully.

Of course, as Marines, our first instinct was usually to attack. As Recon Marines, though, we had to consider the possibility that sneaking away and staying out of sight might be the better course. After all, the mission was the Sword of Categyrn, not crossing blades with every horror out of time and space that might stand between us and it. Speed, surprise, and violence of action can accomplish a lot, but sometimes the mission is better served by avoiding compromise and going undetected.

Now that we knew that someone or something was in that hollow, we could avoid it.

After about another twenty minutes or so, I started back down the rise, Rodeffer following after the briefest pause. So far, there was no sign that we'd been spotted. I hoped that held.

Once we were back below the crest, it was a quick scramble to return to the horses. I quickly reported what I'd seen to Gunny, Mathghaman, Galan, and Cailtarni. "We need to stay to the north and keep to the low ground wherever we can." I glanced at the sky. We still had several hours of daylight remaining, which might be a help or might be a hindrance. The horses would probably handle the footing better in the light, but that ran the risk of raising dust that the enemy could see. On the other hand, darkness was not the protection here that it had been back in The World.

Sometimes waiting until dark in this place was as bad as jumping into chummed waters just after a shark ripped somebody's leg off and you can see the fins in the water.

"There will be spies in the sky." Galan looked up at the faint haze overhead grimly. "Our best hope would be to outrun them."

"Bah." Cailtarni spat. "All this running and hiding chafes my hide."

"You would rather face entire regiments of the imperial army with fewer than forty men?" Galan wasn't having it, and Cailtarni shrugged his acquiescence. He'd been complaining, not suggesting a course of action.

It made him an awful lot more like a Marine than a dignified knight, let alone one of the Tuacha. After all, if Marines ain't bitching, there's something wrong, as my first team leader once said.

Mathghaman held his peace, looking to Gunny, who was still chewing on the problem. Finally, with a tightening of his jaw, Gunny nodded. "We'd better make tracks. If the bulk of the army's only a few miles away, our best bet is going to be to open that gap as wide as we can as fast as we can." He looked to the horizon. "Doesn't look like we're going to get any storms to cover our tracks anytime soon, so speed is gonna have to be security. Mount up and get ready to move."

My team took point again. We stayed low as much as we could, working our way around the north side of the rise and shying away from that hollow where I'd seen the bird move away.

Whatever was there, it had fixated us a little too much on that hollow.

With a shrill yell, a dozen Avur riders came up over the next rise, arrows already nocked, turning their horses as they caught sight of us and drew their bows.

Fortunately, while we'd been moving fast, not quite at a gallop, but more than a canter, we'd been ready for contact. I dropped the reins, snatched my rifle up, and fired just as the first arrow left the string.

My bullet took the lead rider high in the chest, punching through his lamellar armor. The iron scales probably slowed it down enough that it just went into his lung instead of punching out his back. He jerked, dropping his bow as he grabbed for his saddle, blood spraying from his mouth and nose a moment later as he slumped in the saddle, already dying.

His arrow had been shot true, though, and it slammed into Rodeffer's chest rig. He doubled over with a grunt, and then I was spurring my mount forward, holding on with my knees as I surged in front of him, firing at another one of the Avurs on the move. It wasn't easy shooting, and trying to control my skittish horse—boy, I missed Myrsky—while I tried to cover Rodeffer was even worse. Fortunately, after everything else we'd been through so far, the horses weren't really bothered by gunfire anymore. Even so, while we had brought a decent amount of ammo, we'd already burned through an awful lot of it. I still needed to rely on immediate fire superiority right then, though, which meant dumping the mag along the top of the rise, hoping I hit a few of them in the process.

I nailed one through the leg, I knew, because I heard the yell, saw the spray of blood, and saw the horse stumble and go down. Then the rest of them were running for their lives, the *crack*s of my bullets around their ears urging them along.

I twisted around in my saddle, but Rodeffer was straightening up, pulling the arrow out of his chest rig, where it was bound up in between two of his mag pouches. "It skipped off a mag and then the mail stopped it." He gasped a little. "Oh, shit, that hurts. Might have bruised a rib."

"Can you ride?" I let my rifle hang and grabbed his reins as Santos and Farrar covered us.

He nodded. "If it's a choice between riding with some pain and staying here to wait for the bad guys to come collect me, you'd better believe I can ride."

I checked where the Avurs had disappeared. The first one I'd shot lay on the top of the rise, staring sightlessly at the sky. The others had vanished, leaving only their dust behind. "Farrar, you've got point. Let's get out of here."

Even as the rest of the platoon caught up, we headed out again, angling even farther north to avoid the Avurs we'd just clashed with.

The chase was on.

* * *

We rode hard until dark. When we halted, we circled up on ansother rise, a rocky outcrop with a small water hole and a good view of the plains for miles around. We'd caught glimpses of the Avurs pacing us, but they'd always kept their distance, as if they were simply shadowing us for the imperials behind them. They were never *quite* far enough away that we couldn't reach out and touch them, but that would still have meant a halt, and we couldn't really afford it.

The army was still behind us, and it had clearly gotten moving, dust rising in a vast pall above, but we were opening the gap. The imperial troops could only travel as fast as the foot soldiers, and so we had them outpaced already.

We could still see their fires, though, glittering in the dark on the horizon behind us. We hadn't gained as much distance as we'd hoped.

It was a cold camp that night. It was a risk, since we had more than just mortal enemies to worry about, but those mortal enemies couldn't be dismissed, either. We crouched in the dark, watching the night on NVGs, waiting for the Avurs to send raiders.

They didn't, though. We couldn't see their fires, but I knew they were out there. Those guys were tough, and we'd already seen that they weren't even stampeded by gunfire. The fact that they *had* retreated so fast as soon as I'd opened fire told me that they were spooked, though, and I didn't think it was necessarily because of us.

While the Avurs and their Peruni masters didn't appear to stir from their camps that night, the plains were not quiet or still.

The wind never stopped, and while its incessant whispers could sometimes sound eerie enough, it was carrying other sounds with it, sounds that weren't made by the enemy huddled around their fires. Howls and screeches echoed across the grasslands, and at least once, on watch, I was sure I saw a pack of wolves circle our hill, black against the lighter green of the plains around us, under the stars.

From what we'd seen so far, I didn't think those were ordinary, natural wolves. From the way the horses were acting, they didn't seem to think so, either.

Nobody got much rest that night.

* * *

So it went for the next week. We managed to keep our distance from the army and even steadily opened the gap. By the time we neared the river that lay between us and Myrgarak, the Borala plateau cloaked with firs and looming blue in the haze in the distance, we'd pulled ahead by a good five more miles. They were still pursuing, guided by their Avur scouts, but they were falling behind.

The Avurs were keeping up, but they still hadn't closed the distance since I'd shot those two just outside the badlands. Either they had decided that discretion was the better part of valor, or they had been told specifically to shadow and report, and nothing else.

Since there were more of them than there were of us, I strongly suspected the latter.

When we reached the low bluffs above the river, though, the Avurs kind of ceased to be an immediate concern.

It was midafternoon, but there seemed to be a deeper gloom down on the riverbank than could be explained by the shadows of the clouds that had gotten thicker overhead over the last day. It looked like twilight under the eaves of the pines—or something similar; like most of the trees in this place, they were darker than any Ponderosas I'd ever seen—and the wind blew colder even as we reined in and prepared to scout out the river crossing.

The trees had gotten more common as we'd gotten closer to the plateau, though they were still mostly short and in isolated stands when they weren't clumped in the low ground, usually close to the thin streams that wound their way toward this river. Now we halted under just such a stand, which provided some concealment from ordinary observers.

From the figures down below, on the far side of the ford, however, there would be no such concealment.

Ten of the Thirty sat on hellish, skeletal horses on the riverbank, swathed in shadow. No two were exactly alike, except that they all held those grisly whips of vertebrae, and none had a head on its shoulders. One carried its head by the hair. Another had it in a sling across its chest. Yet another had mounted it to a pole that it carried in its other hand, the end thrust into a socket on the outside of its stirrup.

The one in the middle had its head suspended in a column of greenish-blue flame that erupted from its gorget.

Their dress and armor ranged from robes not unlike the revenant's in Barmanak, to mail, to lamellar, to bronze-age panoply, to what looked like full plate, to what looked disturbingly like a plate carrier and black cammies. A few carried swords and axes, but every one had that whip of human spines.

All those severed heads were looking across the river at us. Their eyes gleamed red, purple, or icy blue, and right then I was sure that they could see through the trees and the shadows. They knew we were there.

We had to get across that river. This ford was the only place we knew where we could.

And it was held against us by ten of the nastiest things I'd seen since Dragon Mask had summoned Vaelor's horrors out of the Outer Dark.

CHAPTER 28

THEY didn't move, every one of them looking fixedly up at the bluffs. We crept into observation positions, concealed among the trees, and watched them, trying to think of some way to get past them. They might have been statutes, they were so still. Even their horses didn't so much as twitch.

That was probably because the horses were dead, their withered carcasses instead inhabited by something far less natural.

Gunny, Bailey, Galan, and I crouched behind the largest tree, its windswept crown towering high above the rest of the stumpy evergreens, watching, while Conall began to chant, low and melodious, behind us. His voice was quiet, and the sound couldn't travel very far, but it seemed to penetrate anyway. There was a feeling of strength, comfort, and protection in those ancient words, even though I couldn't understand them.

"Ten of them." Galan was trying really hard not to sound scared, but any sane man would be scared, looking at that. There's a certain degree of weirdness that you can get used to, sort of, but creatures that look like men but without their heads tickle a primal sort of fear in the human mind. Those things were chaos and death personified, even if they weren't quite as bad as Vaelor or even the Deep One. To face ten of them was even worse.

"At a guess, I'd say we're going to have a hard time shooting our way through these guys." Gunny said it as Mathghaman and Bearrac joined us. "I do wonder what the mortars might do, though."

"Little enough." Mathghaman smoothed his beard with one hand, his eyes narrowed as he studied the enemy below. The Dullahans were alone, holding the ford by themselves. No Peruni troops or any other monsters or goblins backed them up. Just the ten of them.

Something told me, even from a distance, that ten of those things would probably be more than enough.

Still, we couldn't just sit there and watch them forever. Even as Conall continued to chant, dispelling some of the raw, visceral terror that accompanied the sight of those things, we had to plan and move, as quickly as possible. The longer we stayed there, the closer the Peruni army and their Avur auxiliaries got.

That might be the plan, after all. We were caught between the hammer and the anvil, unless we kept going north and tried to find another crossing.

Could we cross elsewhere without those abominations down there catching us, anyway?

"We've got to either punch through or break contact." Gunny wasn't briefing so much as he was thinking out loud. He looked at Galan. "Do we know of any other crossings?"

The knight shrugged. "Who can tell, anymore? There is an old story about a lone warrior holding a bridge to the north of here, during one of the civil wars among the lords of Commagan, but who can say whether it was not thrown down into the river long since?"

"*Can* we break contact?" Bailey's eyes were fixed on the specters on the other side of the river. "They know we're here."

"We shall see." Mathghaman was once again the quiet and phlegmatic King's Champion. "If Tigharn wills it." He drew back from the tree trunk. "We should mount and get moving."

I reflected on those words for a moment as I moved back to the team and our horses. I'd come up through the ranks in a Marine Corps strongly influenced by the wars in Afghanistan, Iraq, and Syria. We all knew the Islamist enemy and the ordinary Muslims they moved through and often terrorized, and the "Insh'allah" attitude that pervaded that culture. It had become synonymous with a carelessness and a laziness that we'd all despised. On the surface, Mathghaman's calm, quiet, "If Tigharn wills it," might seem to be much the same thing.

Yet it wasn't. We knew the Tuacha as well as any ordinary man can know one of their tribe by then, and we knew Mathghaman to be a careful, thoughtful man who never moved without having a plan, not to mention multiple contingencies in mind. No, those words were more than a dismissive surrender to the vagaries of fate. They were an acknowledgement that try as we might, nothing is entirely within our control, and that sometimes you've just got to roll with the punches as best you can.

As with everything else, there's a balance to be struck. The Tuacha were better at striking that balance of planning, preparation, and simple acceptance that the world and everything in and above it is bigger than they are than anyone else I'd ever met.

I quickly outlined the plan. Farrar was up in a tree, binoculars to his eyes, watching our back trail. When he scrambled down, he nodded that he'd heard and understood. "The bad guys haven't slowed down. I think you're right; they want to catch us in a pincer movement between them and those freaks on the river."

I swung into the saddle. A year before, I never would have thought I'd be so comfortable on a horse. "Well, we'd better ride fast, then."

Gurke's team was already on point, leading out through the scattered stands of trees, trying to get far enough from the bluffs to conceal our movement from the figures of the Dullahans down on the riverbank. They were moving quickly, but not quite at a gallop. We still had a long way to go, even longer on the way back, and killing the horses from overexertion didn't enter into our calculations.

Unfortunately, the enemy always gets a vote, too.

With an eerie keening, all ten spectral horses suddenly leaped across the river and darted up the bluffs, cresting the hill above the river in moments. They hardly seemed to touch the ground, and there was an eerie sort of black smoke around their hooves and pouring from their nostrils. A bone whip cracked, though the Dullahans themselves were deadly silent.

Gurke's team was closest, and Gurke's horse suddenly bolted with a scream of terror. If we hadn't practiced riding for the better part of the last six months, he would have been unseated, but he stayed in the saddle, barely, his weapons flapping around him as he held on for dear life. In moments, the other horses were joining the stampede, as our worst fears from working with the animals came true.

Cailtarni was already spurring his own mount, pulling his spare horse along behind him, riding hell bent for leather to catch up with the team. I didn't think he was running from fear, except for what might happen to the men or the horses. The old man was rough around the edges and hard to take sometimes, but he had guts, and he rarely thought of himself first.

I put my heels to my own mount, quickly seeing what Cailtarni had already figured out. If we got scattered, we were done. Those monstrosities would be able to hunt us down at leisure.

Not that they couldn't already, but better to face them as a unit, anyway.

Hooves thundering, those horses that hadn't panicked yet awfully close to it, we charged out of the trees and after Gurke's team, even as the Dullahans swept toward us from the bluffs. Those grisly whips cracked again, reaching out far enough that one of them parted the air over Orava's head. He ducked close to his horse's neck, holding on tight to keep the animal from completely losing it. His horse's eyes were rolling, its ears back as it galloped away, conscious of little but the screaming need to get away from those unearthly *things*.

Cailtarni was catching up to Gurke's team, despite their head start and the mind-shredding panic that had their animals trying blindly to just get *away*. He was an older man, but he'd been riding since he'd been knee high to a grasshopper, and his horses were presumably better trained and better attuned to him than the loaners we'd been riding for the last few weeks were to us. He came alongside Gurke's horse and seized the reins, hauling back and gaining some modicum of control without slowing much.

By then, though, most of our beasts were almost out of their heads. Those whips cracked again, and the Dullahans' horses screeched even louder, their hoofbeats drumming on the grassy ground despite the fact that they still didn't seem to quite be touching it. We were just trying to ride the whirlwind at that point, keeping our horses under just enough control that we hopefully didn't get thrown or scattered.

I drove hard toward the flank, trying to get between the Dullahans and those of us whose horses were really losing their heads. Whether that was going to work or not was debatable, but I had to try. Despite my unfavorable comparisons of the roan under me with Myrsky, the stout Menninkai mountain horse I'd ridden in the north, months before, he was doing his best and hadn't completely freaked. Yet.

One of those whips *crack*ed over my head, sounding more like a bullet than a whip. I risked a glance over my shoulder to see the Dullahan in the Bronze Age panoply, its head suspended in a column of blue fire above its shoulders, grinning maniacally, its eyes burning like points of blue-green flame. It cracked that whip at me again, and I ducked, barely avoiding the tip as it snapped just over my head. Somehow, I knew that if it had been making any noise at all, it would have been laughing with a demonic, insane cackle.

We fled upriver, into the deepening woods and the hills, and hell followed after.

CHAPTER 29

IT took several miles of rough terrain and the exhaustion brought on by running that far to finally bring some of the horses to a quivering, sweat-lathered halt. Gurke's horse collapsed as soon as it stopped, and he barely got clear with a jump and a curse.

We had halted on a narrow shoulder halfway up a tall ridge, dotted with more trees and outcrops of rock, within sight and earshot of a thunderous waterfall where the river we'd been paralleling on our headlong flight plunged down from the shoulders of the plateau that was now closer and seemingly even taller. We couldn't see the ruins of Myrgarak from there, but we probably still had a couple of days to go before we reached it.

What we could see was the imperial army of Ar-Annator on the plain below us, still advancing after us. They might have picked up some reinforcements, since the army looked bigger than it had before. Or maybe that was just perspective, since we had a better view from up on that mountainside.

Strangely, it appeared that the Dullahans had joined them instead of keeping up the pursuit. For no reason we'd been able to see, they'd fallen back as we'd run ahead of them, more trying to keep up with the panicked horses than anything else. Diarmodh had twisted around in his saddle and taken a shot at one of them, and, knowing Diarmodh, I was sure he'd hit it. It hadn't had any more effect than I think any of us had expected.

Now that we had a breather and could take stock, Gunny called a short halt and we set security while the rest of us figured out what we'd lost and where to go from here.

"They didn't fall back because they're scared of us." I glowered down into the valley below and at the cloud of dust rising above that mass of men, horses, and worse.

"No, they did not." There was a certainty to those words, but if Mathghaman had an idea of why our hellish pursuers had seemingly given up the chase, he wasn't immediately forthcoming. I'd learned to get used to that. A little.

Cailtarni had joined us at the edge of the cliff. "They're toying with us." The fury in his voice was palpable as he folded his arms across his coat of scales and glared down into the valley. His graying hair and beard had gotten scragglier as we'd gone on through the wilds. "Damn them! What are they playing at?"

When Mathghaman didn't offer an answer, I ventured my own theory, as half-formed as it was. "For some reason, they're not sure that they'll be able to get the Sword of Categyrn themselves, at least not without taking losses they're not willing to endure. They're hoping that we find it and try to run for Cor Legear with it, at which point they think they can ambush us and take it and the Sword of Iudicael from us. We must seem like easier prey than whatever might be guarding the Sword."

Cailtarni had looked over at me with a frown as I'd spoken, and when I finished, he flashed a fierce grin under his beard and gripped my shoulder, hard. "Ah, but with you Marines and our Tuacha friends, we have a bite far beyond our size! Let them try!"

I glanced at Gunny, who was still watching the enemy beneath us. He scanned the whole plain as far as we could see, and if he took any pride or amusement in Cailtarni's boisterous optimism about our capabilities—or our chances—he didn't show it. "The other possibility is that they *don't* know where the Sword is, but because we're out here with the Sword of Iudicael, then maybe we do. They know they've got us outnumbered, and those headless freaks know we can't hurt them." He finally glanced at Mathghaman, just for a moment. "Well, not with most of our weapons."

"That seems most likely." Mathghaman turned his gaze up toward the plateau above. Unless I missed my guess, the Borala Plateau stood a good four thousand feet above sea level. Still pretty low compared to some of the places I'd lived, worked, and fought in, but awfully high after we'd spent so long at sea level.

"We've still got to get across that river, regardless." Bailey nodded toward the waterfall. "Which brings up another question. If they really just wanted to keep track of us, then why push us away from the ford?"

"It's a good question," Gunny allowed, looking back down toward the ford and the twisted foothills of the plateau, dark with scree and more patches of woods. Without speculating, he turned back toward the ridge above us. "I guess we're gonna find out, aren't we?"

With one more backward look at the enemy forces still following, and a glance up at the forbidding silhou-

ette of the plateau above us, nearly black against the setting sun, we moved back to the horses.

* * *

We'd lost three more of the pack animals on the way up,
either to broken legs from the rocky terrain or simply to
exhaustion. Pursued by the Dullahans, we hadn't been able
to stop and retrieve any of the gear and supplies. That was
going to cut our capabilities still more, and we were a long
way from home or relief.

We'd been in worse situations, but not by much.

Switching off to maintain security, we swapped
mounts, those of us who still could. The spares were all
tired, though not nearly as exhausted as the horses that
had run like hell with armed and armored riders on their
backs. We'd still have to slow down if we were going to
keep any of them alive.

I wasn't convinced we weren't going to be on foot,
eating the horses for lack of anything else, before this
was over. I wasn't looking forward to it, given the sheer
number of miles we had to cover to get back to Cor
Legear, but the farther we went and the more supplies
we went through or lost, the more likely it became.

There was nothing for it, though. The mission was
still unfinished, and this wasn't some random half-baked
idea put forward by an officer whose hide wasn't on the
line but just needed something for his Marines to do
for the last two weeks of a deployment. The Sword of
Categyrn might not be quite the superweapon that some
might think it was, but it was still a powerful symbol,
and, if things were stirring the way Mathghaman said

they were, then those symbols might turn out to be vital in the days to come.

I thought about that as I fell in behind Gunny and we rode higher up the ridge, which turned out to be more of a tableland on the shoulder of the plateau, still dotted with dark stands of trees amid grass turned golden in the late summer.

While most people don't think of enlisted Marines as being "big picture" thinkers, the fact of the matter is that most of us really are. Some of it is simply because the reality of working in a small team means that you can accomplish the commander's intent a lot better if you understand it, as well as the context that you're working in. *Especially* if you're in an irregular warfare environment like Syria had been.

Some of that also comes from the realities of a largely NCO-led force. Countries like Russia might be happy to have their soldiers dumb, vicious, and obedient, but when those are the guys who are going to be squad leaders and platoon sergeants, who might have to handle situations on their own, then you want a bit more.

So, I was thinking about the big picture as we rode deeper into the high country, still following the river, which was narrower and faster up there.

I didn't have a lot of the pieces, but something was definitely happening, and we were somehow caught up in it. Someone or something had drawn us through time and space to this place, and that wasn't ordinary, even in a world overrun with sorcery and monsters. The vampire Unsterbanak had known we'd come from somewhere else, and he had wanted to know why. He'd taken Sister Sebeal and the Staff of Nechtan specifically to bait a trap for us, just to find out. He'd fully intended to drain our blood and kill us, or worse, but he also wanted to know who or what had brought us there. We weren't there by sheer happenstance.

At least, I didn't think so. Mathghaman didn't, either, and I tended to take his opinion pretty seriously.

Furthermore, the Deep Ones had tried to assault the Isle of Riamog again, one of the old and terrible Outsiders had nearly gotten loose, and now the Empire of Ar-Annator, one of the big geopolitical heavy hitters in this part of the world, had awakened the Thirty. That hadn't meant much to me before, but after seeing those headless abominations, it sure meant something now.

Something was happening. Something big, by all accounts. I didn't know much of the history of the Thirty, but if they'd been The Summoner's first servants, and hadn't been seen in hundreds of years, then their return was a big deal.

I looked up at the plateau above us. I wasn't just woolgathering; I'd learned a long time before how to think things through on the move while still staying alert and maintaining security. My eyes moved from river to rock to tree, systematically scanning from near to far and back again while my mind chewed on the problem.

I didn't think we were the fulfillment of some ancient prophecy. If we were, for one thing, Mathghaman would probably have said something about it.

Or maybe he wouldn't have. The Tuacha could be pretty closed-mouthed.

Still, I suspected that we wouldn't have taken quite the horrific casualties we'd endured since crossing through the mists if we were some long-foretold band of

Chosen Ones. No, I didn't know why we'd been drawn here, but I didn't think it was that.

I wondered, as we rode higher, if I'd ever find out at all, or if I'd die in this strange place without any answers.

CHAPTER 30

WE got a couple more miles along the tableland before nightfall. The rear-guard element, mainly made up of Orava's team, reported that they thought they'd spotted Avur scouts a handful of times, but if so, the nomads were keeping their distance and trying to stay hidden. We lit fires that night, despite the risk.

The Avurs weren't the only things that we'd seen moving through the woods.

We did spot a bridge across the river just before we halted. It appeared to be intact, but it was getting too dark to see it well enough. We would have to wait until morning to be sure.

"I should take Baldinus and go check it out. It's less than a mile." Bailey already had his NVGs down, even as Applegate got the fire started. The ferrous rod fire starters we'd all carried in our on-body survival kits had come in a lot handier than we'd ever thought they would back on the *Makin Island*.

"It's less than a mile, but it's also well after dark, and I don't know if you noticed, but we've got shadow people following us as well as the Avurs." Gunny shook his head as Applegate's sparks caught in the tinder and he bent to blow gently on the embers. "I know we still have some old habits about the cover of darkness, but it's not likely to be a good idea here. We'll wait until sunup."

Bailey blew a deep breath out of his nose, but he knew better than to object when Gunny used that tone of voice. We might not have argued it out, but Gunny had decided that we'd "slapped the table," and that was that. The plan was as he'd outlined, and we were going to stick to it.

Bearrac loomed out of the dark. "Do not worry, Sean." He pointed south, back the way we'd come. "The Avurs will not stir far from their fires in this country, either." Sure enough, the reddish glimmer of another fire flickered through the trees in the distance. We might be above the haunted plains and badlands around Barmanak, but Myrgarak had still fallen in the madness and chaos of the collapse of the Commagan Empire. These places were weird, and while I hadn't noticed the strange vertigo that had occasionally afflicted us down on the plains, there was still an unsettling quality to the high country that didn't ever quite go away. It only got worse once the sun went down.

It was very quiet up there. The strange noises we'd heard on the wind down on the plains had stopped, and the wind had died down to nothing. The fire crackled loudly in the deathly silence.

My team had first watch, and we set in to cover the approaches as the others went down for a much-needed rest, once the horses were tended to. We'd found a stand of trees to tie them to that also provided some shelter if something came out of the dark to try to eat them.

It was odd. This country was spooky and dangerous, but it was open enough that we didn't have the same worries about big flesh-eating monsters that we'd had in the woods and mountains in the north. That might change as we got deeper into the high country, but the brush and tree barriers we'd needed up there didn't seem that important here. We were still set up inside a couple of the thicker stands of trees, and on a slight rise, well back from the river. It was decent defensive ground, just in case.

I scanned the woods and meadows through my NVGs, glad enough that I could hold security while sitting against a tree. If I'd been more fatigued, that might not have been a good idea, but my brain was still going a mile a minute on all the questions that the Dullahans' presence had brought up, so I wasn't too worried about passing out.

Riding is different from rucking, anyway. Sure, I was stiff and sore and tired, but it wasn't quite the same sort of stiff, sore, and tired.

Movement. A shadow slipped through the trees between us and the Avurs' fire. I saw it as only an eclipse of the flame for a moment, but as I followed it I saw it was a roughly human silhouette, much closer than the fire, gliding rather than walking across the clearing between where I'd first seen it and the next stand of trees, much closer to our position. Too close.

I flicked on my PEQ-16 and shone the laser at it. We hadn't used our lasers much since coming here. For one thing, we hadn't trained much with them, on the assumption that we'd be potentially fighting the Russians, and therefore passive IR was better than active. They were still zeroed, though, which meant that we could be confident that we'd hit anything we pointed them at.

Not that a shadow man would be hurt by an ordinary bullet, but in this case, the figure stopped as soon as I put that bright, green dot on it.

That's right, punk. I see you.

While it was only a shadow, without visible features, I suddenly got the impression that it had turned to look at me. I wondered, then, just how smart pointing the laser at it had ultimately been. I remembered what one of these things had done to Vihattu.

I sent up a wordless prayer that I hadn't just screwed us all with my bad temper. Fortunately, my threat had about the same effect that it had had on the blurry thing that had stalked us that first day in the Land of Ice and Monsters. All of a sudden, that shadow just seemed to melt into the ground and was gone.

Sometimes, you've just got to be meaner than them. "Good" doesn't necessarily mean "nice."

The entire exchange had happened in absolute silence. Come to think of it, I hadn't heard the shadow men make any sound so far, though there had been enough going on in Barmanak that I hadn't noticed before.

The night was just as oppressively silent as it had been since the sun had gone down. I could hear my pulse and my breathing. It was downright eerie. No night birds, no wind, nothing. It was as if everything but us in the entire area was dead.

Dead, or hiding.

As if to punctuate that thought, I saw a flicker of light out of the corner of my eye. Twisting my head, I looked up toward the top of the plateau, toward Myrgarak itself, still out of sight beyond the high ground and the forests on its flanks.

At first, I couldn't see anything out of the ordinary. The plateau was dark and silent, looming black against the sky, visible only as a deeper darkness that eclipsed those few stars I could see through the scattered clouds. Everything was motionless and quiet.

I turned back to my sector. Not because I didn't think there had been anything up there, but because I was getting paranoid as hell, and I had a sudden hunch that maybe whatever I'd seen in my peripheral vision had been a distraction to get me looking the wrong way. Especially in a world where sorcery could conjure up all sorts of illusions, it was a real possibility.

Yet the meadow in front of me was just as empty and still as it had been since that shadow man had disappeared into the ground.

I caught another flicker. This time, when I looked up, I saw what it was.

An eerie light was dancing on the rim of the ridgeline above us. It was faintly blue out of the corner of my eye, though it was as green as any other light through my NVGs. It moved from treetop to rock outcrop, came partway down the steep mountainside, then went back up.

Something about the way it moved was somehow even more disturbing than the presence of the light itself. It didn't move smoothly, but seemed to fritz from place to place, like a video was glitching out and skipping forward.

I tore my eyes away from it and checked the meadow again. Despite the freaky way it was moving, there was something dangerously mesmerizing about that light.

Whatever it was, though, it didn't appear to be a distraction to cover for an attack. Not yet.

When I glanced up once more, just to make sure it wasn't coming down on us, it was gone.

Gooseflesh went up on my arms as I returned to my watch, glancing at the stars I could see to try to figure out how much longer I had to go. I didn't know what had happened up there, but I didn't think it was anything good.

* * *

We approached the bridge through the early morning mists.

The silence had persisted with the dawn, and every creak of saddle leather, every clink of equipment, every hoofbeat sounded deafeningly loud. We were still alert, weapons out and eyes scanning every bush, every rock, every shadow, just in case. We'd been around enough that none of us trusted the apparent stillness.

The bridge was a solid, blocky structure, the arches thick and brutal, without much artistry. It looked almost like concrete, except that no concrete I was familiar with would have lasted this long. The road that had led up to the bridge was all but gone, only the faintest traces still visible in the dirt and the grass.

Bailey's team had already moved up on foot through the rocks and brush on one flank and were holding overwatch. If anything stirred on either side of the bridge, we'd have advance warning.

Whether it died when you shot it or stabbed it was another problem that we'd have to deal with once the threat was identified.

Galan, Cailtarni, and the other Galel knights had demanded that they take point across the bridge. We'd been out front for most of this quest so far, and it had to chafe on men who were the warrior elite of their society. They could fight, too; we knew that. They just weren't quite as well equipped to solve problems at a distance as we were.

Gunny hadn't argued. After all, Bailey, Applegate, Baldinus, and Synar were covering them.

While the rest of us spread out, weapons ready, Galan led the way out onto the bridge. His horse's hooves rang on the stones, the short banner hanging from his spear limp in the utter stillness of the morning. Sunlight turned golden by the mists gleamed off his helmet and armor as he rode out into the center of the bridge and halted.

It wasn't just bravado. His armor was proof against most arrows—at least the non-cursed kind—and he had space to maneuver. There was a fair bit of brush on the far side of the bridge, brush that might conceal an ambush.

His horsehair crest shifted from side to side as he scanned the far side. After a moment, when nothing moved and no sound revealed anyone or anything lying in wait, he spurred his horse forward, Cailtarni and Cinid riding behind him, shoulder to shoulder, the other four in a double column behind them.

If it seems like they were riding in a column right into a choke point, that was exactly what they were doing. Unfortunately, that's the nature of bridge crossings, and at least we could easily engage anything on the other side as soon as it popped up.

I lifted my rifle as something moved higher up the hill beyond the riverbank. For a moment, it looked like a man. Or a shadow man. I couldn't see much. I snapped my weapon to my shoulder and peered through the scope.

Just then, a raven flapped into the air with a harsh *caw* that echoed off the mountains beyond and winged its way toward the top of the plateau.

I wasn't alone in my suspicions. Three of us shot the thing a split second later. At least, we tried. It kept flapping through the air toward the plateau and Myrgarak as if nothing had happened.

Somebody was up there, and that somebody knew we were coming.

There wasn't much more we could do about it. The Galel knights reached the far side without incident, spreading out into a battle line higher up on the bank, leaving enough room for the rest of us to get across and deploy on the far side.

While Bailey and his team held their position, the rest of us rode across and prepared to climb up that mountain toward Myrgarak.

Hopefully we'd find our objective there, before the imperial army behind us caught up.

CHAPTER 31

IT was a hard ride up the mountain. There *had* been a road, once, but erosion, landslides, and fallen trees had long since turned it into an obstacle course. I'd been up worse mountains, not to mention considerably taller ones, but that didn't make it easy or comfortable.

Fortunately, we only had the terrain to worry about as we ascended. The mountainside was silent and while it still felt like we were being watched, we saw no movement, and nothing opposed our advance.

It still took the entire day to get to the top. We had eyes on the imperial army down below almost the entire way, though they seemed to have found a different route. They were crossing the river at the ford the Dullahans had chased us away from, and their advance elements were already nearing the shoulder of the mountains a few miles to our south. I wondered if that wasn't precisely why the Dullahans had held the ford. It was easier to get an army across there than via the bridge.

I also wondered if they didn't have an easier route up the mountain, where they could get more men and horses up the slope faster. I wondered if we weren't going to face the entire Peruni army at the top.

But then, why let us get away in the first place, when the Dullahans could have conceivably torn us to pieces at the ford?

The slope got steeper, and the remains of the road vanished just short of the top. We all had to dismount and lead the horses, and my team handed ours off while we pushed up to the crest on foot, angling off to one side and making for a tall mound of rocks beneath wind-twisted, lightning-blasted trees, where we might be able to get good eyes on the higher ground.

Being able to leave our rucks on our horses made the movement a little easier than it might have been, but footing was treacherous, between loose rocks and thick, tough brush beneath the clumps of trees. We still had to do our utmost to stay quiet, too, which was hard when one of us tripped or had a rock roll out from underfoot every few yards.

Finally, we made it into position, carefully checking the crevices in the rocks before we climbed up to the higher perch where we could overwatch the top.

And there we saw Myrgarak.

It was less a ruin than a mound of rubble. It took some looking to see where walls and towers might have once stood, and after some careful examination, I could still see plenty of darkened openings that probably led deep into that hill. Judging by how far away we still were, some of them were pretty big.

There was a lot of activity, too. I couldn't see who or what was running around at that distance, but that mound looked like a disturbed anthill.

Myrgarak was far from abandoned, it seemed.

"Five, this is One. Be advised, we've got a lot of movement in the city."

"Good copy, One." Gunny didn't sound especially surprised or stressed. After all, I don't think any of us figured that any ruined city in this cursed land would be nice and empty and quiet.

We stayed in place and watched as the rest of the platoon came up over the crest and onto the relatively flat top of the plateau. So far, no welcoming party had come out onto the roughly two-mile open plain between us and the remains of the city to meet us. So far.

That crow flapped overhead with another mocking *caw*. We were expected.

And there was a lot of open ground between us and the city.

* * *

The plateau wasn't actually quite as flat as it looked, though it had been, once. Whatever had happened here, it had opened massive cracks in the plateau, cracks that we had to get around. They were too wide to jump the horses across, particularly the pack animals. Meanwhile, as we got closer, we started to see just what was moving around in the wreckage of Myrgarak.

Two short, stumpy creatures, that looked a lot like some weird cross between pigs and apes, suddenly burst out of a low line of brush along what had once been the road leading to Myrgarak. They didn't attack, but ran squealing toward the city. Bailey snapped his rifle up, but Bearrac put out a hand to restrain him.

"Do not waste the bullet." He squinted at the flee-ing creatures. "They seem little more than beasts, and whoever their master is already knows we are here." He pointed up at the sky. "Unless you thought that was sim-ply another crow?"

Bailey glanced up at the dark winged silhouette above us as another *caw* drifted down out of the sky. That thing seemed to be laughing at us. "I haven't assumed anything is *just* another crow since the first time we went up against shamans."

The creatures were on the other side of another crack, so we couldn't run them down and try to capture them, even if they'd spoken any language that any of us could even try to speak. The noises they were making, despite the fact that they were running on two feet, their long, heavy arms pumping like crazy, didn't sound especially intelligent. Bearrac was right. Those things seemed a lot more like animals than thinking beings.

Weird, but hardly the weirdest thing we'd run into.

I looked down into the crack as we rode around it, but only saw blackness below. Whatever had happened to open the ground on this plateau, it had been something big.

Of course, Myrgarak was in far worse shape than Barmanak had been, so that probably stood to reason. What sorcery had been unleashed here? Even Ground Zero for a nuclear bomb wouldn't look like this.

That impression only got stronger as we got closer to the city. Some of the stones were *melted*, but not just melted as if they'd been exposed to high heat. They were twisted and warped, some stretched, others flattened. It was almost as if the laws of physics had ceased to apply for a few moments, and this was what was left when the madness passed.

I shook the thought off as we rode up from the open ground and into the weirdly twisted rubble, advancing in a wedge toward the first cave. As I looked around, I frowned. Something was bugging me about this.

The last chapel. If the Sword was in such a place, it would have to still be somewhat intact, and nothing about this ruin looked like it fit the bill. Unlike Barmanak, which still at least had the ziggurat standing against the east wall, there were no intact structures at all that I could see. Just melted, smashed walls, open to the sky, and the caves.

The caves were the part we needed to worry about.

Six of the stumpy, pig-faced creatures came rushing out of that first cave as we passed it, squealing and brandishing spears that were basically just long sticks with fire-hardened points. One of them hit Eoghain in the side, though it couldn't hope to penetrate his mail.

He didn't even bother to shoot it, but simply swept his sword from its scabbard and split its skull. Another one swung at Bearrac, and he kicked the spear aside as he wheeled his horse. He didn't even need to draw a weapon, as his horse reared and dashed the creature's brains out with its hooves.

Then Bailey shot the third one, and all hell broke loose.

The gunshot *crack*ed loudly, echoing across the ruins, and the pig-ape-man tumbled away with a pained squeal, curling up around the wound, shuddering out its death as it huddled on the stony ground.

The rest quickly panicked and dashed back into the cave, disappearing into the dark with panicked squeals.

The echoes hadn't even died when a new sound rumbled out of the depths and the hillside quivered, just a little. The horses reacted, getting even more nervous than they had been before, and it took some work to keep them moving forward. They'd started to get used to the suppressed gunfire, but the weird, sorcerous stuff still wore on their nerves, especially after weeks of travel through this eerie, haunted country.

With a cascade of rocks, one of the real rulers of Myrgarak—what was left of it—burst out of the cave just ahead of and above us.

We'd met a giant before, though that five-eyed, frost-covered, skeletal eldritch abomination in the pass in the Land of Ice and Monsters hadn't been anything like this.

Easily twenty feet tall, it was proportioned like a man, though its head was slightly too large. It was built like a powerlifter, with ash gray skin, and completely hairless. Its head was a little more square than a man's, with small ears set high up near the crown of its skull, a wide, lipless gash of a mouth, a faintly piggish nose, and small, mean eyes that glared down at us as it came out of the cave and straightened up.

Actually, it didn't seem to see us at first. It was looking around, apparently trying to find the source of all the noise, when its eyes alighted on the knights, a ray of sunlight having chosen just that moment to pierce the clouds and shine off Galan's helmet.

Opening its massive maw to reveal crooked, jagged teeth, it roared its hate and came storming down the slope from its cave.

The horses started to freak, kept in line purely by strength of will, while I threw my leg over the saddle and slid to the ground, dashing to cover behind a warped, knife-edged rock formation just ahead. Not that I expected that thing to shoot at me, but I wanted *something* between me and it. Even if it was just a strangely twisted, upswept chunk of rock that might break its hand when it tried to hit me.

I didn't bother trying to shoot it in the chest. That thing had a chest the size of a bison. I *might* hit something vital, but its head was a much more likely target. I put my red dot on its forehead and squeezed the trigger.

I hit it. I know I hit it. It recoiled, slowing its onward rush and stumbling as it slapped at its head like a mosquito had just bitten it.

"Oh, hell."

Santos laid into it with a long burst, but our rounds weren't doing much. That thing had a hide thicker than a rhino's, and while 7.62 NATO is a good, hard-hitting round, I wouldn't want to hunt elephants with it. Or giants.

Time for something bigger.

Our bullets *were* throwing the giant off balance, a little. Imagine getting swarmed by hornets. That seemed to be about what this thing was feeling, and it waved its hands in front of its face as it took a step back, stepped on a sharp-edged rock, and staggered. It caught itself, leaned forward and roared its fury.

I dashed back to my horse and yanked the M79 out of its scabbard alongside my saddle.

I wasn't the greatest shot with the thumper, I'll admit. The odds that I was going to get that egg into its mouth were pretty slim. And I didn't. I hit it in the cheek, the grenade detonating with a flash and a puff of black and gray smoke.

The explosion hit that thing like a punch in the jaw with a claw hammer. It didn't kill it, but it tore the hell out of the side of its face. It put a massive hand to the wound, then looked down at me with its one remaining good eye, blood and fluid streaming from the other, bellowed its hate, and lunged for me.

Santos and Farrar were pouring fire into it, punching dimpled holes in its upper chest and face, but it was too enraged and didn't even notice. This time, though, I was dead on with the thumper.

As it roared, I lobbed the 40mm grenade into that cavernous maw and threw myself flat, in case it managed to take a swipe at me. Its arms had to be ten feet long, and it was coming on fast.

It was right at the ragged edge of the grenade's arming distance, but it was enough. The HE grenade hit the back of its throat and went off, blowing a massive chunk of the base of its skull and its spine out its back while it belched smoke and blood as frag tore the inside of its mouth apart.

The giant dropped like a felled tree, hitting the rocky ground hard enough to smash one of the few remaining walls that was still standing.

I gulped air, only then realizing how hard my heart was beating. That thing's shattered skull lay less than three feet away from my cover. That had been a little too close.

A harsh, guttural, hate-filled laugh echoed across the ruins. Looking up, I saw another giant, similar enough to the first that they might have been brothers, looming above another cluster of ruins a little bit higher up the mound and about another five hundred yards away. It was pointing at the fallen giant's corpse and laughing spitefully, its scornful mirth a thunderstorm rumble that I could feel in my chest from even that far away.

Then it was coming for us, striding over the ruins and the shattered, twisted stones, cracking its knuckles as it came.

We were ready this time, though, and three 40mm rounds hammered at it, gouging pits in its flesh and knocking it around like it was getting hammered by the world's biggest prizefighter. None of them penetrated deep enough for that knockout punch, though.

"Fuck this." I barely heard Bailey swear over the racket of the detonating grenades and the giant's roars of fury, but then he was at my packhorse, unstrapping the long weapons case that contained the .50.

There had been a few places I could have used the weapon on this trip, but it had always seemed just a little too long and heavy for the situation, or else we had gotten stuck in before I could get to it. Bailey wasn't letting that stop him, though, even as my horse shifted and tried to rear, held in place by the rocks more than Rodeffer's hands on the reins.

"Hey!" That *was* my rifle, after all.

"You're not using it!" He hauled the *Coira Ansec*'s facsimile of the Barret M107 clear, reached back into the case for a mag, slapped it home, racked the bolt, and then threw the rifle over a rock as the giant staggered again under a renewed volley of 40mm fire.

Bailey proceeded to dump half the mag into the giant. The big RAUFOSS rounds slammed into it with flashes and smaller puffs of smoke, blood, and pulverized bone. The 40mm was doing a job on it, but the explosives didn't have quite the penetration of the .50 caliber rounds. They tore bloody holes through the giant's hand, throat, and jaw before one blew through its eye. That one must have hit something vital. It was a "circuitry kill," a central nervous system hit. The giant crumpled, folding like a cheap suit and sending a cloud of dust billowing into the air as it hit the ground with an impact that made the little rocks at my feet jump.

"You're cleaning that." I didn't look at Bailey as I circled behind him, moving up to higher ground for a better position. I could hear more booming shouts in the distance, most of them as full of hate and contempt as that last giant's laughter had been. "You know the rules."

Bailey didn't leave his position or put the big rifle back. "Like I said, you weren't using it." I paused just long enough to give him a look. "Fine. I'll clean it. Happy? You got one, I got one. Just because I had to borrow your .50 isn't any reason to get snippy."

"We need to get to the top of this hill." Gunny was suddenly beside me, having moved almost invisibly while we were focused on the giants, as he did. "If the Sword is here, it's got to be somewhere near the citadel, right?" He looked at Mathghaman and Bearrac as he said it.

"One might think." Mathghaman scanned the ruins above us, and the caves that had been scooped out of the detritus. Another giant's voice rose in a hooting call. There were words in that shout, but there was no way I could understand them. "Getting there might be more easily said than done. Giants such as these hate each other as much as they hate us and their smaller servants, so they will not work together, but they are formidable, and will not lightly let us move through their territory, now that they know we are here."

Almost as if it had heard him, another giant loomed out of the wreckage above us, climbing over a long ridge of debris and fallen walls that had cascaded down the mound from higher up. This one was a little bigger, its skin somewhat green instead of the pale ash gray of the first two.

I looked over at Bailey as I fed another 40mm egg into the M79 and snapped the action closed. "Tag team?"

"Sure." He hefted the big rifle, pivoting to bring it to bear as I started to clamber up the hillside of debris toward the oncoming giant. My rifle was slung on my back, the Sword of Iudicael at my side. Farrar and Santos flanked me to either side, rifle and machinegun held ready, just in case.

It was a good thing, too, because as I got to the top of that little mound, I came within sight of a smaller cave. Eyes glittered from inside, and a moment later, four of the pig-men came swarming out of the cave, swinging clubs and fire-hardened spears.

They got about ten feet before Santos raked them with a roaring burst that cut two of them off at the knees before he walked his rounds up into the third one's chest and the fourth's face.

That giant was coming on fast, though. I slid to the bottom of the hill in a cloud of dust while Farrar shifted to cover the cave entrance, brought the M79 to my shoulder, and lobbed a grenade at the giant with a *thunk*.

Bailey had better range with my .50 cal, so he beat me to the shot. His first round hit the giant in the chest, making it stagger. My grenade might have taken it in the throat except that when it stepped back under the impact of that big RAUFOSS round, it ducked its head a little.

The ogive hit it right on the crown of its massive skull and detonated.

For a moment, I thought that maybe I'd managed to kill it with that one shot. It reeled and fell as the smoke cleared, crashing onto its face in the rock and dirt with an impact that shook the ground. A moment later, though, it groaned, one massive hand coming up to grope at the rock and dirt, trying to pull itself up.

We'd covered half the distance to it as it started to lift its head, black blood leaking from the gouge that my grenade had blown in its forehead. I'd reloaded, but we were too close for me to want to crank off another HE grenade at that distance.

So, I slung the thumper, letting it bang against my leg as I sprinted up the hill as best I could, drawing the Sword as I went. This was going to get hairy, but I was committed.

When in doubt, attack.

The giant blinked through the blood streaming down its face, and its piggish eyes focused on me. In a moment, they sharpened, and I could *feel* the hatred there.

Its other hand slammed down on the ground, closer to its body, as it started to lever itself up out of the pile of ruined stones and walls it had fallen into.

I had just climbed onto slightly more level ground and got my feet more solidly under me as I rushed it. I was alone and unafraid at that point. Nobody behind me could engage this thing, both because of the terrain and my position. I had to finish it myself.

Putting my palm against the pommel, I moved in as it opened its mouth to roar at me, and rammed the point of the Sword through its eye.

The blade sank to the hilts, the eyeball gushing fluid and black blood all over my hands. I twisted the blade as the point penetrated something vital. The giant spasmed, nearly ripping the sword hilt out of my hands, and I hastily drew it out. Any other sword might have gotten stuck, necessitating a boot against the skull to wrench it clear. The Sword of Iudicael, though, just like it never took a stain or a nick, had never gotten stuck, and this time was no exception. It slid out, nice as you please, and my gloves were the only thing that had taken a stain from the ichor. The giant shuddered once more, its hand grasping at the dust and rocks beneath it, and then it went still.

One more down. The only question was, how many were we going to have to fight? Would we need to clear the entire warren of caves and tunnels beneath the ruined city before we could search for the Sword of Categyrn?

I'd barely had the thought, sliding the Sword back in its scabbard, when the biggest giant yet rose up on the crest of the great mound, still about a hundred sixty yards away. That thing was probably a good five feet taller than any of the others we'd fought so far, and its skin was shading toward blue. It also had a pair of huge, yellowed tusks jutting up from its lower lip.

I hefted the M79, but Bailey was ahead of me again, and probably had a better shot.

With a rolling, staccato thunder, he dumped the rest of the mag into the giant, the high explosive penetrator rounds hitting with hammer blows and bright flashes. One blew off a tusk, another smashed a chunk out of its sternum, and the third struck right at the roof of the thing's mouth as it roared its defiance.

That did it. The giant stopped as the RAUFOSS round smashed through its brain and punched a hole in the back of its skull. It stood and wavered for a moment, then crashed over onto its back.

The entire ruined mound that had been Myrgarak went quiet then. If any of the other giants had wanted a piece, they reconsidered real fast.

Gunny, Mathghaman, and Bearrac joined my team up on the hillside. "Looks like we might have just knocked off the biggest, and the rest don't want to screw with us now."

"That seems likely." Mathghaman didn't put as much stock in kill counts as some the rest of us might, but he seemed sardonically impressed that Bailey and I had just gone through four giants like a buzzsaw. One of us might have been a little put out at not getting a crack at them, but Mathghaman was Mathghaman.

He nodded toward the top of the hill where the big one had gone down. "If the last chapel truly stood here, it should be in what is left of the old city. We should search there."

"You don't sound too confident," Gunny observed.

Mathghaman shook his head gravely as he looked around the ruins. The quiet was almost as eerily complete as it had been down below, near the river. The death of that big bruiser of a giant had put a hell of a damper on the moods of the pig-men and the giants both.

Not the Peruni, though. When I happened to glance down the hill, I saw their lead ranks appear from the south, just visible around the shoulder of the ruined mound. They were still a good distance off, but they'd have this place surrounded soon.

We needed to move.

"This place is not a ruin. It is a burial mound." Mathghaman started up the hill as he spoke. "Picked over by creatures such as these. Grave robbers and gnawers of bones. If the Sword is here, then Tigharn has a grimmer sense of humor than I had thought."

CHAPTER 32

THAT hundred fifty yards or so was a harder climb than it looked. The ruins were smashed and melted in a way that left no intact boulevards or streets. The giants didn't care; they could step over just about any of the melted walls or piles of debris. We weren't so lucky. We had to scramble and climb over all of it, including the less stable parts.

Most of the platoon actually stayed down near the base of the mound with the horses. My team, along with Mathghaman, Bearrac, Gunny, and Galan, made the climb by ourselves, still watching every crevice and waiting for the pig-men or more giants to decide to take a crack at the champs.

Cailtarni had taken a look at the hillside and de-murred. He didn't actually seem all that concerned with the quest for the Sword. It was as if he had come along for honor's sake and little more.

Orava and his team were setting up their mortars, while Pöllö climbed up onto a shoulder of the mound to get a better view of the oncoming Peruni army and start pre-registering target points. If we had to break out, some quick mortar fire might be in order.

Of course, we were getting lower on mortar rounds than we were on just about anything else, so that support would be limited. Still, it's nice to have the support when you can get it.

The top of the mound loomed above us, draped with the corpse of the big blue giant. It got really steep toward the top, almost as if we were looking at the old citadel, or what was left of it. Scaling that was going to be a bear for ordinary-sized humans like us. The giant hadn't had a problem, because its arms and legs had been six to eight feet long.

Fortunately, the cave it had crawled out of was right in front of us and the opening stood almost twenty feet high. The giant had probably had to stoop to pass in and out, but we didn't.

Weapon lights on, we advanced into the dark.

This *had* been the citadel. That was almost certain within the first few yards. The remains of columns hung from the ceiling like stalactites in several places, and there were bits of mosaic on the floor, where the piles of rubble had been swept aside enough that we could see them. There was something about the small bits of the designs that I could see that were disturbing. I couldn't put my finger on it, but there was a curious asymmetry to the designs, and the choice of colors was weird. Lots of purple and black, even under white light.

As we went deeper, we started to see bits of frescoes on the walls—those that were intact. The entire interior seemed to have been hollowed out by sheer violence, the giant flailing about to clear out a den. Walls had been smashed, ceilings broken and torn down, the detritus swept aside to pile against the outer edges of the structure. Only bits and pieces of the interior were left, though it seemed almost like the outer rooms had all been crushed and compacted in the cataclysm that had claimed Myrgarak.

Those frescoes I could see were worse than the bits of mosaic on the floor. Their smashed scraps gave only hints of what they had portrayed, but those hints were all of meticulously detailed depictions of horrible violence and worse monsters.

Just thinking about what little we could see still turns my stomach a little.

The place wasn't just ruins and rubble. It smelled like a wild animal's den, and the parts of the floor where the giant hadn't walked regularly were piled with bones and skulls. The skulls ranged from horned ungulates to the pig-men to human to even a couple that had to have belonged to smaller giants.

The firepit in the center had to be three yards across. Coals still smoldered on it, and there was the remnant of a carcass, still with some shriveled, charred meat on its bones, on the spit.

From the size and the shape, it *might* have been an animal, but I suddenly suspected it had been another giant.

There were bits and pieces of treasure amid the debris of death. Gold and silver gleamed, some of it piled up to one side, some still adorning bones with scraps of flesh, rotting or dried out to the consistency of shoe leather, still attached. Some weapons lay shattered on the floor, others had been put in places of some honor, if a row of skulls with finely crafted swords, spears, and axes buried in their crowns could be called "honor."

It didn't take long to clear the cave. At first glance there appeared to be a lot of little side passages leading off from the main den, but they were all caved in, dead ends. The massive cavern was the only real chamber.

"If there was a chapel here, I think it was wrecked a long time before the giant took up residence." Just from looking around, I was getting a bad feeling about this place that had nothing to do with the giant's leavings. This had been a place of darkness and evil long before that monster had crawled in here to make its den.

"I think you are right." Mathghaman was looking over the weapons in the dark, not bothering, with his strange Tuacha eyes, to even use a light. "The Sword is not here."

"Are we sure?" Gunny's voice was tight. "Because it's almost two hundred miles to Gremman and another two hundred miles back if *it* turns out to be a dry hole."

"I am certain." Mathghaman straightened. "Myrgarak the city may have fallen to the wars after Gremman, but those faithful to Tigharn were long gone by the time the city was destroyed. We will find no last chapel here." He looked at the carcass on the spit. "The giant would have taken all such treasures to itself, blessed or not, anyway."

"If the sword is blessed, and it's reappeared in this 'last chapel' by some mystical means..." Santos was reaching, and I think he knew it. He didn't really want to go all the way to Gremman with the Peruni and the Dullahans on our heels, and I couldn't exactly blame him. Not that we'd necessarily find it any easier to shake them on the way back to Cor Legear from Myrgarak, but adding another several hundred miles of wilderness to fight our way across while our supplies dwindled was not an appealing thought.

Mathghaman didn't have any reassurance for him. "The giant was not like the vampire. It would have been undeterred by a chapel, unless there was a messenger of Tigharn there to guard the sword. There may be, but look around you. Any such chapel would have been here, or else hidden somewhere outside the walls." He shook his head. "Besides that, I cannot explain it fully. I can *feel* that the Sword is not here."

Coming from just about anyone else, that might not have been sufficient. But the Tuacha are more… maybe *attuned* is the word. If Mathghaman was sure that we weren't going to find the Sword of Categyrn in Myrgarak, now that we were on the ground, then we probably weren't.

"We still need to search the ruins as thoroughly as possible." Gunny wasn't dismissing Mathghaman's hunch, but he didn't want to go running across the plains and the highlands to Gremman and the shores of the Cardeleven Sea—where the half-insane remnants of the Commagan were supposed to still lurk—any more than Santos did.

"That should not take long, unless you wish to search every cave, which might be more difficult than antici-pated." Mathghaman didn't appear slighted at Gunny's insistence. "And expend more munitions than we are perhaps prepared to do without."

He was right. There had to be more giants in this mound of ruin and madness. Not to mention the pig-men. I was kind of surprised that we hadn't run into any of the squealing little nuisances in the main cave, but just as happy that we hadn't.

"I trust you, Mathghaman, but we have to be absolutely sure." Gunny ordinarily wasn't one to justify his decisions, but with Mathghaman it always seemed polite, if not necessary. "We're not on the far end of a long, thin supply line; we have no supply line. If the Sword isn't here, I want to be absolutely, one hundred percent sure before we go even farther."

"I understand." Mathghaman knew what was at stake.

Galan didn't, but he understood not wanting to declare a target site a dry hole only to possibly have to come back to it. He bowed slightly. "I thank you, though I do fear that attempting to fight our way through this entire city may be more than we are prepared for."

"Let us go." Mathghaman turned back toward the exit. Farrar was looking around at some of the gold and the weapons, though.

"Should we... I mean..."

"Forget it, Farrar. We're going to strain the horses enough getting back as it is." I understood what he was getting at, though. It wasn't as if Recon Marine was exactly a paying job in this world. There was no S1 to process our pay, even if there had been anywhere to spend it. I was pretty sure we were all still carrying our wallets out of sheer habit, but nobody here was going to take the handful of soggy dollar bills we still had in them, not to mention the worthless plastic that was our credit cards. Gold and silver were tangible, something that we could possibly build a life with.

This wasn't the time or the place, though. Especially since it looked like we had a lot farther to go, all of it through hostile territory.

Bearrac put a big hand on his shoulder. "There will be other times and places, young Michael. Chances at treasures that are not cursed."

Farrar recoiled at that, having been reaching out toward one of the golden bracelets on a whitened, nicked tib/fib. "Really?"

I couldn't tell if Bearrac was kidding or not. He was the most likely of the Tuacha to make a joke, but even he would do it in such a deadpan manner that you could never be entirely sure.

"It is possible." Mathghaman pointed to some of the frescoes on the walls, and then toward a corner that Farrar hadn't looked too closely at. "That giant that lies dead above our heads was a sorcerer. Its paraphernalia lie there. I would not wish to own anything that it had touched."

Farrar backed away from the glitter of the precious metals then, and Bearrac let him go. "Come, my friends. If it is to be a search through the cursed rubble of this once-mighty city, then let us be about it."

* * *

When we came out into the open again, though, the situation had changed.

"If we're going to get clear of this place, we're going to need to move now." Bailey was watching the perimeter through the .50's scope, the bipods resting on a pile of rubble. "The Peruni are moving to encircle us, and the natives are getting restless."

I could hear what he was talking about. A booming voice, dripping with sardonic hate, was shouting just over the hill, and I could hear squeals and grunts in response. It sounded like one of the giants was about to send a pig-man-wave attack at us.

The imperial army had spread out across the plateau, too. Their dust rose high into the sky, and where the clouds didn't hide the sun, the light glittered off spearpoints and helmets. Bailey was right. If we didn't break out soon, we never would.

Gunny grimaced. Cailtarni came up to Galan. "Did you find it?"

Galan shook his head. The older man scowled and looked down at the Peruni. "I know the vow you took, my lord Galan, but perhaps at this moment, it would be better to depart and see if we can draw the Peruni dogs away, then circle back and search more carefully. The giants and their minions are making a great deal of noise, but if they cause us more trouble, I am sure our friends from across the mists can show them the error of their ways again. I am not so sure about the Thirty."

Galan looked at Gunny, whose expression was thunderous, but our senior NCO nodded. This wasn't the hill to die on, especially not if Mathghaman was convinced that it was a dry hole. The man had uncanny senses that extended past his eagle-sharp eyesight and extremely acute hearing. If Mathghaman said it was so, it probably was. "Saddle up! We need to go!"

We had less time than we thought.

The squealing and the giant's roars got louder and more frantic, but we still didn't see any sign of the imminent attack as we scrambled back down to the horses. The squeals turned to screams of panic, cut off abruptly one by one. The giant roared again, shouting its hate, but was answered by a whip crack that made my blood run cold.

The Peruni were still deploying, but at least one of the Dullahans was already inside Myrgarak.

The ground shook as the giant roared again, but there was a note of pain in that thunderous bellow, and the horses were getting increasingly restive. It would be a miracle if half of them didn't drop dead of fright before we got halfway across the plains.

"Ride!" Mathghaman's bellow echoed across the ruins. "The enemy is upon us!"

Sure enough, even as I wheeled my horse toward the north, a pair of Dullahans appeared, riding their monstrous horses around the wreckage of what might once have been a tower, before stone had flowed like molten metal. The one in a long black cloak had its head hanging from its saddle bow, the other, in a coat of plates, carried its own in a sling, held up like a lantern, its fiery eyes gleaming like torches.

The horses started to freak, but we were already making tracks. Gurke was on point, since he'd been stuck in the rear anyway, to his obvious frustration.

It was a risk to run with already-tired horses, but we had no choice, and if we'd tried to restrain them, I think they would have bolted, regardless. Fortunately, the rucks on the packhorses were tied down really well, or we would have lost a lot on that hell-bent-for-leather breakout.

Breakout. That's what I'll call it. In truth, it was a retreat, just short of a rout. We weren't in much order, we had no covering fire, and two of the Menninkai were carrying the mortars across their saddles in front of them while their rifles beat at their backs.

If we'd taken the horses deeper into the ruin of the city, we probably never would have made it out. Those unearthly things wearing the carcasses of horses leaped after us, spurred on by the Dullahans, as those whips cracked overhead. A single, high-pitched cry went up, so shrill that just the sound of it felt like someone was driving an ice pick into my ear. The sense of it was worse, though, and I thought I felt blood trickle down out of my nose as I leaped my horse over a lump of warped rock and onto the plain below.

Horns and drums sounded behind us as the Peruni army took up the alarm. We had to turn west a little way to get around a crack, and as we went, those two Dullahans rode after us, their cloaks flapping behind them as they came, closing the distance with alarming swiftness.

It took every bit of willpower Gurke had to haul his horse around to the north again, around the end of the huge crevice. Franks managed the turn a little more smoothly, but Applegate nearly went down as his horse stumbled.

The rest of us swept around the end of that crack without much order or formation and headed for the north of the plateau, where there was supposed to be another way down, if erosion and the convulsions of the earth hadn't destroyed it. We couldn't go back the way we'd come, not yet.

The Dullahans came after, in deadly silence except for the cracks of their gruesome whips.

CHAPTER 33

AS we thundered across the plateau, I started to despair that we'd make it. Sure, the Peruni army hadn't managed to completely encircle the city yet, but the Dullahans were right on our heels.

They began to fall back, though, as we turned toward the north. I twisted around in my saddle to check our six and saw that the two that had pursued us from the bottom of the mound were now more than a hundred yards behind us, keeping pace but no more.

I didn't know what had bought us the reprieve, but I'd take it. All the same, I gritted my teeth. They were still toying with us, and it wasn't a good feeling.

Of course, then I started to wonder what kind of nasty surprise was waiting for us, if the Dullahans didn't want to pursue that closely. I could say that I was learning not to take anything for granted in this place, but I'd been thinking like that since Syria.

Still, as we neared the northern edge of the plateau, they seemed content to keep pace. And we hadn't been jumped by anything else yet.

Key word: Yet.

The plateau wasn't nearly as steep to the north as the southwestern slope that we'd had to climb to reach Myrgarak. The terrain wasn't gentle, exactly, but the

slope to the north was far more gradual, leading into rolling hills and eventually a wide, grassy plain not unlike
the one we'd crossed from the coastal mountains toward
Barmanak. The faint glitter of sunlight on water in the
distance was the river that we'd crossed in the distance.

In minutes, we were down amid the windswept,
stunted evergreens, thundering off the tableland and
down toward the plain, leaving Myrgarak's warped,
smashed ruin behind us.

* * *

Those plains were as eerie and haunted as the territory
around Barmanak. The wind whispered through the grass
and the low, scrubby brush, and we were stalked every step
of the way.

The Dullahans stayed behind us, though they fell
back farther as we got out onto the plains. The imperial
army followed behind, at an ever-greater distance, until
we could just see the haze of their dust over the horizon,
and little more.

They weren't the only stalkers we had out there,
though. The shadow people were back, though they kept
their distance almost as much as the Dullahans did. The
Tuacha were even more alert, Conall especially taking
the extra time to pace around the perimeter whenever we
halted, quietly chanting as he went. The shadow people
never seemed to want to come too close after that.

On the third day after Myrgarak, though, we spotted
a new threat.

Howls went up from ahead, and a pack of black wolves, running low and fast over the grassland, burst out of the low ground and raced at us.

Eoghain spotted them at the same moment I did. "Turn! Ride to face them!" He probably knew more about what was going on than we did, but we could all get behind the decision to attack. It's a good immediate action drill.

They didn't scatter, but just kept coming, even as we wheeled and spurred our horses toward them, drawing swords and axes, since it's a lot easier to hit something with an edged weapon as you ride by than to shoot at it at full gallop. That was a sign.

Wolves are smart critters. They don't do frontal attacks. The wolves I'd confronted high in the Rockies would back off and scatter when confronted. They hunted by surrounding and flanking their prey, with one or more demonstrating and keeping out of reach of the prey's weapons in front while the real killers got in on the side.

These things didn't do that. They came right on, snarling and howling, teeth bared and eyes burning like coals amid fur so black that it seemed to just drink the light, even in the middle of the day.

Eoghain had pushed to the front of the wedge that we'd formed more by habit and inclination than training, his sword in his hand as he leaned forward over his horse's neck. While these wolves didn't seem to be the natural predators I was used to, they must not have been nearly as bad as some of the things we'd been facing recently, because the Galel's horses weren't freaking out. They were going after these things like warhorses charging into battle.

Eoghain dipped to one side, leaning in to meet the lead wolf as it leaped at him, fangs bared and snarling. His swing met it mid-jump, the Tuacha blade catching it in the mouth, cleaving flesh and bone clear to its spine. He followed through as his horse charged down on another, and the entire top of the wolf's head came away.

I caught just a glimpse of it as it fell, just before I brought the Sword of Iudicael crashing down on another wolf in front of me. Maybe it was my imagination, but it seemed as if a shadow, in the rough shape of a wolf, rose from the crumpled carcass and raced away over the plain.

We slammed through the pack, blades rising and falling, chopping the creatures down. One of them dodged and leaped onto the back of Synar's horse. It clamped its jaws onto Synar's arm, and only his mail and the padded jerkin beneath it kept him from getting the arm torn off. Bailey dropped back and tried to stab the thing, but with both horses running hard—Synar's now starting to panic with the snarling, possessed predator on its back—he missed, the blade skipping along the thing's back, drawing blood but hardly inflicting a fatal wound.

Synar kept his head, though. He couldn't reach his axe, since the wolf was clamped onto his weapon hand, but he snatched his Strider BN-SS knife off his chest rig with his off hand, twisting in his saddle as he went Singer sewing machine on the thing's neck.

It let go and fell away, thrashing in agony, as the same dim black cloud raced away with a subsonic snarl. There was definitely something else inside these animals, but even as I wrenched the Sword of Iudicael out of the one that I'd just killed and swiftly brought it back up just in time to ram the point down the gullet of another, whatever it was apparently decided that this wasn't working. With a rush and a scream that sounded like fingernails on a blackboard, the black smoky things raced out of the remaining wolves. The predators suddenly seemed to shrink and get slightly less black, and then they were running, scattering away from the men on horseback with weapons that tore them apart and armor that they couldn't quite bite through.

We slowed our headlong rush then, as the wolves fled, some of them yelping in fear.

"Everybody in one piece? Nobody dropped a weapon?" Gunny wouldn't harass anyone who had, not then, but there would probably be some eight-counts in their future once we stopped.

Nobody had. It had been a short, sharp fight, but our mail had protected us from claws and fangs, and everyone had stayed on their mounts.

He peered at the sky. We had increasingly come to rely more on the position of the sun to tell time, since none of our watches quite matched the length of days or nights here. "Well, we've got about four hours of daylight left. Let's not waste it." He turned his horse back toward the northeast and got moving again.

While the rest of us followed, I looked back, just in time to see a figure on horseback silhouetted against the sky, about a mile behind us. It was a long way, but somehow, I could tell that the rider didn't have a head.

We still hadn't shaken them.

* * *

The next four days passed without much in the way of incident, despite the fact that we never got away from that sepulchral shadow on the horizon. My belief that the Dullahans were following us, hoping that we'd find the Sword of Categyrn for them, was getting stronger by the day.

After the descent off the Borala plateau, the terrain started to move upward again, the closer we got to the north and the Cardeleven Sea. We couldn't see the sea itself, but the mountains rose, blue in the distance but getting darker and more jagged the closer we got.

The flankers still spotted the dark wolves from time to time, shadowing us at a distance, but they didn't attack again.

As we entered the woods that spread across the foothills of the highlands that lay between us and the Cardeleven Sea, and Gremman on its shore, I couldn't help but wonder if this wasn't going a little too smoothly.

* * *

The woods started as scattered and patchy as they had been around Myrgarak, but quickly thickened, becoming dark and tangled. Most of the trees were some variety of evergreen, though darker than anything back in The World, some with bark that was downright black, and needles shading toward blue, a paler green underneath, but not the silver that I was used to from the Rockies, or the trees on the slopes of the mountains of the Isle of Riamog. The shadows beneath were deeper, though this wasn't the same sort of gloom that we'd seen in Lost Colcand.

The undergrowth made for some rough going. Those woods were entirely wild, and we had to cut our way through when we didn't have to divert around fallen trees. There were a lot of blowdowns in that forest. It had stood for a long time, undisturbed. The terrain wasn't gentle, either, and we weren't even heading for the main crest of the mountains. We were going over the lowest spur, heading for the sea.

We'd just crested that spur, getting glimpses of the wide expanse of the water in the distance, when we got hit.

They were short and skinny, their hair long and matted, and they were so covered in mud that I took them to be goblins at first. They seemed to erupt out of the forest floor to either side of us, hooting and yelling, brandishing stone-tipped spears, axes, and clubs. They charged without tactics or formation.

They'd jumped up a little too far away for their health.

I'd been riding with my rifle slung around my neck, the handguards resting on my thigh, and it really didn't take much more than a second to snap it up to my shoulder, canting it just far enough to pick up the red dot just as it covered the first one's chest, bare except for a thick coating of mud.

I stroked the trigger, having twisted in my saddle enough to get my shoulders solidly behind the rifle, and it surged with a harsh *crack*, blowing a red hole through the mud and the figure's sternum. He took two more steps, bloody froth erupting from his lips, before he fell on his face.

The ragged echoes of the crash of gunfire died more quickly in the forest than I would have expected, but then the mud-caked figures were gone, disappearing into the forest with only a single yelp of fear, as fast as they'd appeared.

"What the hell were those?" Gurke sounded pissed as he scanned the forest over his rifle. I could relate. The attackers had just *appeared* before we'd spotted any sign of their presence.

"They're men." Diarmodh had urged his horse closer to one of the fallen attackers, and was looking down at the corpse thoughtfully. "Camouflaged with mud, but they are men."

"That explains why they went down so easily." Bailey was scanning the woods. "Everything else around here we've got to shoot five or six times, or else blow it up. Or call in Conor with that sword to cut it to pieces because nothing else will do the trick."

"Strange to find men in these woods." Galan had ridden up to join us at the body. It was clearly a man, just covered in mud, most of it dried and cracked. It didn't look like he was just dirty. It looked like he'd deliberately daubed his entire body, except for the ratty breechcloth around his loins, for either camouflage or ritual purposes. Possibly both. "We have seen no others except for the Peruni and the Avurs since we crossed the borderlands, and none of them live here."

"These guys might not, either. They might be another tribe of Peruni auxiliaries." Gunny wasn't dismissing any possibilities, though. "Let's slow down and keep an eye out. I don't want to get surprised again."

Gurke muttered a curse under his breath as he and his team led out again.

CHAPTER 34

IT was the next day before we came down the last ridge and got a look at the ruins of Gremman.

The mud men hadn't made another appearance yet. It seemed like we'd scared them off with the sudden crash of gunfire that had wiped half their assault force off the face of the earth in seconds. While it doesn't *always* happen that someone who's never seen firearms panics, it does sometimes.

If they were shadowing us, they were being really careful about it, too. We saw no movement, at least no human movement, for the entire next day.

Now, though, as my team moved up to take our turn on point, I thought I saw smoke ahead. I reined in a little, lifting my hand to call a halt. Rodeffer hadn't seen it yet, but he slowed as he sniffed the air, then turned and saw me with my hand up. He stopped his horse, then swung a leg over the saddle and slid to the ground. "Leader's recon?"

I nodded. "Leader's recon." I turned back to Santos and Gunny, who had, as was his wont, simply appeared where there might be trouble. I would have thought the man was getting as spooky as the Tuacha, except that he'd always been this way. "I'm taking Rodeffer up to that little rocky hill there, to get eyes on wherever that smoke's coming from. If we've got more company, I think we want to know *before* we walk into an ambush this time. We won't penetrate past those rocks, and we should be back in half an hour." That was, of course, a bit of guesswork without watches, but we were getting pretty good at keeping track of time. "If we take contact, we'll fall back to you."

Neither Gunny nor Santos said anything about the fact that I was kind of stating the obvious. The contingency plan was standard operating procedure for any time you split up a unit. Sometimes you've got to break things down Barney style, not because the guys around you are dumb, but just to make sure nothing gets overlooked.

Especially when you've been in the field, riding and fighting, for weeks, with no real end in sight, and you're getting that close to the objective. That's a bad time to make mistakes. And when you gloss over the details, mistakes get made.

I turned and nodded to Rodeffer, who stepped it out, moving slowly, carefully, and quietly. There was a lot of debris on the forest floor, and it would be all too easy to make noise and compromise ourselves.

Presuming that we hadn't already *been* compromised. How had those mud men found us in that wilderness, anyway? We hadn't exactly been following any sort of road.

As kind of pathetic as these guys were, they might be more dangerous than they'd initially appeared. We needed to step carefully.

It still didn't take that long to reach the pile of rocks that I'd picked out for our OP, carefully keeping as much of the terrain and the trees between us and that thin column of smoke as possible. We had already been pretty good at moving in the bush when we'd first deployed aboard the *Makin Island*. The months since then hadn't dulled that edge.

Getting up on the hill took a little climbing. It wasn't strictly speaking a hill; it was more like a boulder that had rolled down from the mountains above and embedded itself in the ground, slowly cracking under the influence of frost and tree roots in the years since. We had to sling our rifles to our backs, cinching them down tight to keep them from knocking against rock or tree trunks as we climbed. I just hoped and prayed that there weren't any monsters lurking up there.

In that place, who knew?

We reached the top and got down on our bellies. A couple of stunted trees or bushes grew in the cracks in the boulder, but there wasn't a whole lot of other concealment available. Creeping forward, we finally got a view of the valley below.

Myrgarak had been relatively small, surprisingly so for a place that was supposed to be as important as it had been. Granted, it looked like a lot of it might have been ground to dust in the cataclysm that had destroyed it, but the entire city had only been about half a mile wide, even if that entire mound had been honeycombed with tunnels and chambers at one time.

Gremman had been a metropolis. The ruins sprawled across a short spur of land that jutted out into the wide expanse of the Cardeleven Sea, forming a series of concentric rings, connected by lanes like the spokes of a wheel, all emanating from a point somewhere up on the other side of the mountain that loomed to our northeast. That was probably where the citadel had stood.

We weren't actually all that far from the edge of the ruins. In fact, we were far closer than I'd imagined. It was a good thing Rodeffer and I had climbed up there. I wouldn't have wanted to stumble into the open like that, which would have happened if we'd kept riding the way we'd been going.

Not only that, but the ruins at the near edge of the city weren't abandoned.

Crude huts were clustered under a single, smashed wall, almost like they were hiding from the rest of the ruins. The smoke rose from there, and the mud men were moving furtively around them, one of them peering over a low point in the wall from atop a pile of rubble from time to time.

Bringing my rifle around, slowly and carefully, I brought my eye to the scope and started to scan the place.

I counted about three dozen men and a handful of women and children. This was definitely a village, though the longer I watched them, the more their existence started to turn my stomach.

One of the women, just as caked in mud as the men and with a little kid tagging along behind her, got in one of the men's way and was cuffed to the ground and kicked for it. The longer I watched, the more such scenes I saw. The women were doing all the hard work, while the men that weren't on watch clustered around what looked like an altar against the wall.

I won't describe exactly what they were doing on the altar. There's only so much I want to recall. I've seen some pretty horrible things in this world, as well as the one we came from, but human sacrifice and ritual cannibalism will always carry a unique horror.

Even as we got ready to fall back and move, they appeared to finish the ritual, breaking up and picking up their spears and stone axes. Then, while the women cowered away from their blood-streaked, mud-caked visages, they slipped furtively around the wall and out into the ruins.

"We should just kill all of 'em, just to be sure." Rodeffer sounded like he was having a hard time stomaching what we'd just witnessed, too.

"Not the mission." I could sympathize, though. I'd felt the same thing a few times in Syria, when we'd been surveilling some of the nastier jihadis and their allies. This was worse. Orders of magnitude worse.

We couldn't save everybody, though, and from what I'd seen, I suspected that even if we killed all the men, the women, as beaten down and cowed as they were, would probably throw themselves at us with bare hands and teeth. Tribes like that aren't exactly rational.

No, better to try to slip past and into the city, find the Sword, and get out. "Look at it this way. If the Peruni come this way, they'll have to fight these...*people* first. Might buy us some time." It was cold-hearted, but it was viable strategy.

Sometimes it's not a matter of good guys and bad guys. Sometimes, you've got to realize that there are no good guys in a given situation.

We crept back from the top of the boulder and hastily made our way back down to rejoin the team and the rest of the platoon. I was pretty sure we didn't have to worry about an ambush at the moment, but we still needed to move as if they were watching from the weeds. I hadn't seen or heard any of the sorcerous aerial spies that had been such a problem in the north and the corsair lands, but *something* had put them into a position to ambush us before.

Strangely, though, it appeared that they had either completely lost interest in us after that ambush, or they were simply too scared to cross swords with us again. Nothing moved, nothing showed itself as we moved back to the rest of the unit.

I briefed the knights and the team leaders on what we'd seen. Cailtarni frowned, his beard bristling as he looked up toward the ridgeline we still had to get over. "Did you see what they might have been sacrificing to? Or for?"

I shook my head. "To be perfectly honest, I was trying not to look too closely. I've seen too much of that stuff already."

Mathghaman nodded gravely. He'd been there too, at the foot of the Teeth of Winter, when we'd found Captain Sorenson's body, torn open on the altar to Vaelor.

He'd seen what had come next, too.

For a long moment after that, nobody said anything. I think everyone was mulling it over in their heads. Sometimes that doesn't happen enough during planning sessions. Sometimes it happens too much.

"They all appeared to be going *into* the city?" Gunny wanted to be clear. "Not up into the hills to come at us on the flank?"

Rodeffer nodded. "Looked like they were getting ready for a raid or something, but they were definitely going into the ruins. Didn't even look up at the hills, here."

"That doesn't necessarily mean anything. If they pulled a J-turn and came back as soon as they were out of sight?" Bailey wasn't quite buying it.

"These critters don't look like they know about J-turns, Sean." Gurke had regained some of his assurance, after getting angry about how close that ambush had been. "I'm not sure we need to worry about that."

Mathghaman's eyebrow went up, but he didn't say anything. Cailtarni glanced at Galan, then shot me a look, as if to say what most of us were probably thinking at that moment. Gunny was the one to say it. "Don't get cocky, Ross."

He looked up at the hills. "We'll turn east, move up this ridgeline, below the military crest, then pop over about a mile up. From what Conor said, that still won't put us in the middle of the city, so we should have some standoff from both the mud men and anything that might be lurking in the citadel, or whatever's there. I don't want to stumble on something like that big giant this time. We'll take it slow and careful, scout out every danger area before we cross it."

"We should move quickly, nevertheless." Mathghaman spoke with some foreboding in his voice as he looked back the way we'd come, even though we couldn't see very far through the woods. "I doubt our Peruni friends have slowed."

* * *

We rode up the hillside in single file, weapons ready and eyes scanning our surroundings carefully. The black wolves had appeared on a promontory high above, about two miles away, but they stayed put, just watching. I suddenly felt like they were waiting for something. Like all the pieces were almost in place, and at any moment things were going to go down. I felt myself starting to tense, my eyes moving from shadow to shadow, searching for whatever was going to come after us next.

To make matters worse, thick, dark clouds were building over the Cardeleven Sea. There was a storm coming, and given what I could see over the ridge to our immediate left flank, it was going to be a humdinger.

We reached the low saddle where Gunny wanted to cross. Diarmodh and Fennean slipped ahead this time, scouting it out. They vanished beneath those Tuacha cloaks almost as soon as they stepped off.

Moments later, they were back. They reported in with quick, silent nods. The coast was clear. They mounted up while we headed over the crest.

The city sprawled below us, a maze of roofless buildings and collapsed piles of rubble.

Some of those piles of rubble looked nearly as melted as the walls of Myrgarak.

No, there was something different, here. The strange, warped sculptures of Myrgarak's ruins weren't here. This looked a lot more straightforward, as if a volcano or lava flow had run through the city.

Except there were no volcanos that we knew of in the highlands behind us.

I had a really bad feeling as we rode down into the ruins, weapons held at the ready and eyes searching for any sign of our mud-caked adversaries. Or anyone or anything else, for that matter.

There was another finger on the east side of the saddle that cut off some of our view of the center of the city. As we rode farther down, however, we cleared that spur of the mountains, and the citadel came into view. Its towers still stood tall above a thick, sloping curtain wall where it perched on the shoulder of the mountain that rose sheer and black behind it.

We hardly noticed the citadel itself, though. The giant, winged serpent uncoiling out of that curtain wall kind of arrested our attention.

CHAPTER 35

RED, shading to black, and glistening dully in the gathering gloom of the oncoming storm, the dragon slithered up out of the ruins of the citadel, its wings spreading as it cleared the walls, overshadowing the rubble with their vast, leathery span. It did have short, alligator-like legs, and two taloned feet gripped the wall for a moment as its long neck wove upward until its head, its eyes like burning coals, stood above the half-fallen tower. Its tail was easily as long as its neck. The thing really looked like a gigantic red and black pit viper with wings and short legs.

"That's not good." Santos seemed to be going for understatement today.

"Is that where we're supposed to be going?" Farrar's eyes were fixed on the dragon. I supposed there might be another name for it, but I figured a winged serpent the size of a B-52 could only be called a dragon.

"Probably." I wasn't entirely sure; if the Commagan had been as corrupted and as far gone down the road to savagery and madness by the end as the stories we'd been told said they had been, then the odds that a chapel might have survived in the central citadel seemed to be slim. But at the same time, I didn't think it was necessarily a coincidence that the dragon was there, in all this ruin, in a place where we hoped to find the Sword.

Maybe the prophecy was off. Wouldn't be the first time the intel turned out to be bad. Or maybe things had changed. After all, I'd found the Sword of Iudicael on the body of a minor Dovo warrior. Who was to say that the dragon hadn't taken it from the last chapel? Mathghaman had even said that if it had been in Myrgarak, the giant would probably have taken it.

Right then, however, we had to deal with the immediate problem that there was a dragon taking off entirely too close to us, and the horses were really starting to freak.

Those animals had had a rough go of it this trip.

We quickly steered them into the shelter of a small, ruined compound about a half mile from the citadel's outer wall, partially sheltered by another finger coming off the west side of the citadel's hill. There were fairly tall evergreens growing through the broken cobblestones, which provided at least some overhead concealment.

It was a struggle to keep the horses quiet and get security set as the dragon rose above the ancient fortress in ever higher circles. Its head swayed from side to side, its burning eyes scanning the ruins beneath it. We finally had to tie the animals to the trees, to the knights' extreme chagrin.

"We shall have to fight on foot like men at arms." Cailtarni looked over at me. "No offense."

"None taken." I looked up at the dragon, which was now a good five hundred feet up. That it still looked like a flying calamity even at that altitude said something about its size. "Gunny, how the hell are we supposed to kill that? We didn't bring any MANPADs."

"I'll let you know when I have an idea, Conor." Gunny wasn't pissed, exactly, but he also didn't have any answers, and that was frustrating in and of itself.

Conall was watching the dragon, his eyes narrowed. "That is no mere beast." There was a haunted note in his voice. "There is an ancient and malevolent spirit within it." He shook his head grimly. "It will take more than explosives and bullets to kill that."

Bailey, however, was undeterred. "Maybe enough concentrated machinegun fire might cut its wings up. Force it down."

"That still will not be enough." Conall looked around at all of us. Mathghaman was watching him keenly, his own gray eyes narrowed. Conall had been quiet, though he had increasingly taken the lead on the mystical side of the combat we'd been engaged in. That he was so insistent was telling. He sensed something that the rest of us didn't, and we'd probably better pay attention to him.

"How do we kill it, then?" Gunny came back up to our vantage point after checking on the security at the entrance to our temporary refuge. "Or do we need to avoid it at all costs?"

Even as he said it, the big serpent twisted its head around to look toward the west, its tongue flicking out to taste the air. It wasn't looking at us. Maybe it wasn't even looking for us.

With a hiss that crackled like a hot skillet, clearly audible from as far away as we were, it suddenly flapped its massive wings hard and darted through the sky to the west, stretching them out to glide toward the edge of the ruins, slowly banking in a wide circle.

"It's hunting." It might be a snake with wings, but I'd seen hawks and eagles fly like that over the mountains and fields. "Question is, is it hunting for us, or for the mud men?"

"Does it matter?" Galan had torn his eyes away from the dragon itself and looked toward the citadel. "If it is diverted, perhaps we can get inside and find what we came for." He turned to face the rest of us, his hawkish features set. "To kill the dragon is not the quest. To find the Sword of Categyrn and keep it out of the hands of the Empire of Ar-Annator and the foul wickednesses they have awakened—that is the quest. Let us take advantage of the dragon's hunger for the mud men, or whatever it is hunting out there, get in, get what we came for, and get out."

Bailey grinned then, and he stepped up to clap Galan on the shoulder. "For a knight, you're a sneaky bastard, Galan. I like it." He glanced over his shoulder at me. "No MANPADs required."

"I hope." I looked down across the ruins. The dragon was a couple miles away by now, still circling above the western edge of the ruins and the forest beyond. I was acutely aware of just how fast it had covered that distance, and if it really wasn't just a big flying dinosaur, but was, in fact, something more akin to the Outsiders, like Conall had made it sound, then I didn't think it was going to be easy to hide from it. "We'll have to move fast and keep our footprint as small as we can. That means one team, on foot. Won't be as fast as on horseback, but..." I gestured to the restive horses, their eyes still rolling, nostrils flared. "I don't think trying to ride in there is going to work all that well."

"I will go." Galan was adamant. He was the last of the original quest takers, after all. "I would have the Bearer of the Sword of Iudicael come with me, if he is willing."

He got more formal in situations like this, apparently.

The civilized part of me, the part that had to admit that I'd been thinking about Derelei in the quiet moments since we'd left Cor Legear, didn't necessarily want to go in there. The old, atavistic part, however, that side of me that had been reveling in this world of vast wilderness and weird, wild threats, wouldn't miss this infiltration for the world.

I simply nodded.

"Team One's up, then." Gunny wasn't going to split teams, not yet, even as battered as we were. We might only have three understrength teams left, but it was what it was.

"I shall go, as well." Of course Mathghaman was coming. The only reason Bearrac wasn't, though I could see the big man's scowl, was because there were only so many who *could* go, without taking so many that we'd be sure to get spotted.

Of course, as we got ready to move, I hoped that there weren't all sorts of other nasty surprises waiting inside.

If the dragon hadn't been the only monster in the citadel, this could get mighty hairy, mighty fast.

* * *

We moved quickly from wall to fallen arch to pile of rubble. The wind had picked up, and thunder rumbled out over the sea. That storm was coming in fast, and it looked nastier with every passing moment. Lightning flickered in the distance, dark gray curtains of rain were already sweeping down from the billowing black clouds, and I could see the whitecaps on the sea from there.

That could make things interesting, if the weather forced us to ground at the same time as the dragon.

It was still circling out there, turning lazy figure eights over the edge of the city. Even as I looked up, I saw it dip toward the ruins with another sizzling hiss, audible even miles away.

I'd been expecting it to breathe fire. Instead, I saw it strike, quick as lightning, just like the venomous snake it resembled, as it leveled off and glided over the ruins. When its head came up, a tiny shape was writhing in agony in its jaws.

I forced myself to look away as we neared the wall of the citadel.

The place had been ravaged, and there were plenty of good-sized gaps in the wall. I pointed Rodeffer toward the closest one, and he nodded. We started up the slide of rubble that had fallen down from the hole in the barrier, careful to keep low and keep as much cover as possible between us and the dragon.

Looking up, I reminded myself that the dragon wasn't the only threat, and if we got too fixated on it, then we'd probably stumble on something worse. I was glad to see that Rodeffer hadn't lost track of his surroundings, and that he was shying to one side of the hole in the wall, his rifle up to clear as much of the inside as he could see without exposing himself directly in the fatal funnel.

We hadn't heard a sound or seen a single flicker of movement from the citadel since the dragon had taken off. Good tactics are good tactics, though. Even if there was nothing up there, I wasn't ever going to berate him for being cautious.

He waited, watching the scorched and blackened courtyard over his weapon, as I worked my way up to join him. The stench was brutal. I hadn't expected it, but it smelled like sulfur, ash, and rotting meat. There was something else, too, underlying it. Something metallic.

Something that reminded me all too much of the servants of the Outer Dark, summoned into this world by sorcery that defied all that was good and natural.

With Mathghaman right behind me, Galan beside him, gripping his sword behind his oval shield, and Santos and Farrar taking up the rear, I gave Rodeffer's shoulder a squeeze. He ducked through the gap in the wall, quickly pivoting to cover the part he hadn't been able to see, while I crossed the gap and held on the opening that faced the main gates, toward the sea.

Everything was silent and still. If the dragon had minions, they weren't showing themselves. Something about that thing made me suspect it wasn't the sort of creature to have minions. It looked like the mud men offered sacrifices to keep it off them while they scavenged through the ruins, and look how that was working out for them.

We spread out across the burned out, rubble-strewn courtyard. The bulk of the citadel still loomed above us, crumbling where it wasn't melted, the remains of the square tower at the pinnacle still towering nearly ten stories into the sky. This had been an impressive structure in its day. Hell, that outer curtain wall had been fifteen feet thick. It had taken a considerable amount of force to smash through that.

That dragon looked like it could have done it easily.

"The entrance will be on the north side, facing the sea." Galan kept his voice hushed, despite the fact that the dragon was still a good five to six miles away and on the other side of thick stone walls. "If it has not been blocked up."

I took point, since time was of the essence and Rodeffer was currently in the rear. Sometimes, spots in the stack just have to go to whoever's closest. Initiative rules.

It was a long hike around that massive ruin. Not nearly as long as it would have taken to go around even the upper and smallest circle of Vahavah Paykhah, but this place had been bigger than the fortress of Cor Legear. I moved as fast as I could without sacrificing security, covering each danger area with my muzzle as I passed it. I passed a few cracks in the wall that we might be able to get through, but if there was a gateway that wasn't quite so much of a choke point, I'd take that.

Sure enough, as we came around the north side, the cavernous, darkened portal yawned overhead. That gate was big enough that you could probably have driven two Abrams tanks through it, side by side.

The first few spatters of rain hit us, and thunder rumbled again over the water, louder this time. The storm was almost on us.

We held on the doorway for a moment. It was pitch black inside, almost like the inside of the ziggurat in Barmanak. The dragon stench was worse there, as if we were looking into its den.

I finally decided to risk it, and flicked on my white light.

At first, all I could see was stone and rusted metal, discolored and blackened as if it had been burned. Deeper in, though, my light gleamed off something brighter. Maybe gold. Maybe silver. It was hard to tell.

Another gust came in off the sea, hard enough that I swayed a little when it hit me. The rain was still light, but I could smell the storm, and feel the hair on my neck standing on end. This was going to be bad.

"We have to go in there. If the Sword is here…" Galan didn't sound eager, but he was committed. The look on his face, half in shadow under the looming arch of the gateway, was determined.

"White lights on. It's just one more CQB environment. Watch your angles." I shouldn't have to say it, but we hadn't really done a lot of Close Quarters Battle lately. "We'll move slow, cover our angles, and keep track of where we are. It's going to be easy to get lost in this place."

"Unless it's like the cave in Myrgarak," Santos muttered.

Weapons up, cones of white light stabbing out into the gloom, we made entry.

Into the dragon's lair.

CHAPTER 36

THE gatehouse had been smashed by the dragon's passage, just like the citadel in Myrgarak. Shattered pillars lay heaped to the sides, and the rubble of the floors above had been scraped and shoved against them, leaving heaps of smashed and blackened stone against the remaining walls, turning what had once been a guardhouse and a great hall into a darkened cave.

Darkened except for the massive heap of treasure lying piled halfway to the broken ceiling in the center of the open space.

Gold, silver, gems, weapons, statues, suits of armor, artifacts I had no name for—but that made me vaguely uneasy, looking at them—were piled and heaped in the center. Even though they gleamed in our lights, showing none of the blackening and soot that covered the stones of the walls and ceiling, they were still tarnished, dented, and chipped. Except for some of the more gruesome-looking artifacts, anyway.

That pile was the very picture of "I don't care about it except to the extent that I possess it, and no one else." It fit some of the old stories about dragons that I vaguely remembered, stories in which they were the personification of greed itself.

Rodeffer looked back and I signaled him to go around the pile. It might be quicker to go over it, but the footing looked pretty bad, and the last thing we wanted was to get caught on top of that, unable to move quickly or smoothly, when something popped out of the dark and tried to eat us.

He moved to the right, passing another gaping opening in the wall that might have once been a tall doorway. He paused just before it, then popped the corner, rifle in his shoulder, triggering the white light to shine inside. Then he passed it by, continuing on the way around the shattered ruin of the old hall.

When I followed after him, I saw why he'd bypassed the opening. It had indeed been a hallway once upon a time, but it had caved in a long time ago, and was completely choked with rubble only a few yards in. A dead end.

This place was looking more and more like the giant's den in Myrgarak by the minute.

The reason we were running white light instead of IR and NVGs was because of Galan. He was the only one of us who *couldn't* see in the dark. Even so, as we went deeper, I wondered just how much we would have been able to see through our PVS-15s, anyway. The stones of the walls and floor were so blackened that they seemed to drink the light as we moved. This place would still be dark even on NVGs.

Yet something gleamed ahead of us, beyond the reflected glitter of the pile of treasure. It took me a second to see that it hadn't just been a reflection of Rodeffer's weapon light. There was a steady line of golden light on the stone floor ahead, spilling out through the crack beneath a door.

"That's a bit out of place here." Rodeffer's voice was still hushed as he neared the door, his weapon still covering down on it, just in case. We'd trained for a long time that doorways are danger areas, and we weren't about to drop that alertness here.

Still, there was definitely something odd about that tall, double door. It was wood, bound with iron, but it showed not a single scorch or burn mark, in decided contrast to the soot-covered stone around it. A double rune, identical to that on the pommel of the Sword of Iudicael, was impressed in gold on the door.

"This is it." Galan stepped forward, sheathing his sword as he did so, and lifted a hand toward the door, halting only a few inches away. "The last chapel."

"Are you sure?" I couldn't be, and it seemed more than a little weird that the last chapel would be right off a dragon's lair in the center of a citadel of the Commagan Empire. Mathghaman had told us about the madness and slaughter that had brought that empire down to the dust.

"The rune is formed of the first and last letters of the name of Tigharn. And it has not been touched." He nodded, awe written all over his features. "I am sure."

Mathghaman stepped forward, letting his rifle hang from its sling, and reached out to put his hand to the door. His eyes narrowed, but when he stepped back, he nodded, his eyes still fixed on that gleaming, untarnished golden rune. "This place has not been touched by the dragon, or any other forces of the Outer Dark." He shook his head, his voice low. "I cannot say how, or why. But it is true."

I wasn't in the habit of discussing how to take a door right there next to the fatal funnel, but something about this place was just spooky. "Okay, how do you want to do this?"

In response, Galan reached out and pushed the doors open.

I bit back a curse. Even if this *was* the last chapel, we had no way to know what was on the other side of that door. Rodeffer was thinking the same thing, and as the doors swung open, the two of us pushed in front of Galan, riding the doors to their stops, clearing the corners with our rifle muzzles before pivoting back toward the center, fingers hovering near triggers, eyes just above our sights.

It *was* a chapel, though apparently anyone who came there had either stood or knelt on the flagstones on the floor. There were no pews. The ceiling rose impossibly high above us, making the room about three times as tall as it was wide. A stained-glass window let in a dim, multicolored light from high above, somehow miraculously unbroken after all this time.

The stench of the dragon hadn't penetrated in here. It smelled clean, with a touch of incense.

A curtain had been drawn across the head of the chamber, and candles glowed behind and before it. I wondered where they had come from, or how they were replaced when they burned down.

There was one chair in the chapel, and it stood just before the curtain, facing it. High-backed and intricately carved, it completely concealed anyone or anything that might be sitting on it.

By that time Mathghaman, Santos, and Farrar had made entry, and Santos and Farrar had turned to cover the door. That doorway was the only way in or out.

With an exchange of short nods, Rodeffer and I moved up the outer walls toward that chair, weapons leveled, ready for anything.

At least, I thought we were ready for anything.

The man who sat in that chair was ancient. A snow-white beard spilled down over his cuirass, which appeared to be solid bronze above the sternum, with scales beneath. Massive bronze pauldrons, trimmed in red tassels, covered his shoulders. A blue-dyed horsetail cascaded down from the top of his three-ridged bronze helm. His face, browned by wind and sun, was deeply lined, and his eyes were closed.

He held a sword across his knees, sheathed in a richly tooled scabbard. The hilt was identical to that of the Sword of Iudicael, except the accents were silver, rather than gold.

He was as still as a statute, but the two of us angled out to either side of him, our backs to the curtain, covering him with our rifles, careful to make sure none of our companions were directly behind him, maintaining our distance. This man—if he was a man—was sitting right in the heart of a dragon's lair, deep within the ruins of an empire that had turned entirely to the worship of the Outsider Thoggudan, an eldritch abomination from the Outer Dark, before that same abomination had ripped it apart, apparently for shits and giggles. I wasn't taking any chances.

Galan came around behind me, having learned not to cross in front of a rifle muzzle. He stepped toward the chair and paused, his hand partway extended, but still hesitant to reach out to take the Sword.

The old man's eyes opened.

Just judging by the ruins and the dragon outside, I'd more than halfway expected them to be either entirely black or glowing red, or something. Instead, they were a piercing, icy blue, but entirely human, nevertheless. He locked his gaze on Galan.

"It has been many, many lives of men since anyone has dared set foot here." His voice was hoarse and faint, but his *Tenga Tuacha* was clear enough. He seemed to straighten still farther, and I realized that he was uncommonly tall. Even sitting, his helmet came nearly to my eye level. "You are not touched by the dragon, or by the worship of the Outer Dark. Why have you come?"

"The Thirty have been awakened." Galan, to his credit, maintained his equilibrium, even when speaking to a man who really shouldn't be there. Maybe all that knighthood stuff meant he maintained his bearing no matter what. "They seek the Sword of Categyrn. We came to find it before they did, to carry it safe to Cor Legear."

The old man snorted. "And you assumed that you are worthy to carry the Sword yourself?"

That seemed to take Galan back somewhat. He didn't have an answer. The old man's eyes shifted to me, then to the hilt of the weapon at my side.

Something changed in them, then. He recognized the Sword of Iudicael. He almost seemed to sigh. "So, the Swords are to be reunited at long last." He searched my eyes. I still had my rifle pointed at his heart, and it wasn't moving an inch. He didn't seem fazed by it.

He did, however, seem to see something that made him think. "So. It seems the plan is not quite as I believed it to be."

Something about that stung. I'd been carrying that blessed blade for months, and doing my best to stay on the good guys' side that entire time. "What plan?"

He raised a white, bushy eyebrow. "If you need me to tell you that, then you still have some way to go on the path." He looked back at Galan. "You would bear the Sword of Categyrn?"

Galan bowed. "I make no presumption to being worthy to be its Bearer. I only seek to see it safe from the enemy."

"Perhaps there is hope for you." The ancient looked at me again. "You, though, *are* a Sword Bearer. With all the dangers that come with it." He tilted his head slightly, as if trying to get a better look at me. "Yes. You have come through fire, shadow, and death. Not entirely willingly, yet your feet *are* upon the path." His gaze sharpened. "You must take care, young one. It is easy to stray from that path and fall into darkness." He looked down at the Sword on my hip again. "Such happened to the last Bearer of that blade."

Galan had drawn his hands back, his sword sheathed, one hand resting on his shield, the rim of which he had set on the floor at his foot. Now he knelt, going down to one knee, looking up at the ancient in his chair. "How came you to this place, old man?"

The ancient leaned back, his helmet touching the back of the chair. "I was a warrior of Commagan, a companion to Soorenard. They said he was a pretender to the throne, that he stole the Sword of Categyrn. That was only a tale spread by those who would control the king in his old age. The king knew they were tightening the noose around him, that Thoggudan was slowly strangling the faithful. He sent us away with the Sword. Better that it should wander through the wilds, fighting evil as it had been bestowed upon Man to do, than to allow it to fall into the hands of evil men.

"Far we journeyed, and long and hard we fought. We scattered the Cult of Yog, threw the Warlords of Forek into the wilds, and slew the Beast of Turia. Always we were hunted. Finally, the Thirty cornered us in the high passes of the Wall of Scath. Soorenard, Rollory, and Mommolek all were slain. I alone of the Sentinels still stood, though I was wounded in many places. Soorenard, as he fell, threw me the Sword and bid me return here."

He looked around the chapel. "It was a long, hard fight to get clear of there. I wandered long, longer than I had believed. We had all sworn a solemn vow to safeguard the Sword until its next Bearer could receive it. It seemed that Tigharn would have me remain until the vow is fulfilled.

"Through many dangers and many years I sojourned, until finally I returned to the shores of the Cardeleven Sea and Gremman, only to find the city in ruins and only madmen and monsters haunting the outskirts. Yet the prophet Meliboe had foretold that this place would remain inviolate. So I came through the nightmare of these ruins, and finally I found it. I have been here ever since, waiting, besieged by the dragon which came out of the north with a blast of hate a year after I arrived."

He locked gazes with Galan. "Not every man is worthy to bear such a blade. The Sword of Iudicael has been through tragedy and fire, because the man who bore it before proved unworthy, and lost it to the enemy. Should I surrender it to you, are you ready for the burden you would take upon yourself?"

"As I said, my lord, I come not to take the Sword to myself, but only to take it to a place of safety." Galan bowed his head more deeply. "I am but the last man of those twenty first charged by my king to secure it."

But the old man shook his head. "There can be no mere courier. You bear the Sword or you do not. There is no middle ground."

Even though his eyes were on the floor, I could see the anguish in Galan. He really didn't think that he was worthy to do this, even given how far he'd already come.

Before he could answer, though, the ruined citadel shook. A crackling, sizzling hiss reached us through the open door. "Uh, guys?" Farrar's voice rose sharply. "We've got some company."

The dragon had returned.

And we were cut off.

CHAPTER 37

NEITHER Santos nor Farrar had opened fire, which told me that they didn't have a target. That was odd, since there hadn't seemed to be any place in that hall where a beast the size of that dragon could hide. Both were still barricaded on the doorway, searching the darkness over their sights.

"*So.*" The voice was somehow a volcano rumble and a sibilant hiss all at the same time. "*The mouse has snuck into the trap.*" Another steam explosion hiss rattled the stones outside the door. "*So simple to bring both of the Swords into my grasp.*" Something out in the dark shifted and part of the pile of treasure slid down to the floor with a clatter. I was doing my utmost to stay out of the fatal funnel of the door, but I still thought that, just for a moment, I could see a burning eye out there in the dark.

"*Sword Bearer.*" Even though there were technically two of us who could be said to hold that title in the chapel, I knew it was talking to me. "*You do not carry the same curse as the other. He may not die until he has passed the Sword of Categyrn on to another Bearer. So has he been my unwilling guest for all these turnings of the world. You, however, must choose to wither and die within his refuge, or come out and face me. Why sacrifice yourself to a long, lingering death from hunger and thirst, even after you have succumbed to the madness of ravenous starvation and killed and consumed your comrades raw? Come out, lay the blade down upon my hoard, and I will grant you a quick, and relatively painless, death.*"

"That sounds like the offer of a lifetime, right there." Santos had increased his offset from the door, barely exposing one eye, his Mk 48 pointed out into the dark, looking for a target, any target. "Only thing better is the car salesman off base offering that sweet new Camaro at thirty-eight percent interest."

"I should go." Galan had straightened and drawn his sword, stepping in front of me. "I brought us here. I must face it."

"Hold up, Galan." I probably should have called him *Lord* Galan, but we'd been through enough that I didn't think that the slight informality would get his back up, particularly now. "That thing will have you for lunch, armor or not. Let's not get Active Stupid before the situation calls for it."

A laugh sounded out there in the dark, deep, sibilant, and dripping with malice like poison from that thing's fangs. "*Brave, and yet so foolish. Do you think I left a single one of your pathetic companions outside alive? Oh, how they writhed as my venom flowed into their veins. They cursed you, you know, as they died, knowing that you had brought them to their deaths.*" Something quivered in the dark, sounding a little like a sheet flapping. It must have stretched its wings.

Galan took a step forward then, his teeth clenched, but Mathghaman stopped him. "Remember what Conall said. That is no mere beast. It is a thing of the Outer Dark, and so everything it speaks is lies."

"*Everything?*" The dragon's voice was mocking. "*You underestimate me, later child of that cursed meddler from above. I do not lie. The withered husks of every man in these ruins lies outside—those whose bones I did not strip before I returned."*

Galan tried to surge forward then, but Mathghaman's grip was like a vise. He merely shook his head when the knight turned desperate and rage-filled eyes to look at him.

Mathghaman wasn't going to give that monstrosity anything more to work with. I could understand that.

"As long as we're in here, it can't—or won't—come in after us. That gives us an advantage." I wasn't entirely sure what that advantage might be, especially since I'd left the thumper on my horse, a decision I was currently cursing silently. We had four rifles, a machinegun with a 100-round nutsack and two 200-round drums, a few grenades, four swords and two axes. Five swords if you counted the Sword of Categyrn, but the old timer holding it hadn't stirred from his chair, and he didn't look like he was quite up for a round of dragon slaying. His vow might have kept him alive—somehow—but it didn't seem to have kept him in fighting shape.

I might be wrong. I'd been mistaken about people and creatures in this world before. But I didn't think we should necessarily count on him to join us.

I also wasn't convinced that the dragon was telling the truth, either. Like Mathghaman had said, if it was an Outsider, or akin to them, then lies were its lifeblood. I'd seen enough to be dead certain of that.

And a moment later, we got our confirmation.

"One, this is Five. Confirm if you're still alive in there."

Santos still had his earpiece in, too, and shot me a quick, sardonic look before turning that glare on the darkness outside the door. "'*I do not lie,*' my ass."

"Five, this is One. We're all still intact. Objective located, but we've got a big snake outside that kind of has us trapped."

"Good copy. Are you clear of the gateway?" I could hear the calculation in Gunny's voice even over the radio.

"Nowhere near it. Fire for effect."

The ripple of explosions came almost immediately after I let off the radio, as Gunny, Bailey, and Gurke lobbed 40mm grenades in through the gateway. The *thud*s still sounded muted inside the chapel. The detonations seemed miniscule compared to the impact of the dragon's return.

The dragon's hiss, however, made the very walls vibrate. "*So be it. I shall deal with you in time. Do not think this is anything but a brief reprieve, Sword Bearer.*"

With a crash of noise, the dragon burst out through the gateway. We felt the wind of its passage, rank with its sulfurous, rotting blood stench, as it burst out with another steam-boiler hiss.

"Time to move." I looked at Galan and then back at the ancient. "What are we going to do about the Sword?"

The ancient was on his feet. "I may not give it up unless the new Bearer prove worthy."

Galan looked at me and smiled tightly. "We kill the dragon first. The fate of the Sword comes later." He glanced at the ancient guardian, and bowed his head slightly in deference, as if to acknowledge that the decision as to that fate largely lay in the old man's hands.

I gave Santos the nod, and he and Farrar led the way out, guns up and NVGs down. We hadn't even addressed the use of white light. With the dragon out there, flashing white lights around didn't feel like a good idea. Galan figured it out fast, and he had a hand on my shoulder as I followed Santos out.

More gunfire thundered outside, answered by that same sizzling hiss. Our guys were putting up a hell of a fight, but it didn't sound like the dragon was going down easily. No surprise there.

When we came out into the sunlight—what there was of it, as the dark clouds of the storm now covered almost the entire sky, the wind whipping off the sea as more stinging drops of rain hammered down on us—the dragon was perched on the wall, its wings spread, its head held low, its neck bunched to strike.

Below, in the partial cover of the ruins of the curtain wall and some of the smashed structures below it, Team Tuacha, Team Two, and Team Three poured fire into the giant serpent while Cailtarni led the remaining knights toward the lee of the fallen curtain wall, spears held ready. They were pretty long weapons, but whether they were long enough to get inside the dragon's striking distance was anybody's guess.

They weren't. Even as I barricaded myself on the gateway and drew a bead on the dragon, it struck.

I hadn't gotten to know Urchnid very well on the journey. Like most of the younger knights, he'd kept to himself, rarely speaking to us or getting near us. It had seemed to be a tossup as to whether it was awe or conceit. Cailtarni and Galan had mingled with the rest of us easily, but sometimes the Galel could be just as clannish as the Menninkai. Maybe even more so.

Still, we'd been through hell since crossing the mountains, and when the dragon bit him in half, it hit me almost as hard as losing any of our brother Marines since we'd come though the mists.

His entire upper body just disappeared, spear and all, and blood showered his companions as the dragon snapped its head around, flinging his legs out over the ruins. "Tight formation!" Cailtarni roared, and the knights closed in, spears bristling from behind their shields. The dragon gulped down the top half of Urchnid's corpse, then arched its neck again, rearing its head high and letting its jaws gape.

I didn't know for sure, but I'd seen a spitting cobra do something like that before, so I thought I knew what was coming. And the Galel's armor wasn't going to save them.

Putting my crosshairs on the dragon's eye, I fired.

It was a hasty shot, at a relatively small target that was in motion. I missed. Instead of popping its eyeball like a grape, my bullet disintegrated with a puff against the bony ridge just above it, like hitting a reactive steel target.

The hit distracted it for a second, though. It reared back again, turning toward us, and Cailtarni used the momentary breather to pull his men back. It wouldn't do anyone any good if the Galel knights all got choked to death or melted in a shower of that thing's venom.

Presuming it didn't breathe fire, but I still hadn't seen it do that yet.

A moment later, my suspicions were confirmed as it twisted around, fast as lightning, and spat twin streams of milky liquid at the gateway. I ducked back just in time as the stuff spattered on the stones, smoking and eating away at the rock. The fumes were intense, and I started to cough as they burned my esophagus. "Get out of the gateway!"

Ordinary men might have fallen back into the darkness of the great hall, even back to the chapel. Recon Marines, though, don't react that way.

When in doubt, attack.

We burst out through the fumes, eyes watering, coughing and gagging, but still putting fire on that thing as we went. Our bullets weren't doing anything to it. They smacked against its scales without effect, but it wasn't attacking again, not yet.

It had turned its attention back to the knights, spreading its wings and heaving itself into the air. "*I will scatter you across the land and hunt you down one by one. This promises to be great sport.*" Another 40mm hit it in the neck, throwing its head to one side, but aside from a scorch mark on its scales, it was unfazed. "*I have not had such prey to hunt in oh, such a long time.*"

I slowed down as I skidded to a halt behind another pile of rubble. Sheer firepower wasn't going to stop this thing. We may as well be shooting 7.62 at an Abrams tank.

"It's got to have a weak point." I hadn't realized I'd said it out loud until Santos grunted next to me.

"Maybe it does, maybe it doesn't. The ones in fantasy novels always do. But this thing's not like those, is it?"

"What do you know about fantasy novels, Vince?" I ducked out from behind cover and hammered another pair at it. I hit it, but with about as much effect as before.

As I ducked back, Santos let rip with another burst. "I'm better read than you think, Conor." He ducked as the dragon swooped overhead, and I braced myself for another stream of corrosive venom, but it simply laughed that evil, hissing laugh. "We have to keep moving. There's no overhead cover here."

There wasn't any overhead cover anywhere but inside the dragon's den itself.

I considered it. But there was one thing I'd learned in Syria, long before coming to this strange, monster-haunted place. Never go in somewhere you don't know how to get out of. Taking refuge in there would only get us trapped and eaten.

My .50 *boom*ed. Bailey had come loaded for bear. The RAUFOSS round hit with a flash, and this time, it seemed to do some damage. It tore through the leathery wing just outside the wing root, blasting a ragged hole through the reddish membrane. The dragon hissed as it wheeled suddenly, and only a storm of machinegun fire, accompanied by the thunder of those elegant Tuacha rifles, drove it off, just long enough for my friend to avoid getting his head bitten off.

But it could be hurt. We just had to hurt it badly enough.

"The joints. Maybe if we hit it there." I was trying to draw a bead, but that thing was moving *fast*. My next shot came close, but not close enough.

Then Bailey got a good shot with that .50, punching into the dragon's body just under the wing. It *roared* then, twisting and writhing across the sky as it flapped higher, getting more distance.

"We cannot kill it while it is still in the air." Galan had joined us behind our meager cover. He'd seen what that venom had done and apparently wanted no part of it. "If we get it on the ground, we'll have a better chance."

"Still not much of one." I reloaded, realizing just how few full mags I still had left, even with the extras we'd brought by packhorse. "As long as it's in the sky, we might have a shot at its underbelly. If it comes down here…"

"I have an idea." Galan was suddenly moving, dashing toward where the knights had formed a shield wall beneath the ruined defensive works, bristling with spears. "Lord Cailtarni! Give me a spear!"

Cailtarni didn't ask questions. That didn't seem to be the Galel way, anyway. He tossed one of the six-foot long, leaf-bladed spears through the air, and Galan caught it, coming to a halt in the middle of the muddy courtyard, bracing himself behind his shield, the spear held over his shoulder, ready to strike.

"I am Galan, son of Ciniath! Warrior of Cor Legear! Loyal servant of Tigharn, and our anointed King, Uven, son of Drosten! I am he who was tasked to bear the Sword of Categyrn, worm! If you would have me…" He took a deep breath, staring defiantly at the dragon as it came back around toward the citadel. *"COME AND TAKE ME!"*

The dragon circled around, and I could have sworn that it *hovered* for a moment, its wings flapping ferociously, holding its own against the storm that was sweeping in behind it. *"So be it, Son of Ciniath."*

Then it struck.

It dove so fast that it was a blur, its jaws gaping wide, its fangs glistening in that brief moment of violent movement. It was so fast that Galan couldn't possibly dodge out of the way.

He didn't try. Instead, he struck back.

Both hit at the same instant. A fang easily three feet long pierced through his body at the same time that, with every ounce of strength he had, he thrust that spear into the roof of the serpent's mouth.

It shrieked then, an ear-piercing, tearing sound that almost drove me to my knees. Its massive body twisted and thrashed in agony, smashing rocks and stone walls with its tail, its wings beating as if to lift it off the ground. Somehow, though, it was as if it was pinned there, held in place by that spear that transfixed its mouth.

I had the Sword of Iudicael out before I even knew for sure what I was doing, and I was moving, rifle hammering against my back, sword in one hand, buckler in the other.

Just for a moment, I might have seen a flash of white light out of the corner of my eye.

I wasn't alone. Bailey had come through the nearest gap in the wall, my M107 in his hands. Leaning into the big weapon, he proceeded to mag-dump the last seven rounds in the magazine into the serpent, punching deep into its body, just beneath the root of one of those enormous wings.

I reached Galan an instant later, despite the risk attendant to being that close to something that Bailey was shooting RAUFOSS rounds at. The dragon, hurt though it was, was still very much alive—as much as anything like it could be "alive." It had started to draw itself up, even against what seemed like the suddenly immense weight of Galan's body.

I ducked under its fang and drove the Sword of Iudicael deep into the bottom jaw, pinning it to the ground. I didn't know that it would do anything except punch a hole and possibly get the sword ripped out of my hand, but I prayed, wordlessly, that this would work.

It did. The thing screamed again, the caustic fumes of its breath practically knocking me over, but the flesh began to blacken and crack around the wound I'd just inflicted. Faint blue flames flickered in the shadow of the storm. It thrashed even harder, but I was a Sword Bearer, with a blade gifted to mankind by a messenger of Tigharn, and I held it.

Bailey was at the other side a second later. He'd let the M107 fall, the magazine empty, and as I held the dragon, he reached up, past Galan, and grabbed the spear.

Galan was clearly dead, his eyes rolled back in his head, bloody foam around his mouth, his flesh already whitening and withering under the assault of the venom. Yet he had still held the haft of the spear with a death grip, until Bailey put his hand on it. Then, as if finally relinquishing the quest, Galan's dead hand relaxed, and Bailey pulled the spear out.

Our eyes met between the monster's jaws. "Hold it a few more seconds, Conor. I got this."

Was there a new gleam to that spearhead as Bailey ducked away, barely avoiding the lashing wing that battered the ground and cracked the curtain wall? The knights were closing in, with Marines and Tuacha on their flanks, but Bailey was ahead of all of them, running toward the wounds he'd inflicted with that .50, Galan's spear in his hands.

I couldn't see what happened next, my view obscured by the bulk of the dragon's head and body. That thing was truly enormous. But I knew what was going on.

Bailey ran, crouched almost double, toward the root of that vast wing, and then, gripping the spear with both hands, he drove it deep into the monster's body, through a bloody crater that he'd blasted in its more tender scales with a .50 caliber RAUFOSS round.

The spear dug deep, plunging between unearthly ribs, and pierced the blackened, oily, unnatural thing that was the dragon's heart.

If the monster's shrieks had been painful before, that was nothing compared to the unholy noise that tore through it now. The blast of foul wind knocked me over, and only the fact that I'd been holding onto the sword as tightly as Galan had held onto his spear kept it in my hand.

I hit the mud hard, the wind practically knocked out of me, and the driving rain nearly blinded me for a moment.

When I struggled back to one knee, gasping for breath, dashing the water out of my eyes, I saw the last spasm of the dying monster. Its eyes were still open, still burning, though that unholy light was already fading, as the dragon itself seemed to shrink, almost as if it was falling in on itself.

A thick, oily smoke seemed to come from its nostrils then, rising and spreading out until it formed a shadow of the dragon in the air above it, just for a moment, before the wind blew it to tatters and it faded.

Slowly, painfully, I levered myself to my feet. Bailey was pulling himself up by the fallen dragon's wing. He looked worse than I felt, a nasty burn across one cheek and several superficial wounds bleeding freely in the rain.

He looked down, then, and he frowned. With a faint wince, he bent down and picked something up off the ground. "Conor? Gunny?"

I stepped forward, limping a little. I might have wrenched something when I'd fallen. Mathghaman joined me, his rifle in one hand and his sword in the other, and we moved to join Bailey.

I got a couple of steps and stopped. He was holding the Sword of Categyrn in his hands.

"Get security set on the walls!" Gunny was already taking charge of consolidation. "Get the horses inside! Orava, I want those mortars up and ready to go thirty seconds ago!"

Something about the urgency in his voice drew my eyes away from Bailey and the dragon's carcass. I looked past him, through a gap in the walls, squinting against the blowing rain. Sheets of gray obscured the ruins past a few hundred yards, but as lightning forked across the sky, an instant before the thunderclap hit us, I saw why.

The imperial army was moving up the lanes of the ruined city, in good order, led by the Dullahans.

CHAPTER 38

THERE were thousands of them. Even if we hadn't been low on ammo, we never could have held them off. Yet there we were, up against the mountain, with nowhere to run but the haunted highlands above the Cardeleven Sea, even as the storm's ferocity redoubled.

There wasn't time to consider what it might mean that Sean Bailey had just picked up the Sword of Categyrn off the ground outside of the last chapel.

Orava was on it. With a series of *thunk*s, mortar rounds arced skyward, whickering down through the rain to slam into the ruins just short of the first ranks, throwing mud and shrapnel skyward in ugly black fountains, the *thump*s of the detonations reaching us a moment later, dwarfed by the cataclysmic roll of thunder that rumbled across the sky.

Orava was spotting, squinting unflinchingly against the driving rain, and already calling out corrections. The rest of us moved quickly to defensive positions.

I sheathed the Sword of Iudicael and grabbed my M107 out of the mud, ripping the empty magazine out as I ran to my packhorse, pulling two fresh mags out and stuffing them into the front of my chest rig. If it had been an original M107, I'd have been more worried about the mud and the zero, since Bailey had just dropped it once the mag had gone dry, but this was a *Coira Ansec* weapon. It would hold up to a lot worse.

Santos had found a ramp leading up to the top of a still-intact section of wall, and already had Rodeffer and Farrar set in there. I started for it, the M107 over my shoulder, and saw that Bailey hadn't moved yet. "Sean! You okay, buddy?"

Even as I turned to him, though, a voice echoed across the ruins, high-pitched and deadly cold. The words were foreign, but it wasn't surprising that the Dullahans could wield the sorcery that mimics the Tuacha's mind speech. "Rebels against the true Elder Gods. Hear me. There is no escape. You will be crushed beneath the might of our power. Surrender the Swords, and I will allow you the mercy of a quick death."

"They really can't think up a better deal than that, can they?" I moved to Bailey's side, where he was staring at the Sword in his hands. "We need to get up there on the defense, buddy."

He shook himself. I saw that the spear he'd driven into the dragon's heart had exploded, splinters scattered around the dirt beneath the rapidly shriveling carcass and probably accounting for a couple of his wounds. "Right." He thrust the sword into his belt, next to the Tuacha weapon he'd been carrying for a while, and brought his M110 back around from where it had been slung across his back. "Let's get to it."

Even as we mounted the wall, though, I wondered if this wasn't it. We'd found the Sword of Categyrn, but it had become entirely too evident to me that the Swords by themselves, while potent weapons, weren't going to get us out of this scrape. They were still only weapons, and there were only two of them.

As I got up on the wall, I saw the full extent of the threat we faced. It was worse than I'd thought.

I could only count fifteen Dullahans, but that was enough. We had more men than that, but even at two to one, we couldn't handle those specters.

Never mind the masses of armed and armored men and beasts behind them.

Aside from the Dullahans at their head, the army of the Empire of Ar-Annator was probably the most normal-looking force that we'd faced since coming through the mists. Square formations of spearmen marched behind and to the flanks of masses of heavily-armored cataphracts. Rank upon rank of archers marched behind, and much more ragged-looking auxiliaries, poorly armored and carrying a mishmash of different weapons, spread out on the farther flanks to either side. Avur horsemen ranged along the ridgeline above.

That massive army was spreading out through the ruins, their ranks thinning ever so slightly as they wrapped around the citadel. They hadn't quite completely encircled it yet, though the Dullahans had moved ahead, and there weren't many avenues left if to us we were going to try to break out.

"Gurke! Take your team and find us a way out!" Gunny wasn't getting sucked into the immediate threat, fortunately. I realized I'd been just sort of gaping at that vast force and wondering what the hell we were going to do for the last few seconds.

"Where?" Gurke, apparently, was having the same problem.

Gunny was at his side in an instant, grabbing him roughly by the shoulder and turning him around to look up at the mountain behind us. "Find a spot that they don't have covered yet." He gave Gurke a bit of a shove. "Now."

Shaken out of his reverie, Gurke immediately set to and started barking at his team. Meanwhile, Orava had called out his corrections, and the next salvo of mortar rounds landed on target, smashing into the lead ranks of the cataphracts that were riding up the main boulevard to the west, behind the Dullahan with its head floating in blue flames. Explosions tore through armored men and horses alike, and in a moment, as the smoke and mud was driven down by the rain, the boulevard was a mass of bleeding men, thrashing, maimed animals, and blood-stained metal.

The Dullahan was unfazed. Naturally.

The curtain wall was plenty thick, but there weren't really any battlements left, so I got down in the prone as I flipped out the M107's bipods, and got down behind the rifle. The Sword of Iudicael was a little awkward, though not nearly so much as my M110, as the suppressor knocked against the back of my helmet. Loading the bipods as best I could on the cracked and partially-melted stone, I searched for a Dullahan.

I didn't know for sure that a RAUFOSS round would even scratch that thing, but it wasn't an Outsider, and I'd blown the guts out of a Fohoriman with that .50, so I was willing to give it the old college try. Gurke may or may not find us a route out, but if we were well and truly trapped, we were going to take as many of these bastards with us as possible.

Eventually, every man has to face the fact that he's going to die, and when matters less than how.

Applegate and Santos were already laying into the nearest ranks of cataphracts and spearmen with tight, short bursts of Mk 48 fire. I was focused and strangely calm as I searched for that Dullahan through my scope.

We needed to keep them at a distance for as long as possible. I hoped that dropping a Dullahan would do even more than knocking dozens of the Peruni and their auxiliaries into the mud with bullets and mortars.

I found it after a moment's scanning. That blue flame filled my scope, those glaring eyes, without pupil or iris, simply points of bright blue fire, fixed on me. Its maniacal grin hadn't changed a whit since I'd first seen it back near Barmanak.

It was staring right at me. It knew I was there and that I was aiming in at it. Even though I was a good six hundred yards off, low to the top of the wall, all of my bulk behind the weapon, it knew precisely who I was and where I was.

If it hoped that that knowledge was going to intimidate me, it was dead wrong. I squeezed the trigger.

The massive .50 cal slammed back into my shoulder, the shock of the shot and the cycling action feeling somewhat like getting punched in the jaw. I lost my sight picture for a moment, despite how good my position was.

When I got it back, the head was gone. No, not quite gone. I dialed the magnification back just a little, to see that there was still a tendril of blue fire rising from the stub of a neck, and the head itself was on the ground, twenty feet away, screaming curses.

Well, I hadn't killed it, but the reaction nearby was telling. The cataphracts had drawn back from the head and had halted their advance. A moment later, as I shifted my point of aim and blew a fist-sized hole through the armored torso of the foremost cataphract, they scattered into the ruins, desperately looking for any available cover, anything to put between themselves and the invisible, thunderous death that we could deal at a distance. We'd bought some time. But only some.

"Shift fire to the archers!" Gunny was keeping an eye on the big picture. If we kept the archers off, they couldn't reach out to suppress us or try to kill us at range. We had a significant range advantage, but they had numbers. So far, they hadn't tried to just to swamp us with bodies, but if those Dullahans were as scary as I thought they were, it was probably only a matter of time.

I was looking for another Dullahan. They were suddenly elusive as hell. As soon as I thought I spotted one, and shifted to get it in my scope, it wasn't there anymore.

I dumped another cataphract as my sights steadied, the M107's massive muzzle blast somewhat attenuated by the rain, so at least we didn't get hit by a blast of grit. The round took him in the neck, blowing his scaled aventail to pieces and practically decapitating him.

I could shoot cataphracts until I was out of .50 cal ammo, though, and do absolutely nothing. There were just too many of them. The Dullahans were the only target that might get us out of this, and they weren't cooperating.

At least, they weren't cooperating with us.

High, rasping voices began to chant down there in the ruins. The words made my ears ache and my eyes sting. The wind got even more ferocious, lashing us with rain and hail as it plucked at our cloaks and battered at our weapons, throwing more than a few shots off. The dark clouds overhead began to swirl, and lighting struck the mountainside above the citadel.

I'd seen this before. A corsair shaman had yanked a storm down to ground level to cover for the corsair fighters so that they could close the distance without getting shot. This promised to be worse. Far worse.

Three more lightning strikes hit the mountain, one of them shattering a dark pine with a *bang* that was only eclipsed by the artillery-shell *boom* of the thunderclap itself.

I thought I spotted another Dullahan through the worsening blur of water on my scope, but it slipped away before I could draw a bead on it. It was almost as if they weren't quite there.

Something made me look up, then, coming off the scope to squint through the blowing water and ice in the air, scanning the ruins below. Something had changed.

Before I could figure out exactly what, a flickering barrage of lighting hammered the citadel behind us. Stone exploded where it didn't run and flow, and the top of the tower burst apart, shattered stones tumbling violently through the air. After a moment, the entire tower collapsed with a grinding groan, falling in on itself with a thunderous crash.

When I looked back toward the enemy, squinting against the rage of the storm, I saw a new figure walking down the slope from the citadel, toward the ruins of the city. It took a moment to realize that it was the ancient who had held the Sword of Categyrn. He walked tall, his head held high, unfazed by the storm. He held a spear in his hands, rather than a sword. Naturally. The Sword of Categyrn was now on Bailey's belt.

He paused, just for a moment, and looked back at us. He seemed limned in light, a faint, golden corona around him and his weapon. "Ride." It was the only word he said, before he lifted that spear and ran at the nearest Dullahan, silently and more swiftly than a man on horseback could charge.

It took a second to realize what was happening. The Dullahans parted like the Red Sea, their mounts suddenly freaking out and leaping away, going over even the cataphracts' heads, racing to get clear before that gleaming, glowing spear could touch any of them. A few of the cataphracts tried to stand their ground and fight, but none of them could touch the old man, while one took that glowing spear right through the chest and died instantly.

"Mount up!" Gunny had seen our opening, and we raced to reach our horses and take advantage before it closed.

I paused. Galan's body was still propped up on its knees, impaled by that long, venomous fang. I didn't know if there was still enough poison there to hurt me, but I couldn't just leave him there. He'd bought us the chance to kill the dragon. I couldn't help but think that he'd known he was sacrificing himself, right at that moment, and had chosen to challenge the beast anyway.

"Farrar!" I tossed him the M107, and he caught it, staggering a little as he ran toward the horses. Then I turned, drew the Sword of Iudicael, and severed that fang with one blow. Fortunately, none of that corrosive venom leaked out. It was as if the dragon's carcass had dried out completely, despite the rain.

Galan's body slumped to one side, and I hastily swung it up into a fireman's carry, then ran for the horses.

There were so many that I wished I could have done this for. So many of our guys who were lost in unmarked graves somewhere in the north, or even picked over by scavengers where they hadn't been devoured by the monsters that had killed them. But I could take Galan's body back, at least.

It was the work of seconds to throw the corpse over his saddle, Cailtarni already holding the reins. The older knight gave me one brief nod, and then I was running to my horse.

The army of Ar-Annator was in utter disarray, the glowing figure of the Sword of Categyrn's last Bearer still ahead of Gurke's team, who had taken point. The Dullahans' flight had broken their morale more than any gunfire or falling mortar rounds could have.

Without much of a formation or order, we drove right down the hillside from the citadel, through the rain and the hail and the mud, hooves thundering as we slung rifles and machineguns and drew swords and axes. Bailey and I found ourselves riding side by side, the Sword of Categyrn in his hand, the Sword of Iudicael in mine. We raced down the boulevard, hacking at any enemies that were foolish enough to try to intercept us.

Halfway down the boulevard, I saw the head of the Dullahan I'd shot. It was lying in the mud, cursing, its eyes still glowing balefully. I leaned down to one side, the Sword of Iudicael held ready like a polo player's mallet, and saw those eyes widen just before I hit it.

The Sword split that evil face like a melon. The scream was deafening, and blue fire flared from the thing just before I was past and racing after Gunny and Gurke's team.

That glowing figure went ahead of us for miles, always in front despite the fact that he was on foot and we were on horseback, driving a wedge through the enemy until we were through and had only empty country ahead of us, harsh voices and horns sounding behind as the Peruni cataphracts tried to rally their troops. In another mile, the army of the Empire of Ar-Annator had vanished into the ruins behind us. The Avurs seemed even more reluctant to follow than the Peruni.

At the edge of the ruins, just before the forest, the glowing figure stopped and turned to face us, lifting that spear in salute. He said nothing, but simply faded from sight.

"Let's ride." Gunny had reined in just long enough to look back and make sure we had everybody. The mortar tubes had been left behind. There hadn't been time to pack them back up, and we were out of ammo for them, anyway. We had just about everything else, though. "They'll get themselves sorted out soon enough, and they'll be pissed."

We rode into the forest, leaving the ruins of Gremman and the last chapel behind.

EPILOGUE

FOR days we rode as hard as we could, pausing only for brief rests of an hour or two, swapping horses and moving on. The army of Ar-Annator was still behind us, though they'd lost a lot of ground.

The Dullahans were still there, too, though they had slowed considerably. I hoped that the Thirty was now the Twenty-Nine, but there was no telling. It seemed likely. There was no other reason I could see for their reluctance, now that they knew we had both of the Swords.

Finally, we had to halt and rest, or else guys were going to start dropping dead. The horses weren't in great shape, either. Fortunately, we hadn't seen the Peruni or the Avurs behind us for most of the last day.

"If we reach Cor Legear, we will be safe." Cailtarni was a lot more confident than I felt. "Even the Thirty will think twice about assailing the Rock."

"That will depend on the emperor, I think," Bearrac mused, looking past the fire at the darkness to the east. Now that we were back on the plains, north of Myrgarak, we had a chance to lose them, especially since we'd seen no sign of the Avurs since we'd escaped from Gremman. "Can he afford to start an all-out war?"

"Why wouldn't he?" Gurke had learned. He wasn't looking into the fire anymore. "He's got the numbers."

"He must consider more than mere numbers, but that he has awakened the Thirty, wherever he found them, is not a good sign." Mathghaman stood with his back to the fire, but he was looking south, deep into the heart of the Empire of Ar-Annator. "No sane man would wake them at all, but for him to have taken such a step bodes ill. I hardly expected them to walk the waking world again so soon."

"They're worse than the Warlock Kings, aren't they?" I asked.

Mathghaman nodded without turning around. "Much worse."

"Any chance I actually killed that thing when I hit its head with the Sword?"

"There is a chance, since it was the Sword of Iudicael. There is no way to know for sure, though, unless it does not appear again. Many men have tried to kill those ancient evils over the centuries." He looked up at the stars above. We'd left the storm behind us days before. "We have accomplished the quest, for now, but I fear much darker times loom upon the horizon. And we still have not returned to Cor Legear just yet."

It was rare to see Mathghaman this gloomy. He had to see a lot that we didn't understand just yet.

I looked over at Bailey. We were all tired, and already, most of those who weren't on security were passed out. He was sitting by the fire, though, staring at the Sword of Categyrn.

"You okay, Sean?" Gunny, as always, was going to be the last man to go down, and he'd noticed Bailey's reverie.

"I don't know." He ran a finger over the handguard with its carved lions, set in silver. "I don't understand how I ended up with this. I mean, the last I saw it, that old guy was holding onto it like it was his lifeline, talking about being worthy. Then it was right there. At my feet."

"You killed the dragon," I pointed out.

"Only because I was the one guy who was close enough to do it." He looked up, a faint frown on his face. "Galan sacrificed himself to bring it close enough, and Conor, somehow, managed to pin it to the ground. Speaking of which, bro, I still have no idea how you did that. That damned thing was the size of an airliner." He looked down at the Sword again. "I was just close enough, I had the .50, and then I had my hands free once that was empty."

"What made you think of using Galan's spear?" I had the beginnings of an idea.

He shrugged. "It just seemed like the thing to do."

I looked up at the stars. There were a few that might have been the same as those I'd grown up looking at, but if they were, they'd changed position a lot. "I don't know, brother. I sure as hell wasn't expecting to be the guy to pick this up." I touched the hilt of the Sword of Iudicael at my side. "I still don't feel like I'm the *Sword Bearer*. If anybody around this fire is supposed to be, it's Mathghaman." He didn't respond except to faintly shake his head. "But maybe that's not the point."

I was searching for the words. Something that Mathghaman had said, coupled with the old man's words in the Last Chapel. "Maybe it's not so much about being worthy when we pick it up, as it is about *becoming* worthy to carry it. We've been handed the burden, now it's up to us to live up to it." I wasn't quite hitting the mark that I thought I could see, murkily, in my head. "What was it the old man said? 'Your feet are upon the path. You have to be careful not to stray from it.' Or something like that."

I met Bailey's eyes. He was thinking it through, that frown still furrowing his brow. "Maybe things don't work by the kind of neat, 'chosen one' prophecies we got used to from Hollywood, back in The World. Maybe there really *is* a reason that we're supposed to be here, now, and why you and I are supposed to carry these Swords. We just can't see it yet."

There was a long silence after that, broken only by the popping of the fire. Mathghaman finally broke it. "You speak well, Conor. And I think you are right. Except that you must also understand and accept that you may *never* know the reasons in this life. Destiny is not so easily examined while a man still lives."

"Well, destiny or not, we've got a long way to go yet." Gunny, as always, was eminently practical. "If you're not on security, hit the sack."

In the distance, something howled. Gunny was right. We had a long way to go, through plains and mountains filled with monsters and worse.

The wind was cold, that night.

Peter Nealen is a former United States Marine
who now writes full time for a living.

https://www.americanpraetorians.com/

Other WarGate Titles Available now:

Forgotten Ruin
Tier 1000

For Updates, New Releases, and Other Titles,
visit
www.WarGateBooks.com

www.ingramcontent.com/pod-product-compliance
Lightning Source LLC
Chambersburg PA
CBHW031032030726
47497CB00004B/1100